The Secret Fire

C. J. DAUGHERTY and CARINA ROZENFELD

www.atombooks.net

ATOM

First published in Great Britain in 2015 by Atom

1 3 5 7 9 10 8 6 4 2

Copyright © 2015 by C. J. Daugherty and Carina Rozenfeld

The moral right of the author has been asserted.

A CIP catalogue record for this book
is available from the British Library.

ISBN: 978-0-349-002-19-4 [paperback]
ISBN: 978-0-349-002-20-0 [eBook]

Typeset in Bodoni by M Rules
Printed and bound in Great Britain by
Clays Ltd, St Ives plc

Papers used by Atom are from well-managed forests
and other responsible sources.

MIX
Paper from
responsible sources
FSC® C104740

Atom
An imprint of
Little, Brown Book Group
Carmelite House
50 Victoria Embankment
London EC4Y 0DZ

An Hachette UK Company
www.hachette.co.uk

www.atombooks.net

For Jack, and for Leo

The
Secret Fire

ONE

'Jump!'

The voice was as cool as the night.

Sacha turned around – he looked more amused than afraid.

'You really want me to do it?' Clutching his chest, he pretended to quiver. 'But ... but ... I might get hurt.'

'Shut up.' Antoine took a warning step towards him; the gun in his hand glinted in the moonlight. 'Stop wasting my time, kid. You lost the bet. You chose this option. Now ...' He shrugged. 'You have to jump. Just do it, Sacha. Let's get this over with.'

Sacha held up his hands. 'OK, OK. Don't get excited.'

He was tall and slim, in a faded black T-shirt and jeans. His broad smile made him look even younger than he was as he stepped fearlessly to the edge of the warehouse roof. A breeze blew his straight brown hair into his eyes and he shoved it back to peer into the darkness.

Antoine knew the ground below would be lost in the midnight shadows. The roof they stood on was five storeys high.

Too far to fall and survive.

Crouching low, Sacha prepared to spring forward into the void.

Antoine's breath caught. He admired the kid's bravery and hated to see him die. But a bet's a bet, and the kid had pushed him to the limit this time. Taking his money and not paying him back. Messing with him like he wasn't for real. He couldn't let that happen; couldn't let the guys see someone treat him like that. He had to make an example of him. When his body was found tomorrow they'd know who was behind it.

They'd respect him.

Twenty feet away, Sacha swung his arms out like a diver . . . then stopped abruptly and turned back, his eyes dancing.

'Hey, I've got an idea. Let's make another bet.'

Antoine's hand tightened on the gun.

He couldn't understand any of this. Why wasn't he afraid? Didn't he care that he was about to die? It made no sense.

Antoine didn't like things that didn't make sense.

'What? Now?' Anger made his voice high-pitched. He forced it down a register. 'You're about to smash your face into the ground and you want to renegotiate?'

'Yeah,' the boy said with cool determination. 'Right now.'

Muttering a litany of colourful swear words, Antoine lowered the gun and switched on the torch he held in his left hand.

Its bright white light revealed the warehouse roof, littered with dirt and rubble. In the distance he could just make out the hulking shapes of other warehouses, along with the parked lorries and rubbish bins that marked this unlovely suburb of Paris.

During the day the area would be crawling with workers, but not at this hour. They were alone save for the rats crawling in from the harbour and the pigeons cooing their complaints from the rafters beneath their feet.

'What do you want to bet now, when you're about to die?' Antoine growled.

Reaching into his pocket, Sacha pulled out his phone. 'First, I need you to hold this. My mum just bought it for me and she'll kill me if I break it.'

Antoine waved the gun. 'I don't give a shit about your ...'

'Tsk.' Sacha tapped his index finger against his lips. 'Language. I'm not done yet. As part of the bet, you take the phone. Then I'll jump, since you really, really want me to. But I won't die. Instead, I'll get up and go home. When I do, you'll give me my phone back, forgive all my debts and give me 500 euros for my trouble.' He rocked back onto his heels, eyes daring Antoine to refuse. 'Have we got a deal?'

Antoine barked a laugh, although he wasn't finding any of this funny. The gun twitched in his hand.

'You really think you're ever using a phone again? Can dead fingers dial?'

Looking increasingly bored, Sacha dusted his hands against the legs of his faded jeans. 'Do you take the bet or not?'

Antoine stopped laughing.

He knew from long experience Sacha would bet on any-thing. He didn't care if he lost – that's why he was here now. Sacha had cost him money, a lot of money, messing around with the kinds of guys who don't like being messed with.

He didn't know what was wrong with him but if Sacha hated life so much, Antoine would do him the favour of help-ing him part with it. He'd outlived his usefulness anyway.

Maybe that would appease the men who were after him now because of Sacha's little stunts.

'Sure.' Antoine shrugged. 'I've got nothing to lose making a bet with a dead boy. It's a deal. I'll meet you downstairs with your phone and the money. All you have to do is jump and then get up from your grave and take them from me.'

'Great.' Sacha looked pleased. 'I'll do that.'

He held out the phone. For a second, Antoine hesitated, sensing a trick. The boy could grab his arm; throw him over the edge.

But he'd known Sacha for more than a year. He'd never seemed the type. He was actually a good kid. He just didn't care who he pissed off.

Shoving the torch into his pocket, Antoine picked his way across the roof to where Sacha stood waiting.

'Come on, come on,' he said, waving the phone. 'I don't have all night.'

Reaching out gingerly, Antoine plucked the device from his hand and scuttled back out of reach.

Sacha shot him a look that said he knew Antoine was more scared than him.

4

Antoine's face darkened.

'Enough talking.' He took a step back and raised the gun. 'Now, smart-ass. Jump.'

'OK.' Sacha said.

Then he jumped.

He jumped with no hesitation, no trace of fear. He didn't scream. In fact, he made no sound at all; the leap was chillingly silent. The last thing Antoine saw was the top of his head, a mop of sandy brown hair blown by the wind as he fell.

Stunned, Antoine reeled backwards. '*Merde*. He did it.'

As he stared at the empty space where Sacha had just been standing, some part of him felt a twinge of regret. He was brave, that kid.

Stupid. But brave.

Whirling, he ran across the rubble-strewn roof to the staircase, hurtling down the wide, cement steps, half-laughing in nervous shock.

He'd offered Sacha a range of options. Payment plans. Deals. He could apologise to the guy whose sports car he'd stolen and wrecked. Make it up to him. Do some work for him.

But he said he wanted to die. In the end, Antoine had agreed mostly to see what he'd do when it came right down to it. The whole time he thought the kid was gaming him. Playing him. That in the end he'd admit it was another big joke.

I never thought he'd do it, he told himself. *Maybe he thought he could fly.*

It was a long way down, and Antoine was breathless by the time he reached the warehouse floor. He sped across the dark, cavernous space, eager to get out before anyone discovered the body.

He reached for the door handle.

Just as he did, someone opened it from the other side.

A silhouette appeared in front of him, backlit by a distant streetlamp: tall, lean, dishevelled, but very much alive. And cocky as ever.

'Can I have my phone, please?' Sacha held out his hand.

Drawing a sharp breath, Antoine stumbled backward, tripping over a piece of rusted machinery that lay forgotten on the dirty concrete floor. Regaining his balance he reached behind him as he continued to back away, never taking his eyes off him.

'*Non.* It's impossible! You can't . . . '

Sacha frowned. 'Did you bring my phone, or what? I'd like to go home. It's late, you know.'

His mouth agape, Antoine stared.

Sacha couldn't have survived that fall. It wasn't possible. But aside from a couple of bloody scrapes on his face and hands, he looked . . . fine.

It wasn't possible.

Shoving past him, Antoine stumbled out to the point of impact, where Sacha should be spread like marmalade on the ground, soaked in his own blood.

Nothing.

He turned back. The boy stood in the doorway, watching him with open amusement.

'But . . . but . . . ' Antoine couldn't seem to form a coherent sentence.

Sacha rolled his eyes. 'Come on, Antoine. Give me my money and my phone. We had a deal.'

With a shaking hand, Antoine reached into his pocket and pulled out the phone. Then he counted out the bills.

But he tried not to touch the kid's hand as he handed it all over.

There was something very wrong with him.

Two

'What are you wearing tomorrow night?'

Standing at the mirror in the utilitarian school bathroom, Taylor ran a brush through her hopeless blonde curls.

'Dunno. I haven't thought about it.' She spoke absently; the brush had become trapped in a tangle and she struggled to tug it free without yanking out a clump of hair.

This happened all the time.

On more than one occasion she'd had to cut the brush free and walk around with an empty space on her head for weeks. She could really do without that happening right now.

In the mirror she could see Georgie's perplexed expression.

'I don't see how you can do that,' Georgie said. 'I've planned my entire outfit already. Down to the nail varnish. Ocean pink.'

'*Ocean* pink?' Taylor laughed. 'That doesn't make any sense. Who gives nail polishes such crappy names?'

She yanked the brush free at last, and stared in dismay at the mirror. Her hair seemed to be responding to some unseen force, frizzing in front of her eyes. It was enraging. Blonde hair should be straight and silky. Hers was a hot mess.

With a sigh, she gave up, shoving the brush into her handbag. 'It's just Tom, anyway. He already knows what I look like.'

'It is traditional,' Georgie said primly, 'to care what your boyfriend thinks of your appearance.'

Taylor didn't reply. As if she had time to worry about clothes. After studying for her A-levels, tutoring, volunteering . . . there was no time left to think about anything else. In fact, she wouldn't even go on this stupid double-date at all if she hadn't promised Georgie she'd be there.

'I'll wear something, Georgie,' she said. 'I promise.'

'Or you could go naked,' Georgie suggested, studying her perfect brown skin in the mirror. 'You'd be famous forever.'

Taylor headed for the door. 'You know, advice like this is why I go elsewhere when I have real problems.'

'Oh, Tay. You wound me.' Georgie followed her out. 'Hey, are we still studying tonight after dinner? I have that history essay . . .'

'And you want me to write it for you?' Taylor finished the thought for her.

Georgie beamed, dimples deepening. 'If you're not too busy.'

They walked out into the school hallway, crowded as

9

students rushed from the dining room to their next class after lunch.

Two boys punched each other as they passed, looking to see if Georgie had noticed. But she didn't even glance at them.

'You tosser,' one of them shouted at the other.

'Whatever,' the first boy said, and they took off down the corridor.

Taylor cast a sideways glance at her friend. She knew they made an odd pair. Georgie's glossy, dark ponytail bounced with each step. As always, she looked perfect. She'd altered her outfit herself – a low-cut white blouse nipped in at the waist, emphasising her slim figure and smooth, espresso-dark skin. Her pleated skirt had been shortened to better display her long legs.

Taylor's own clothes were much less ... well, less. Her straight skirt ended below her knees making her legs look short, but she didn't have long legs to show off anyway. Her top was too baggy to do anything with her curves except make her look lumpy.

The fact was, she didn't know how to do what Georgie did with clothes. How to make them her friend instead of her enemy. She just put them on ... and despaired.

Georgie wanted to work in fashion when she finished school. Taylor wanted to be an archaeologist. On the surface they had little in common but for some reason, when Georgie had first arrived in town at the beginning of year nine, they'd just hit it off.

Ever since then, Georgie had kept her from getting too lost in her books. And she'd kept Georgie from failing everything.

It just ... worked.

'Yeah,' she said, smiling. 'We're still studying tonight.'

'Miss Montclair, could I speak to you for a moment?'

Mr Finlay's nasal voice came from behind them. Turning, Taylor saw the French teacher hurrying towards her, his wiry grey hair dishevelled as usual, tie utterly askew. He looked distracted.

She made a pained face only Georgie could see.

With a responding sympathetic grimace, Georgie melted into the crowds before she could get roped into one of Mr Finlay's scattered conversations.

Taylor composed her face before turning back to the French teacher. 'Yes, Mr Finlay?'

The students were funnelling off into their classrooms now. The hallway was clearing. A few students hurtled by, feet thudding on the linoleum floor, hoping to avoid the late bell.

'Miss Montclair, I realise you're busy at the moment with your studies and your other admirable activities ...' In his hand, Mr Finlay clutched a handful of crumpled papers — Taylor got the impression he'd forgotten he was holding them. 'But a tutoring opportunity has just come up.'

Taylor suppressed an inward sigh. She was already up to her eyebrows in work. And teachers were always giving her more to do. It was like an education conspiracy. But she kept her expression neutral. French was one of her best classes.

'Is it a new student?'

'Not exactly.' The teacher shoved his wire-framed glasses up his nose with the hand holding the papers. This served to

11

remind him that they existed and he shuffled through them. 'I've got it here somewhere. Where is it? Oh yes.' Holding up a folded sheet of paper, he waved it triumphantly. 'It's a French boy.'

Taylor blinked. 'I'm going to tutor a French boy in how to speak ... French?'

'Of course not.' He squinted at her. 'That would be pointless. You're going to tutor him in English.' He unfolded the page. 'Here's the information. You'll do it all over the Internet. It's a modern world.' From the way he said it, Taylor got the impression he had no idea what the 'Internet' was. 'Now, Miss Montclair.' His tone changed, becoming more serious. 'You'll need to be sensitive. I'm told this boy's having a rum time of it – something about his father.' He cleared his throat as if even the merest hint of emotion made him uncomfortable. 'Anyway, he's struggling. He needs guidance and help. I'm sure you'll handle it with aplomb.'

He held out the page.

Taylor didn't have time to teach English to some messed up French kid. But she also couldn't bring herself to refuse. She needed good grades in French, and she wanted Finlay on her side.

Reluctantly, she took the crumpled paper from his hand.

'Get in touch with him tonight, please.' As he spoke, Mr Finlay resumed his distracted ambulation down the hallway. 'And if his grades improve, you can take credit for it. Oxford looks very kindly on that sort of initiative ...'

All Taylor's teachers knew she was pinning her hopes on getting into Oxford. Her grandfather was a professor there.

Ever since she was a little girl, it had been her dream to study with him.

The bell rang at that moment, drowning out whatever else Finlay had to say. He turned a corner, disappearing into the depths of the school.

As the halls emptied, Taylor stared at the piece of paper.

One word was scrawled at the top: Sacha.

♊

As soon as Taylor walked into her house after school, a grey-and-white terrier launched itself at her. Wagging its tail furiously, the dog rubbed against her legs, its fur curly, warm and soft against her skin.

Dropping her book bag, Taylor stroked its back. 'Hey, Fizz,' she crooned. 'Hey, Fizziwig.'

Wriggling with delight, the dog licked Taylor's cheek as she scooped her up and carried her towards the light-filled kitchen.

Her mother was still at work. Her younger sister, Emily, was busy with after-school activities. She had the house to herself.

Flipping the locks on the back door, she pulled it open, smiling as Fizz hurtled across the grass like a fluffy bullet.

It was a warm day, so she left the door open as she poured a glass of orange juice and dumped her books on the old, pine kitchen table. The crumpled piece of paper tumbled out last, landing on top of her calculus text book.

Taylor spread it flat, smoothing the wrinkles. Frowning, she read again the words written in Mr Finlay's uneven hand-writing. It was sparse; just the most basic details. But the teacher had said the boy was having a hard time – *something about his father ...*

A wave of empathy took her by surprise. She felt sorry for this unknown French boy. Something bad must have happened.

Fizz returned from the garden and wound around her ankles, panting happily, before curling up in her basket near the radiator.

Taylor flipped open her laptop, drumming her fingers as it churned. Finally, a photo of a lighthouse appeared on the screen.

She opened a new email, and copied the address from the piece of paper. Then she stared at the blank screen for a moment before typing rapidly.

Dear Sacha,

My name is Taylor Montclair. I am a student in England. I've been given your name by my French teacher. He says I'm to tutor you in English. We could start on Sunday if that is convenient?

I think we should start by reading a book in English together. Anything you would like. Within reason, of course.

Kind regards,

Taylor Montclair

When she'd finished, she read it over again, tapping a fingertip against her lips. Then, with a shrug, she hit 'send'.

♊

'So, Georgie and I are going on this double-date thing on Friday. Is that Ok?' Taylor spoke loudly to be heard over the sound of stir-fry sizzling.

She and her sister were sitting at the kitchen table. Her mother was at the stove. She was still in her work skirt and blouse, although she'd hung her blazer over the back of a chair and abandoned her heels under the table.

'How nice,' her mother said, checking the rice. 'With Tom and who else?'

'His friend Paul. From rugby.' Taylor wrinkled her nose. She found Paul boring, but Georgie was dazzled by his muscles.

'I want to go on a double date.' Across the table, Emily sighed, resting her head on one hand.

She was 13, and wanted to do everything Taylor did.

'You can,' Taylor said. 'In three years.'

'Too long,' Emily muttered. Her long blonde hair fell over one shoulder. Unlike Taylor's unruly locks, Emily's hair was thick and straight; a sheet of gold. The unfairness of this genetic good fortune drove Taylor crazy.

Leaning against the counter, Taylor's mother took a sip from her glass of white wine. It was warm in the kitchen, and condensation made the wine glass look frosted.

'Actually, you have my permission to go on a double-date when you're 15, Emily,' she announced. 'So only two years to wait.'

As blonde as her daughters, their mother wore her own hair cut short to her collar, where it curled just a little. 'And yes, Taylor, that will be fine. How is Tom? He hasn't been over to study with you lately.'

Taylor gave a careless shrug. 'Fine, I guess. I'm too busy to study with him right now. He slows me down.'

Her mother gave her an odd look. 'Is everything OK with you two?'

'Yeah,' A touch of defensiveness entered Taylor's voice. 'We've just got a lot going on. Exams. Life.'

'Well.' Her mother began serving food onto three plates. 'As long as you're home by twelve, of course you can go.'

Taylor's phone buzzed. She glanced down to see she had a new email. It was a reply from that French boy, Sacha.

'No phones at the table, Taylor,' her mother chided as she set the steaming plate in front of her. The sharp tang of soy sauce filled the air.

But Taylor barely noticed. She was staring at the message.

```
Yo. Thanks for the email and everything, but I
speak perfect English and I don't really have
time for this stuff. Later. S
```

'That is so rude,' Georgie said, frowning. 'Where are his *manners*? I thought French guys were, like ... suave.'

They were in Taylor's room, studying. Or, at least, Taylor was studying. Georgie was stretched out on the bed, looking at something on her iPad, while Taylor sat at the desk, writing Georgie's history essay.

'I know!' Taylor was still fuming. 'What a wanker. I just can't believe Finlay's doing this to me.'

She stared down at her laptop, the words blurring. For some

reason Sacha's cold response had really stung. The whole situation was infuriating.

'What are you going to do?'

'I have no idea. I could tell Finlay but he'll just blame me for not trying hard enough.' Taylor blew out a long breath. 'I guess I'll write to French boy again and beg him to let me help him study. Because I cannot afford to get in trouble in this stupid class.' Taylor pressed her fingertips to her temples. 'God, I hate him. He's messing up my life.'

'Uh-uh. Give me your phone.' Georgie held her hand, glossy nails gleaming magenta.

Taylor glanced up at her suspiciously. 'Why?'

Georgie crooked her fingers. 'Come on, Tay. Trust me.'

Hesitantly, Taylor handed her the phone.

'Excellent.' With practiced ease, Georgie opened her email and navigated through it. 'Is this him here?' She held up the phone so Taylor could see the screen. 'What's his name, Sacha?'

Taylor nodded doubtfully. 'What are you going to do? I don't think ...'

'I am,' Georgie said, frowning to herself as she typed, 'sending him a message.'

'Oh George ...' Taylor bit her lip. Georgie was much more outspoken than she was. 'Don't make it a thing.'

Georgie hit send and then held the phone out to her, her brown eyes defiant. 'He made it a thing when he wrote you that bitchy message. Nobody talks to my friend like that.'

Fumbling with the keys, Taylor navigated to the message to see what Georgie had written.

Despite everything, the words she saw there made her laugh.

```
Hi Sacha. That's cool. If you want to stay
stupid, no problem. Laters. T
```

'I guess he'll never want to be tutored by me now.' Taylor dropped the phone onto the desk.

'Good.' Georgie returned to her spot on Taylor's bed.

Taylor turned back to her computer. It felt good to stand up to the French guy. Or at least to have Georgie stand up on her behalf. But as Taylor tried to focus on the history essay, she wondered how Sacha would handle the stone-cold brush-off. And whether Georgie's words would find their way back to Finlay.

THREE

The day after the jump, the bruises and scrapes on Sacha's face and hands were the only visible evidence of his flying leap the night before. His wrist ached but the bone had healed already.

He was only in a little pain now. Last night had been a different story.

His bravura act had lasted until Antoine scuttled down the street like a startled rat. As soon as he was out of sight, Sacha had sagged back against the warehouse wall, clutching his broken arm. His breath hissed between his teeth.

It might not kill him, but dying sure hurt like hell.

And if his mother saw the cuts on his face she'd lose it.

With effort, he'd straightened and begun limping down the street towards home. He was halfway there when his phone buzzed.

'Not now, Antoine,' he'd muttered, pulling the device from his pocket.

But it wasn't Antoine. It was an email from that English chick.

As he read it, his face had creased, first in outrage, then in bemused laughter.

The laugh had sent pain shooting through his ribs, which he was pretty sure were broken, too. Clutching his sides, he shoved the phone back in his pocket and limped on.

The English girl had attitude.

That was when he'd decided to let her teach him after all.

Still, he needed a little information first. How did she find him? Who gave her his email address?

He had his suspicions, but there was only one place to get those answers.

Luckily, his mother was working nights this week, and she'd already gone to bed by the time he got up. She wouldn't see the telltale marks on his face.

In the shower he leaned against the white, tiled wall and let the hot water wash away the last of the dried blood. He ran soap across his skin, his fingertips finding bumps and ridges – each pale scar a reminder of another chance taken. Another death.

There was a long slim scar on his left arm, from the time he crashed a stolen car into a lamp post on purpose for a bet. He'd made 150 euros for that.

A slight scooped scar on his thigh served as reminder of the time he got jumped after a poker game. The guys he'd defeated in that game hadn't liked losing.

He turned off the water and stood for a moment, dripping. Then he reached for a towel.

Now, he had to do something much worse than just crashing a car.

A short while later, clad in jeans and a faded black T-shirt, he left the flat and headed to school for the first time in weeks.

In the bright morning sunshine the workaday city street bustled. The trees danced in the breeze. Crowds of Parisians hurried around him.

He'd become so nocturnal lately – he'd forgotten how pleasant mornings could be.

He was already late for class, but when he passed a bakery the smell of warm bread made his mouth water.

He had some of Antoine's money in his pocket, so he bought a croissant and ate as he walked. The buttery pastry melted in his mouth; he devoured it in four bites.

When he reached the school a few minutes later, the tall brick building swarmed with students hurrying to class. Sacha didn't rush. He strolled through the crowd, sunglasses on. An island of cool in a frantic teenage stream.

He looked neither right nor left – there was no one here he knew well anymore. He had no friends. What was the point in friends if you weren't going to be here to hang out with them?

Even their conversations seemed so childish to him now.

'Did you see Justine last night? That *dress*?'

'If you don't do your essay, Lanton will kill you . . . '

'You have to come! Everyone's going to be there.'

It was laughable, really. The things they worried about.

His presence didn't go unnoticed. The sunglasses, and the bruises on his face, made him stand out. He could feel people staring; hear the whispers as he passed.

But no one stopped to ask what happened.

Sacha's teachers were so surprised to see him they didn't bother to hide their shock. In his first class, the teacher rifled through the class list frantically. 'But I thought you transferred to another school last month ... ?'

His maths teacher, on the other hand, just arched one sardonic eyebrow. 'And to what do we owe the honour of your presence today, Sacha? Is it a holiday?'

None of this really bothered him. He let the words roll over him.

What was the point in learning things he'd never have a chance to use?

He couldn't blame his teachers. He had all but dropped out of school last term. Only deep curiosity could have brought him here now. That and irritation. He didn't like people giving out his email address and he had a feeling he knew who'd done it.

By the time he reached Mr Deide's English class, his sudden reappearance had obviously been discussed in the staff room. Mr Deide made no comment – he just pointed to an empty seat at the back of the room.

When the lesson was over and the other students left, though, Sacha didn't get up. This didn't seem to surprise his teacher.

'I haven't seen much of you lately,' Mr Deide said, closing the door. His sharp, intense gaze seemed to miss nothing.

Sacha shrugged. His long legs sprawled out into the aisle but he took off the sunglasses.

Deide was the only teacher he rated. No matter what happened, however long he disappeared, he always welcomed Sacha back. Tried to help him. Asked about his family. Unlike the other teachers, he really seemed to care. And Sacha was absolutely certain Deide was behind this new tutoring thing.

He just wondered when he was going to tell him.

'I had ... stuff to do,' Sacha said, keeping his reply vague.

'That's rather obvious.' Deide gestured at his bruised face. 'What happened? Did you take up boxing?'

Deide was shorter than Sacha and muscular – Sacha had always wondered if he played some kind of sport. His thick dark hair was neatly brushed, and his sharply defined jaw smooth. His narrow glasses were surprisingly trendy.

'You could say that. I do a bit of base-jumping now, too ...' Sacha smiled at his own joke.

'Interesting.' Deide's tone said he didn't really think it was interesting.

Silence fell. Sacha waited for Deide to tell him what was going on. He knew if he was patient, eventually the truth would come out.

Perching on top of a nearby desk the teacher regarded him earnestly.

'Listen, I understand school has never been your ... kind of thing, as kids say. And that's a shame because I believe you're actually much smarter than you let on. In my class you should be making perfect scores. You were until last year. And then you just ... ' He held up his hands. 'Quit.'

Lowering his gaze, Sacha toyed with the strap of his book bag.

'You dropped your friends. Stopped studying. Disappeared. You didn't just quit school. It was more like you quit life.' Deide leaned towards him. 'I don't like to see a 17-year-old boy quit life.'

Sacha couldn't argue with his assessment. But he couldn't tell him the truth, either.

'I guess you're right,' he said with utter insincerity. 'I should try. I promise I'll do my work ...'

'That's not enough,' Deide said, cutting him off. 'I know you speak English well – you used to love this class. I don't know why you're not trying any more, but it can't go on. You need to catch up. Get back on track.'

'How?' Sacha scoffed. 'It's too late. I'm too far behind now.' He slouched low in his chair. 'What's the point anyway?'

'Don't be ridiculous.' The teacher flipped through his papers. 'It's not too late. I've got someone who will help you.'

Here we go, Sacha thought.

Finding the paper he was looking for, Deide glanced up at him, his brow furrowed. 'It'll mean extra work.'

Sacha, who did no school work at all, almost smiled at that. 'You can't be serious.'

'I *am* serious,' the teacher said. 'You're still a student, and I don't see why you should get out of working. Besides ... wasn't your father English?'

Sacha's smile faded. He didn't talk about his father.

'Uh ... I guess,' he shrugged, retreating into his cool, hard shell.

His father had been British by birth, and that information would have been on Sacha's school records. Along with the date of his death.

'Then you should honour his memory by learning his language,' Deide said. 'And by not giving up.'

He held out a slip of paper with something written on it.

For a split second, Sacha thought of telling him exactly what he could do with that paper. But he just couldn't do that to the only teacher left who still gave a damn about him.

With an exaggerated sigh, he held out his hand for the notepaper. It only contained a few words. An email address. And a now familiar name: 'Taylor Montclair'.

Just as he'd suspected, Deide was behind this.

'That is the email address of your tutor.' The teacher sounded pleased with himself. 'She's a student your age in England. You're to contact her online and write emails to her, chat with her in English. She'll help you with your grammar. Help you catch up.' He gathered his books into a stack. 'It's a nice way to learn, *non*? No more teachers shouting at you.'

'Actually, she already got in touch with me,' Sacha said.

'Oh really?' Deide glanced up at him.

'I told her to get lost. And, by the way, I don't like people giving out my email address.'

The teacher leaned back against his desk with a sigh. 'You know, you could try being nice for a change, Sacha.'

Sacha shot him a withering look. 'I *am* nice.'

'I don't want to play games with you,' the teacher snapped. And Sacha straightened – it wasn't like Deide to lose his temper. 'I'm not asking very much here. I'm just asking you to give her a chance. Talk to her. I really think she could help . . . if you let her.'

Frowning, Sacha stared at the piece of paper in his hand.

Deide was always trying to find new ways to save him. Even though this was all pointless for reasons Deide could never understand, it mattered that he cared.

Maybe he should at least pretend to try. Just to give him something back.

But he wouldn't make it easy for him.

'We'll see,' he said.

Deide sighed and began stacking papers. 'It is impossible to help you.'

He didn't know how right he was.

As he walked down the corridor a few minutes later, alone in a crowd, some part of Sacha wished he could tell the English teacher the truth. To make him understand that he wasn't just being difficult. He had a reason.

You can't help me. No one can.

♊

By the time school ended, Sacha was completely healed, aside from the very worst bruises. Those always took longest to fade. He'd never been able to figure out why his bones healed faster than bruises. It just always worked out that way.

He walked home with his usual cool slouch, sunglasses black and forbidding, head tucked inside a hoody, though the day was warm and sunny. He didn't talk to anyone and no one talked to him.

Just the way he liked it.

The apartment building where he lived with his mother and sister was typically Parisian – wedding-cake white and five storeys high. It was all so familiar to him, he walked into the lobby without really noticing how the sun made long shadows on the linoleum floor, or the way it smelled faintly of dust and floor cleaner.

Climbing into the small lift, panelled in fake wood, he punched number three. The doors slid shut with a soft thud. For a brief moment nothing happened, then it rose with a creak.

His family's apartment had the slightly dishevelled feel it got when his mother was working nights at the hospital. There were still a few dishes in the sink, the mail hadn't been put away, and the striped blue and grey throw lay rumpled on the sofa, instead of being folded away as it normally would be.

Everything was quiet. His mother's bedroom door stood open, light pouring through it onto the wood floor in the hallway. She must be out. His little sister, Laura, often had late classes or after-school activities.

He had the place to himself.

After heading to the kitchen to make a sandwich, he made his way to his bedroom.

By mutual agreement his mother never cleaned in here, and the room could, at the moment, best be described as post-apocalyptic. Clothes strewn on the floor, the bed unmade, books and papers everywhere, along with DVDs, computer games, a football.

Sacha made his way through the chaos to the small desk near the window. After unearthing the half-buried computer by swiping an avalanche of clutter to the floor, he switched it on and waited.

As soon as it came to life, he opened the message from the English girl and read it again, his lips pursed with thought.

After a second, he hit reply and typed with quick expert strokes: 'Let's talk.'

Then he added his chat name and told her where to find him.

He left it at that. No need to go into more detail until he knew more about her.

Deide had asked him to give her a chance, and he would. But that was all he'd give her.

Taking a huge bite of the sandwich, he chewed thoughtfully. Something about this English girl nagged at him. Her last name seemed oddly familiar. As if he knew her from somewhere.

He set the sandwich down on the desktop and, dragging the keyboard closer, entered 'Taylor Montclair' into a search engine.

Most of the results were random – a university in America, a cleaning company.

But it also returned one article from a local newspaper in a town called Woodbury in England.

'Local student Taylor Montclair was presented with the national Youth Volunteer of the Year Award at a ceremony on Friday night,' the article stated. 'The award includes a scholarship towards higher education and a plaque. Last year Taylor, who is only seventeen, raised thousands of pounds for national charities, and volunteered more than a hundred hours of her time ...'

There was no picture, and no more useful information. But something told him it had to be her. The email he'd received was so formal. So prim. So . . . volunteer of the year.

Little do-gooder Taylor Montclair.

It didn't explain why her name had struck such a chord with him. But . . . still.

A wicked grin spread across his face.

This is going to be interesting.

Four

Taylor saw the message from Sacha as soon as she logged into her email after school.

'Let's talk,' it said.

It was insulting that he'd think she'd even want to talk to him after the idiotic email he'd sent yesterday. But she was trapped. Finlay had read her the riot act when she told him Sacha didn't want her help.

'You can't agree to take on an assignment and then give up the moment it gets difficult,' he'd chided her. 'I'd be forced to lower your marks for something like this. How can you expect to make it into Oxford if the second you encounter adversity you simply quit?' He'd given her his sternest look – the one he reserved for the most difficult students. 'I must say I expected more of you, Miss Montclair.'

The whole thing had been oddly out of character – he was

usually mild-mannered. But he seemed to really care whether or not she tutored this French creep.

With a sigh, she clicked on the link in Sacha's email. It opened a website called 'Revolution Chat'. She'd never heard of it.

Of course he'd choose something like this, she thought irritably.

The website had a plain black background with few graphics or images. Its logo was a blood-red fist. The motto at the top said: 'CONVERSATION WITHOUT CONSEQUENCES'.

It promised all web conversations on the site were free and could not be monitored 'BY ANY GOVERNMENT OR CORPORATE ENTITY.'

It looked spectacularly dodgy.

She tried to navigate to Sacha's page, but a black skull and bones flashed across the screen. Below it was a message reading: 'REGISTER OR DIE.'

Taylor wrinkled her nose.

She put in only the most basic facts but then, it didn't ask for much. Name. Email address. Picture.

She chose a photo at random from her pictures file and uploaded it. Georgie had taken it a couple of weeks ago in the park. In it, she was sitting on the grass, laughing. The sun was so bright on her blonde hair it looked like a halo around her head.

A green, smiling skull swam onto the screen. 'You're in'.

'Cuh-reepy,' Taylor murmured to herself.

She typed Sacha's screen name in. This time his profile page popped up instantly. A message in red said 'OFFLINE'.

But there was a picture.

Taylor leaned forward to get a better look.

A boy stared back at her from beneath a tangle of silky brown hair. He was slim – his cheekbones and jaw sharply defined, his neck almost fragile-looking – but his eyes were what arrested her attention. Clear blue and defiant. Challenging.

What are you looking at?

She had to admit he was attractive. Compelling, somehow. He looked so angry. Rebellious. He wore a faded T-shirt and jeans, his hands stuffed into his pockets as he glared at the lens like he loathed whoever was taking the picture.

Suddenly, the profile page disappeared, and Sacha's real face loomed, much bigger, in front of her.

Caught off guard, Taylor recoiled.

He looked as surprised to see her as she was to see him but recovered quickly. Leaning back in his chair, he studied her with a guarded expression.

For a second they just stared at each other.

He spoke first.

'*Salut,* professor.' His lips curved into a sardonic smile that made Taylor's hackles rise. 'You wanted to talk to me, and here I am.'

His voice was surprisingly deep, his French accent velvety. But his tone was abrupt and she sensed dismissal within it.

'I . . . what?' Thrown, Taylor stumbled over her words before recovering. 'You're the one who said we should talk.'

'Only because you seemed desperate.'

'*Desperate?*' She bristled. 'I am not desperate. I have to do this for class. I don't want to talk to you at all. My teacher's *making me* do this.'

A wicked smile quirked his lips.

'Do you always do what you're told?' His tone was condemning – as if being obedient was the worst thing he could think of.

The blood rushed to her cheeks.

'Just because I care about my education and my future ...'

His smile widened.

Taylor knew she sounded the very cliché of a prim English school girl but she couldn't seem to stop herself.

Why was he being so *awkward*?

Sacha waved a hand; on the computer screen the motion was a blur.

'Oh, come on. Don't lecture me on the ...' he paused, looking for the English word, 'importance of education. It's boring.'

Taylor glowered at him. She could happily punch Finlay right about now.

Sacha didn't need a teacher. He needed a *warden*.

She replied with icy dignity. 'I wasn't going to lecture you. You asked a question and I answered it. Besides, if you don't want to talk to me, then why are you talking to me?'

To her surprise, he laughed at that. A real, not at all sarcastic, laugh.

'*Touché*,' he said, and for a split second he didn't look defensive.

Spotting a chink in his armour, Taylor leaned towards the screen. 'Seriously. It's obvious you don't want to do this. Why are you even here?'

'I don't know.' His gaze swept across her face. 'I suppose I was . . . curious. And my teacher told me I had to.'

'Do you always do everything you're told?' she asked, throwing his own words back at him.

Again he laughed. There was something disarming about the sound of it – a deep, pleasing rumble.

None the less, Taylor watched him warily, waiting for him to snap at her again.

He didn't.

'OK, OK.' He held up his hands. 'I'm sorry I was so grumpy. I'm just not really . . . ' Sacha paused. 'How do you say it in English? *Into* school right now. But it's not your fault we have to do this. I shouldn't take it out on you.'

His mood swings were dizzying.

'You're right. You shouldn't.'

She kept her tone tart. But with his blue eyes watching her with lively interest, she couldn't stay angry.

Besides, she needed him.

'Your teacher sounds a lot like my teacher. He's obsessed with me tutoring you.' She glanced at him curiously. 'You actually speak really good English, so I don't know what his problem is.'

He looked pleased. 'Thank you.'

Despite herself, Taylor couldn't help noticing that when Sacha smiled he was really good looking. His cheekbones were ridiculous.

'My teacher's always on my back; wanting me to study more. I never listen to him.' He gestured at the computer. 'This is my punishment.'

There was something reckless in the loose way he held

himself, and the way he looked at her – even when he was being nice – like he was assessing her. Deciding if she was cool enough.

It made her nervous.

She was certain he'd rather be looking at someone like Georgie – a girl with perfect hair, perfect makeup, a perfect figure.

Someone who was everything Taylor wasn't.

'You're a real do-gooder, I hear,' he said now, as if he'd heard her thoughts and wanted to prove her right.

She frowned. 'I don't know what you mean.'

'Taylor Montclair, of Woodbury, England; Volunteer of the Year. That's you, right?' Her surprise must have shown on her face because he added as explanation, 'I looked you up.'

Taylor found herself flushing, as if the award she was proud of – which was displayed on a shelf above her bedroom desk – was suddenly embarrassing.

She hated that he was making her feel like this. She'd worked hard for that award. It meant something.

She forced herself to hold his gaze. 'Yeah. So what? I care about things. I'm smart. Are you jealous?'

If she'd thought snapping at him would put him off, she was wrong. Leaning forward, Sacha rested his chin on one hand and studied her with new interest.

'I think I like you, Taylor Montclair of Woodbury, England. If I needed an English tutor, I would choose you. But I don't. As you can see, I speak English well.'

She couldn't argue with that.

'So . . . why does your teacher think you need my help?'

He looked away. 'I don't know. I haven't been going to school lately. I'm just not interested in it. I think he's trying to make me get involved again. It's pointless.'

She couldn't disguise how baffling this explanation seemed to her.

'I don't get it. Why?'

His smile disappeared. 'I have my reasons. I know you won't believe me, but they're good reasons.'

Despite his even tone, Taylor got the feeling they'd chanced into dangerous territory here. He looked bitter again, only this time, beneath the bitterness, she detected something else: fear. And pain.

She leaned back in her chair, her thoughts whirling.

It was hard to decide what to make of him. He was prickly and defensive. Anarchic and confused. Smart as a whip but uninterested in school. He wasn't like anyone she'd ever met.

He intrigued her.

She wanted to know more. But to do that, she'd have to convince him to study with her.

'Well, this isn't school.' She tapped her keyboard. 'This is just two people talking. I'm not tutoring you.' Sacha watched her with interest as she continued talking rapidly. 'Here's the thing. We'll both get shouted at if we don't at least pretend to do this tutoring thing. So ... why don't we? Pretend, I mean. We can talk on this *really* dodgy, by the way, website, maybe read a book in English. It'll get our teachers off our backs. We don't really have to study.' She held up her hands. 'Everyone wins.'

He didn't reply immediately. His eyes scanned her face as if he was looking for something.

Taylor didn't understand why but, for reasons that had nothing at all to do with Finlay or Oxford, she wanted him to say yes.

'OK, Taylor Montclair,' he said finally. 'I will be your student.' His grin was rakish. 'As long as you don't try to teach me anything, we're cool.'

FIVE

'**A**re you eating those?' Tom gestured at the untouched fries on Taylor's plate.

Shaking her head, she pushed the plate towards him.

Seeing how little she'd eaten, Georgie shot her a questioning look from across the table. Taylor dodged her eyes. However true it might be, she didn't want to shout over the music, 'I'M HAVING A RUBBISH TIME.'

But she was. First they'd gone to a film that contained so much shooting her head had begun to ache from the noise. Taylor hated violent films but everyone except her had wanted to see this one, so she'd given in.

Now they were in one of those retro American-style diners, where the only thing on the menu was hamburgers and milkshakes. The music was cranked up so loudly she couldn't hear herself think. This had all made her headache worse.

She'd been getting these weird headaches for the last couple of months. Once one started, the only thing for it was to take pain pills and hide in a dark room until it stopped. Her mother said they were migraines. All Taylor knew was they hurt like hell.

As another song began with a drum roll, she pressed her fingertips against her temples. It felt like someone was inside her skull, excavating her brain.

Next to her, Tom was oblivious, eating her fries and laughing at something Paul was saying. Georgie smiled and rested one hand on Paul's arm as if to remind him she was there. She'd had a thing for him for ages and this was their first date. Unfortunately, he and Tom had spent much of the night talking to each other about yesterday's rugby practice and next week's game.

Still, Georgie looked happy. In fact, everyone else seemed to be having a fine time.

Except me.

Taylor didn't want to ruin their night but she had to get out of there. So when the waitress came over to ask if they wanted anything else, she leaned forward before the others could speak.

'Could we get the bill, please?' she asked.

'Seriously, Tay?' Tom said, as the woman sashayed away, mini-skirt swishing. 'It's only ten o'clock. I thought we'd stick around for a while.'

Georgie looked disappointed, too. 'It *is* awfully early.'

Quickly, Taylor thought up a reasonable lie. 'I thought you all knew I had to get back early tonight. I've got a thing with my mum first thing in the morning. I'm really sorry. But you guys can stay.'

If her head hadn't been pounding a rhythm comparable to the drum solo emanating from the sound system, she would have been quite pleased with that spontaneous and believable lie. In normal circumstances she found it almost impossible to deceive anyone.

Tonight, desperation made it easy.

'Come on,' Tom pleaded. 'Don't go.'

'We could go to the pub on my road,' Paul suggested, looking at Georgie as if he'd just noticed she was rather pretty. 'It's open for another hour.'

Taylor's heart sank.

'We're under-age,' she protested. 'They'll just kick us out.'

But Paul's smile was confident. 'I know the owner – he's friends with my uncle. I go in there all the time.'

Georgie beamed. 'That sounds brill. Don't you think, Taylor?'

'I think it sounds like trouble.' Taylor reached for her bag.

'Don't be such a wuss.' Tom didn't hide his irritation. 'You never want to have any fun. All you ever do is study.'

Her head throbbing, Taylor stared at him. Couldn't he tell she was in pain? She'd mentioned her headache earlier. But he paid no attention. All he cared about was rugby.

'Thanks for the support, Tom.' Her voice was heavy with sarcasm.

The waitress returned, the bill fluttering from her hand. Taking in the unhappy scene – arms folded, faces turned away from each other – she dropped it on the table. 'I'll come back for this when you're ready.'

Pulling money from her wallet, Taylor threw it down on the tray without looking at the numbers. She didn't care if she paid too much or too little.

She just needed to get away.

'You do whatever you want. I'm going home.' She stood so abruptly the chair made a shrill noise against the tile floor, but the sound was lost in the chorus of the pop song, which seemed to be sung by a choir of thousands.

The deafening music swirled in her head like a flock of crows, pecking at her brain. Making it hard to think, to move.

Taylor clapped her hands to her ears.

She just wanted it to *stop*.

A tremendous *bang* shook the room.

Everybody gasped. Someone dropped a glass and it shattered with a crystalline crash.

Then ... silence.

Slim wisps of grey smoke trailed along the ceiling. Waiters scurried around the room, which now smelled faintly of burning plastic.

'The bloody sound system,' she heard one waiter say to another. 'It just exploded.'

♊

Taylor was halfway home before she slowed to a walk. The cool night air chilled the sweat on her back and she breathed deep, as if the oxygen could fix her.

She hadn't waited to find out how the explosion had

happened or what the others thought of it. She'd made her excuses in the blessed quiet and fled.

Her head still pounded. Even the clicking of her heels on the concrete was too loud. She needed to be home in bed. Soon.

She picked up her pace again.

Woodbury was a typical English town with lots of old stone and brick buildings, winding streets and little churches. A narrow river ran through the middle, flanked by leafy parks. It was pretty, she supposed, but she'd grown up here. To her it was just ... home.

As she walked, she went over the evening's events, questioning her every decision. She knew Georgie could tell she wasn't feeling well and would forgive; but Tom? Tom was another issue.

When they first got together it had been so exciting. Tom was one of the school's best athletes. He had a professional trainer and was serious about making a career out of rugby.

He was tall and muscular with golden hair – a teenage Adonis. All the girls at school were after him. When he'd first shown interest in Taylor, neither she nor Georgie could believe it.

One day he'd come up to her to ask if she'd done an English essay due that afternoon.

'Of course,' she'd replied, baffled.

'Uh ... Well. Good. Me too,' he'd said then, looking suddenly flustered. After that he'd left in a rush.

'Bloody hell,' Georgie had said, watching him go. 'He fancies you.'

Taylor, who that day was wearing a T-shirt bearing the slogan 'Books are my life' and a pair of worn jeans, made a disbelieving noise.

'That's ridiculous. He's really good looking and popular.'

'I know,' Georgie had replied, straightening her perfect pony tail. 'And he fancies the pants off you.'

Taylor hadn't believed it at first, but Tom persisted – sitting with her at lunch and assembly, doing homework with her in the library, and generally trying to win her over. He had a good smile and she found his determination hard to resist. Eventually he convinced her it wasn't some kind of a hoax, and she'd given in and gone to a party with him. Georgie chose her outfit for her that night from her own wardrobe – a short, black dress that created the illusion of long legs and made the most of Taylor's curves.

She'd wrestled her curls into an updo, and worn new cherry red lip gloss.

When she'd stood in front of a mirror, she hardly recognised herself. She felt like an imposter.

She didn't usually go to parties, and as she'd walked in the door with Tom, she could hear the other girls whispering about her.

'Look it's that geek, Taylor Thingy.'

'What's *she* doing with Tom?'

All that night, Tom stuck to her side; he only had eyes for her. She'd been glad he was there. In such unfamiliar territory, he suddenly seemed like safe ground to her.

That was the first night they'd kissed.

After that, they were an item. Tom and Taylor. Their

relationship had always been perfectly fine. For Taylor, though, that was all it had been. Just ... fine.

She found it hard to feel comfortable in the relationship. She tried not to think about it – tried to just accept that things were the way they were. But in her most honest moments, she couldn't figure out why they were together. He didn't like studying. She wasn't interested in sport. He had no career ambitions that she recognised – she didn't consider rugby a valid career path.

He was short tempered with her when she didn't want to go to parties on weekends. Once, he hid her science textbook before an important exam, telling her, 'You need to loosen up.' He refused to give it back, even when she pleaded with him.

She'd nearly broken up with him that day. But Georgie talked her out of it. She believed they could work it out.

Taylor wasn't so certain. She didn't feel like she loved him. She didn't have butterflies when he phoned, the way books and films said she should. She didn't feel breathless when he looked at her. She didn't get excited when he texted or sad when he didn't. Sometimes she forgot about him altogether.

Secretly, she'd begun to believe something was wrong with her. If you didn't get excited about Tom Berenson calling you, with his blue eyes and blond hair and bulging muscles ... then you really must have issues. Right?

At least, that's the way it seemed.

Maybe this was all perfectly normal, as Georgie said. Tom was Taylor's first boyfriend. Maybe everybody in a relationship felt just like her – confused and a little lost.

Or maybe not. Maybe she really needed to break up with him, once and for all.

She turned off the main road into the long, quiet side street where her family lived. The curved road held a mix of Victorian terrace houses and more modern brick homes, each with a tiny front garden overflowing with creamy roses and fat pink hydrangeas.

It was quiet at this hour – the street was dark and empty. She was almost at her house when she suddenly got the strangest feeling she was being followed.

The hairs on the back of her neck stood on end. Her skin tingled as if something had rubbed against it the wrong way.

She knew with absolute clarity that she wasn't alone. Someone was watching her.

She spun around, hands raised defensively. The street was empty.

She cleared her throat. 'Is someone there?'

Nothing stirred.

She turned back around, half-running now. With each step the feeling worsened. It was hard to describe – a sharp coldness on her back – as if someone was pressing an ice cube between her shoulder blades.

She didn't know what was going on. She only knew she had to get home.

When she heard footsteps rushing towards her, panic threatened to overtake her. She tried to run, but it was as if she'd tumbled into a nightmare – she couldn't seem to make her feet work.

In panic, she tripped over a kerbstone and nearly went sprawling.

Someone grabbed her arm, and she screamed, struggling to free herself.

'Taylor, what the hell?'

Tearful, Taylor peered up at the familiar face. 'Georgie ... ?'

Georgie stared at her, brown eyes worried.

'Of course it's me.' Georgie appeared dumbfounded. 'Are you OK? Did something happen?'

'I just ...' She didn't know how to answer that question because, actually, what *was* the matter with her?

She tried to look composed, knowing it was hopeless.

'I'm fine. You just scared me,' she said. 'What are you doing here? I left you at the restaurant.'

Georgie's expression was doubtful. 'I came to check on you. You ran out in such a rush, I was worried about you.'

The tension drained from Taylor's shoulders all at once. This headache was making her crazy.

'Oh, George ...' she sighed. 'I'm sorry. I just have this stupid headache, and then I thought someone was following me ... I didn't know it was you. I got scared.' She held up her hands. 'I hope I didn't ruin your night with Paul.'

Georgie's expression softened. 'Oh you goose. I can go out with Paul any time. Why didn't you tell me you had another of those headaches? Come on.' Putting her arm around her, she steered Taylor down the pavement. 'Let's get you home.'

♊

Once they were inside, Georgie distracted Taylor's mother and made them both cups of hot chocolate.

'Now,' she said, when they were in Taylor's room alone. 'Are you really OK? You've been acting kind of weird all day. Is anything else going on?'

'I'm fine,' Taylor insisted. And indeed, now that she was inside and clutching a warm mug, her headache had begun to fade a little. She did feel more like herself.

Still, she didn't understand what had happened on the street. She'd been absolutely certain someone was watching her, and she was convinced that someone wasn't Georgie. She'd never experienced anything like it.

It made no sense. Maybe the headache caused a panic attack. Maybe she was stressed about Tom.

Either way, she couldn't begin to explain it to Georgie right now.

She decided to change the subject. 'What happened to the guys? Seriously, I feel so lame about ruining your big night with my stupid head.'

'I left the guys at the restaurant,' Georgie said with a careless wave of her perfectly manicured (Ocean Pink) hand. 'You were what mattered. Not some boring date.'

Taylor grimaced. 'George, you are the worst liar. Never attempt a life of crime.'

'I'm serious,' Georgie insisted. 'You're having a bad night. I belong with you.'

Taylor wasn't buying it. She settled herself onto the bed more comfortably. 'You and Paul seemed to be getting along OK. What do you think? Were there sparks?'

47

Georgie's eyes lit up. 'Oh my God. Is he the hottest hottie in Hot-town or what?' She fanned herself. 'I can't even . . .'

Taylor regarded her indulgently. Georgie was prone to frequent, passionate crushes. She'd seen all of this before.

'Did you make plans to go out again? You looked good together.'

'We exchanged numbers. He said he'd call.' Georgie's face fell just a little.

Boys could not be trusted when it came to calling.

'He will,' Taylor assured her. 'He's not a complete moron. Besides, I saw the way he looked at you.'

Before Georgie could reply, her phone jangled, and she glanced down at a text message.

'What are you, a witch?' A smile spread across her face.

'Is it him?' Taylor guessed. 'Blimey, that was fast. Must be the nail polish.'

Georgie ignored that. 'He and Tom have gone to that pub and he wants to know if I'll meet them there.' She was aglow with excitement. 'Tay, I think he really likes me.'

Taylor wanted to be happy for her but she couldn't help feeling a little deflated. She didn't want to be alone right now. Her disappointment must have shown, because Georgie's smile disappeared.

'But . . . I'll say no, of course. I should stay. Make sure you're OK.'

Taylor sighed. She was being selfish. She'd already ruined Georgie's date night. She couldn't now screw up her chance to do some underage drinking and heavy petting. Friendship only went so far.

'Don't be ridiculous,' she said firmly. 'I'm absolutely fine and swimming in chocolate. You go. Have a good time.'

Georgie's expression was a tangle of hope and doubt. 'Are you absolutely certain?'

'Go,' Taylor commanded, waving her cup. 'Be gone. I wish to be alone with my hot, creamy drink and a stack of books. This is my happy place.'

Bounding to her feet, Georgie headed to the door, stopping only to say, 'If you start feeling bad again call me, OK?'

'I promise,' Taylor said. But she wondered if she would.

♊

After Georgie had gone, Taylor curled up in bed with a book and tried to fall asleep, but she tossed and turned as the evening's events replayed themselves on a loop in her brain.

At one in the morning she finally gave up. Kicking the covers off, she grabbed her laptop from the floor next to her bed and propped herself up on pillows as it powered up.

She opened her inbox. There was an email from Georgie, sent at midnight:

You OK, Tay? Hope you're feeling better. I have so much to tell you about PAUL!! G xxx

Idly, she scrolled through her messages until she reached Sacha's last. Her cursor hovered over his name.

They hadn't spoken since their online chat a few days ago, but she hadn't been able to get him out of her mind. Everything about him had been so unexpected.

And she'd really liked his laugh.

He made her nervous in a way she didn't understand.

She *liked* the kind of nervous he made her.

She thought again of the look he'd given her when the conversation got too personal. He'd seemed so wounded.

There was more to him than he wanted anyone to know.

She drummed her fingers on the edge of the keyboard. Then she opened a new blank email.

Dear Sacha,

It was nice talking to you the other day. I've been thinking about it, and maybe what we should do is read a book together.

Could you find a copy of *The Catcher in the Rye* in English? I think you might like it.

Should we chat about it tomorrow on that creepy website?

Kind regards,

Taylor

She hit 'send'.

Six

Sacha was sound asleep when the insect-like buzzing of his phone roused him. He picked it up automatically.

'Mmphhhh ... ?' he said, by way of hello.

'Sacha, I have an idea.' It was Antoine.

'Mmphhhh ... ?' Sacha said again, closing his eyes.

Antoine shouted into the phone. '*Sacha*, are you listening?' His voice was nasal and jarring; Sacha flinched.

'Yeah, yeah, I'm listening. *Merde*, Antoine ... What the hell do you want? And why are you calling so early?'

'Early?' Antoine barked a disbelieving laugh. 'It's four in the afternoon! You're still asleep?'

Sacha sat bolt upright. He'd slept all day?

'Not anymore,' he said, rubbing sleep from his eyes. 'What's your idea, Antoine? You want me to jump off the Eiffel Tower?'

There was a pause. 'Look, Sacha ... About that night. It

was just business, you know? I didn't think you'd really do it. I just needed you to understand how serious those guys are. You can't mess with them.'

It was as sincere an apology as he was capable of giving. To be fair, jumping *had* been mostly Sacha's idea – he'd thought it would be funny – so he couldn't entirely blame Antoine. But he still didn't trust him.

Sacha ran a hand through his bed-rumpled hair. 'It's cool. I'm over it. So what's all this about?'

The eagerness returned to Antoine's voice. 'That fake jump . . . ?'

'It wasn't fake.'

Antoine brushed that aside. 'Whatever. Could you do it again?'

Sacha snorted. 'You can't be serious.'

'I can't stop thinking about it. I don't care how you did it – that can be your secret – but . . . man. Do you have any idea how cool it *looked*? It was impossible. Genius. It got me thinking – those guys who have it in for you? They might back off if they saw it. Also, we could make some serious money off this.'

Antoine was a player – into gambling, into drugs, into everything. Sacha knew getting mixed up with him again was not a good idea at all – he ran with some very unpleasant people.

His lips curved up in a dangerous smile. He liked messing with dangerous people.

Still, he kept his tone vague. 'I don't know, Antoine . . . '

'It's like this.' Antoine spoke rapidly, afraid Sacha might not let him finish the pitch. 'You jumped off a roof and survived. I don't know how, but you did and it was mind-blowing. To see you just ... walk away from that? *Putain* ... ' There was admiration in his voice. 'Here's my idea. We should work together, you and me. We should put on a show. I could set it up, bring in some people to see you do it again. People with money. People who like to gamble. They will place bets on your death. They'll be nervous, want to know the catch – but they'll do it anyway. Curiosity always wins out. I'll drum up the tension, then you jump and ... *wham*!' He shouted the word so loudly Sacha flinched and held the phone away from his ear. 'You dust yourself off and stroll into the sunset. All the money will be ours.'

By now, Sacha was fully awake. Swinging his feet off the bed, he sat on the edge of the mattress, scratching his bare chest thoughtfully.

It was a crazy plan. They could both get killed. Well ... Antoine could get killed, anyway. Those guys didn't mess around.

Still, Antoine was right – they could make a *lot* of money. Six months ago he'd helped Antoine out with a few high-stakes poker games, and ended up with a sweet Yamaha motorcycle for his efforts. They could make even more off something like this.

Besides, he didn't have anything better to do.

Still, he wasn't going to let Antoine think it was an easy decision.

'You realise it hurts, right?' He tried to sound reluctant, fearful. 'I mean ... Jumping that far. It's not easy.'

He could almost hear Antoine's shrug at the other end of the line. 'Come on. What do you want? A medal? It's not like you died.'

Sacha had to laugh. That guy really could not care less.

Sensing he'd gone too far, Antoine changed tactics. His voice took on a wheedling tone. 'Look, Sacha, you don't have to do it every night. You just have to jump once. Then we pick up our money and we're done.'

Antoine knew all the gangs on this side of Paris. Those guys gambled on anything. Horses, dogs, dice ... They'd gamble on death. No question about it.

Anyway, what did he have to lose? There was so little time left.

Less than eight weeks.

With the money he'd make, he could buy whatever he wanted. Maybe take a trip. Get out of France. Somewhere far away. Escape his whole messed-up life. See the world, before it was too late.

'Fine. I'll jump, but not further than the last time. Deal?'

Antoine shouted into the phone. 'Are you kidding me? This is going to be perfect. We'll do it at the same place.'

'But I want 60 per cent,' Sacha said, cutting him off.

Antoine's voice trailed off. 'Huh? What? Why?'

With a languid stretch, Sacha stood up.

'Because I'm the one who jumps.'

♊

Rendezvous at midnight. Same place as last
time. 17 guys coming. They all bet you're
gonna die. We're going to be rich.

Sitting at the kitchen table, Sacha read Antoine's text message surreptitiously as his mother and sister talked around him. His mother was at the sink cleaning the dinner dishes. She was already in her green nursing scrubs, ready for work. Laura, his sister, was across the table from him.

Excited butterflies swarmed in his stomach. *Seventeen* gamblers. Antoine would have made them each put up at least a thousand euros – it was always the minimum. And some of the crazy ones would bet more to show off.

They could make twenty grand.

Twenty grand.

He found it impossible to imagine that much money. How big the stack would be. How much it would weigh. What it could buy. What it would mean to his family.

Since his father's death, they'd struggled a bit. His mother worked hard – often pulling double shifts at the hospital. But after rent, bills and food, there was never much left over.

His mother tried to shield them from the realities of their situation, but Sacha knew they'd had to move into this flat because it was cheaper than the house where they'd lived when his dad was alive.

He looked up at his mother, her dark hair shining in the sun that streamed through the window behind her. She was laughing at something Laura had just said, but he could see how much the last few years had aged her. The tell-tale lines pain had carved into her skin.

It hurt his heart.

She deserved to be happy. But life had denied her that.

The thought came to him suddenly: he could save the

money he made from jumping for her. Make sure she and Laura were taken care of when he was gone.

The idea was heartening. If he could somehow help his family, then maybe it wasn't all for nothing.

Laura chatted without pausing for breath about her day at school. She was 13 but looked younger with her golden-brown hair pulled back in a ponytail. Like him, she was tall, and they shared the same blue eyes and sharp cheekbones, but she had a scattering of freckles on her cheeks, while he had none.

The youngest child and a girl – those two factors meant she was safe. He was glad of that.

Along with his father's sister, Annie, this was his whole family. There was no one else – no grandparents. No other aunts or uncles. No one to help his mother after he was gone.

Sacha would jump from the top of the tallest skyscraper in the city if it would make their lives even a little bit better.

His mother dried her hands on a tea towel and glanced at her watch with a reluctant sigh. It was nearly time for her to leave. Working the night shift paid better, but it wore her down.

'I'd better get going.'

She left the room to gather her things, reappearing at the kitchen door a few minutes later, her bag on her shoulder.

She shot Sacha a warning look. 'Stay home tonight, yes? Don't leave Laura alone.'

Laura made a face. 'Come on, *Maman*. I'm old enough to stay by myself.'

'Don't encourage your brother,' their mother said darkly. 'If he goes out tonight, I want to be informed. I still make the rules around here, don't I?'

'Yes, *Maman*,' they chorused unconvincingly.

Blowing kisses to them, she turned to leave.

Behind her back, Sacha winked at his sister. She winked back with the well-practiced grin of an accomplice.

♊

The cavernous old warehouse at the edge of the Pantin Harbour was in dire need of repair. It stood five storeys high and had once welcomed deliveries of cotton, coffee and huge crates of rubber. In those days it had been a bustling, noisy place day and night.

But times had changed.

Whereas many of the warehouses around it had been knocked down and replaced by modern structures with air conditioning, tall fences and advance security systems, this particular building had been left alone. Many of the enormous windows were broken. No one bothered to guard it. It spent most of its time empty of all but the water rats and pigeons seeking shelter.

Tonight, though, the warehouse roof was unusually crowded.

A cluster of tough-looking men stood as far as was seemly from the edge of the roof.

'It's very high, *non*?' muttered one of them.

'The kid's crazy,' said another, without sympathy or interest. 'Either we win this bet or it's a set-up.'

'I just don't see how he'd fix it.' The first man waved a lighted cigarette, its tip a red glowing eye blinking in the darkness. 'I've got guys upstairs, downstairs, *on* the stairs ... Nothing's getting by me. He plays us, I'll know.'

Antoine had taken care of everything: the bets were all recorded, he'd even arranged for the men to inspect the warehouse to prove there were no wires; no ropes. Just steep, straight walls and concrete death below.

They had haggled over the grimmest details: What if Sacha was alive but paralysed? What if he was brain dead? All such enquiries were dealt with, the odds agreed.

At the edge of the roof, Sacha stood alone and perfectly relaxed with his feet half in the void. A cool breeze ruffled his fine hair and sent his black T-shirt fluttering around him. He never once looked at the men behind him.

None of them would admit it but they found this unnerving.

In hopes of higher bets, Antoine was haranguing the crowd. 'Five storeys. That is the distance between us and the ground, gentlemen. Five long storeys without a net, or a mattress to land on. Without a rope or a trick up his sleeve. My friend here' – he pointed at Sacha – 'is going to jump at my signal.'

A whisper of excitement shuddered through the crowd. Gamblers loved this moment. The fleeting second when everything was on the line. This was what made them feel alive, made them feel powerful. They'd win or they'd lose – the attraction was in the thrill. The risk.

Tonight, though, was a sure bet. Tonight they were here to watch a boy die.

For some of them, this wasn't a first. Others before Sacha had tried impossible feats for their money and failed. But for a few, this was a new sensation, as sharp and vertiginous as the fall Sacha now faced.

They were the ones who looked a little green; whose hands shook as they lit cigarette after cigarette.

♊

Sacha stared into the dark at the landing spot five storeys down. In the fog it looked hazy. Like something from a dream.

He could just make out the figures of the men clustered at the foot of the building, stationed there to make sure everything was legit. He would crash to his death in front of them. Then they would collect their money.

He didn't listen to a word Antoine said behind him. He just waited for his cue.

He felt focused and unafraid. What was there to be scared of?

Finally, as if from far away, the words he waited for rose in the night air. 'And now, gentlemen, he is going to jump. You will see what he's capable of. In three . . . two . . . *one* . . . '

Sacha jumped.

After last time, he knew what to expect. The wind whistling in his ears seemed unnaturally loud, like it was screaming. He gritted his teeth to keep from biting his tongue. His shirt flew up. He squeezed his toes hard to keep his trainers on his feet.

The ground shot towards him so fast. Too fast.

His heart contracted. Instinctively, he twisted in the air to slow down. To stop.

Then he hit.

From miles away, he heard the crunching sound his body

made as it began to break. He would have screamed if he could.

After that, for a brief second ... nothing.

Just peace.

♊

Sacha blinked.

The ground was cold – ice cold. Rough concrete pressed against his torn skin.

Every part of him hurt. Every inch of flesh. Every muscle. Every bone.

He felt destroyed.

This is worse than last time. Worse than anything before.

His feet shifted, scraping against the ground. Voices gasped and murmured as he stirred.

'Holy Mother, he's alive.' A male voice. Deep. It sounded frightened.

That voice sliced through the haze of pain, reminding Sacha where he was. How he'd got here. What was expected of him.

Vaguely, he wondered how long he'd been out.

Not long enough.

He could sense eyes on him, hear the uncomfortable rustle as the men clustered together.

Stifling a groan, he raised one hand slowly to shield his eyes.

At first he could see little – everything was blurred. As his vision cleared, though, he could see the small crowd recoiling from him, as if he might be contagious.

He couldn't blame them. He must look like hell.

He longed to stay on the pavement but he had to get up.

He had an audience to impress.

With grim determination he struggled to his feet, forcing himself not to look as broken as he felt.

Each tiny movement sent a stab of pain shooting through him. He'd never felt agony like this. Surely, some internal organs must have exploded. He knew some bones had broken and his heart definitely stopped beating for a short time – he'd noticed its absence. An odd, sinking stillness.

But everything was repairing itself now. He could feel his body healing, shattered bones knitting back together. Rebuilding what he'd so recklessly destroyed. Whether he wanted it to or not.

Nearby, the crowd of men grew restive.

'How?' One man murmured.

A thug in a leather jacket crossed himself.

'It's a trick,' someone said.

'Yeah, but *how*?' The first one looked at the others, bewildered. 'I heard him hit. You all saw it. No one survives that.' He pointed at Sacha from a safe distance, his hand trembling. Sacha just blinked at him. 'That boy was dead. Now he ... isn't.'

'That's impossible,' the other one said stubbornly. 'It's a con.'

Sacha could have told them it wasn't a trick, wasn't magic or illusion. It was just the way things were: he would die on the day of his eighteenth birthday and not one day sooner. What would kill him later, today saved his life.

But he said nothing. They'd never believe it anyway.

Suppressing the pain, he forced himself to offer the crowd a sardonic bow.

They stared at him in horrified bewilderment.

One thing was certain: they'd be talking about this for years.

Behind them, the rest of the group – those who'd watched the show from the roof – began to emerge from the warehouse, guided by Antoine, his face glowing with the smug contentment bestowed by huge profit.

Antoine shot Sacha a wink before turning to the group.

'Gentlemen, I'll collect your money now . . . '

SEVEN

It was early evening when Sacha finally climbed out of bed the next day, whimpering a little with each movement. It wasn't as bad as last night but he still felt stiff and sore. It was like his body was punishing him.

Through the curtains he could see the last of the day's sunlight flooding the street with gold. He was in no mood for sunshine. Last night should have filled him with exhilaration. Instead he felt more hopeless than ever. He felt freakish. Lost.

Damned.

The jump had taken a toll not only on his body but also on his mind.

He shut the curtains so no bright rays could filter into the darkness of his room. Then he stood there, surrounded by clutter.

Dirty clothes lay on the floor along with empty crisp bags,

used plates, papers, and empty soda bottles. With the tip of his bare foot, he pushed over a pile of books, watching dispassionately as they toppled onto the carpet.

There'd been a time when he had loved to read. These days he was increasingly afraid that, one day he'd start to read a story he really loved, and he'd never have the chance to finish it.

For similar reasons he'd given up almost everything that once brought him joy: friendships, school. Love.

Amid the floor detritus, his book bag lay open, spilling bundles of banknotes, bound with rubber bands.

The men had bet much more than Antoine expected. There were twenty thousand euros in that bag. Enough for his mother to buy a really nice car. Or a hell of a lot of groceries.

He knew which one *he'd* spend it on.

Picking up the bag he sat on the bed and carefully, almost tenderly, pulled the money into a thick stack. Now he knew what it felt like to touch that much cash. How much it weighed.

Grabbing a wad of bills, he ruffled them with his thumb, letting the light breeze move across his face. It smelled of cool ink and old paper. He liked that smell.

Each time he died, it got harder. Each time it hurt more.

But, *damn*. It was worth it.

Imagine how much he could make if he could jump two to three times a week. It would be excruciating but the money would flow. If he died a few more times, maybe his mum could buy a better flat.

Reality quickly chased that dream away, though. Money brought trouble. Somehow, he had to keep this cash safe and hidden. If his mother discovered it she'd want to know where it came from. And that was a story he didn't intend to tell.

There weren't many hiding places in this flat. So he had to keep it simple.

Crossing to his desk, he pulled out one of the lower drawers, dumping its contents onto the floor without ceremony. He stuffed the cash all the way at the back before disguising it with old school papers and books.

That done, he cleared the top of his desk with a sweep of his arm, sending papers and books flying, and switched on his computer.

It opened automatically to his email inbox. More than a hundred unread messages blinked at him accusingly. He scanned the names without opening them. Emails from the school, ads for things he didn't want ... nothing interesting. Then a name caught his eye.

Taylor.

He clicked on it. When he'd read the message, he leaned back in his chair and stared up at the ceiling, considering his options.

This tutoring thing was such a hassle. He had much more important things on his mind right now than humouring Deide and some random English girl who knew nothing about him.

Still, he didn't close the email.

He tried to imagine telling her the truth about his life. What would she think? What if she could have seen him last night?

She'd run screaming.

His lifestyle was so far removed from her perfect world. She was so clean. So ... *normal*. It was as if their teachers had selected the two most unlikely people on the planet and forced them to work together.

He knew he should focus on this deal with Antoine, and making more money for his family. He knew he should be living it up in his last remaining days. Still, he couldn't help remembering the way she'd looked at him. She wasn't beautiful in the Hollywood way, but she was pretty, in that unconscious way of girls who didn't know they were pretty. She had a heart-shaped face and those extraordinary eyes, green as lake water.

Maybe it would help him to talk to someone who didn't know what a wreck he was. Someone who signed their emails 'kind regards', as if polite formality came easily.

If nothing else, it was fun to tease her. She was cute when she was outraged.

That decided it. He'd give her another chance before making up his mind.

He typed a terse reply:

Meet me tonight. Ten o'clock England time. You know where. Sacha.

When he'd finished, he headed to the kitchen to make himself a sandwich. That was where his mother intercepted him.

'Will you have dinner with us tonight?' she asked. 'It's my night off. It would be nice to have a real family dinner for a change.'

'Sure,' he said. 'I've got nothing special on tonight. I just have to chat with my English tutor, that's all.'

Surprise flickered across her face. '*You* have a tutor?'

He shrugged as if being tutored was an everyday thing with him, and affected an insulted tone. 'I'm not an idiot, you know. I really care about my mind.'

His mother snorted and, from the living room down the hall, he heard Laura laughing. 'Sacha has a *tutor*? Is the world ending? Should we pack?'

He held up his hands. 'Laugh if you want to, but it's true. We're going to read books in English together.'

'Well, I think it's wonderful,' his mother said. 'I'm just a little shocked.'

Sacha took a bite of his sandwich and spoke with his mouth full. 'I can't believe you ever doubted my love of education.'

Laura came into the kitchen and leaned against the door frame. 'That is the funniest thing I've heard all year.'

'OK. That's enough.' Sacha threw a piece of bread at her and she snatched it from the air.

'No throwing food,' their mother ordered, but her smile softened her words. 'Who is this tutor? Someone from school?'

Sacha swallowed the bite he'd just taken. 'No – Deide set it up. She's some English girl. Her name's Taylor. Taylor Montclair.'

A glass slipped from his mother's hand and shattered on the tile.

For a long second she didn't move, but stood looking dumbly at the glass shards at her feet.

Laura and Sacha exchanged a puzzled glance.

'*Maman?*' Laura looked at her mother with concern. 'Are you hurt?'

Their mother reached for a dustpan.

'So clumsy,' she murmured. 'I really liked that glass.'

Her voice was oddly strained.

Sacha said nothing but, as he watched her, his brow creased. Something about Taylor's name had startled her. He was sure of it.

Before he could ask her about it, the phone in his pocket buzzed angrily.

Sacha glanced at the screen then, cursing under his breath, hurried back towards his room holding the phone to his ear. 'Antoine. What is it? I'm busy right now.'

All he could hear at the end of the line was hoarse, heavy breathing and the sound of footsteps, as if someone was running.

Sacha froze. 'Antoine? What's going on?'

'We've got ... trouble.' Antoine's voice echoed oddly. It sounded like he was at the bottom of a cavern.

In the background Sacha could hear the sound of his panicked footsteps, and something dripping.

'What kind of trouble?'

'The guys from the other night – they're after me.' Antoine's voice was taut 'Come quick or I'm a dead man.'

Sacha's stomach flipped. This was bad. Nothing scared Antoine. Right now he sounded terrified.

'What the hell happened?' he asked, keeping his voice low.

'They think we cheated them. They want the money back but I haven't got it. Anyway, they'll kill me – and they say they're coming for you next. I believe them.' Antoine drew a shaky breath. 'We're screwed, Sacha.'

Sacha closed his eyes, squeezing the phone tight. 'Where are you?'

♊

A few minutes later, Sacha pulled on his trainers, shoved his arms into a black hoody and headed for the door. As soon as his mother spotted the keys in his hand, her good mood evaporated.

'Where are you going?'

'Don't worry,' he said with forced nonchalance. 'Someone needs my help but it's no big deal – I'll be back in time for dinner.'

His mother sighed. Whatever he thought he'd seen in her face when he'd said Taylor's name was gone now. She just looked disappointed.

'I hope you will.' She paused, as if considering whether to say more. 'Sometimes I think you're avoiding me now so I won't miss you later. I hate it. It's like you're gone already.' She bit her lip; her eyes searching his. 'Please don't do this. Not anymore. I want us to have all the time together we can. To be a family.'

Sacha stood in the doorway, keys gripped tightly in one hand. This was the worst time for her to decide she wanted to talk about this. Antoine could be dead already.

None the less, guilt unfurled inside his chest. She wasn't

entirely wrong. He had been avoiding his family, but not because he knew how much they would miss him. More because he knew how much *he* would miss *them*.

It had been a little over a year since she first told him what was going to happen to him. At first, he hadn't believed her. It sounded insane. He'd been confused and hurt. The first time he died, though, he realised it was true.

He'd been fighting with some guys – guys much bigger than him. He was angry. He wanted to get into trouble. Wanted to cause pain. In the end, they were the ones who hurt him.

A single punch to the jaw was all it took. He'd gone flying, hitting the curb at just the wrong angle. Snapping his neck clean through. The last thing he'd heard was the *crack* as it broke.

When he woke up a few minutes later feeling like he'd been run over by a truck, the boys were gone.

After that he believed.

From then on, he'd avoided his family, quit going to school, dropped his friends, broke up with his girlfriend.

He couldn't see the point of any of it. His entire life was a lie.

His entire life was nearly over.

Even as he'd withdrawn, though, his mother grew more determinedly cheery. Everything at home became hyper-normal. His impending fate was so rarely mentioned, at times he wondered if she'd forgotten it entirely.

What he couldn't forgive was that she didn't try to fight it. He knew his father had tried. She'd told him that much. But after he died it was as if his mother just ... gave up.

Sacha knew she loved him, but she never tried to save him. That hurt more than dying.

So he'd avoided her. Avoided his old life. Avoided school. For months now he'd done his best to disappear. Only now the end was nearing did he regret it.

If he was only to have seventeen years with his family, he could at least try to make them seventeen good years.

Finally he spoke, his voice steady.

'I promise, *Maman*. I'll be here for dinner.'

The longing in her eyes for more – more information, more truth – was painful to see. But he didn't have time. 'I've got to go.'

He kissed her cheek and left the flat, running at full speed.

♊

The basement car park was quiet and dim, the flickering fluorescent lights darkened by the bodies of countless suicidal insects.

He'd parked his motorcycle in its usual space behind the bins, safe from any distracted drivers who might back up without looking.

Even in the bad light it gleamed like black gold.

He'd won it a few months ago off one of Antoine's associates, after a particularly perilous night of gambling, and he loved it more than just about anything except his family. It was a Yamaha FJR 1300 – the most perfect bike in the world.

Pulling his helmet on with the swift ease of practice, he climbed on the bike and gunned it.

The address Antoine had given him turned out to be a

decrepit 1960s tower block in a very dodgy suburb a few miles away.

Most people who've never lived in Paris think the entire city is one gigantic tourist attraction – all milky white buildings and tree-lined streets. In reality, outside the centre, the city is like any other. Strip malls. Big, ugly retail outlets. Miles of car parks.

There are good Paris neighbourhoods and bad.

This was a very bad one.

Sacha made his way between crowded modern apartment blocks, blighted with graffiti. His tires crunched over trash in the street.

A small gang of guys hung out in front of the building, looking for trouble.

Sacha drove by without stopping – they all turned to watch him pass. He didn't like the way they looked at his bike.

He longed to turn around and go right back home. But he had no choice. Antoine was not his friend, but if those guys planned to off him and then come looking for Sacha, they might find his family in the process. That couldn't happen.

After a short search, he found a place to hide the bike behind a garage a few blocks away, then returned to the building on foot with his hoody up, running past the guys without looking at them. They jeered as he passed, but none followed as he headed down the concrete stairs to the basement level.

At the foot of the steps, he threw his shoulder against a set of grey, metal double doors scratched with graffiti. They opened with a shriek of protest.

On the other side, he found himself in a narrow, industrial passageway. Faint light was provided by flickering bare bulbs set intermittently in the ceiling.

The concrete walls were covered in spray paint but he couldn't make out what was written. Over time, one word had been painted on top of another over and over until it was too chaotic to read. Like written screaming.

On one side the wall was lined with a series of doors, each of which had, it seemed, been kicked in.

Once upon a time, this must have been storage for the building above. But nobody kept anything good down here now.

After a while the bulbs ran out and he walked into the dark. The whole place stank of urine. And something else. Something worse.

At first he heard nothing but his own footsteps. Then strident voices echoed in the distance. A scream split the air.

Pulling his phone from his pocket, Sacha held it up as a makeshift torch and quickened his pace. When he reached a fractured wooden door marked with the number thirty-seven, he stopped.

'Antoine?'

The only reply was the sound of his heart thudding in his ears.

Cautiously, he placed his fingertips against the door and pushed. It swung open too easily, revealing a yawning darkness on the other side.

The stench was worse here. Covering his mouth and nose with one hand, Sacha stepped inside.

His phone cast a wash of pale blue light across the small, cube-shaped room. Damp oozed from the concrete walls. The floor was littered with trash and shapes he could just make out but would rather not think about.

The perfect setting for a murder, he thought.

It was a second before he spotted Antoine, sitting in a chair, his head slumped to his chest. A huge man stood next to him, holding a gun to his temple.

The man's tattoos and scowl perfectly matched the setting. He was, Sacha thought with mild hysteria, born for this job.

Stay cool, Sacha.

Shoving his hands into the pockets of his jeans, he adopted a confident, dismissive expression.

'You guys really know how to party.'

The big guy turned the gun on him, almost as a reflex.

Antoine's head jerked up; relief filled his eyes. 'Sacha! You came.'

Blood ran down his face from his nose, giving the bizarre impression that he had a red moustache and beard. One of his eyes was swollen shut.

'Of course.' Sacha shrugged, like he came to this sort of place every day.

Antoine squinted at the gunman. 'See? I told you he'd come. So we can all calm down now. Everything's fine.'

At that moment, a second man, hidden until then in a dark corner, stepped into the dim light from Sacha's phone.

Physically, he was the opposite of the first one: as short and lean as the other was tall and muscular. He, too, seemed perfectly suited to a dank, rancid cellar.

'Shut up,' he said to Antoine, who did as he was told.

He's the boss, Sacha thought.

He could hear something dripping. He hoped it was water.

'I have to say the casting is amazing,' he said, looking back and forth between the two thugs. 'You are both . . . terrifying.'

'What the hell is he talking about?' asked the big guy, gesturing with his gun. Sacha tried not to flinch as the barrel flashed at him.

'So you're a smart ass, are you?' The small one grinned. In the dimness, his teeth looked sharp.

Sacha sauntered closer.

'Look. It's like this. You've got my business partner and I've got some money. Why don't you let him go? And I'll give you the cash.' He gestured at Antoine. 'He really had nothing to do with the scam anyway. He's an idiot. I told him I could survive the fall and he believed me.'

The small, ugly man turned to Antoine. 'Is that true?'

'It's all true.' Antoine spoke eagerly, seizing Sacha's story like a lifeline. 'He's the bastard who set it up. He took all the cash and left me with nothing.'

The short guy studied Sacha with new interest.

'Hand it over, kid,' he said. 'And your friend here goes free.'

He made a quick gesture Sacha didn't really see. Suddenly, the big guy struck Antoine on the side of the head with the gun. The cracking sound echoed through the concrete chamber.

Antoine's head snapped to one side. A new trickle of blood ran down the side of his face.

Sacha swallowed hard. He didn't like this at all. Odds were

they'd kill both of them. Or at least, they'd kill Antoine. And they'd try to kill him, too.

He had to play this smart.

'Let's do this another way,' he said, as if an idea had just occurred to him. 'Let him go first.' He nodded at Antoine. 'Then I'll give you the money.'

The smaller guy studied him for a second, then he pulled a pack of cigarettes from his pocket.

Frowning, the big guy swung the gun towards Sacha. 'I don't think he's going to give it to us.'

The smaller guy squinted at Sacha as he placed a cigarette in his mouth.

There was a click of a button, and a sudden flash of flame as he lit it with a silver lighter. He took his time, inhaling deeply, then blowing the smoke out in a thin, pale stream. All the while he kept his gaze on Sacha.

'No,' he said at last. 'I don't either. Let's just take it.' He waved the hand holding the cigarette in a careless gesture. 'Get on with it.'

In the square, concrete room, the gun's retort was deafening. Sacha thought he heard someone scream.

The bullet hit the left side of his forehead near the hairline, travelled through his skull and perforated his brain.

He felt heat first. Agonising pain speared him.

Then darkness spread over him with the comforting warmth of a blanket.

The nightmarish cellar scene vanished.

♊

The first thing Sacha heard when he came to was Antoine's voice.

'*Merde, merde, merde . . .* '

Someone was pushing him. Shoving him hard. It took a moment to realise it was hands, going through his pockets roughly, turning them inside out. Frantic and desperate.

He couldn't open his eyes. It was hard to think. He thought he might puke.

'Where is it?' Antoine muttered to himself. 'It's got to be here . . .'

Sacha licked his lips, swimming slowly back to full consciousness. His head pounded sickeningly. Something stank. Everything was sticky and cold.

With a groan, he raised his hand to his head, forcing his eyes to open. 'God . . . did he *have* to shoot me?'

Antoine jumped as if he'd been stung. He scuttled away; his feet made an awful skidding sound on the damp floor.

In the dimness, he stared at Sacha with a look of horror. 'You're . . . You can't be . . . alive?'

Sacha struggled to sit up, but the room swam and he had to brace himself on his elbows and wait for the nausea to pass.

'I think so. Unless my ghost is talking to you. Which is always possible. I believe in ghosts, you know. And you won't find the money. I didn't bring it.' He clutched his temples. 'God, my *head.*'

'No, no, no . . . ' Antoine shook his head violently. 'He shot you in the *face*. I saw the whole thing. You've lost a . . . a lot of blood . . . '

As if to prove it, he held up a red-stained hand.

Sacha's head throbbed. This was such a mess. He felt too sick to lie. Too tired to make anything up.

'I know, I know . . . It's a long story. I'd explain but I've got this awful headache.'

He almost laughed, but his head throbbed with such viciousness he thought laughing might kill him again.

With difficulty, he staggered to his feet, swaying a little, as if he stood on the deck of a ship. Gingerly, he ran his fingers across his forehead. There was nothing left: no hole. Just a smooth shallow dimple where the bullet had gone in. He didn't know how his body did this . . . this . . . healing. This regeneration. But it always did.

Still, he must look a sight. His face, his neck, his forehead, his shirt – all were covered in blood. It was disgusting.

Antoine cowered like a trapped animal, watching him with terrified eyes.

Sacha held up a hand reassuringly. 'I'll be OK, seriously. No need to panic.' Turning his wrist, he glanced at his watch, wincing. It had taken him a while to wake up this time. It was late. 'Look, I have to go. I promised my mother I'd be back for dinner.' He looked around. 'What happened to those guys? Did they leave after they killed me?'

Antoine nodded slowly as if emerging from a dream.

'The big one was too quick on the trigger. I think they just planned to scare you so you'd hand over the cash. When they saw you were . . . dead . . . they legged it. They didn't even try to find the money.'

'Those assholes.' Sacha looked down at his bloodied clothes. 'They absolutely *ruined* this shirt.'

Antoine backed up until he was pressed against the sticky wall.

'Sacha. *Putain* ... You were dead. Weren't you?'

There would be no getting out of this without an explanation – that much was obvious. Antoine had been willing to accept the jumping thing – he'd convinced himself Sacha was some kind of trickster – an illusionist – but this time ... this time he knew it was real.

'Not completely.' Sacha struggled to find the words. He'd never told anyone the truth. Only he and his family knew. 'It's hard to explain but I ... I kind of can't die. Yet.'

Silence fell in the filthy cellar. Then Antoine spoke again, his voice quivering but resolute.

'Thank you for coming when I called you.' He stopped for a second, before seeming to regain courage. 'But I never want to see you again. OK? You understand? You scare the hell out of me. I don't know what you are but ... just ... never call me again. Forget I exist. I'll do the same with you. It's better this way.'

Without waiting for a reply, he ran from the room.

Sacha stood still, listening as the footsteps receded in the distance. He heard the rusty, metallic screech of a door opening on atrophied hinges. The thud as it closed.

And then he was alone in the middle of the most horrible room he'd ever seen, standing in a puddle of his own blood.

EiGHT

'Come on, Taylor.' Georgie's voice took on a wheedling tone. 'Mum says I can't study with Paul in my room unless you're here, too. Tom says he'll come over if you do . . .'

With the phone tucked between her shoulder and her ear, Taylor rinsed the last dinner plate and slid it into the dishwasher. A few pale strands of hair had escaped from her ponytail holder. In the steam from the hot water they curled until they tickled her cheek. She swiped at them ineffectually.

'I'd love to, George,' she said. 'But I've got to do this tutoring thing. It's been scheduled for ages.'

'Come on, Tay. Cancel it. The French random's a total jerk anyway. Finlay will get over it.'

Taylor shook her head, nearly dropping the phone. 'I need this for my Oxford application . . .'

'God.' Georgie didn't try to hide her irritation. 'That bloody application. It's all you ever talk about. It ruins your *life*.'

Turning off the tap, Taylor switched the phone to her other ear. 'It doesn't ruin my life,' she said patiently. 'But it is important. And this has been scheduled . . .'

'I know, I know. You said. For ages.' Georgie sighed. 'But how am I supposed to get anything going with Paul if I can't spend any time with him?'

'You were out with him the other night,' Taylor pointed out. She knew it wasn't fair. Georgie was deep in crush, and desperate to see Paul again. But she didn't want to spend another night hanging out listening to Paul and Tom talk about sport.

'That's why I want him to come over tonight,' Georgie explained. 'That night, Paul and I really got on. I felt like we just . . . I don't know . . . connected, you know? It was like he finally noticed me. But then Tom came back and . . .'

The boys talked mostly to each other, Taylor guessed. She knew that situation all too well.

'Look, if Tom's there tonight the same thing will happen. Seriously. Sometimes I think they should just go out with each other.'

Dropping the soap into the dishwasher, she closed it and turned it on, leaning back against the counter as it rumbled to life. In the background she could hear applause and laughter from whatever reality show her mother and sister were watching in the living room.

'What's up with you and Tom anyway?' Georgie asked. 'You never want to see him lately.'

Taylor twisted a damp tea towel until it looked like blue

81

and white rope. Then let it go, watching as it untangled itself, reforming into a towel again.

'I don't know, George. I just . . . I don't think it's working.'

As soon as she said it she instantly felt better. All her muscles seemed to loosen, like that towel. And spin free.

'Are you serious, Tay?' Georgie sounded shocked. 'Do you think you'll really break up with him?'

Taylor let out a long breath. She'd never broken up with anyone in her life.

Tom was her first real boyfriend. She didn't want to make him sad. She just didn't want to be his girlfriend any more.

'Oh, I don't know, Georgie. It's a mess. I don't think either of us is happy any more. And we should probably make it official. Or unofficial. Whatever you call it when you really break up. So I can't come tonight and hang out with him until I've sorted this out. I'm really sorry. I hope you and Paul still find a way to get together.'

Recognising defeat, Georgie finally gave up. 'I'm sorry about you and Tom, Tay. But you have to do what makes you happy.'

After ending the call, Taylor sat down at the table, and flipped open her laptop. The clock above the stove said it was nine o'clock. Still an hour until the chat with Sacha and she had plenty of homework – which didn't stop her typing in the address of the dodgy chatroom, just to see if maybe he was around early.

A skittering sound and a whimper outside the kitchen door made her stop, just as the grinning green skull and bones floated onto the screen.

'Hey, Fizzy.' Opening the door, she picked up the little dog, carrying her back to the table. Fizz sat in her lap, panting at the computer screen. Taylor stroked her fur with one hand as she typed Sacha's screen name with the other.

His profile page popped up – he was offline. But Taylor didn't close the window. Instead, she leaned forward to study his picture more closely.

His ocean-blue gaze seemed to hold hers. The photo had been taken on a city street, in front of a dirty, grey wall spray-painted with a meaningless jumble of letters and symbols. She wondered if he was the one who'd painted it. He looked the type. Tough. And antagonistic; a giant chip on his shoulder.

He looked dangerous. And that danger had a magnetic force.

When the kitchen door opened with a creak, it startled her so much she nearly dropped Fizz, who she'd forgotten was still in her lap.

Her mother frowned. 'Is that homework? Or are you playing?'

Taylor's eyes landed on the kitchen clock again. Her heart stuttered. It was half past nine.

Had she been staring at that photo for half an hour?

She looked down at her computer – its glowing white numbers told her the same thing: 21:30.

But that simply wasn't possible. She'd sat down, picked up Fizz, opened the computer ...

And half an hour had disappeared.

Confusion made her feel panicked, dizzy. She looked around the room for an explanation but found none.

She realised her mother was watching her, puzzlement and suspicion making narrow lines on her forehead.

When Taylor forced herself to reply to her mother's question, her voice came out high-pitched and anxious.

'Homework . . . I was just getting started but . . . ' But what? *I got lost in the kitchen and thirty minutes disappeared?* ' . . . I got distracted.'

Clearly not impressed, her mother put a tea bag in a mug and reached for the milk jug. 'Well, I'm sure you have other work to do. Don't spend all night on that thing . . . ' She pointed accusingly at the laptop.

Taylor's mother believed phones and computers were bad for people's brains. She'd read some article about it in Flake Out International Magazine or something like that, and would not stop going on about it.

But given that she'd just lost half an hour of actual time, Taylor decided not to argue about that stuff right now. Instead, she shut down her web browser with a decisive click.

'Don't worry. I won't.'

She spent the next thirty minutes half-doing her physics homework, half-trying to figure out what had happened. She'd sat down. Turned on her laptop. And lost time. No matter how often she tried, she came back to the same black hole.

At ten o'clock, when she found herself Googling 'brain tumour', she made herself stop. She wasn't really in the mood to teach anyone anything right now but she'd promised.

She opened Sacha's profile page again. The 'offline' message glared at her.

She left the screen open while she read over her history

essay again, to pass the time. Every few minutes she glanced up to check, but he wasn't there.

After a while it started to bother her.

Where is he? How could he be so totally unreliable?

This tutoring thing was not going to work out if he didn't take it seriously at all. Georgie was right – it was a waste of time.

She opened her email to check one more time. He'd definitely said ten o'clock. And he definitely wasn't there. And it was definitely half past ten.

Enough.

Finlay would go mental but she didn't have to put up with this.

Her fingers moved with quick efficient irritation as she opened a blank email.

Sacha,

I don't appreciate being ignored. I turned down a date tonight for you. Then waited around for half an hour like an idiot.

I should have guessed you wouldn't take this seriously.

Fine, whatever. Let's just forget this whole thing. Find another tutor. I quit.

Taylor

Before she could change her mind, she clicked 'send' decisively.

Still, despite herself, she checked his Revolution Chat profile page one last time.

Offline.

She slammed the laptop shut.

At that moment, a white-hot pain seared her head with such force she cried out, crumpling to the floor.

Fizz gave a surprised yap but Taylor didn't notice. All she was aware of was pain like nothing she'd ever felt. As if she'd been stabbed or shot. She could hear someone moaning and wondered who it was.

Fizz had begun to bark frantically but the sound was faint, as if it had travelled to her from a great distance away.

The kitchen door opened.

'Taylor . . . ?' Her mother's panicked voice seemed to come from the bottom of a well.

Taylor tried to reply but she couldn't speak. She felt as if she was dying.

The walls closed in. Then everything went dark. And she was glad.

Nine

Taylor tried to blink, but her eyelids felt heavy, as if they were weighted down. Her head thudded with such viciousness it made her stomach churn. She could hear voices around her – frightened familiar voices.

With tremendous effort, she opened her eyes.

Bright light pierced her skull with the sharpness of a chisel. She groaned.

The blurry figure of her sister Emily hovered into view. She was on the floor at Taylor's side, holding her hand. She looked frightened, tearful.

What is she doing in my bedroom? Taylor wondered.

The bed was cold and hard beneath her cheek. She spread her fingers out flat against it.

Not the bed. The floor.

She turned her head to one side.

Table legs. Chairs. The kitchen.

It all came back to her.

'Are you awake?' Emily asked, and Taylor could hear relief in her voice. Before she could reply, her sister turned to look up at their mother who Taylor saw now was behind her, talking into the phone. 'Mum.'

'No.' Taylor heard her mother say into the phone. 'She just collapsed.'

'*Mum*,' Emily called more urgently. 'She's awake.'

'Oh, thank God.' Her mother's pale, worried face loomed into view. 'Taylor, can you hear me? Do you know who I am?'

'Of course I know who you are, Mum.'

She struggled to sit up and found it surprisingly difficult with the floor swinging like that. Emily helped her, tugging at her arm, and eventually she was up, her back against a table leg. She seemed to have bruised every part of her body.

'Ouch,' Taylor said. 'I guess I fell.'

Her mother shot her an odd look, as if that wasn't the right thing to say. Taylor wondered what the right thing to say was.

She still felt groggy. Like she'd got drunk and been hit in the head by a hammer simultaneously.

'Yes,' her mother said into the phone, 'she's conscious but I think you should send the ambulance anyway.'

'*Ambulance*?' Suddenly Taylor felt wide awake. 'No, Mum. Seriously. I'm fine. I just didn't eat enough today. I hardly drank any water. I was just dizzy.'

It wasn't at all true – she'd eaten plenty. But she really didn't want to go to a hospital for one tiny little collapse.

Holding the phone away from her ear, her mother looked at her doubtfully. 'Are you sure?'

'I'm *fine*,' Taylor insisted, trying to look fine. 'Just give me a biscuit and I'll be good. Promise.'

For a long moment her mother held her gaze with worried eyes. Taylor could hear the faint squawk of the 999 operator on the end of the line. Finally, she lifted the phone back to her ear.

'Let's cancel the ambulance for now. She says she hasn't eaten. It could be blood sugar. She's a teenager.' She added the last bit as if it explained everything.

Taylor climbed to her feet without help. The dizziness was receding. Her head still ached and a biscuit actually wouldn't have gone amiss. Otherwise, she felt fine. Just a bit dazed.

She stared at the laptop on the table in front of her. The last thing she could remember was closing it.

It was like it had punched her.

Her mother shuffled through the cupboards, emerging with a packet of digestive biscuits. She looked over her shoulder at her.

'Sit. Don't take things too fast. I'll get you some tea.'

'Can I have tea and biscuits, too?' Emily asked, taking the seat across from Taylor.

'Naturally.' Their mother filled the kettle, talking over the splash of the water. 'Don't need you fainting, too.'

She placed the biscuits onto a plate and set it on the table between the two of them. 'Eat.'

Dutifully, Taylor took a biscuit and devoured it. She grabbed another.

Maybe I really was hungry, she thought.

In truth, though, she knew something was wrong. She just didn't want to think about what that something might be.

Her mother returned with three cups of milky tea, setting one in front of each of them. She took the seat at the table next to Taylor. Her hazel eyes fixed her with a penetrating look. 'Tell me what happened.'

Taylor hesitated.

For the first time she could remember, she made a conscious decision to lie to her mother.

'I don't really know,' she said, which was almost true. 'I was doing my homework. I'd felt kind of dizzy earlier and I kept meaning to get up and eat something but I didn't. I was working on my history essay and I wanted to finish it.'

Trying to keep her expression a good balance of innocence and mild martyrdom, she blinked wanly.

Her mother's eyes narrowed. 'Then what?'

Taylor sipped her tea. It had lots of sugar in it. Just the way she liked it.

'I stood up too fast, I guess. Because I felt super dizzy. I tried to call you. And . . . that's all I remember.'

'Hmm,' her mother said, still watching her. After a moment she seemed to make up her mind. 'Well, obviously you're not eating enough. No more skipping meals. And I'll be limiting your time on that thing.'

She pointed at the laptop.

Taylor's stomach dropped.

'But I need the computer for homework,' she protested. 'I have exams.'

Her mother was unmoved. 'Too much time on the computer is bad for you. I told you about the article I read. It's scientifically proven. You'll just have to use your time on it more wisely from now on. You can have two hours of computer a night, no more.'

She might as well have said she would have to spend twenty-two hours a day in prison. Taylor stared at her in horror.

'But, *Mum*. That's not nearly enough.'

'It will have to be enough.' Her mind made up, her mother picked up the laptop and placed it on top of the kitchen cupboard. 'Because that is all you can have.'

TEN

Sacha's mother was waiting for him when he got home. She sat alone in the dark at the kitchen table as he paused uncertainly in the doorway. He knew she'd heard him come in, was sure she knew he was standing in the corridor, but she didn't look at him.

'You promised, Sacha. You did promise.' Her voice was muffled. 'One family night, that's all I asked. Just one. I knew I couldn't trust you. I shouldn't have let you go out. I should have forbidden it.'

The pain in her voice hurt Sacha nearly as much as the bullet had.

Exhausted, he leaned against a wall in the shadows outside the kitchen, hoping she wouldn't get a good look at him. His T-shirt was sticky with half-dried blood. The coppery stench of death was all over him. On the journey back, his helmet had hidden the gore from the world but now he knew he must look like a monster.

'Come on, *Maman* ... ' His voice was weak, and she cut him off, her tone sharpening.

'I know you don't value your own life anymore. But you could at least keep your word. You could show me some respect. Is that too much to ask?'

Sacha flinched. How could she say that to him? Why should he value his life when it was going to be taken from him in just a few weeks? He couldn't pretend everything was fine. He couldn't lie to himself like that.

But he didn't have the strength to argue with her right now.

'I'm sorry, *Maman*.' He spoke in a raspy whisper. 'Tonight didn't turn out the way it was supposed to. It was ... '

The sentence trailed off. He didn't know what to say.

When his mother spoke again, anger took the place of disappointment.

'You're *sorry*? Well, it's easy to say you're sorry. But that doesn't fix anything. Laura begged me to hold dinner for you. We sat here waiting for you for an hour.' She pounded the table with her fingers; each thud made Sacha wince. 'We both wanted to believe. We both just wanted to be a family.'

She spun around to face him, her pale blue eyes narrow with anger. At the same moment, Sacha stepped into a pool of light spilling out into the hallway.

All the colour drained from his mother's face. She clapped a hand over her mouth to muffle a scream.

'My God, Sacha,' she whispered. 'What happened to you?'

She rushed to his side but when she reached out to touch his bloodied shoulder he recoiled. He didn't want her to have any contact with the blood and filth that coated his clothes, his skin.

'It's nothing. I just fell off my bike. Some place really horrible.'

But she wasn't about to believe that. Her nurses' eyes scanned him for wounds. 'All this blood? Is it yours?'

He couldn't bear the look on her face – the fear and confusion.

Dropping the act, he nodded ashamedly.

'What really happened, Sacha?' she asked.

'I got shot.'

'*What*?'

'I'm fine now.' His eyes pleaded for her to understand. 'See?' He held out his blood-encrusted arms.

His mother stared at him with horror – as if she was looking at a stranger.

'This,' she said, 'is not fine.'

Anger tore through Sacha, giving him strength.

'Well, it's as fine as I get,' he fired back. 'You know, if you don't like the way I live, maybe you should try and help me, instead of pretending everything is perfect. Did you ever consider that?'

Her jaw dropped. For a split second he thought she might slap him.

'That's *enough*,' she said instead. 'Enough of your excuses.

Enough of your miserable behaviour.' Her voice was firm but not shrill. 'I'm fed up with your attitude. Whatever future you face, right now you're still a child. And you're my responsibility. You're grounded, Sacha. You will not leave this house at night. And you will go to school like every other teenager does.' Her lips tightened. 'I've been lax with you. It hasn't done either of us any good.' She pointed down the hallway. 'Go to your room.'

She hadn't talked to him like this in years. Not since they found out the truth about him. In a strange way he found it comforting.

Besides, there was no point in arguing about this right now, when all he really wanted to do was get back to his room and wash off the blood.

She said nothing more. But he thought he heard her stifle a sob as he walked away.

♊

A few minutes later, Sacha stood in the shower trying to wash the night's damage away. He'd turned the temperature up as hot as he could bear; the scalding water lashing his back made him wince but this kind of pain was good, reminding him he really was still alive.

The dried blood on his skin dissolved in the steaming cascade; the water swirling at his feet looked like liquid rust.

His scars were pale against his tawny skin. Each one a reminder of his recklessness. Or bad luck.

Closing his eyes he leaned against the shower wall. He felt drained. Mostly because of the shock his body had taken tonight, but not just that. He was tired of everything. Of knowing the day he would die. Of being a freak. Of scaring people away.

As soon as Antoine really understood what he was, he'd been disgusted. Terrified. Twice he'd seen Sacha leap from impossible heights and walk away unscathed. He must have known there was something going on.

Tonight though ... Sacha ran his hands through his wet hair. *Things were different.*

The sight of his skull bashed in by the bullet – the time it took his body to repair itself, to keep him in perfect shape until D-day – there was no way to unsee that. It must have all been too much. Even for someone like Antoine.

And then there was his mother. Who, in the middle of all this, wanted him to pretend to be a normal kid.

As if that were possible.

With a rough twist of his wrist he shut off the water.

Wrapped in a towel he made his way back to his cluttered bedroom and surveyed the mess with bitter eyes.

Maybe he should just stay in here. There was no one left to go out with anyway. No one to keep him company on long nights when flirting with death was the only way to stay sane.

He didn't understand the world. Didn't understand how he could be like he was. But there was one thing he was certain of: no one should have to live like this.

He felt completely alone.

He didn't know what to do now. Adrenaline still raced in his veins, leaving him jittery and restless. His head ached from the gunshot, making it hard for him to think straight.

Spotting the aspirin amid the mess on top of his desk, he

reached for it, jarring the computer mouse in the process. The monitor lit up. His email inbox was open. A message at the top blinked at him. It was from Taylor.

'*Merde.*'

Clutching the aspirin bottle, Sacha sank down in the chair. He'd forgotten all about their planned tutorial.

Was there no one he hadn't let down today?

Shaking out two of the tablets he swallowed them dry. Then, steeling himself, he reached out for the cool plastic of the mouse and opened the email.

It was as he'd expected. The irritation and disappointment in her message were clear. She was giving up, she wouldn't help him.

On any other night, Sacha would have laughed at the wounded pride in her words. He would have called her boring. A nag.

But right now, when it was nearly midnight, when he'd taken a bullet in the head, when he'd seen the horror of his situation reflected in someone else's eyes – he didn't laugh.

He couldn't change most of the things that were wrong in his life. But he could fix this.

First he checked Revolution Chat, but her profile page said she was offline.

No surprise there ... They were meant to talk more than an hour ago.

Returning to his inbox he replied to her email.

Dear Taylor,

I'm truly sorry I wasn't here for our meeting. I can

assure you I wanted to be there but I got caught up in something and I couldn't get away.

There's no reason for you to believe me, but it really wasn't my fault. And I did want to be here tonight as we'd planned.

Right now I'm going to log in to chat and I'll stay there until you come back. Please contact me. This time, I will be there.

Catcher in the Rye is a very good choice. I read it in French last year. *L'Attrape-Cœur* is its title in my language. It means *The Heart Catcher.* I think I prefer the English title. Anyway. It's a story I would read again with you with great pleasure.

If you can forgive me.

Sacha

His fingers hovered over the send button, but then he thought of something, and he added one line before his name: 'Kind regards.'

Then he pushed the send button.

As soon as the message had gone, he checked her profile page again.

Suddenly, he was desperate for her to come back, to talk to him. To lecture him about the importance of learning.

He wanted to know what her life was like. It had to be different from his.

It was clear to him that Taylor was intelligent. She had to be if she was chosen as a tutor. She was a normal person with a normal life and a normal family. And right now he needed to know that was real. That for someone out there, normal was possible.

He needed to be reassured that the rest of the world was different from his messed-up universe.

ELEVEN

Taylor lay still in her darkened bedroom searching for ways to make herself sleepy. She tried all her usual tricks. Listing the names of the planets. Remembering the names of every teacher she'd ever had, in order. Conjugating French verbs.

Nothing worked. She was wide awake.

The clock on the bedside table mocked her, reading 2.24 a.m. for what must have been an hour before finally advancing to 2.25.

'That's *it*,' Taylor muttered, sitting up in bed.

Sleep wasn't going to happen.

Switching on the lamp, she pulled her history book out of the bag leaning against the wall. For a while she tried to catch up on her reading, squinting at the words in the light. But she was thirsty and her head had begun to ache again, making it difficult to concentrate.

Finally, she climbed out of bed and went downstairs in search of something to drink.

The hallway had the quiet, otherworldly atmosphere all houses take on at night when everyone is asleep. What was safe and familiar during the day felt foreign and threatening in the dark.

Taylor tiptoed down the stairs, as if trying not to disturb the walls.

In the kitchen, the refrigerator hummed. The clock on the wall ticked at what seemed a deafening volume. In a basket by the radiator, Fizz snored.

Taylor filled a glass with water, downed it and filled it again before heading back.

She'd just reached the hallway when she thought of it.

The laptop.

She could see it from the kitchen doorway, one corner jutting out from atop the cupboard.

She stopped, looking over her shoulder. But the house was still. Everyone was sound asleep. No one would know.

Careful not to make a sound, she lifted the laptop down. Tucking it under one arm, she hurried up the stairs.

She never did things like this. Ever since her dad left, she and her mother had been a team. Working together, taking care of Emily. She'd never gone through a teenage rebellion phase because it hadn't seemed right. Her mother worked too hard. Besides, they just ... got along.

Now she felt like a criminal. A cheat. She wondered again about brain tumours. But surely if she had a brain tumour there'd be more serious symptoms than fainting, occasional headaches, a sudden urge to disobey her mother and use the laptop.

She wouldn't stay on the computer for long. She'd just check her email, see if Georgie was online anywhere, and put it back.

The laptop powered up with a quiet whirr. It opened to the last page she'd looked at. Revolution Chat. Sacha's profile page.

Only now it didn't say he was offline.

The picture of an angry boy had disappeared, replaced by a real boy who appeared to be at a desk, his head resting on one arm, sound asleep.

Taylor's breath caught. She'd never seen a boy sleep before.

Leaning forward, she studied him with interest. His silky brown hair was tangled. His eyes were closed. He had the longest lashes she could ever remember seeing. Like black feathers against his cheeks.

His fingers were curled in such a childlike pose of innocence, it hurt her heart.

It was impossible to find the cynical, angry young man she'd met the other day in the boy in front of her now.

Taylor knew it was super-stalky to just sit there watching him sleep. She had to do something. Wake him up, maybe. Or she could just turn the computer off and walk away; pretend she never saw him. But somehow the idea seemed absurd. After all, he was *right there*.

Besides, she needed to tutor him.

She rifled through a desk drawer for her headphones. After plugging them into the computer she placed the earpieces in her ears. Then she leaned closer to the computer until her lips were near the microphone.

'Hello? Sacha?' she whispered.

He didn't stir.

This was a conundrum. She couldn't raise her voice or even talk much at all without waking her mother, whose bedroom was two doors down. But suddenly she very much wanted to talk to this innocent-looking boy with the eyelashes and cheekbones.

'Sacha,' she hissed again, more sharply this time. '*Wake. Up.*'

He leapt to his feet like she'd electrocuted him. Startled, Taylor leaned away from the computer screen, watching as he spun around with surprising speed, searching his room as if he expected to find monsters there.

Taylor wondered what could be happening in his life right now to make him react like that to a whisper.

'Sacha,' she said again, her voice softer now. 'It's me, Taylor.' She waved at the webcam to attract his attention. 'Over here.'

Slowly he turned back to the computer and met her gaze. His eyes were wide and blue.

Taylor forgot to breathe.

He didn't look sarcastic now. He looked scared.

For a long moment they just stared at each other.

'Taylor?' There was wonder in his voice. As if he had woken from a deep sleep and wasn't sure which was real – this world or that one. 'You startled me.'

'I'm sorry,' she said. 'I couldn't wake you up.'

He sank into the desk chair.

'It's OK.' He rubbed his eyes as if trying to clear the cobwebs. 'Did you get my email?'

What email? Taylor wondered.

'No,' she said, careful to keep her voice just above a whisper. 'I just opened my computer and you were there. Or ... here.'

'Oh.' He seemed disappointed. Suddenly she itched to see that email. 'I apologised for not being here last night. It was ... unavoidable. But I am sorry. It was ... ' he paused, searching for the right word, 'unforgivably rude.'

His apology seemed genuine, and any anger Taylor might have held onto after everything that had happened that night melted away.

Suddenly she remembered her tartly worded email from earlier that night.

'I'm sorry I wrote you such a snippy email, too,' she said. 'I was cross.'

A faint hint of a smile softened his features. 'What does it mean, "snippy"?'

Taylor thought for a moment, trying and failing to come up with an exact French equivalent. She chose the closest word she knew. *'Désagréable.'*

He chuckled. 'No – it was not *désagréable* at all. I deserved it. It's not nice for someone to not be there when you expect them. When they have promised. I keep my promises. It is my ... How do you say it? My thing.'

His laugh was fleeting. But she liked it as much as she had last time.

'Mine too,' she whispered with a tentative smile.

She liked this new, gentler Sacha.

He leaned forward, studying her. His gaze was so intense it was impossible to look away.

'Why are you awake so late? It's nearly four in the morning here. It must be three there, *non*?'

Taylor didn't know how to respond to this. So she kept her reply vague. 'I couldn't sleep. Something happened earlier tonight and I ... Well. Now I can't sleep.'

'What happened?' He looked genuinely interested. 'Something happened to me tonight, too.'

'You go first.' Taylor didn't like the idea of telling him about fainting. He'd think she was completely flaky.

He hesitated, as if he didn't want to tell his story either.

'Oh, it was nothing. Just a fight with some guys. I hit my head.'

He gestured vaguely at his forehead above his left eye. Taylor thought she could make out a faint red mark near the hairline, surrounded by bruising.

'Why did you fight?' she asked, frowning.

'It was nothing that mattered. Money.' Sacha shrugged. 'It's fine now.'

A guarded look appeared suddenly on his face, indicating that, whatever had really happened earlier that night, it wasn't fine at all. But he hurried on before she could ask more questions.

'Now it's your turn. What happened to you?'

Maybe it was the late hour. Or the fact that she didn't know him. Or the strange intimacy of sitting in her bedroom,

105

whispering to him. Or the brain tumour she was beginning to believe she had. But Taylor found it impossible not to tell him the truth.

'I was waiting for you to talk to me,' she began. 'I wrote you that email. Then I just . . . fainted, I guess.' She sighed. 'My mum freaked out. Now it's this big drama. She thinks the internet is eating my brain or something. And I'm forbidden to use the laptop . . . ' She considered this for a second before adding, 'That I'm using now.'

'Fainted?' Sacha squinted at her. 'Girls really do that?'

Taylor made an apologetic gesture. 'I guess so.'

'But you're OK?'

Her gaze darted up to his. He looked concerned.

'I'm fine, I guess,' she said, with an embarrassed smile. 'It was just weird. I'm not much of a swooner normally.'

That made him grin. 'You don't seem weak to me.' Resting his chin on his hand he studied her with a frank curiosity that sent heat rushing to her face. 'Tell me about yourself, Taylor Montclair. Who are you?'

She liked the way her name sounded when he said it.

'What do you mean?' she asked, hoping he would say it again.

'Oh you know,' he said, 'what do you like? What do you hate? Who's your best friend? Parents?'

Taylor hesitated. She knew if she told the truth he'd think she was a geek. But she didn't feel like lying.

'I like . . . books,' she admitted after a second. 'And history. I want to be an archaeologist.'

He accepted this with a nod, as if he'd expected nothing

less. 'That's cool. A good goal. And friends, boyfriend?'

Their eyes locked. Heat crept to Taylor's cheeks.

When she answered she dropped her gaze to her keyboard. 'My best friend is Georgie. She's actually the one who wrote the bitchy text about being stupid.' She wrinkled her nose. 'She's the cheeky one. I'm the earnest one.'

She didn't answer the boyfriend question. Did she have one or didn't she? Technically yes. But she was planning to break up with him at the first opportunity so she was really in transition.

Pre-rebound. Soon-to-be single.

'What about your family?' he asked, letting the boyfriend question go.

'One sister,' she said. 'She's 12. I live with my mum. Dad left a couple of years ago. He has a shiny new family now.'

She could hear the bitterness in her own tone, and Sacha's eyebrows arched. Before he could ask for more details she turned the tables on him.

'What about you?'

He bit his lip and, for a long moment didn't answer. When he finally did speak, his voice was hesitant.

'I was really into history and languages when I was younger but I guess I . . . ' His voice trailed off and he seemed to be searching for the right words. 'I . . . I kind of got lost. Some things happened, in my life.'

He spoke haltingly, with a kind of painful honesty. Taylor found herself leaning forward, willing him to continue.

He exhaled. 'Anyway. I live with my mother and my sister.

She is 13 now. I don't have many friends. No real plans.' The dark smile she was beginning to know well, reappeared. 'No future. I'm probably your mother's worst nightmare.'

His words fizzed through Taylor's veins, but she kept her expression neutral.

'Of course you have a future,' she said. 'There's lots of time to decide what you want to do . . .'

The look he gave her then was so empty and hopeless, her voice trailed off.

'I don't understand.' She searched his face for clues. 'Why wouldn't you have a future?'

At that moment, a faint sound from the corridor – just a whisper of footsteps – drew her attention away from Sacha.

Turning, she pulled the headphones out of her ears to listen, then turned back to him in a panic.

'Bugger,' she hissed. 'It's my mum. I have to go.'

She could see he was saying something to her but she couldn't wait to hear what it was.

Hurriedly shutting the laptop, she picked it up and dived into bed, sliding under the covers, where she closed her eyes and feigned sleep.

A split second later, the bedroom door opened with a sound like a sigh.

'Taylor?' her mother said softly.

Shifting to be sure the sheets hid the computer, Taylor blinked at her.

'Mum?' she said groggily.

'I thought I heard voices.'

'Mmph.' Taylor rolled over in bed as if too weary to speak.

She was now lying on top of the laptop. She pretended this was very comfortable.

After a moment, the door closed again. Silence returned.

Taylor didn't move. She needed to get the laptop back downstairs before morning, but she'd wait a while first to make sure her mother had fallen asleep again.

While she waited, she thought about Sacha, with his blue eyes and his cheekbones.

'I'm probably your mother's worst nightmare ... '

And it struck her that her headache was completely gone. In fact, she felt great.

TWELVE

Despite his promise to his mother, Sacha didn't go to
school the next day.

In fact, it was midday by the time he awoke, to find
himself alone in the flat.

Wearing only his pyjama bottoms, he padded along the hall
to the kitchen. A fresh baguette lay on the counter – his
mother must have gone to the bakery before heading out.
While the coffee brewed, he cut himself a big chunk, spread
butter on it lavishly and added a thick slice of cheese.
Carrying this and a cup of strong black coffee, he ambled
back to his room.

A dull pain above his left eye was the only obvious reminder
of last night's carnage. Before going to sleep, he'd stuffed his
bloody clothes into the bins downstairs, and cleaned the bathroom, so Laura would see no sign of what had occurred.

Now, sitting at his desk, he ran his fingertips across the spot where the bullet had entered his skull, finding, with effort, a shallow indentation. It didn't hurt. But he suspected his brain was still mending – his thoughts were sluggish. But that could have been because he was tired.

After Taylor disappeared from his screen the night before, he'd sat up for nearly an hour in case she came back. It was silly, he knew. She wouldn't expect him to wait at four in the morning.

But he kept seeing her face in his mind, skin luminous in the dark, tousled golden curls tumbling everywhere.

He went over their conversation in his mind, remembering the things she'd said. The way she'd looked at him when he said he had no future. Like a superhero in a movie looking at an innocent person standing in front of a bus, right before they swooped down to rescue them.

It had been the first real conversation they'd had – when each of them wasn't trying to insult or impress the other.

He had to admit it had been ... good.

In some ways she was exactly as he'd imagined. Her mum, her sister, her neatly decorated bedroom in shadows behind her. But then there was the way her face darkened when she mentioned her father, and the fact that she was defying her mother by talking to him when she'd been forbidden to use the computer.

It was more than that, though. There was something about her.

She'd looked at him with those serious green eyes that pierced straight through, and he'd wanted to tell her the truth. He'd wanted to tell her everything.

Taking a bite of his sandwich, he opened her profile page

and leaned in to see the small picture better. She was sitting in a park, or somewhere green. It was a bright, sunny day. She was laughing.

As he looked at her, an unexpected stab of jealousy pierced him. When he asked if she had a boyfriend she'd dodged the question.

He shouldn't be surprised. Of course she had a boyfriend. Girls like her always did. Probably some good-looking athlete. A future lawyer. Someone reliable.

She'd never like someone like him – a loser, counting the days, minutes, seconds down to zero.

If that's true then … why didn't she answer the question?

It wasn't just her appearance that intrigued him. Her name – he knew it from somewhere. His mother recognised it, too. More than that – the name seemed to frighten her.

He leaned back in the chair until he was staring at the white emptiness of his bedroom ceiling.

'Who are you, Taylor Montclair?' he asked aloud.

It was time to find out.

After throwing on some jeans and a black T-shirt with a hole in the shoulder, he made himself another cup of coffee. Then he got down to work.

First, just in case the answer was screamingly obvious, he searched his inbox for any emails containing the name 'Montclair', but found only Taylor's messages.

He dug out his list of school contact numbers and scanned the M's. Again, nothing.

After that he looked through his desk drawers, his papers. Notebooks.

Nothing. Nothing. Nothing.

The more he came up empty, the more it bothered him.

Where have I heard that name? Was it on TV? In a book?

He didn't think so. He wouldn't remember it so clearly if that's all it was.

A friend of my parents?

That seemed more likely.

He headed to the living room, where his mother's desk sat in one corner, out of the way. Feeling a bit like a burglar, he searched through the neatly organised drawers, filled with bills, old pay slips and receipts, until he found her address book.

He flipped to the M's.

No Montclair.

He looked through every business card. Every paper. Nothing.

Drumming his fingers, he leaned back in the chair, considering his options. The apartment was comfortably quiet. A warm breeze blew in through the half-open window. He could hear the sound of cars on the narrow street below. Somewhere in the distance a dog barked.

There was one other place in the flat to search.

Bending down, he reached beneath the desk and pulled out a cardboard box tucked away at the back.

His father's personal papers were kept here. They were rarely disturbed.

From the back of the box, he drew out a large notebook bound in black leather.

He ran his fingers tentatively across the smooth cover. The

leather was soft, finely made. The initials 'AW' were embossed in gold on the cover.

His father had taken this notebook with him whenever he'd left for one of his research trips. He was rarely without it.

Except on that last trip.

That was one of the odd things about the accident that killed him. When his body was extracted from the tangled metal remnants of a rental car on a country lane near Oxford, not a single paper had been found on him.

Lifting the book to his nose, Sacha closed his eyes and inhaled. The scent – paper and ink, old leather and the faint musk of cigarette smoke – was so evocative, he could actually *see* his father, scooping him up in his arms and swinging him around. Smiling as Sacha laughed.

With a sigh, he set the notebook down and opened it.

The first page held only two words 'Adam Winters', in his father's elegant handwriting. Below that, his title:

Historien médiéviste, maître de conférence à l'Université Paris 1, Panthéon Sorbonne. Medieval History Consultant, University of Oxford.

Just those words were enough to summon memories of countless nights in the old stone house, sitting in front of the fire listening to his father's tales of kings and castles, of knights and witches burned on pyres.

'It's true,' he would insist, when Sacha said such things couldn't really happen. 'It's all true.'

When his father died, Sacha dropped out of history class.

In the late night hush, the paper crinkled as he turned a page.

His father had used this notebook for everything – diary, address book and journal. His handwriting covered every inch of the page. Words swam at Sacha from all angles – notes climbed vertically in the margin, and crept diagonally in the corners.

It was too much information. Names, places, thoughts, dates ...

He flipped through the pages faster, searching for the section of the book used for addresses, and then for one particular name. But nothing was in alphabetical order, and he frowned as he struggled to understand his father's complex system.

As he traced the words with his fingertips, he saw familiar names, unfamiliar names, English, French, Spanish, Italian.

More than an hour had passed before he finally found what he was looking for:

'Aldrich Montclair, Oxford University.' Next to it a phone number and an address.

Sacha's heart began to pound.

Suddenly he knew where he'd heard it before.

His father, standing in the doorway, a leather travelling bag in his hand. 'Montclair thinks he's on to something. I have to find out if he's right.'

'Again?' His mother, frowning at him. 'You were just there last month. You know it's not safe.'

Both of them glancing to where Sacha sat doing his homework, only half listening to them. Then walking outside together, talking in whispers.

He flipped through the rest of the book, looking for other references, but found none. There was no mention of Taylor or any other Montclair.

Sacha closed the book, resting his fingers thoughtfully on the cover.

'Who are you, Taylor Montclair?'

Thirteen

'Wait. You were chatting with Sacha at 3 a.m.?' Pushing her salad away, Georgie looked at Taylor with avid interest. 'Were your clothes on or off at the time?'

'Shut up!' Taylor laughed as heat rushed to her face. 'We were both fully dressed. I'm not *you*, George.'

They were having lunch outside Caffeine Daze, a coffee shop near the school. It was a grey day, the air was heavy with impending rain, but Georgie had insisted on touching up her makeup after morning classes so all the tables inside had been taken by the time they arrived.

Georgie regarded her steadily.

'Seriously, Tay, this is all a bit convenient. One minute you're thinking of breaking up with Tom and the next you're up all night talking to some French guy.' She leaned forward.

'What's going on? Tell me everything. And I do mean *every-thing*.'

Confusion fluttered in Taylor's stomach.

She didn't really understand her own emotions right now. How could she explain them to Georgie?

Georgie's brown eyes widened.

'Oh my God,' she said. 'You fancy this French boy.'

'Don't be silly,' Taylor said. 'I don't even know him. We've talked, like, twice. It was nothing. I was supposed to tutor him but he didn't show, and he apologised. I told him about the weird fainting thing, and we talked about that for a few minutes. That was it.'

So why does it feel like more?

Georgia shot her sceptical look. 'If you say so.' She stirred her skinny latte. 'Are you going to talk to him again tonight?'

'No,' Taylor said, and she meant it.

As soon as she said it, though, her head began to throb.

♊

The headache worsened as the day went on. When her lessons ended that afternoon, Taylor rushed to the girls' loos, downing two painkillers with water she cupped in her hands. She splashed cool water on her face, studying herself in the mirror.

She had a date to meet Tom. She was thinking seriously about breaking up with him then. She needed to hurry – she couldn't be late for her own break-up.

She pressed her fingers against her temples and closed her eyes. Truthfully, she was starting to panic. This pain couldn't be normal. She would have to tell her mother about it. See a doctor.

For the first time she considered the possibility that it could be something really serious. She'd never been ill. She rarely even had colds.

Every news item about a fatal illness seemed to race through her mind at once.

Imagine being seventeen and it all just … ending. One minute you're worried about your exams. The next?

Click.

Out go the lights.

In the mirror her wide green eyes looked scared. Her golden hair waved and curled wildly around her face. The shadows under her eyes betrayed her lack of sleep. She looked terrible.

She glanced at her watch. Fifteen minutes had passed.

It had happened again.

'Bollocks,' she whispered, genuinely scared now.

Losing time was not OK. None of this was OK.

Grabbing her bag, she rushed from the room, shoving the door hard.

It thudded against something soft. The soft thing gave a small squeak.

Scrabbling for the handle, Taylor yanked the door back.

On the other side, Mr Finlay stood amid a circle of fallen papers, rubbing his shoulder and glaring at her resentfully.

'I'm so sorry, Mr Finlay,' she said. 'Are you OK?'

'Young people,' he said with great deliberation, 'should watch where they are going.'

'Yes, they … I mean … we should,' Taylor agreed. 'I hope you're not hurt.'

'Hmmph.'

He still looked cross as Taylor helped him gather his papers into a rumpled stack.

'Thank you.' His clipped tone indicated it was the least she could do.

'Well.' Taylor took a sideways step. 'I should be . . . '

'I've been meaning to ask you, Miss Montclair,' he said, 'how your tutoring is going with that French boy?'

'Yes – Sacha,' she said. 'We've spoken several times.'

She tried not to show her impatience. Tom was going to kill her.

'Good, good.' His head bobbed approvingly. 'I'm glad to hear you're working with him. Now if you pay attention in class and watch where you're going you might just get into Oxford after all.'

With that, he turned and walked away.

'Bye to you, too,' Taylor muttered.

Why were teachers so *odd*?

She rushed outside to find Tom standing on the school steps staring at his phone. It had begun to rain, and he was already soaked.

He held himself stiffly; muscles tense.

'Tom,' she said. He spun around to glower at her. Before he could speak she rushed into an apology. 'I'm really sorry. Finlay grabbed me and I couldn't get away. You know what he's like . . . '

He held up one hand, cutting off her explanation. 'Whatever, Taylor.'

He stared at her. 'I don't know what's going on with you lately but this is not cool.'

His tone was glacial.

'I'm so sorry,' she said again. 'I should have called you or . . . something.'

She wasn't handling this well, but her head was pounding in earnest now, making it hard to think.

'To be honest, I don't feel so great. In fact, I think I'm going to beg off from studying with you today. I think I should just go home.'

'God's *sake*, Taylor.' He shook his head in disgust. 'You leave me standing in the rain for twenty minutes for no reason whatsoever, ignore the text messages I send you, and then say you're going home?'

'Come on, Tom . . . '

'No, seriously, Taylor.' He rounded on her. 'You treat me like dirt, do you know that? My friends can't believe I put up with it.'

The anger in his voice made her flinch.

This was going very badly. She'd planned to break up with him but he was so furious right now it looked like he might break up with *her*.

'Tom . . . ' she began, but he didn't wait for her to finish.

'You take me for granted,' he said. 'And I don't like it.'

Taylor was stunned to silence. Before she could think of the right thing to say, he turned away.

'You know what? Forget it. I don't have time for this right now. Just . . . do what you want, Taylor.'

He ran down the steps with the muscular stride of an athlete, disappearing across the playing fields.

♊

Taylor slept the rest of the afternoon, and by that evening her headache was gone. She felt normal again.

Her argument with Tom had left her shaken. He was so resentful. Maybe he could sense she was pulling away. It was time to do something about it.

As soon as dinner was over, she went up to her room to call Georgie.

She answered on the first ring. 'What's up, Tay?'

Taylor could hear the television in the background, turned up so loud Georgie's parents were likely to begin complaining at any moment.

'It's nothing, I guess. I just had this stupid row with Tom today.' Taylor kept her voice low. She didn't want her mother to hear any of this. 'And I'm a bit ... I don't know.' She sighed. 'Confused, I guess.'

'Uh-oh,' Georgie said. The televised audience roared, drowning her out momentarily. Taylor heard her scrambling for the remote. Then the TV sound diminished to a hush. 'What happened?'

Taylor told her the basics, leaving out the part about losing time.

When she finished, Georgie sighed. 'He's got a short temper. Paul and I were talking about it the other day. He shouldn't talk to you like that.' She paused. 'But, then again, aren't you going to break up with him? Maybe he, like, senses it. Don't animals do that?'

'What? Sense when other animals are going to break up with them?'

'You know what I mean.'

Taylor leaned back against her pillows. 'Oh, I don't know, George. It's all a mess.'

'At least you still have French boy,' Georgie teased her. 'To keep you warm at night.'

A pinprick of panic made Taylor straighten.

'Look, George. Don't mention Sacha to Tom, OK? The last thing I need right now is him getting jealous. Things are bad enough.'

'Of course not.' Georgie sounded insulted. 'Who do you think I am?'

'Seriously, George.' Taylor said. 'You know what he's like. He's not a bad guy but he's really jealous.'

'God,' Georgie said. 'I won't tell anyone. Chill *out*.'

There was a pause. When she spoke again, Georgie's tone was practical. As if she was giving directions to her house. 'Here's the deal. If you're going to break up with Tom, do it fast. Don't let this grow into a thing where you both really hate each other. Do it fast, keep it nice.'

In the background the TV audience applauded something.

'I'll do it tomorrow,' Taylor promised.

But the very idea made her feel ill.

♊

Taylor sat bolt upright in bed, clutching her duvet to her chest, her heart racing hard as if she'd been running. She couldn't seem to catch her breath.

The last seconds of her nightmare were crystal clear in her mind. She'd been standing on the edge of a cliff and Finlay had pushed her off.

It had been so vivid and terrifying, so real.

When her breathing quieted, she lay back down but every time she closed her eyes she saw the ground racing up towards her.

Her eyes snapped open. It was no use. She wouldn't get back to sleep.

A glance at the alarm clock told her it was just after one in the morning.

I wonder if Sacha is up? The thought entered her mind unbidden, as if it had lurked there, waiting for a chance.

She flushed again, remembering Georgie's accusing voice; *'You fancy this French boy'*.

She shook her head. Of course she didn't. She'd never even met him in real life. Then she thought of Sacha's blue eyes. His long, dark lashes. The way his accent made words sound velvety.

Her stomach flipped.

Do I?

There was one way to find out.

She swung her feet to the floor and made her way carefully across the room. Cracking open the door, she paused to listen.

The house was quiet.

She tiptoed downstairs, careful to skip the step that squeaked, and slipped along the dark hallway, quiet as a wraith.

It occurred to her that for someone who'd never sneaked around at night in her life, she was rather good at it.

She was almost to the kitchen when she heard a noise, very faint, coming from the study. It sounded like papers rustling. As if someone were turning the pages of a large book.

Odd. Her mother was almost always asleep by ten, up by six.

With a puzzled frown, she crept closer.

As she neared the room, the rustling grew louder and she could hear someone whispering, too – a faint but ominous susurration that made her head fuzzy, made it difficult to focus.

She reached for the door handle. 'Mum?'

The sound stopped. A second later, all the air seemed to leave her lungs. She felt her throat constricting, hands squeezing her windpipe, pressing against her larynx.

She couldn't breathe.

She clawed at her throat but found no fingers to prise away. She twisted around and swung her fists wildly but there was no one there.

She was alone.

She tried to scream but no sound came out.

Panic sent adrenaline rushing into her veins, bringing everything into clear and terrifying focus. There was no one to fight. And yet someone was killing her.

Spots appeared at the edges of her vision as the world began to go black. She slapped at the air with increasing futility.

She was going to faint. To die.

She'd begun seeing stars – golden lights in the darkness. No – strands of gold, like silken threads. She stared at them in wonder. They were so real, she found herself reaching for one.

That slim strand seemed to pulsate with power.

Electricity surged through her body with a force that should have killed her.

From somewhere came a strange sound, like a muffled shriek.

The hands released her.

Gasping, Taylor collapsed to the floor. The strands of gold had disappeared

And whatever had attacked her was gone.

Fourteen

Taylor sat on the floor in the hallway sobbing and shaking. She kept hearing sounds – seeing things moving in the shadows. But there was no one. It was all in her mind.

Finally summoning the courage to move, she ran up the stairs to her mother's door. When she reached it, though, she stopped. What was she going to say? 'Someone invisible tried to kill me?'

It was insane. She would sound insane.

She was so scared.

Sobbing silently, she pressed her forehead against the cool wood of the closed door behind which her mother slept peacefully, just a few paces away.

'I'm going crazy,' she whispered through her tears, too quietly to wake anyone. 'Mummy, please help me, I'm going crazy.'

She stayed there for a long moment. Then she took a shaky breath and walked unsteadily down the dark corridor to her own room.

She spent the night huddled in her bed, shaking violently. Trying to understand what was happening to her.

♊

Taylor didn't go to school the next day.

She'd hardly slept at all. Her head felt strangely light, like a balloon on a string.

She got up early and stood in front of the mirror for a long time. The marks on her neck had been red last night but now had turned into purpling bruises. They snaked around her pale throat, the unmistakeable size and shape of long, thin fingers.

As she touched them lightly, her breath hissed between her teeth. It was hard to imagine the force needed to leave impressions like that. To rupture capillaries and send the blood coursing to her skin.

But I was alone.

A tear slipped down her cheek and she struck it away. She had to stop crying.

She needed to focus. To figure this out. To understand.

Things like this just don't happen.

But it had happened.

And all she knew was she had to get out of this house.

Moving quickly, she pulled on a pair of shorts and a vest top. She tied a white scarf around her neck to hide the bruises.

Then, before her mother had made it downstairs for breakfast, she slipped out the front door into the morning light.

♊

The Woodbury Library was in a rambling two-storey Victorian building at the edge of the town centre with the word 'Library' in pale stone on the front just below the steep, gabled roof.

Taylor crossed the busy street out front, and hurried up the front steps. She'd spent a lot of time here over the years. When she was young, she'd be here every day in the summer holidays, looking for new books to read. It still felt like a safe place. A place of knowledge. Sanctuary.

She could figure it out here. She had to.

When she reached the front door, she grabbed the heavy, iron door handle. It was locked solid.

Taylor's shoulders drooped. She'd forgotten opening hours. A glance at her watch showed it wasn't even eight o'clock yet. The library didn't open until nine.

Slowly, she sank down onto the top step and buried her head in her arms. How could she wait an *hour*?

She wasn't without options. She could go home for an hour, or to the coffee shop. But home meant her mother and the coffee shop was full of people she didn't want to see. So she didn't move. She just sat there, her forehead resting on her folded arms as the traffic rumbled by.

'Taylor?'

Taylor lifted her head to find a woman in a plain, blue dress with short, greying hair standing on the steps in front of her. A heavy bag hung from one shoulder and a huge set of keys jangled in her hand. She was studying her with a puzzled expression.

'What are you doing here?'

129

Surreptitiously, Taylor wiped her cheeks before rising to her feet.

'Uh ... Hi Mrs Atkinson,' she said. 'I just need to do some research today.'

The librarian's astute gaze swept across her face. She'd known Taylor since she was a toddler. Woodbury was a small town. When she was still too young to stay at home alone, her mother had sometimes left her here in Mrs Atkinson's care while she went shopping.

'She's no trouble,' the librarian would say breezily. 'All readers are welcome.'

Taylor would sit happily with books in the children's section for hours. It was safe there.

She needed that safety now.

Mrs Atkinson bustled past her and unlocked the door with a clattering of keys.

'Let's get you inside.'

♊

The old building held a series of shadowy rooms with high ceilings that had changed little over the century or more it had stood here. All still had original ornate plaster work and fireplaces, although the lights had been replaced with modern fixtures that stood out starkly amid the ramshackle beauty. It was cool inside, and the familiar smell of paper and ink, wood polish and dust, was deeply comforting.

'I don't normally do this, as you know.' Mrs Atkinson's voice floated out from the little supply room behind the librarian's desk. 'But you look like you could use a cup of tea.'

Faintly, Taylor heard a kettle rumble to life, and the sounds of cupboards opening and closing. Teaspoons jangling against ceramic mugs.

She set her bag down on one of the battered wooden tables and lowered herself onto a chair. The plastic was cold beneath her legs.

A wave of exhaustion swept over her. She could have put her head down on the table and slept right there.

'Here you go.' The mug the librarian handed her was covered in a motif of cheery yellow sunflowers.

She sat for a long while without drinking it, just staring into its milky depths, as if it could help her know what to do.

From across the table, Mrs Atkinson watched her, a frown creasing her brow.

'My dear, are you quite all right?' Her tone was just gentle enough to make Taylor feel like crying again.

'I don't know,' she whispered. 'I'm having a *really* bad day. I need to look some things up, and then I think ... I think maybe I'll feel better. I hope, anyway.'

The woman considered this – Taylor suspected she was deciding whether or not to intervene further. But she wasn't a little girl anymore. You couldn't call her mother every time she cried.

After a moment, the librarian stood with obvious reluctance and headed to her overcrowded desk.

'Whatever's happening in your life, I hope you figure it out. At any rate, it's nice to see you again. We've missed you around here.'

Taylor wondered who 'we' were – Mrs Atkinson essentially *was* the library.

The tea was hot and sweet, the way she liked it. After a few sips she began to feel more herself.

By then, the librarian had disappeared into the depths of the building. Occasionally, she could hear the reassuring thump of books being reshelved.

Taylor was tempted to stay right where she was. But there was work to do.

With heavy steps she made her way upstairs to the non-fiction section, flipping the light switch by the door. The fluorescent bulbs flickered and came on with a mechanical buzz.

The small room was crowded with books, stacked on shelves six feet high, covering every inch of wall space. A window on one wall let in a glare of sunlight.

She traced the shelves around the room, looking at the section titles until she found the one she sought.

The non-fiction paranormal section at the Woodbury town library was one short shelf of books, mostly about witches and ghosts. Taylor didn't believe in ghosts. In fact, she wasn't the believing kind. She'd first become convinced Santa Claus was an outrageous fraud when she was 4. By then she'd already long since ceased believing in the tooth fairy. She'd become an atheist at 8 after her father explained the Big Bang theory to her one winter night when they were out in the back garden looking at the stars. Although, as she got older she wasn't sure she was right about that one.

Still, when you got right down to it, she didn't believe in much of anything.

From downstairs she could hear the faint murmur of conversation – someone else must have come in early today.

She moved across the room, still scanning section names. This time she stopped where the section card read 'Psychology and Psychotherapy'.

It looked much more promising. A whole bookcase filled with volumes of all shapes and sizes.

The first book she chose was entitled, simply, *Schizophrenia*.

She flipped through frightening pages about the disease with increasing apprehension.

The case studies were the worst:

Patient X suffered contusions, haematoma and lacerations to his upper body after an episode lasting twenty minutes. During that time he believed himself to be under attack, or fighting an unseen assailant. Medical staff who witnessed the incident said all the injuries were self-inflicted, but the patient later insisted he was fending off an attack ...

She slammed the book shut.

She didn't want to know any more. This couldn't be her fate.

You don't just wake up with a mental illness all of a sudden at 17, do you?

She decided not to research that.

Whatever it was that attacked her last night was not a figment of her mind. It was real. She hadn't made those marks on her own neck.

She turned back to the paranormal shelf. Slowly, reluctantly, she reached for a book about poltergeists.

'You won't find what you're looking for there.'

Taylor jumped, dropping the book.

A man stepped out of the shadows into the narrow doorway. He was barely taller than she was, and stocky. Thick, white hair waved around his head in an unkempt cloud that looked as if it would be very soft to touch, though Taylor had never dared. His eyes were the same clear green as her own. He watched her with a discerning alertness that, when she was younger, used to make her nervous.

She was so shocked, at first she couldn't seem to speak. Finally she found her voice.

'Grandfather? What are you doing here?'

Aldrich Montclair smiled, although his eyes remained serious. 'Hello my dear. I think it's time we had a little talk.'

FIFTEEN

T aylor slid a hand down her arm and pinched herself. It hurt.

'I ... I don't u ... understand,' she stammered, looking around the small room as if the shelves would hold the answers. 'How did you know where to find me?'

'It's a little complicated to explain,' her grandfather said. 'But I will tell you all I can. About that, and other things.'

'Other things?' Taylor asked, faintly.

'The incident last night.' She'd never seen him look more serious. 'There *was* an incident last night, was there not?'

A chill ran down Taylor's spine.

'How can you know that?' she whispered.

'Because I've been expecting something like this to happen,' he said. 'Now, I fear, we must move very quickly. I may have waited too long. The others think I have, and they're usually right.'

The others? Move?

Bewildered, Taylor took a step away from him, towards the small window behind her. Despite the warm day, she'd begun to shiver.

Her grandfather's eyes widened. 'My dear, I need you to remain calm.'

The urgency in his voice only made her feel more panicked. When he took a step towards her she thrust up one hand in caution.

'*Don't.*'

The overhead light flickered ominously. Her grandfather stopped in his tracks and held up his hands.

The light flickered again and Taylor looked up at the long fluorescent tube, wondering what was wrong with it.

'Listen to me, my dear.' Aldrich's voice was low and calm. 'These things that have been happening to you – headaches, fainting, tingling hands, lost time – they are real. The attack last night was real, too. What's happening to you is very dangerous, and could be deadly if we are not careful.'

Taylor's lips moved but no words came out.

She hadn't told anyone – not even her mother – about the lost time.

'How . . . ?' she whispered.

'Because it happened to me, and to my father before me, and to my sister and her children,' Aldrich said. 'It is in your blood.'

Taylor gripped the window sill behind her with such force it hurt.

'What is in my blood?'

'Power,' he said simply.

The lights flickered once then went out with a bang.

'Oh dear.' Her grandfather sighed. 'I was afraid of that.'

Through the floor they heard Mrs Atkinson exclaim, 'What on *earth*?'

'We should go outside,' her grandfather said. 'Before anything else happens. And I will tell you what I can.' He held out one hand to her, palm facing downwards, as you would to an injured animal. 'Will you come with me?'

Taylor hesitated. But she had to understand what was happening. And her grandfather seemed to know.

She took his hand.

♊

'I still don't get how you found me,' Taylor said as they made their way down the street. The day was warming quickly, and the sun beat down on the concrete.

She hadn't seen her grandfather in nearly a year. Things had been tense since her father left, so this was all coming out of the blue.

'I'm afraid I have a confession to make.' Her grandfather cast a sideways glance at her. 'I've been keeping an eye on you for some time now.'

Taylor stopped walking. 'You have? But how?'

'I have people working with me who are very good at this sort of thing,' he said. 'And they have been keeping you safe. Until last night.'

Someone pushed past them and he stopped talking. He

pointed across the street, where a lush green park sprawled.

'Perhaps we should go in here, and I can explain everything.'

It was a weekday morning and the long, narrow park was still empty. A stream moved slowly through the green grass.

Aldrich led Taylor down towards the water, stopping when they reached an iron bench on the shore. At some point it had been painted green, as if to disguise it. The paint had begun to peel, revealing the black underneath.

'Have a seat,' he said.

Hesitantly, Taylor perched on the edge of the bench. The metal was warm from the sun.

Her grandfather remained standing. 'I knew you would have these headaches, because I had them,' he said. 'And I knew once the headaches started, you would begin experiencing other symptoms – like the impact you have on electricity. Because that is the way it manifests.'

'Huh?' Taylor blinked.

'In the library, when the lights went out.' Aldrich held her gaze. 'That was you.'

She squinted at him, perplexed. 'I had nothing to do with that. How could I? We were upstairs. You were with me the whole time.'

'You didn't do it with your hands.' He pointed at her head. 'You did it with your *brain*.'

Taylor dropped her head to her hands.

She didn't know what she was supposed to think. For just a second there she'd hoped he might have the answers. But he wasn't making any sense.

My grandfather is as crazy as I am.

'Taylor,' he said.

Slowly, she raised her head to meet his gaze.

'This is what's giving you a headache.' He raised his right hand. In it, he held a light bulb.

As she watched, the bulb began to glow. Faintly at first, but then very brightly.

Astounded, she looked around for witnesses but they were all alone. No one was passing to give her some indication if they, too could see the glowing bulb, or if it was just a figment of her imagination.

'All you did in the library was this.' He twirled the bulb between his thumb and forefinger. All the while, the light beamed steadily. 'You did what I am doing now. You moved molecules of energy from where they belonged – the air, the ground – to where they didn't. The lights.'

The bulb went out. He held it out to her.

Too confused to argue, she accepted it.

It appeared to be a normal bulb of the type you'd find in any table lamp. There were no hidden switches or buttons.

She didn't know what to say. This whole situation was too strange for her to accept. Then again, if there was one person she'd always trusted, it was Aldrich Montclair.

Her grandfather was an Oxford don, a specialist in medieval history. He was eccentric and cerebral, but he'd always had time for her and Emily. When she was little, they'd frequently visited him at his cluttered little flat at the university.

Outside, the stone spires of St Wilfred's College soared up and up as if to pierce the sky. Inside, stacks of books mirrored the exterior architecture, towering and teetering from every table and chair.

For Taylor, it had been like Disneyland.

He'd give her old exam papers to draw on. When that lost its charm, he'd hand her heavy books, filled with colourful illustrations to flip through. It would be years before she realised how rare and precious those ancient, leather-bound editions must have been.

He taught her about marginalia – the fanciful doodles monks would draw down the sides of manuscript folios. She would spend ages searching for the tiny cats, mice and dragons hidden at the edges of the thick soft pages.

'You are two peas in a pod,' her mother used to sigh, as Taylor and Aldrich bent over a huge dusty book, examining an image of a snake eating an elaborately detailed letter 'A'.

But after Taylor's dad left them Aldrich had gradually faded from their lives. Taylor was getting older, and had less time to spend with him. And he was very busy with his research and tutoring.

To have him appear now, when she most needed help, could not be a coincidence. Had he really been trying to keep her 'safe'?

Safe from what?

Aldrich sat down on the bench next to her. The breeze toyed with his fine, white hair.

'You're an intelligent girl, Taylor, so I'm going to explain this to you as I would any scientific fact. There is something in your DNA – the same thing I have in mine – that allows you to do unusual things. To manipulate nature. The headaches are the start but it progresses very quickly from here. You need training. Guidance. I can provide that. But . . . ' He paused, his face darkening. 'There are other things happening here as well. Things that put you in tremendous danger. We need to move quickly to protect you.'

Taylor studied him. In his tweed jacket and knotted tie he appeared perfectly rational.

Only his words were bonkers.

'I'm sorry but this is crazy,' she said. '*I'm* crazy. I'm probably imagining this entire conversation right now. I'm delusional.'

'You most certainly are not.' Her grandfather looked offended. 'This is real, Taylor. This is your life. You are not imagining any of it. The attack last night should have made that absolutely clear.' He pointed at the scarf around her neck. 'Take that off.'

'Are you . . . Why?'

'My dear,' he said, 'I need to see what they did to you so I can know precisely what we're dealing with here. That *is* where you were injured, yes? You're hiding the marks with that scarf?'

For some reason Taylor found herself unable to lie to him. She nodded.

'Then please,' he said gently, 'take off the scarf.'

Her fingers were numb and she fumbled with the knot, pulling at the thin material of the scarf until it let go. The air felt cool against her neck.

She lifted her chin.

His lips tightened when he saw the thin, purple marks on her throat. 'It's as I feared. But it could have been worse. Have you told anyone what happened? Your mother? The police?'

She shook her head, hastily retying the scarf.

'Good.' His tone was crisp. 'So difficult to explain these things to the authorities. They simply never understand. Nothing about it in their books. But you can tell me. *I* will understand. And I need to know everything down to the smallest detail.'

The truth was, Taylor longed to tell someone what she'd been through. It had been the most frightening thing she'd ever experienced and she'd had to go through every bit of it entirely alone.

Haltingly at first, and then with increasing confidence, she told him about the attack in the hallway. The invisible hands. The odd strands of power – the lifeline she'd grabbed.

'Explain that to me again,' he said, and there was an undercurrent of excitement in his voice. 'You saw golden filaments and you were able to manipulate them?'

'I don't know if I manipulated them, exactly,' Taylor said. 'It was more like I . . . grabbed one.'

'I see.' She could see the spark of approval in his eyes. 'That is much more impressive than you know.'

She didn't understand why it was impressive. To her it was still all a confusion of pain and fear. And exploding lights.

'Tell me what this is,' she said, leaning towards him. 'You say this is in my DNA and yours. So this is something I inherited? Some genetic . . . defect?'

'Precisely,' he said. 'Although I wouldn't use the word "defect". It's more that there's a gene in your DNA most people don't have. A simple element that might, in other circumstances, have given you blue eyes, or brown hair.'

'In this case it's given me what, though?' Taylor held up her hands. 'What am I?'

They both heard the voices at the same time. Twisting on the bench, Taylor saw two women in business clothes walk into the park.

'This isn't the place to talk about this.' Aldrich's gaze swept the park, looking for others who might overhear them. 'You should come see me in Oxford. Then I can explain in more detail.'

He started to rise, but Taylor reached for his arm, holding him back.

'Wait, you can't just *go*. You have to explain more.'

Lowering himself back onto the bench, he fixed her with a steady look.

'What matters is that you have this genetic trait. I could sense it even when you were a baby – the potential. You *glowed* with it. Others can sense it too. That is the problem.'

Taylor, who didn't understand what she was glowing with, wasn't certain whether or not to be pleased about this.

'That is why I sent Finlay to watch over you,' he continued. 'I knew your ability would appear with suddenness and that it might overwhelm you. Your mother knows nothing about this, and your father has ...' he paused delicately, 'gone, so there had to be someone watching.'

Taylor blinked at him. 'Wait ... Finlay works for *you*?'

He nodded. 'He's the one who notified me you'd begun having ... incidents.'

'But how did you know what happened last night?'

'There has been someone outside your house every night,' Aldrich explained as if this was perfectly rational. 'Ever since you blew out the stereo system in that restaurant with the absurd name. What is it? Jay's Rocket Bar?' He wrinkled his nose. 'Ridiculous.'

'Someone has been outside my *house*?'

Taylor couldn't seem to stop herself from parroting back each piece of news he offered her.

She'd been watched in school. She'd been watched at home. What had they seen? The idea of someone skulking through her life spying made her skin crawl.

'Why didn't you just tell me what was happening?' she asked, her voice rising. 'Why didn't you just explain?'

The smile he gave her then was knowing. 'Would you have believed me? My dear, if I'd told you about this before I fear you would have tried to have me committed.'

Taylor's mouth – which had been open to argue – snapped shut.

'Do you believe me now?' He peered at her. 'Are you ready to take the next step? To let me help you?'

Next step to what?

All she knew was she had a genetic abnormality that made her dangerous around electricity. How was that going to be useful?

'I don't understand what any of this means,' she said. 'I don't know why I got hurt. I don't know why you're here. I don't know why any of this is happening to me.'

144

A tear escaped and rolled down her cheek, and she turned her head away.

For a moment he didn't move. Then, reaching across the space between them, her grandfather rested his hand on her shoulder.

'I know this is confusing. And I will explain everything. We will keep you safe.'

Before Taylor could argue, voices floated towards them on the breeze. This time, an elderly couple walked carefully on the path towards them, arms linked.

'There's so much to tell you.' Aldrich said quietly, his gaze on the grey-haired couple. 'But this isn't the place. I should like you to come to Oxford this Saturday to see me. I'll explain more then, introduce you to others who are like us, and we can begin teaching you to control your power.'

Surprised, Taylor turned to him. 'Others? You mean, this isn't just our family?'

He beamed. 'Oh no, my dear. This isn't just our family. There are many like us. We are not alone in this. *You* are not alone.'

The elderly couple grew closer. Some distance behind them, a woman appeared, pushing a pram.

Her grandfather stood and gestured for her to follow. 'Walk with me as far as the street.'

He moved with surprising swiftness, and Taylor hurried her steps.

'I know you have many questions,' he said. 'And I promise you will have answers. In the meantime, I'm afraid you are not safe. There's much going on that shouldn't be – what happened last night is a clear indication of that. My people were

145

there, but they didn't get to you in time. We've increased our security and that sort of attack should not happen there again. But I must ask that you stay home at night. Even during the day, be aware at all times of who you're with. Don't go anywhere with anyone you're not sure of.' He fixed her with a stern look. 'Do I have your promise?'

'I . . . guess,' she said uncertainly.

They'd reached the pavement now, and he stopped with such suddenness she stumbled.

'One other thing,' he said. 'Your headaches and the other . . . side effects of our condition can be set off by high emotion. Anger. Fear. And so forth.' He waved his hand in a gesture that took in her whole body. 'Try not to get too emotional.'

Try not to have emotions? Taylor thought. *How will I do that?*

'Now,' he said, 'I really must go. Don't worry about Saturday, I'll arrange it all with your mother.' Taking her shoulders he kissed her cheeks warmly. 'It is truly lovely to see you again. So grown up. But . . . no more poltergeist research, please. Those books are a load of old codswallop.'

With that, he headed down the street away from her.

Dumbfounded, Taylor watched him go. Just before he reached the corner, she noticed an odd looking girl with blue hair standing under a lamp post. She had elaborate tattoos on her arms and legs. She looked muscular, fearless.

As Taylor studied her curiously, the girl met her gaze with a challenging stare.

Flustered, Taylor turned away.

♊

The classic white 1965 Jaguar was parked on a quiet side street, sheltered by a high hedge. Aldrich climbed in behind the wheel and closed the door behind him with a satisfying thunk. The dashboard was made of polished wood; it felt warm and alive beneath his hand as he rolled down the window to let in fresh air.

Seconds later, the blue-haired girl opened the other door and slipped into the passenger seat.

'Well?' She held up her hands with barely controlled impatience. The tattooed alchemy symbols on her wrists were black as ink. 'Am I right? Is it happening?'

Aldrich pulled out his handkerchief and wiped the perspiration from his forehead. It really was quite warm today.

'It's happening,' he said.

She exhaled audibly and dropped back against the black leather seat. 'OK. So this is real. What happens now?'

He smiled. His assistant was talented but very young. Only a few years older than his granddaughter. There was nothing he could say that could prepare her for what they were about to face.

'Now,' he said, 'we must keep her alive.'

Sixteen

Sacha checked Taylor's Revolution Chat page for the hundredth time – offline. She hadn't emailed in days.

He knew he needed to talk to her but he was almost relieved. If he told her what he suspected . . .

She'll think I'm crazy.

He'd spent the better part of two days going through his father's papers, looking for more references to Aldrich Montclair. He'd researched Montclair, knew he was a medieval history professor at St Wilfred's College, Oxford. He was held in high regard in the historic and scientific communities. Beyond that, though, there was nothing to tie his historian father to a man with the same last name as Taylor. Nothing that would explain why they were working together.

There had to be something. No way was it pure coincidence

that his teacher and Taylor's teacher had decided to put them in touch with each other, when they could have chosen any of the millions of other students in England and France.

Sacha didn't believe in coincidences.

With a sigh, he opened his father's notebook again. Each page was covered in Adam's tiny precise writing. He had no evident system – it was as if he took notes as he went. So pages contained a mixture of work notes ('meet dean at 7') and personal ('pick up milk at store'). Hidden among these, were the parts Sacha was really looking for.

These lines stood out – each word heavy with desperation.

'Twelve so far. I count twelve boys. There *must* be another.'

He'd found the date of his eighteenth birthday written on page one and circled in red.

He flipped the page. 'Aldrich is looking for the key. Says there must be a way to end this before it's too late. His entire group is committed to this. But time is the enemy.'

'What kind of key?' he wrote in his notes

He knew now that in his last years, his father had devoted his life to trying to find a way to keep him alive. All the trips away, when Sacha thought he was doing research for his work at the university, he'd been looking for clues – ways to break the curse.

The curse. Sacha saw those two words over and over again in his father's papers. But never a full explanation. Never anything that told him *what* or *why*.

When his mother had first told him what she knew, she'd used that word: curse. At first thought he'd thought it was a bizarre joke. Or some sort of weird metaphor. But gradually he realised they used that word because there was no other. They genuinely believed his family was cursed.

He believed it, too.

What else do you call it when you know from birth the date you'll die? What do you call that?

Cursed.

At the beginning, Sacha had made his mother tell him everything she knew about his situation. The problem was, she didn't know very much. All she'd been able to tell him was that first-born sons in his family died on their eighteenth birthdays. Every time. Decade after decade. Century after century. Until then, nothing could kill him.

'This is how things have been as long as anyone can remember,' she'd said the day she told him of his fate. 'The family has tried everything to save the boys but each time ... they die.'

Her eyes had been filled with a grief so stark, it had shaken him.

They'd been sitting on the sofa in the living room, Sacha remembered. The same sofa that was there now, soft, brown and sagging a little in the middle. It had been his sixteenth birthday. That year she'd given him a computer game he really wanted. And a death sentence.

At first he hadn't believed her. He'd been angry, confused.

Once she'd told him all she could, his mother hadn't wanted to talk about it anymore. She was focussed on trying to give him a normal life. She was obsessed with it.

'You will have the best life I can give you,' she used to say. 'It's all I can do.'

But he didn't want a normal life.

He wanted answers. He wanted to stop this thing.

Now he had seven weeks left. Seven weeks.

He needed to talk to Annie. What if she knew more than his mother did? After all, she'd grown up with this in her family. She would at least know more of the family lore about it.

He was certain there was more to it than he'd been able to figure out so far. He was missing something. Dropping the pen, Sacha rubbed his eyes. God, he was tired.

'You could have left me more clues, Papa,' he muttered unfairly, then hated himself for saying it.

There was no way his father could have known he'd die that night five years ago, his car crushed against the trunk of a tree on an English country lane. No reason for him to leave Sacha an explanation. He thought he'd be here to figure it all out.

Only he wasn't.

Sacha slammed his notebook shut. He needed a break from this. And he *really* needed to talk to Taylor.

Turning to his computer, he opened a new email and typed in her address and a terse message:

We need to talk. Tonight, 5 p.m. England time.

When the email was sent, he stretched gingerly – he'd been in that chair a long time. It was after two o'clock. He hadn't eaten since breakfast. No wonder his stomach was grumbling.

The flat was quiet as he headed to the kitchen – his sister was at school, and his mother was back on day shifts.

Day shifts meant order, and the kitchen was spotless.

Grabbing an apple from the bowl on the counter, he took an enormous bite. As he chewed, he leaned across the sink to look out the window to the street below. There wasn't much to see. An old man was walking a small dog on a long, slim leash. A woman pushed a pram at a brisk pace while talking on her phone. Just as he straightened, three men in dark suits turned into his street moving at an oddly rapid pace, but he didn't wait to see where they went.

He pulled his phone from his pocket, and scrolled through the list of contacts. 'Annie' was the first name on the list.

His finger hovered above the call button. He hadn't spoken to his aunt in ages. He'd pushed her away – along with every-one else.

She lived in the countryside, several hours from Paris. She rarely came to the city. It had been easy to just let her slip from his life. But now ...

What if she has the answers?

He had to talk to her.

Before he could push the call button, though, the front door bell rang.

He headed down the hallway, a frown creasing his brow.

It was rare for anyone to come to the house during the day. Their neighbours knew his mother often worked nights. Packages and post were left downstairs.

He was nearly to the door when someone pounded their fist against it so heavily it shook in the frame.

Sacha froze, his gaze fixed on the door. The fine hairs on the back of his neck rose.

The pounding came again. It was more than demanding. It

was as if someone was trying to knock the door off its hinges.

The memory of the men who shot him flickered horribly through his mind.

Do they know I'm alive? Did Antoine tell them?

Cautiously, he bent down to remove his shoes. In his socks, he slipped down the corridor with silent steps, his back to the wall.

When he reached the door, he leaned forward to see through the peephole.

Three men stood in the hallway outside the door. At first, they looked normal. But as Sacha looked closer he drew in a sharp breath. All three were thin to the point of emaciation. All were neatly dressed in long, black coats, although the day was warm. All three were deathly pale.

One of them, the smallest, had a hand pressed against the door. He didn't look strong enough to have made the door shake with his fist.

The pounding came again. The door shook violently.

But Sacha was looking right at him and his fist never moved. No one was hitting that door.

His heart began to pound.

What the hell is going on?

Suddenly, the last of the three, who stood some distance behind the other two, looked straight at him. His eyes were black as coal and piercing.

Much as he wanted to, Sacha couldn't tear his gaze away.

His eyes fixed on Sacha, the man spoke, his voice deep and chilling. 'Stay away from the girl.'

Sacha had the sickening sense the man could see him

through the door. That he knew he was here looking back. That he knew he was afraid.

And worse, that he found it amusing.

The man's lips curved into a rictus grin that seemed to stretch his skin across the bones of his face. It was like staring at a grinning skull.

Sacha took a gasping breath.

The three pivoted in unison and walked away. They had an unnatural gait – so smooth they seemed to glide across the linoleum floor. As one, they turned into the stairwell, before disappearing into the shadows.

Sweating, Sacha sagged back away from the door.

What the hell just happened?

♊

When he'd caught his breath, he pulled his phone from his pocket with shaking hands.

This was getting out of control. Whoever those guys were, they weren't normal. And they knew about Taylor.

It was time to find out what Annie knew.

His aunt picked up her phone after four rings. 'Hello?'

After everything that had just happened, her warm, alto voice was wonderfully familiar. Sacha clutched the phone tightly to his ear. He hadn't realised until that moment how much he'd missed her.

'*Salut*, Annie,' he said, trying to keep his voice steady. 'It's Sacha.'

'Sacha!' Her voice brightened. 'My goodness. I'm so glad to hear from you.'

He could almost see her, sitting in her big country kitchen, her black cat curled up nearby, a cup of coffee perpetually at her elbow.

'I'm sorry I haven't been in touch, lately,' he began, but she didn't wait for him to finish.

'Don't apologise,' she said. 'I know the day is close. I've been expecting to hear from you.'

The day is close. Hearing her say it made it even more real.

'How are you, Sacha?' Her voice grew gentle.

He bit his lip hard. He didn't want her to know how he really was – nearly at the end of his short life, with terrifying men appearing at his door making vague threats. Also killing himself occasionally for cash.

'I don't know. Confused,' he said. 'Scared. Weird things are happening, Annie. And I don't understand any of it. I need help. Can you help me?'

It wasn't like him to be so honest. Or to allow himself to feel how much all of this hurt. But hearing his aunt's voice again had touched a chord. In his memories she was intrinsically connected to a happier time. A time when he thought he would live forever.

She still lived on the family vineyard where she and his father had grown up. Sacha had spent a lot of time there as a child. He wondered if he'd ever get the chance to see it again.

The strands of pain strung around his heart tightened.

Annie's reply was instant. 'What do you need, Sacha? Just say it and it's yours.'

He could have hugged her.

'I need information,' he said eagerly. 'I need to know about my father. His work. How far he got. Everything he knew about what's happening to me.'

'I'll tell you everything I know.'

Sacha's body sagged with relief. He needed an ally very badly right now.

'Thank you,' he whispered.

'Your father didn't tell me everything but he shared some of it,' Annie said. 'You know we call it a curse, but we don't really know what it is. Your father devoted his entire life to trying to figure out what it really was – how this was possible. He told me, right before he died, he thought he was onto something. He'd found information that made him believe there might be a way to stop it. That's why he kept going to England. He told me the key was there. He was looking for the key.'

Sacha's heart skipped a beat.

That must be what his father and Taylor's grandfather were working on together. It had to be.

'*Stay away from the girl*,' those men had said.

Maybe they didn't want him to find what his father was looking for.

He couldn't keep his excitement out of his voice. 'Did he tell you anything else? Has anyone ever stopped it? Lived after they turned eighteen?'

She hesitated.

'No,' she said after a second. 'Not as far as we know.'

Sacha felt some of his hope drain away. 'Never?'

'Never.' Her voice was sorrowful. 'All first-born sons die on their eighteenth birthday. It's just the way things are for us.'

'Oh.'

Why couldn't there ever be good news?

'He found a reference to the curse that said it would end with the thirteenth son. Your father spent years researching old records to figure out which number you were. Trying to see how many had died before you. Hoping it was all over. That you were the fourteenth or the fifteenth and the whole thing was finished. It was difficult because, long ago, deaths weren't always recorded. And then you had that accident.'

'On the swings.' Sacha didn't remember the incident, but he'd heard the story many times.

Annie told it again, anyway.

'You fell and broke your neck. Your mother saw the whole thing. She's a nurse, after all – she knew you were dead. She was absolutely beside herself. Then, after a few minutes, you just got up and started to play again.' Annie paused. 'That was when they knew . . .'

'. . . I couldn't die.' Sacha finished the thought.

They both fell silent for a second.

Sacha tried to get the conversation back on track. 'Some men came to my door today,' he said. 'They were really strange. Pale and thin. Not normal. Did my dad ever see anyone like that? Was anyone following him?'

'If they were, he didn't tell me.' Annie sounded worried. 'Did they hurt you?'

'No. Maybe it was nothing.'

He was deliberately underplaying it. He didn't want Annie to know how awful they'd been. How shaken the incident had left him.

How much danger he thought he might be in now.

His aunt sighed. 'I wish I knew more that could help you, Sacha. I feel so helpless. Your father was a historian. He always understood this better than anyone. He called it a kind of lost knowledge – beliefs that were once common that we now no longer understand so we just ... dismiss them.'

'You are helping, Annie, really. I'm just ...' Sacha pounded one fist softly against his knee, '... getting desperate.'

She paused to think. 'Sacha, why don't you come down here and look at your father's books? There might be something there that would help you. Adam always believed the answers were in those books somewhere.'

'I'll do that.'

His tone was honest, but it was a lie. He was sure he'd never get the chance to see his aunt's house; his father's books.

His time was running out.

Seventeen

Taylor could not get the conversation with her grandfather out of her head.

She went over and over it, trying to figure it out. She kept hearing his voice in her head.

'What's happening to you is very dangerous . . . '

His warning had rattled her. She stayed in at night, despite Georgie's entreaties that she should come over to study. In the morning she walked to school at a fast pace, glancing over her shoulder.

In lessons she sat near the door so she could be the first one out. It was absurd, really, but she did it anyway.

When classes ended for the day, she decided to stay at school and study in the library. Even though her grandfather had promised the house was safe, she didn't see how he could be 100 per cent sure of that. Emily had her after-school activities, her mother was still at work, and she didn't want to be home by herself right now.

And so, at four o'clock, she was sitting at a table in the quiet, bookish environs of the school library when someone stepped up to the table, blocking the light.

She looked up to find Tom towering over her.

'We need to talk.'

His curt tone and dour expression made her heart sink. Despite Georgia's warning to break up with him quickly, she'd been avoiding him for two days. He'd obviously noticed.

'Uh . . . Sure,' she said, trying to sound calm. 'Where . . . ?'

'I know a place.' His voice was cold.

This didn't look good.

Leaving her books behind, Taylor followed him out of the brightly lit, modern school library into the empty corridor. School had been out for nearly an hour and their footsteps echoed as they walked in tense silence.

His silence was unnerving and, when they turned a corner into a shadowy stretch of corridor, Taylor hesitated.

'Where are we going . . . ?'

Tom's reply was clipped. 'Not far.'

Some part of Taylor wanted to refuse but it seemed ridiculous. This was *Tom*. He wouldn't hurt her.

He led the way to the end of the corridor, turning left into the cavernous space of the school gym. Grey afternoon light filtered dimly through a row of windows high on the wall, leaving much of the sprawling room in shadow. Even empty, the smell of sweat and fear still hung in the air.

This was Tom's territory. He was an athlete. Whatever he

had to say to her now, he wanted to be on home turf when he said it.

Taylor folded her arms across her chest.

'What's this about, Tom?' Her voice echoed.

'I should ask you the same question, Taylor.' His face was red. He looked angry. 'I don't understand why you've been acting this way.' He gestured at her body language – her tightly crossed arms. 'You're avoiding me. Ignoring my messages. You're supposed to be my girlfriend.'

He spat out the last word.

'I *am* your girlfriend,' Taylor said. She paused. It was time for her to be honest. 'Or I was.'

'Was.' He glared. 'Just like I thought. So you're breaking up with me but you don't have the guts to tell me? Is that it, Taylor?'

Taylor wanted to argue with that but it was a fair point.

'I'm sorry,' she said, dropping her arms to her sides. 'We should have talked before now. But I've been so busy studying . . . '

'Yeah, I know all about your *studying*,' he sneered. With some French guy. I hear you've been doing more than studying with him.'

Taylor's heart stuttered. How did he know about Sacha? How could he possibly . . . ?

For a split second she was too shocked to think straight, then she put two and two together.

Georgie.

She found herself stammering. 'I . . . What?'

Tom's eyes narrowed as he took a step towards her. The

161

tendons in his neck bulged. 'I'm not some idiot, you know. You can't mess *me* around. Do you know who I am?' He flung out an arm to take in the gym around them. 'I'm the most popular guy at this *school*. You're lucky I ever went out with you at all.'

Taylor had never seen this side of him. He looked like he hated her.

'Tom, I don't know where you got this idea, but I'm not doing anything ...'

'Oh really? That's not what I hear.' He took another step towards her.

He was too close.

Blindly, she took a stumbling step backwards, her eyes sweeping the room for an escape route. But Tom had positioned himself between her and the only door.

She held out placating hands. 'Look ... calm down. Let's talk this through.'

But he wasn't going to listen to reason.

'Everyone wondered what I was doing going out with geeky Taylor Montclair. My mates all made fun of me.' His glare was accusing. 'I thought you were different. Kind of cool ...' He slapped his hand against his forehead and the sound reverberated like a gunshot. 'God. I was such an idiot to waste my time on you.'

Heat rose to Taylor's cheeks. She could hear the hurt and contempt in his voice – one emotion mixing with the other to form a potent rage.

She'd begun to tremble.

'Look, Tom, I'm so sorry,' she said. 'You're right. I haven't been fair.'

162

'Fair?' He glared. 'No you bloody haven't been fair, you slag. You cheated on me . . .'

'Cheated?' Taylor stared. 'I never cheated on you.'

'Don't lie.' He took another step towards her. Again, she moved back. This time, though, she ran into the wall – cold and solid against her back. Now there was nowhere to go. Her heart hammered against her ribs.

When he thrust his finger at her she flinched. 'You've been messing around with some random French guy you met online, you skank. Everyone's talking about it.'

Everyone?

Taylor shook her head violently. 'No, I haven't . . .'

'You're such a liar,' he shouted. 'Who the hell do you think you are? You're *no one*.'

She could feel his breath on her skin, hot and moist, as he towered over her, trapping her with his body.

'I'm going to make you sorry you ever cheated on me.'

Desperately, her eyes flashed up to his, pleading with him to stop. But his face was dark with resentment.

Suddenly, all the fear left her. A calm, otherworldly sense of control descended.

Taylor closed her eyes as power tingled from her heart down her arms. She took a gasping breath.

The muscular boy in front of her seemed small and insignificant now.

She was the strong one.

Was this what her grandfather was talking about? The genetic abnormality?

She thought of his cautioning words, *'There's no way to*

control what could happen . . . ' And, for a brief second, worry flashed across her mind. But, like lightning, it flashed and faded away.

'You're a bitch, you know that?' Tom said.

Taylor's hands began to burn. She forgot to be careful.

'Step back.' Her voice seemed to come from far away. Amplified. Irrefutable.

Tom didn't move, he just stared at her in disbelief. 'What . . . ?'

'Step. Back.'

He took a stiff step away. As he did, he looked down at his legs as if he didn't understand what they were doing. Colour drained from his face.

She watched as if from a distance as he took another jerky step. And another. He moved like a toy. A puppet.

'What the hell?' He sounded scared.

At first, Taylor didn't fully comprehend what was happening. When she did, she felt dizzy with exhilaration.

I'm doing this. I'm making him run.

The power was heady. He couldn't hurt her. She wouldn't let him.

She felt as if she was flying.

He *should* run. He was a creep. He'd threatened and insulted her. He deserved much worse than this.

Tom's jerky steps came faster and faster.

Some part of Taylor knew she should stop now. But she couldn't seem to hear that voice. The energy coursing through her veins was overwhelming. Like nothing she'd ever experienced. She never wanted it to end.

A victorious smile crept across her face. She held out her arms and asked for more.

An unseen power picked Tom up off the polished wood floor. His feet left the ground. He hurtled him towards the back wall.

He gave a strangled cry of fear.

'*Stop.*'

The commanding voice came from the doorway.

Just short of the wall, Tom froze. He hung suspended off the floor, feet swinging, eyes wide with bewilderment and terror. Taylor turned slowly to see a man standing in the doorway.

'Mr Finlay?'

EIGHTEEN

Finlay stood with one hand held out towards Tom, palm facing outwards. But his eyes were on Taylor.

'Miss Montclair, you need to let him go.' He spoke calmly and firmly. 'I cannot save him without your permission. It could tear him in half.'

She couldn't seem to focus. The French teacher was clearly the one stopping Tom from smashing into the wall. But how?

'I sent Finlay to watch you . . . '

'I need your help.' The teacher's voice rose, cutting through the fog in her mind. He sounded strained, as if he was carrying something heavy. 'You must release him *now.*'

'I don't know how,' she whispered.

'It is really rather easy. Find the energy and control it.' Finlay's tone was professorial, as if he was discussing verb conjugations. But he'd begun to sweat. 'The simplest method is to imagine the energy as a physical object and bring it back. Visualise it as a thread you're reeling back, spooling into your hands.'

Taylor closed her eyes. She felt the power swirl around her, more wind than thread.

She held up her hands, which still felt oddly hot, and imagined the wind pouring into them.

It responded, flooding back to her in a rush that made her draw in a breath. Her hair flew into a cloud of golden curls around her face.

'Very good,' Mr Finlay said approvingly.

Across the room, Tom fell to the floor with a crash.

Taylor stared at his limp body in horror.

What have I done?

Now that Tom was down Finlay seemed utterly unperturbed by the situation.

He strolled over to the boy and held out his hand. 'How careless of you, Mr Berenson. I hope you haven't injured yourself.'

Tom lifted his head, his confused gaze swinging from Finlay to Taylor.

'She hit me.' He pointed at Taylor. 'Or . . . something.'

Finlay pulled him to his feet with surprising ease, and ushered him to the door, one hand on his shoulder. The whole time he talked in a low, steady voice. 'You had a quarrel with Taylor. You left in anger. You remember nothing else. A fight with Taylor. You left in anger.'

When they reached the door, he blinked owlishly. 'Take care, Berenson. That floor is slippery in places.'

'Oh . . .' Tom spoke with an odd, slow befuddlement. 'I'm sorry, Mr Finlay. I'll be careful.'

'Good lad.' Finlay patted him on the shoulder. 'Off you go.'

He stood in the doorway until he was certain Tom had gone.

'Now, Miss Montclair.' Finlay turned back to her, eyes glittering. 'Come with me.'

In a fog, she followed him out of the gym down the wide empty corridor.

The staff room had worn red carpet and was decorated with a mismatched array of shabby furniture. It smelled faintly of sour milk.

After directing her to a chair, the teacher flipped on the kettle and bustled around assembling cups and milk.

By the time he returned with two steaming mugs Taylor had begun to tremble violently.

'Oh my God, what have I done?'

'Now, now.' Finlay pressed the mug into her hand, wrapping her fingers around it tightly. 'No need for that. Drink your tea and we'll talk this through.'

Taylor felt too sick to drink. 'I could have killed him.'

'Don't exaggerate.' The teacher's tone was mild. 'You might have stunned him but he's a strong boy. He'll recover.' He fixed her with a stern look. 'I really must insist that you drink your tea.'

Under duress, she took a small sip. The heat seemed to enter her veins, slowing her trembling. She drank more.

Finlay sat in the seat across from her, watching her with

168

sharp eyes. 'Why don't you tell me what happened in there?'

Taylor took a deep breath and tried to remember what had started the whole thing.

'We broke up.'

'Ah.'

'Tom got angry,' Taylor said. 'Really angry. He said things that weren't true. He . . . threatened me.'

'Ruddy cad.' Finlay looked furious. 'I'll have him in detention for the rest of the year.'

'No,' Taylor said hastily. 'Please don't. I've done enough damage.'

'I must say, that was quite a show you put on there,' Finlay said. 'Aldrich is going to be terribly pleased.'

'*Pleased*?' Taylor shuddered. 'I'm a monster.'

'There's no need to be dramatic, Miss Montclair.' Finlay tutted. 'Your abilities are new. You just need to learn how to control them. There's nothing wrong with you.'

'How can you say that? You saw what I did in there. If it wasn't for you . . . ' Suddenly she remembered the image of the teacher standing in the doorway, one hand flung towards Tom. 'Wait. How did you do that? Are you . . . like me?'

'Yes.' He met her gaze with something that looked almost like respect. 'But I think you're much more powerful than I am. I couldn't stop you.'

'What did you do in there?' Taylor asked, going through it all again in her mind. 'Tom was upset but then you . . . did something to him.'

'We have the ability to make people forget, for a little

while.' Finlay took off his glasses and cleaned them with a tissue. 'It's very advanced but once you're trained it's a useful skill.'

Taylor saw Tom's face again, the way his anger and fear had turned to apology in an instant.

Finlay took away his thoughts?

The idea of it made her stomach churn.

'That's horrible,' she said. 'Horrible.'

She didn't want tea anymore. She didn't want to be here talking to her French teacher. But she didn't know where else to go.

Overhead, the lights flickered ominously.

Finlay's eyes widened.

'My dear, calm yourself,' he said soothingly. 'Of course you don't understand and this is all new to you. I know it's upsetting. But I understand you're seeing Aldrich on Saturday?'

Taylor nodded through a haze of tears.

'Well.' Finlay stood and Taylor found herself doing the same. 'Your grandfather will want to explain this himself.' Moving swiftly, he ushered her to the nearest exit. 'In the meantime, you must stay calm. Try not to get upset. Don't worry about Berenson – I'll make certain he leaves you alone.'

Taylor wasn't sure whether she liked the sound of that but they'd reached the door now and, just like that, she found herself standing outside.

Finlay peered at her. 'Are you well enough to go home? Do you need to be escorted?'

She shook her head. She still felt strange – her hands tingled oddly, as if sparks might shoot from her fingertips at any moment. But she didn't want Finlay walking her home.

'I'll be fine.'

'If you're sure,' he said. 'I'll phone your grandfather immediately, he'll want to know what happened. And, please.' He stopped to catch her eye. 'Don't lose your temper.'

♊

Taylor shoved the front door open and locked it behind her.

'Hello?' she called tentatively, though she wasn't surprised when no one answered. It was too early for her mother or Emily to have come home.

Fizz appeared from the kitchen and circled around her ankles, looking up at her anxiously as if she could sense something had happened.

Picking up the terrier, Taylor cradled her in her arms, letting her lick the salty residue of tears from her cheeks.

'Such strange things happened today, Fizz,' she whispered. 'Such strange things.'

She didn't want to be alone right now. She couldn't shake the memory of Tom's face – the look in his eyes when she'd thrown him ...

She longed to go to Caffeine Daze with Georgie. But she couldn't do that, could she?

Taylor bit her lip hard. Hurt and betrayal wrestled inside her. She should have known Georgie wouldn't be able to resist telling Paul about Sacha. And of course, Paul went straight to Tom.

Somewhere along the way the story got twisted.

I begged her not to tell anyone about Sacha, Taylor thought bitterly. *Begged her.*

Fizz yipped as if she'd been stung and leaped out of her arms, hitting the floor with a thud and skittering away.

Standing a safe distance away, she looked back at Taylor resentfully.

Only then did Taylor realise the tingling sensation had returned to her hands. Fizz could sense it.

Above her head the lights flickered.

Her heart began to pound.

She had to stop this. What if her brain trashed the *house*?

She closed her eyes taking steady breaths. *Don't get angry, Taylor. Don't get scared.*

She needed to do something right away. Something ordinary and calming.

With slow even steps, she made her way to the kitchen and sat down carefully at the table with her laptop.

While she waited for the computer to power up, she took deep breaths, the way they did in yoga class. It helped a little. Still, she touched the computer cautiously with the very tips of her fingers.

The last thing she needed was to explode her laptop.

She thought briefly about sending Georgie an email telling her how she felt, but she gave up on that instantly. It would only make her angry again and then, who knew what might happen? She could short out all the electrics. Send Fizz flying through a window.

The message at the top of her inbox blinked at her. It was from Sacha.

We need to talk. Tonight. 5 p.m. England time.

She glanced at the clock. It was nearly half past five.

When she logged in he was there waiting for her.

Her heart jumped at the sight of him, and she was too tired and confused to question why.

'Taylor.' Relief was clear in his voice. 'I thought I'd missed you.'

'Sorry I'm late,' she said. 'I've had a really ... weird day.'

'Me too.'

Taylor leaned forward to see him better. He was pale. His hair was mussed, and he seemed nervous – he kept glancing over his shoulder as if someone might jump out behind him.

'Sacha,' she said. 'What's the matter?'

He hesitated. 'I have to ask you a strange question.'

'OK ...'

He leaned towards the computer screen. His eyes were as blue and deep as the sea. 'Do you know a man named Aldrich Montclair?'

Taylor's mouth went dry.

'He's my grandfather. Why? Do you know him?'

He shook his head. 'I think ... I mean, I *know*, my father knew him.'

Taylor's brow creased. 'Your father knows my grandfather?'

Sacha flinched. '*Knew*,' he said. 'My father is dead.'

She covered her mouth with her fingers. 'Oh, Sacha. I'm sorry. I didn't know.'

He accepted her apology with a grave nod.

'I thought your name sounded familiar,' he explained. 'I couldn't place it, so I did a bit of digging and ... Anyway, I think they were working together.'

173

'What did they work on?' Taylor asked.

Again, Sacha hesitated, and she watched him with growing concern. There was something he wasn't telling her.

'There are things you don't know about my family. It's . . . complicated.' He took a deep breath. 'Taylor, I think I'm in trouble. And I think you're in trouble, too. I don't believe it was a coincidence we were assigned to work together. Someone wanted us to find each other. I just don't know why.' Across the miles their eyes locked. 'I think we might both be in danger.'

Taylor's mind spun. She thought of Finlay's insistence that she should talk to Sacha. Her grandfather's sudden appearance. She thought of Tom flying across the room. And Georgie's betrayal.

Nothing was what she thought it was. Nothing made sense.

Maybe it was time to do something about it.

'Sacha,' she said. 'I think we should meet.'

Nineteen

Amid the hubbub of the Gare du Nord railway station, Sacha leaned against the base of a lamp post and watched the barely controlled chaos of summer travel from behind dark sunglasses.

A family of tourists overloaded with suitcases lumbered by, their rolling cases barely missing his toes. Sacha grimaced.

He hated crowds. You never knew who you might run into.

He'd chosen a spot half-hidden between a sandwich stand and a candy stall. From here he could clearly see the train from England as it arrived, disgorging a mass of people who rushed down the platform, excited to be in Paris on a sunny day.

He scanned their faces as they passed the metal gates. He couldn't see Taylor among them. As the crowd thinned, he grew nervous.

He glanced at his phone – no messages . . .

When he looked up again, she was there. Her curly blonde hair blew around her head in a golden halo as she made her way through the crowd. Her loose, white top fluttered around the curves of her figure.

For a second he stayed where he was, out of sight, studying her.

In person she was much prettier than she'd seemed online. But then, he'd never been able to see all of her before.

When her uncertain eyes searched the cluster of people waiting at the gates, Sacha stepped out of the shadows and threaded his way through the crowd.

A relieved smile lit up her face. Her eyes were the same green as bottle glass when the light shone through it. They took his breath his away.

'Sacha.' She beamed at him. 'You're here.'

'Of course.'

He bent down to kiss her cheeks. She gave a small gasp of surprise.

Suddenly self-conscious, Sacha straightened hurriedly, remembering that English teens didn't kiss each other quite as frequently as French kids. She might read something into it.

Did he want her to read something into it?

For a second, they stood awkwardly as the crowds hustled by them. It was Taylor who broke the silence.

'I can't believe you're really here. And I'm really here.' The broad smile returned to her face, revealing the dimples he'd seen on his computer screen. 'This is crazy.'

'Crazy,' he said soberly. 'But necessary.'

As they talked, her gaze swept across his face, his clothes, taking in his black T-shirt and jeans, the sunglasses he clutched in one hand.

He leaned back against the metal bar of the barricade with elaborate casualness. 'What did you tell your parents?'

'My mum thinks I'm staying at a friend's tonight.' Her gaze flickered away from his. 'I do it all the time … she'll never check. But I have to be back by the time she gets home from work tomorrow. Otherwise she'll …'

Before she could finish the thought, a group of unidentifiable nationality shoved into them, nearly knocking Taylor over.

Sacha pulled her closer, out of the way. For just a second he could feel the warmth of her body against his.

One of the adults offered his apology in broken French. Sacha glowered at him until – realising he wasn't going to be forgiven – the man gave up and wandered away, dragging his bright blue suitcase behind him.

Taylor said nothing through all of this, but her eyes danced with unspoken mirth.

Sacha exhaled. 'Let's get out of here.'

♊

Outside, the sun bleached the statues on the front of the station until they glowed white. Traffic crawled by.

Sacha made his way through the largely stationary cars with practiced ease. Taylor followed with more caution. Whenever he glanced over she was staring at the dingy nineteenth century buildings around them.

'It's beautiful,' she said. 'It looks just like I imagined Paris would look.'

With a dismissive glance at the travel shops and nail salons, Sacha made a face.

'*This* isn't Paris,' he scoffed. 'I will take you to Paris.'

He turned off the noisy main avenue on to a quieter side road lined with pale green trees. The buildings were prettier here, better maintained.

'Do you live around here?' Taylor asked, looking up at the creamy white buildings, with their black, wrought iron balconies spilling over with vivid flowers.

Sacha shook his head. 'We live on the east side.' He waved in the general direction. 'That way.'

'Oh,' Taylor said.

As they walked, Sacha tried to decide how to start. This meeting was his chance to tell her the truth about himself. That was why she was here, after all. It had been two days since Taylor had announced she was coming to Paris, and that she wasn't going to tell anyone. He'd had two days to get ready to tell her the truth.

Now that she was here he couldn't make his mouth form any useful words, much less the hardest words of all. He had no idea how to begin telling her about his life.

When they talked online, everything had been easy. Like they knew each other. He'd felt comfortable and safe. With her here, he suddenly felt too tall, too thin, too clumsy. Her very presence, all cute and English and blonde, was throwing him off his game.

A stunning woman walked a small dog right into their path, requiring them both to veer sharply out of the way.

'Wow. Paris is so ... *Paris*.' Taylor sighed.

Sacha laughed. 'That's good, *non*?'

'Yeah,' she agreed. 'That's good.'

They turned to cross a busy street, pausing as a man in an expensive suit roared by on a scooter.

'I never do things like this,' she announced when they reached the pavement on the other side. 'I've never even sneaked out of my house before. Not once. Today I sneaked out of my *country*.' Her voice was high-pitched – Sacha could hear the tension in it. 'I think maybe I'm going nuts.'

'If you're going crazy,' he said, 'then I am, too. So . . . ' he shrugged. 'At least you're not alone.'

She smiled up at him. 'We can go crazy together in Paris. I guess there are worse ways to spend a Thursday.'

She had even, white teeth and full pink lips, and when she smiled she lit up as if illuminated by some inner light. She was one of those people.

Sacha wanted to make her smile more.

But that wasn't why she'd come all this way.

'When you emailed me that first time?' He glanced over at her. 'Who gave you my email address?'

'My French teacher,' she said. 'Mr Finlay.'

'What did he tell you about me?'

She thought for a second. 'He said you needed to work on your English, and that tutoring you would help me get into Oxford.'

Finlay. The name was completely unfamiliar to Sacha. But he made a mental note to check his father's books later. Just in case.

She glanced at him. 'Why do you ask?'

'Because I don't think any of this,' he gestured back and forth between them, 'happened by chance.' He had to raise his voice to be heard above the traffic. 'Your grandfather knew my father. Out of every student you could have tutored, your teacher chose me. And my teacher urged me to get in touch with you, even though I never go to school anymore and honestly, he knows my English is good.' He shook his head. 'That is a lot of coincidences.'

'I found out this week that Finlay works for my grandfather,' she said. 'He's supposed to be ... watching me.'

Sacha didn't like the sound of this. '*Watching* you?'

'It's a long story.'

'So, let me get this straight,' Sacha said. 'The teacher who gave you my name works for your grandfather. Who knew my father.'

Taylor stopped walking. 'You think my grandfather is behind all of this?'

Sacha turned to face her. 'Don't you?'

The other pedestrians flowed around them like water around stones.

'But ... I don't understand,' she said. 'Why wouldn't he just tell me?'

'That's what we have to find out.' Sacha's jaw was set.

As they resumed their journey, he told her about the pale men who'd come to his house. He didn't mention that they could pound on the door without moving. But he told her what they'd said.

'They told you to stay away from me?' Taylor shuddered.

'Yes. Stay away from the girl. It has to be you.'

'That's terrifying. You're sure?'

Sacha nodded. 'There is no other girl.'

She glanced up at him then quickly away.

Is she blushing?

It was a hot afternoon; they were both flushed. That must be it.

'But who were they?' she asked after a moment. 'And how could they know about us?'

'I have no idea,' he admitted. 'But they scared the hell out of me.'

At some point, they'd left the traffic behind. Now they walked amid trees, in cool shade. Suddenly Sacha knew just where he wanted to take her.

'This way,' he said, turning left.

The Jardin des Tuileries stretched along the banks of the Seine with a kind of lazy elegance, each tree perfectly shaped, each hedge precisely trimmed, each path measured to mathematically balance every other path. It was green and lush and peaceful.

It was one of Sacha's favourite places. He often came here just to sit and watch the people.

When they reached the centre, he held out his arms. 'We're here.'

Taylor turned a slow circle, Sacha watched her take it all in. Statues peeked out from among the trees. Children ran past to play in a fountain. Lovers strolled hand-in-hand.

If she didn't like it, he would know everything he needed to know about her.

'Oh Sacha, it's magical.' She gazed up at him, a delighted smile spreading across her face. 'I love it.'

Her joy was contagious, and he found himself smiling back at her.

This was going to be a good day. He could tell already.

♊

'Your lemonade,' Sacha said, handing Taylor a can.

'*Merci bien*,' she said.

He lowered himself to the ground next to her and opened his own drink.

'*De rien.* Your French is not bad.'

'Thanks.' She could feel the heat rushing to her cheeks again. This was ridiculous. She had to stop blushing at everything he said.

He was so different in person than she'd expected. For one thing, he was taller than she'd thought – when they stood side by side she had to tilt her head back to see his face.

He was also incredibly cool. He didn't so much walk as saunter. His narrow shoulders were perpetually slouched in this kind of rock star way. He could cut people down with a single look. Sometimes it was riveting, sometimes it was dangerous ... sometimes it was both.

She'd never met anyone like him.

Back in the train station, when he'd pulled her close, out of the way of the crowd, she'd felt an unexpected thrill when her body met his.

That had never happened before with anyone.

She took a long drink. The lemonade was cold and fizzy

against her tongue. She loved it. In fact, she loved everything about this whole day.

With a happy sigh, she looked around at the people strolling on the gravel path. From somewhere she could hear music playing.

Paris.

In the end, getting here had been easy. She'd raided money from her university savings account to pay for the tickets. Ordering the tickets online was simple – then she just picked them up at the station in London. The rest was a piece of cake. No one had paid the slightest attention to her on the train, which was so full of young people with backpacks, it was easy to fit right in.

Knowing her family had no clue where she was filled her with a heady mixture of liberation and terror. She was on her own for the first time in her life.

Well, not completely alone.

There was Sacha.

She couldn't get over how comfortable she felt with him. They'd talked and talked. They must have walked miles to get to this park, but she'd hardly noticed. The only problem was, getting together hadn't brought many answers so far.

'Maybe . . . ' she said tentatively then stopped herself.

'Maybe what?' Sacha met her gaze.

'Maybe you should tell me a little about your dad. Maybe we can figure out what he was doing with my grandfather.'

He shrugged as if that was no big deal, but she noticed his jaw tighten at the mention of his father.

'I can tell you his name was Adam Winters. He was a

university professor at the Sorbonne, and he also worked at Oxford,' he said.

'My grandfather works at Oxford,' she offered.

'What does he teach?'

'The history of science,' Taylor said. 'Newton and that sort of thing. What about your dad?'

A lock of silky brown hair tumbled across his forehead; he pushed it back absently.

'Medieval history.' He shot her a sideways glance. 'I think what they were working on together was ... different from their work.'

'How?'

He looked hard at the can in his hand, as if it held the answers.

'I think,' he said slowly, 'they were working on something to do with my family.'

Taylor could sense how hard this was for him. His words came slowly.

'You don't have to tell me if you don't want to.'

Sacha didn't speak for a long moment, his expression was deadly serious.

'There's a problem,' he said finally. 'In my family. Like a health problem. My father was trying to cure it. Before it could ... hurt me. And I wondered if he was working with your grandfather on that. Since he is a scientist.'

He met her gaze then and the look in his eyes made her breath hitch in her throat – he looked utterly vulnerable.

'But my grandfather studies ancient science,' she explained, wishing she had better news. 'Like weird instruments and concoctions made from plants. Leeches . . . '

He exhaled audibly and muttered something in French. Taylor wasn't certain, but she thought he'd said, 'It's an old problem.'

Before she could ask what he'd meant, he crushed the can in his hand with sudden violence and said, 'Let's get out of here.'

Twenty

'Hundreds of years ago, these were castle gardens,' Sacha explained, gesturing at a fountain where children sailed boats made of paper, like a scene from a history book. 'Now it's for everyone.'

Sacha and Taylor emerged from the trees onto a broad path, joining crowds of tourists and Parisians out for a stroll. The gravel crunched satisfyingly beneath their feet; each step raised a fine cloud of dust.

They could hear music playing somewhere and the sound of laughter.

Ahead, an enormous ornate building loomed. They walked into a vast courtyard, enclosed on three sides. In the middle a glass pyramid glinted in the afternoon sunlight.

'Welcome to the Louvre,' Sacha said.

The huge art museum's elaborately carved stone walls appeared to stretch for miles. Taylor couldn't see the end of it.

She craned her neck to see the top windows. 'Bloody hell, it's enormous.'

Their steps slowed. Tourists hurried around them, rushing to join a long queue snaking towards the ticket office.

'We could go in. If you want.' Sacha's tone was doubtful.

'I don't think I could handle it,' she said. 'There must be *miles* of art in there. I could have an art overdose.'

His lips twitched. 'I've never heard of an art overdose.'

'Happens all the time,' she assured him breezily. 'They cover it up.'

'No Louvre then,' he said, turning back. 'Because art is dangerous.'

In his accent the word 'dangerous' sounded amazing.

They walked back across the cool, green park. Taylor felt so comfortable here, in this moment. In the heat and bustle of summertime Paris. The light glinting off the graceful buildings around her.

'This all feels so familiar,' she said, glancing at Sacha. 'Like I've already been here a hundred times. But that must just be from seeing it on TV. It's weird. Like when you see someone on the street and you think you know them, but you don't.'

'We call it *déjà vu*,' he said. 'Maybe you have been here before. In another life.'

She cast him a sceptical glance. 'You don't believe in that stuff, do you?'

'I don't know what to believe, anymore.'

The mood darkened momentarily. He gave a shiver, as if shaking off the gloom.

Moving in sync, they turned towards the river. The air was cooler here. And scented with something delicious, like burned sugar.

It made Taylor's stomach rumble.

'Why do rivers smell like sugar in Paris? Where I'm from they smell like fish.'

Sacha pointed to a stall on the riverside selling crepes. 'We cheat.'

'That smells *incredible*.' Her mouth began to water.

Sacha looked at her, amused. 'Do you want one?'

It was nearly five o'clock and she hadn't eaten anything since breakfast. She'd been too excited to realise she was hungry before. Now she was ravenous.

'Oh my God, yes.'

As they waited for their turn in the short queue in front of the crepe stall, Taylor kept thinking about the things Sacha had told her – and the things he'd left out. She wondered what his health problem was – maybe it was the same thing that killed his father.

It was a horrible thought.

She stole a surreptitious glance at Sacha, who stood, hands shoved deep in his pockets, watching the crepe makers. Taylor followed his gaze. The cooks used long spatulas to scrape the whisper-thin pancakes off the grill and flip them in one move. They made it look so simple.

Nothing is ever as easy as it looks.

'You said your dad sometimes worked at Oxford,' Taylor began. 'Did he spend a lot of time in England?'

His eyes still on the crepes, Sacha nodded. 'He was born

in England, actually. He moved to France after marrying my mother. But he went back a lot for work.'

That explained his last name and his near-perfect English.

The couple ahead of them ordered in the worst French Taylor had ever heard. Sacha winced at every word.

She stifled a laugh.

Turning to face her, he lifted his sunglasses so she could see his outraged expression. She covered her mouth with her hands but couldn't contain her giggles.

'Don't laugh,' he deadpanned. 'It's rude.'

That only made her laugh harder. Soon she was gasping for breath, unable to stop giggling.

When the couple glanced at them curiously, they pretended to be laughing at something happening on the river, where a tourist boat floated by, bristling with cameras.

It was fun. And for a few minutes, Taylor could pretend that they were just ordinary kids out on an ordinary day in Paris.

♊

'It's funny,' Taylor said, wriggling her bare toes. 'I thought something would just sort of happen when I got here. Like, we'd figure out instantly why our teachers wanted us to meet.'

Next to her, Sacha leaned back, stretching his shoulders. 'That would be helpful.'

They were on the Ile de la Cité, a tiny island in the middle of the river Seine, sitting side by side, their feet dangling above the deep green water. The sun was setting now. Most of the tourists who'd crowded the place earlier had gone, and the narrow strip of riverside pavement was slowly filling with teenagers.

'But no such luck.' She stared down at the water. 'I still don't know why my grandfather wanted us to meet. You're just some random French guy.'

He chuckled. 'And you're just some English girl with a leaf in your hair.'

'There's a leaf in my hair?' Reaching up, she felt for objects.

'Here. Let me.' Leaning towards her, Sacha pulled the leaf from a curl carefully. Her hair felt incredibly soft beneath his fingertips. The last rays of the setting sun made each individual gold strand glitter.

'Here.' He held up the incriminating flora so she could see.

She looked self-conscious. 'My hair is so hopeless. You can probably find other things in there. Lost watches. The Bermuda Triangle. The missing link.'

'I don't know,' he said, wishing he had more of an excuse to touch her. 'I think your hair's kind of cool.'

'Hmph,' she scoffed. But she looked pleased.

They'd been wandering the city all evening, talking in circles about their teachers, their lives.

Now, though, it was getting dark, and Sacha wasn't sure what to do.

He hadn't planned this very well. He didn't want to take her home – he didn't know how to explain her presence to his mother. Nor did he want to put Taylor through the inevitable French maternal inquisition.

In the end, he'd brought her here.

They certainly weren't alone. Under a nearby bridge. a group of young musicians in hipster suits played Dixieland jazz on battered instruments. Girls in short skirts jitterbugged in front of them as a small crowd gathered. Some had brought food in baskets, and bottles of wine. The air held the cloying scent of marijuana smoke.

It was a relaxed, happy twilight gathering. Everyone cheered when the street lights came on.

'Paris,' Taylor said, 'is amazing.'

'It is,' Sacha agreed.

A moment passed. A cool breeze stirred his hair.

Then she glanced over at him. 'Tell me something about yourself. What's your family like?'

He shrugged. 'My mother works in a hospital. My little sister is a pain.'

She snorted a laugh. 'Mine, too.'

They exchanged sympathetic glances.

'And you don't go to school much, you said?' She studied him more closely. 'How come?'

Sacha longed to tell her the truth. But he just couldn't seem to form the words. He knew how it would sound. How she would look at him. They were just getting to know each other. He couldn't bear to ruin it now.

'Things went bad a year ago,' he said vaguely. 'Something happened in my family and I just ... lost interest.'

Her cool green eyes searched his face. 'I don't want to lecture you. But you're so smart, Sacha. Do you understand what you'll lose if you drop out?'

'I know everything I'm losing. Believe me.' His bitter tone signalled an end of the conversation.

Taylor looked away. 'Then I won't tell you what to do. But seriously, one thing you do not need is an English tutor. Your

191

English is as good as mine. Your teacher is such a liar.' She stopped then, as if she'd just thought of something. 'Wait. If Finlay works for my grandfather, who does your teacher work for? I mean ... what if he works for my grandfather, too?'

It was a good point.

Was Deide involved with Aldrich Montclair? Or someone else entirely?

'We should go see him,' he murmured, thinking aloud.

She shot him a puzzled look. 'See who?'

'You're right. My teacher. He's got to be part of this whole thing with your teacher and your grandfather. If we catch him by surprise, maybe we can make him tell us what's really going on.'

Her eyes widened as she caught on.

'Of course! He must know something.' She glanced at the delicate silver watch dangling from her wrist. 'It's late, though. How ... ?'

'Tomorrow.' Sacha's mind was made up. 'We'll go to my school before your train leaves.'

He saw a worried frown flit across her delicate features. But she didn't argue.

All day long he'd felt she was keeping something from him. Several times she'd started to say something and then changed her mind. Now he sensed it again. The hesitation. The way she stared into the distance, lost in thought.

She's hiding something.

But then, why shouldn't she? He was hiding things, too.

Their relaxed mood had evaporated with the last rays of sunlight, replaced by the fear that had haunted them both for weeks. Suddenly, the jolly river scene felt false. The laughter and guitars, the dancing and pot smoke – it seemed ridiculous.

'Let's go.' Sacha jumped to his feet.

'Where to?'

'It's Paris.' He reached down a hand to help her up. 'There's always somewhere to go.'

♊

'See?' Sacha pointed at the Eiffel Tower. They were standing in the dark, just across the river from the iconic structure. 'Give it a few seconds. Three . . . Two . . . One. And . . . *Now*.'

Suddenly the tower was ablaze. Lights flashed and sparkled in a violent glitter.

He glanced down to check Taylor's reaction – she seemed bemused.

'It's a bit . . . blingy, don't you think?' she said.

He shot her a look of pure disbelief, and she laughed.

'I'm kidding. It's amazing.' She stretched her arms above her head, as if working out kinks in her shoulders. 'It must be getting late now. It feels quieter.'

Sacha glanced at his watch. 'It's after midnight.'

They were sitting on the grass in a dark park. They'd stopped here to rest and take in the view. Sacha knew they must have walked fifteen kilometres today. Taylor looked as tired as he felt. They needed to rest. They couldn't spend all night in a park.

They were at the edge of his own neighbourhood now. If they walked another ten minutes they could be at his flat, but he didn't suggest it.

The problem was, all the other options were pretty

unpleasant. A squat. A more sheltered park. He couldn't imagine asking Taylor to spend the night at either place.

A cool breeze blew off the Seine. In her filmy top, Taylor began to shiver.

That made up Sacha's mind. They'd go to the squat. If it was empty, it wouldn't be too bad. It was only a few minutes' walk away. At least they'd be inside.

'We should go,' he said. 'I think I know a place where we won't be hassled.'

Wearily, she rubbed a hand across her eyes. 'Is it far?'

'Not too far, I promise.'

They climbed to their feet and headed across the soft grass.

'It's not a pretty place,' he found himself explaining, 'but it's usually empty and it's better than sleeping on the grass . . . '

At that moment, two men melted out of the shadows ahead of them. One tall and meaty, the other small and slim.

'*Merde,*' one of them said. 'I don't believe it.'

Sacha's blood froze in his veins.

'It's that kid,' the big one said, peering at him.

'Can't be,' the small one replied. 'That kid's dead. You killed him yourself.'

It was the two thugs from the cellar – the ones who'd shot him in the face. What the hell were they doing here? How had they found him?

This was his neighbourhood – had Antoine told them where he lived?

'Sacha . . . ' Taylor whispered, and he heard worry in her voice.

This was bad. Taylor couldn't be here. With them.

But she was.

'Hey.' Sacha took a step back, pulling Taylor closer. 'You've made some kind of mistake. I don't know you.'

'Kid.' Squinting at him, the small one pulled a pack of cigarettes from his pocket. 'Anyone ever tell you you're a terrible liar?'

His lighter flared, illuminating a sharp nose and chin, tiny quick eyes.

Sacha's heart began to pound. He had to *think*.

'Look,' he said, changing tack, 'I never told anyone what happened that night. I have no problem with you. Just ... leave us alone.'

At his side, Taylor said nothing, but she clung to his hand with a fierce grip.

The small man cast a lazy glance in her direction.

'Pretty girl,' he said. 'How'd a loser like you get a girl like that?'

'Don't ask stupid questions.' Sacha's fear began to seep away, replaced by cold, clarifying anger. He had to get Taylor out of here.

Then he would deal with Antoine.

'Smart mouth,' the little one said. 'That's what got you in trouble last time.'

'Want me to kill him again?' The big one stepped forward eagerly.

Sacha looked for a gun but his beefy hands were empty.

'Not sure I see the point,' the little one said. He pointed his cigarette at Taylor, its ember a red flash in the dark. 'Maybe we kill *her* this time. See if it lasts longer.'

'Don't you touch her.' Sacha spoke between gritted teeth. 'I let you get away with this once. I won't let it happen again.'

'I don't see this being your decision,' the smaller man said. He turned to his henchman. 'Take her.'

The thug moved fast for a big guy. One minute he was in front of them. The next he had Taylor in a brutal grip and was dragging her away. She held on to Sacha for dear life, but then her grip slipped.

Her terrified scream split the air.

'Taylor!' Sacha scrambled after her.

Across the river the Eiffel Tower's lights went off, plunging them into darkness.

Everything became a shadowy blur. He could see Taylor struggling in the big man's grip, her blonde hair glimmering in the darkness. But before he could reach her, the small guy grabbed his arm. He was stronger than he looked, his fingers dug in to Sacha's flesh. The knife in his hand caught the faint moonlight and glittered.

'You want a job done right ... ' the man said.

Then he shoved the knife into Sacha's stomach.

Twenty-one

'No!' Taylor twisted in the big man's grip, her eyes wide with horror as the smaller man thrust the knife.

It happened so fast – like a film speeded up. It didn't seem real.

Until, with a kind of ethereal grace, Sacha crumpled to the ground.

All the breath seemed to leave Taylor's lungs. He wasn't moving. Why wasn't he moving?

He can't be dead. This can't be happening.

She tried to scream but her throat was too tight – no sound emerged.

'*Maintenant*, pretty girl.' The small man walked towards her, the knife still in his hand. 'I have plans for you.'

The little man reached for her arm. He had blood on his fingers.

Fury welled inside her from someplace deep and primal.

The ground heaved beneath her feet, as if it wanted to fight alongside her.

Her hands burned like fire.

'Don't you touch me.' The voice didn't sound like hers at all. It was strong and cold.

'English . . . ?' The man looked surprised. Before he could complete the thought, she flung out her arm, palm facing him.

A strange energy consumed her – it seemed to come from the grass beneath her feet, wrapping around her ankles like tentacles, climbing her arms. Filling her with unspeakable power.

The small man flew through the air as if carried by the force of an invisible tornado. He was tiny and fragile and he smashed into a tree trunk with an awful thud.

After that, he slid to the ground and didn't move again.

The big man still held her arm in a vice-like grip, but his jaw fell open.

'What . . . ' he began.

'Let go of me,' Taylor ordered.

Instantly, he did as she said. His confused expression reminded her sickeningly of Tom. But she didn't care about that. She didn't care about anything right now, except Sacha.

'Run.'

The big man took a step towards her.

'That way.' She flicked her fingers towards the street at the end of the park.

With confused obedience, he turned, stumbling unsteadily. He moved slowly at first and then faster and faster, across the park. Taylor watched him until she couldn't see him anymore.

Far away she heard the screech of breaks. Someone screaming. But it didn't seem to matter. Nothing mattered.

Numb, she ran across the cold grass – which didn't want to
help her anymore, how could it? It was just grass – to where
Sacha had fallen. Dropping to her knees she reached out to
him with shaking hands.

His eyes were closed, and he breathed with obvious effort.

'Oh God, Sacha,' she whispered, breathless with fear. 'Oh
God. Oh God. You're OK. You're OK.'

She didn't know why she kept saying that, because he
wasn't OK. Not at all. She was just so scared. She couldn't
seem to think.

Her legs felt warm and damp. It took a moment for her to
realise it was his blood, soaking through her clothes.

Nausea rose in her throat and she fought it back.

'Sacha . . . ' She pulled him into her arms.

He made a quiet gasping sound. His lips moved, trying to
form words . . .

She leaned her ear close to his face.

'How the hell,' he whispered very faintly, breath rattling in
his chest, 'did you do *that*?'

Then he died in her arms.

♊

'Sacha, no!' Taylor clutched his lifeless body. 'Don't die.
Please don't die.'

Panic made it hard to breathe. To be rational. But she had to.

'Pulse,' she told herself frantically. 'Check his pulse. Check
his pulse . . . '

She trembled with such violence her teeth chattered. Her fingers seemed frozen, and she had to force her hand to tighten around his wrist. When she did, she felt nothing.

No flutter of blood moving in his veins. No signs of life.

An awful, empty nothing.

'Please Sacha,' she whispered, leaning down to press her cheek to his cool, still lips. 'Please. Breathe. *Please*.'

No air stirred against her skin.

He was dead.

Taylor was too stunned to move. Too shocked to call for help.

She sat on the cold ground in the dark, holding a beautiful corpse in her arms.

Time passed – she didn't know how long. She couldn't seem to do anything but sit there, silent tears tumbling down her cheeks, rocking Sacha's cold body.

What am I going to do now?

At last she understood. *This* was why they weren't meant to be together. This was why those men at his door had told him to stay away from her.

Somehow they knew.

It was too late now, though. Too late.

Some part of her hoped someone would come by. Someone who hadn't just seen their friend die. Someone who could still think. But it was very late now. The city was quiet. No one passed.

The night was utterly still when, out of nowhere, Sacha took a breath.

At first, Taylor thought she must have fallen asleep – that

she was dreaming. Then he did it again – a deep, gasping inhalation.

As she stared down at him in disbelief, his body went rigid in her lap, his spine arcing sharply, as if he were being electrocuted.

Taylor had passed beyond fear now into a kind of frozen terror.

Sacha's eyes flew open.

Stifling a scream, she scrambled back, dumping his body in the grass.

He rolled onto his back.

'*Merde*,' he groaned. 'That really hurt.'

He looked pale but perfectly alive. Perfectly normal.

Taylor's heart hammered against her ribs. This was impossible.

Their eyes met. She saw the recognition in his gaze. A kind of horrified realisation.

He opened his mouth to say something but then doubled over, his body spasming again.

'Don't be scared.' He gasped out the words, his fingertips digging into the soft earth, his features contorted with agony. 'It's really me. I'm not ... a zombie. *Putain*. Forgive ... my language. It just ... really hurts. *Merde*.'

For a while he stayed that way, curled up on the ground, his body racked with pain.

Then, finally, it ended.

He pushed himself up into a sitting position. With the back of one hand he wiped the sweat from his brow. His fingers left a smear of blood on his face.

201

Taylor hadn't moved. She knelt in the cool grass a short distance away, staring at him as if she was watching a ghost. Which, in a way, she was.

'It hurts more every time,' he explained. Strands of hair clung to the perspiration on his forehead. 'How long was I gone?'

She opened her mouth to speak but no sound came out. It took several tries before she could form whole words.

'I don't know,' she whispered.

'Long, I'll bet,' he guessed. 'It's getting longer.'

'What's getting longer?' she asked weakly, although she was afraid she already knew the answer.

His gaze locked on hers. 'Dying.'

There was no way to reply to that. Nothing she could say. On some level Taylor had begun to believe she'd died, too, and this was some sort of nightmarish afterlife.

Or she could be in a coma. That would explain it.

She felt queasy. And so cold. She couldn't seem to stop shivering.

'You're probably wondering what's going on.' Sacha's voice was perfectly reasonable. But Taylor saw that his hands trembled when he ran them through his hair.

'A little.'

She felt like crying again. Crying and never stopping. But she just stayed there. Waiting.

'Do you remember when we were in the park by the Louvre, and you asked me about my father?'

'Yes.'

Everything had been different then.

'I told you there was a family problem, a health thing? And that my father was working with your grandfather to try and fix it?'

She nodded.

'This is the thing I was talking about.'

He looked down at his abdomen. Pulling his T-shirt free of his body he put his fingers through the hole the knife had made in the black fabric.

'Those bastards. Another perfectly good shirt ruined.'

Taylor just stared at him. She wanted to run but felt glued to the earth beneath her knees.

Sacha seemed to notice this.

'Hey,' he said gently, 'are you OK?'

Her lips trembled and she shook her head.

'No.' It came out as a whimper.

'I didn't think so.'

He reached towards her. There was blood on his hands.

Taylor recoiled. 'Don't.'

'Hey.' He dropped back onto his heels, his voice softening. 'Hey. Taylor. It's really me. It's Sacha. Not a ghost. I won't hurt you.'

A tear rolled down her cheek.

'You were *dead*, Sacha. I felt your pulse. You quit breathing.' Her voice shook. 'For a *long* time.'

'And you were all alone.' Understanding shadowed his face. 'I'm so sorry, Taylor. It must have been terrifying. I should have warned you. Given you some idea what might happen. I thought I had time. But those assholes keep killing me and . . .'

He stopped, and she saw the spark of memory in his face.

'Wait.' He straightened and stared at her. 'Before I died. You did a thing. With your hands.' He demonstrated, holding out one hand, like she'd done. 'A superwoman kind of thing. You threw the little one across the park. I didn't dream that, did I?'

Unconsciously, her eyes flashed to where the man still lay at the bottom of the tree trunk, legs sprawled.

Sacha followed her gaze.

'*Merde*. I didn't dream it.' He looked back at her. 'Is he dead?'

She shook her head slowly. 'I don't know.'

'If he's dead, we need to run,' he explained with cool reason. 'What happened to the other one, by the way?'

Taylor gestured vaguely in the direction he'd run. 'I think he might have been hit by a car.' She said it without emotion.

'Right.' Sacha made a calming gesture. 'Stay here, OK? Let me go check the little asshole. See if he's dead. I hope he's dead. He's killed me twice – he should at least die once.'

Climbing unsteadily to his feet he walked toward the tree, stumbling at first but then finding his legs. Taylor watched as he crouched down by the man's body, holding his wrist up for a moment, then letting it drop to the ground.

By the time he returned, Sacha's gait had returned to its usual confident, loping stride. He was himself again.

All better now.

'He's not dead.' He sounded disappointed.

Taylor knew she should be relieved but she felt nothing. It

was as if all her emotions had been hidden away and she hadn't had a chance to unpack them yet.

Her lack of reaction seemed to worry him; he crouched down beside her.

'Taylor, *ma puce*, we need to get out of here. Pretty fast, actually.' His voice was low but urgent. 'Somebody could come along. I think he's badly hurt. There's blood all over both of us. We don't want to spend all night with the police.' He held out his hand. 'Please trust me.'

She looked at it for a long second.

Then she put her hand in his. Whatever had happened in this park tonight, whatever lay ahead of them, he was right about one thing.

They had to run.

Twenty-two

'There are things I didn't tell you,' Sacha said. 'Things I haven't told anyone. And I'm sorry about that.'

Taylor regarded him gravely. 'There are things I didn't tell you, too.'

They were back in the relative safety of the Ile de la Cité, where they'd sat earlier. The dancing crowds were gone now.

In the pale glow of a streetlight, Sacha could see her cheeks were tear-streaked, her eyes hollow.

At least she was talking again.

After they left the park they'd made their way through the dark tangle of Paris streets. When Sacha thought they'd put enough space between themselves and the scene of his death, they'd stopped at a fountain to wash off the blood. Water poured from the mouth of a Greek god, and slowly turned red as they cleaned their hands and faces.

His black T-shirt was stiff with dried blood, but the dark

colour hid the worst of the carnage. Taylor's white top was ruined. She hadn't brought a change of clothes – she was only here for a day. In desperation, she'd turned her top around, until the damage was behind her. Now it was nearly dawn and they sat at the edge of the river, the water lost in the darkness below.

The city was still as if it held its breath waiting for the sun to rise.

'You died.' Taylor's soft English voice broke the quiet. 'Really died.'

Here we go, Sacha thought with a stab of regret. *No more secrets.*

'I died,' he agreed.

'And then you . . . un-died.'

'The thing I didn't tell you,' he said slowly, 'is that I can't die. Not . . . permanently anyway.'

Her brow creased.

'I don't understand,' she said. 'How is that possible?'

Hazarding a sideways glance at her, he saw that she looked confused, but not repulsed or terrified. That was something.

'I can only tell you what I've been told,' he said. 'Something happened long ago in my family. We call it a curse but we don't really understand it. Every first-born son in my father's family dies on his eighteenth birthday. Until that day he can't die. If we are hurt or killed, we heal very quickly. And live again. It seems impossible. But it happens. As you saw.'

He'd never told anyone this. Telling her felt like opening

himself up, and showing her his insides. Leaving himself vulnerable and raw.

He watched her warily for signs of panic, but she just seemed to be processing this as she would any other information.

'So it's genetic, but in an illogical way,' she murmured. 'Genes wouldn't be able to skip girls or second sons . . . ' She glanced up at him again. 'And other boys have had this before you?'

He nodded.

'My father devoted his life to researching this. I found his research notes – it's where I saw your grandfather's name. He said he found evidence of boys before me. All died on their eighteenth birthday.'

She held his gaze. 'Do you believe you'll die on your eighteenth birthday?'

Nobody had ever asked him that before. But Sacha found he didn't hesitate. The truth was there; waiting for him to acknowledge it.

'Yes.'

He waited for her to tell him that things like this didn't happen. Or that it was all too much for her to take.

But that wasn't what she said at all.

'Then we have to stop it.' Her tone was resolute.

Sacha didn't know what to say. He'd just told her his father had spent a lifetime trying and failing to crack this terminal riddle, and yet she still wanted to try.

Something warm and unfamiliar unfurled in his chest. It had been so long since he'd believed he had a chance.

He'd forgotten what hope felt like.

Taylor looked lost in thought – he got the feeling she was making plans, figuring things out.

But he had some questions of his own.

'Before I ... died,' he said, 'you did something to those guys. The little one especially. He *flew*.'

A long silence followed. Taylor kept her gaze on the darkness beneath their feet.

'I have these powers,' she said with obvious reluctance. 'I don't understand them. I don't believe in this stuff, you know? But it just ... keeps happening.' She paused, choosing her words carefully. 'My grandfather says I inherited it. He says he has powers, too. It's in our blood. Like what's happening to you. Only ... different.'

Sacha tried to square this with what he'd seen.

'What kind of powers? Strength?'

'Not exactly.' She glanced at him. 'It's more like ... weird science. Moving molecules. Like, I take bits of energy from the world around me and manipulate that into something else. Like using energy from that river to create fire.'

She held out her hand and for a split second Sacha expected a flame to appear. But her palm stayed empty.

Curling her fingers up again, she dropped her hand.

'The only problem is, I don't know how to control it. I keep, like, shorting the lights when I have a bad day.' She turned to him, her eyes darkening. 'When I'm really scared or angry, like tonight ... awful things happen. I don't want it to happen. But it does. Those guys were hurting you and I knew I wanted them to stop. But the rest of it ... It's just a blur. Like it wasn't me doing it.'

She exhaled audibly. 'I have no idea what happened to the big guy, Sacha. He could be dead.'

'What did you do to him?' Sacha couldn't summon any sympathy for the thugs.

'I honestly don't know. I just remember how much I wanted him to run away – to run and run and run. And, well – he ran. And ran and ran.' She rested her head against the metal safety railing. 'I didn't know how to make him stop. I didn't really want him to.'

The image of the big guy running – possibly for the first time in his life – was darkly funny. Sacha barked a bitter laugh.

Her eyes flashed. 'It's not funny. It's horrible.'

'I know,' he said sobering quickly. 'I'm sorry. I don't mean to laugh. It's just . . . ' He leaned back, his hands against the cold metal railings at the river's edge. He'd never met anyone with problems as odd as his own before. It was almost comforting. 'That's some secret.'

'I hate it,' she whispered. 'I don't understand it and I hate it.'

Sacha, who knew that feeling well, didn't argue.

'Have you always been able to do this?'

She shook her head. 'It started a week ago when I was . . . attacked. It triggered something.'

Sacha's eyes narrowed.

'What happened?'

She told him about the invisible hands, tilting her head to expose a curve of pale, slim neck.

'You can still see the marks, just a bit.'

Sacha leaned forward. It was too dark to make out much, but

he could see the faint hint of bruising on either side of her throat.

His anger flared, like a match struck, and he was surprised by how protective he felt.

'Who did this to you?'

'I don't know,' she said. 'I couldn't see or touch them ... it, whatever. It was like they were ... invisible.'

Sacha didn't know what to say to that.

Clocking the look on his face, she flushed.

'I know,' she said. 'It's crazy. But my grandfather says it's real. He says I'm in danger. I'm going to Oxford this weekend and he's going to help me learn how to use my ... power or whatever. So I can be safe.'

Sacha was quiet for a moment.

'Do you trust your grandfather?'

She hesitated only slightly before replying. 'Yes.'

'Good,' he said. 'Just ... be careful. I don't trust anyone right now.'

'I'll be careful,' she held his gaze. 'But you have to be careful, too.'

'Nothing can kill me,' he reminded her. He half hoped she'd smile but she didn't. Instead she studied him, the concern in her eyes visible even in the gloaming.

'Does it hurt now?' She pointed at his stomach.

Sacha had to think about it. The wound ached a little, but in that not unpleasurable way of an injury in the process of healing. The cells were knitting themselves together again, reforming skin and muscle.

'Only a little.'

He scooted closer, lifting his shirt so she could see there

was nothing to be afraid of – no deep gouge or oozing wound.

Taylor stared at the thin, red scar where the knife had gone in. 'It's not possible,' she breathed. Slowly, tentatively, she brushed her fingertips against the skin near the wound.

The taut skin of his abdomen quivered involuntarily at her touch, and she jerked her hand back.

'I'm sorry,' she said, flushing.

He reached for her hand, taking it in his. 'Don't be. You didn't hurt me.'

Her body was close to his now, he could feel the heat of her skin through the fabric of her top. He thought she would pull away, instead she leaned against him.

'What happened to you tonight was the worst thing I have ever seen,' she whispered.

He pulled her closer still until he cradled her against him. 'I know,' he said.

'I'm glad you're not dead.'

'Me too.' So lightly that she couldn't possibly notice, he brushed his lips against her hair, breathing in her scent.

He thought she smelled like lemons and sunlight.

They sat like that for a long time, until he felt his body relax against hers.

'I forgot to ask,' she said, her voice a tired whisper, 'When's your eighteenth birthday?'

'In seven weeks.'

'*Seven weeks*?' She leaned back to see his face. 'But . . . '

'Yes, I know.' He pulled her close again, resting his chin against her shoulder. 'If we don't figure this out, I'm dead in seven weeks.'

A long moment passed before Taylor spoke again. 'We'll figure it out, Sacha.'

They huddled together at the river's edge, as the first rays of sunlight appeared above their heads, turning the sky glorious pink. The ornate Paris architecture faded into view.

The long night was over.

Twenty-three

Taylor and Sacha walked side by side through the school's swinging front doors.

God, Sacha thought, *I hate the way this place smells.* The squat, brick building had a perpetual scent of industrial disinfectant, school lunches and teenage alienation.

'Your school is so different from mine.' Next to him, Taylor was gazing around with avid interest. 'It's so . . . *European.*'

Sacha wasn't sure he knew what that meant.

He couldn't believe how focussed and calm Taylor was.

As soon as the shops opened, they'd purchased new clothes – Sacha insisted on paying.

'I have plenty of money,' he'd said when Taylor protested. 'And it's my fault your clothes were ruined.'

He wouldn't go to just any shop, though. He took her to an expensive boutique not far from the Louvre.

When they'd walked through the door, dirty and tired, he'd

thought for a second the staff might call the police. But he'd already planned his explanation.

'You'll have to forgive us,' he told the shop assistant, when she teetered towards him on perilously high heels, eyebrows winging upward. 'We've been filming all night around the corner – you probably saw the film crew – and the wardrobe department left us in these ridiculous clothes. We can't go home like this.' He'd gestured at his blood-stained shirt. 'This fake blood is disgusting.'

When she still appeared dubious, he pulled a thick wad of cash from his pocket. 'Money is not a problem.'

The woman gaped at him. Then, recovering, she turned on her heel and led them both to a rack of dark clothes.

'You might find what you're looking for here, sir.'

Now Taylor wore a short, black skirt and a sleeveless dark top. He'd been a little surprised by her choices – these new clothes had a much edgier look than those she'd worn when she arrived in Paris.

Sacha had new jeans and a new black T-shirt, exactly like the ruined ones. Only much more expensive.

They'd changed in the dressing rooms at the shop, stuffing their bloodied clothes into a bin on a street corner.

Taylor even threw away her sandals, replacing them with sturdy, black ankle boots.

When he'd mentioned that, she'd said, 'I need shoes I can run in.'

But he thought it was more than that. She was making a statement: Life is dangerous. If you want to survive, you get strong.

It was mid-morning; class was in session. Behind the long line of closed doors on either side of the wide, main corridor they could hear the murmur of teachers lecturing, and an occasional burst of explosive conversation from students.

When they reached Deide's room, they loitered beside the door, waiting for the bell to ring. Sacha found it difficult not to stare at Taylor.

She'd pulled her hair back into a loose pony tail from which curls were already escaping and tumbling around her cheeks. Her golden hair and pale skin stood out in sharp contrast to the black top. She looked beautiful; intense.

Paris had changed her.

Holding her in his arms last night had felt so right. He hated the idea that, in a couple of hours, she'd get on a train. And he'd be alone again.

They were linked, somehow. He could sense it. They just had to figure out how.

The shriek of the school bell made them both jump.

From inside the classroom, Taylor heard Deide bark last-minute instructions ('essays are due tomorrow, lateness will not be excused ... '). Then the doors flew open and the students flooded out.

A couple cast curious glances at Taylor and Sacha, but no one spoke to them.

They rushed by, their teenage conversations utterly foreign.

'Meet you in the lunch room?'

'Did you finish your chemistry work?'

'Who's that blonde girl?'

He noticed a couple of the boys casting appreciative looks at Taylor, but she didn't seem to see it.

Her eyes were on him. Waiting for the signal.

When the room was empty, he nodded.

Turning in unison, they walked into the classroom.

Deide stood at the front of the room, stacking papers and books into neat piles.

The whiteboard behind the teacher bore the telltale notes of an English class: 'I am going to the park. The park is near the lake. Will you meet me at the park?'

As Taylor and Sacha arrayed themselves side by side in front of the teacher's desk, he glanced up at them enquiringly. When he saw Sacha, his eyes widened. But his voice betrayed no surprise.

'How are you, Sacha? I've been sorry not to see you in class.'

'I've been busy,' Sacha said shortly.

Deide's gaze turned to Taylor. 'And who's this?' He peered at her through his glasses. 'I don't think you're a student here, are you?'

'*Bonjour*,' Taylor said. '*Je m'appelle Taylor Montclair.*'

Deide blanched.

He took an involuntary step back, and stared at her with something like horror.

'*Non*,' he whispered. 'You can't be here.'

'But she is.' Sacha moved closer to Taylor. 'And we both want to know what the hell is going on.'

A fine sheen of sweat formed on Deide's forehead.

'Dear God, Sacha ... what have you done?'

Sacha and Taylor exchanged a worried look. They'd expected a strong reaction ... but not this.

'We've come here for answers,' Sacha said. 'And we're not leaving until we get them.'

Deide didn't seem to be listening. 'She has to go,' he told Sacha in rapid-fire French. 'She cannot be here in this school. She can't be in Paris at all. She has to go home. Now. What you've done is very dangerous. For her.' He pointed at Taylor. 'And for you.'

Sacha watched him closely, looking for signs of deception, but he saw none. Deide appeared to be genuinely afraid.

'You have to tell us more,' Taylor said in English. 'We don't understand what's happening. And people keep trying to kill us. Who are you? Do you work for my grandfather?'

Deide hesitated. 'Not exactly,' he said finally. 'But Aldrich is an associate of mine.'

So they'd been right. This was all connected.

'Why did you want us to meet?' Sacha demanded. 'What do you know?'

The corridors were noisy with students heading to their next class. The hubbub filtered through the door into the classroom.

Deide turned on his heel and crossed to the door, locking it with a solid click.

Rejoining them in front of his desk, he removed his glasses and shoved them into his shirt pocket.

'I'll tell you what I know,' he said. Turning to Taylor he added, 'But you must go back to England. There are people here who mean you harm, I am sorry to say. Very dangerous people.'

Taylor didn't flinch. 'There are people in England who mean me harm, too.'

The teacher's expression softened.

'I know. And I'm sorry. These are dangerous times.' He looked back and forth between them. 'I apologise for the subterfuge but I hope you'll understand it was necessary. You see, getting you to meet was a kind of ... experiment, I suppose.'

'Experiment?' Taylor frowned. 'What do you mean?'

Deide looked at Sacha. 'We believe she can help with your ... situation.'

Sacha's heart stuttered.

'What situation?' he asked coolly. 'And who is "we"?'

'I know about the curse, Sacha.' Deide's voice was low. 'I knew your father. I've been trying to help you for the last five years ...'

Sacha's ribs seemed to close around his lungs. 'You knew my father?'

Deide nodded. 'I was working with him when he died. I am a member of an organisation of sorts.' Deide glanced at Taylor. 'The same organisation your grandfather is in, in Oxford. We were all working with Adam to try and understand what was happening to you, Sacha. When Adam died, I volunteered to work at your school, to keep an eye on you.'

Sacha couldn't seem to think. He just reacted; grabbing his teacher by the shirt front in a vicious grip.

'You're lying,' he said through gritted teeth. 'My father

never mentioned you. My mother never mentioned you. This is bullshit.'

'Sacha . . . ' Taylor's voice held a warning. But he didn't let go.

Deide didn't look intimidated. He held his gaze steadily, hands loose at his sides.

'Sacha, I'm telling you the truth. I knew your father well. He was a good man. A friend. He believed there was a way to stop this thing from killing you. I think he was right.'

There was no deception in his expression. He appeared utterly candid.

Sacha released his grip.

He felt unaccountably angry with his father.

Why didn't he tell me more? Why didn't he leave us clues? Instead he told total strangers secrets he kept from us.

The teacher had stepped away, straightening his shirt. Taylor followed him.

'Mr Deide,' she said, 'please tell us all that you know. Are you what my grandfather is? What *I* am? Do you have some sort of . . . power?'

The teacher studied her with open curiosity. 'I suppose I am, although I'm nowhere near as skilled as Aldrich Montclair.' He said the name with reverence. 'Your own abilities . . . have they manifested?'

Taylor made a wry face. 'A little. But it's not great. I kind of . . . blow things up by mistake.'

'That's normal,' he assured her. 'You'll get better with practice.'

'I hope so.' Taylor leaned against a desk near Sacha. 'Mr

Deide, what did you think would happen when we met? How can I help Sacha?'

The school bell clanged again. Outside the classroom, the hallways had grown quiet.

Deide lifted himself up until he was sitting on top of his own desk facing them.

'We don't know as much as we'd like,' he admitted. 'We know the curse on Sacha's family was issued by a Dark practitioner.' He glanced at Taylor. 'Someone with powers, like you and me, who has dabbled in the dark arts. Using demonic techniques to gain additional power.'

'*Demonic*?' Taylor's voice was faint.

Sacha thought of the men who'd come to his door and suppressed a shiver. That would, at least, explain them.

'The curse affecting Sacha's family was issued, we believe, in the seventeenth century,' Deide continued. 'We've found little written about it at that time, but some mentions in later books that allow us to place the time and location.' He included Sacha in his gaze. 'Our modern scepticism made it harder for us to realise – or even accept – what was happening. These ancient beliefs – we just dismiss them out of hand. Call them fairy tales. Fantasies. Attribute death to coincidence. But your father was an excellent researcher, Sacha. His work on this subject was exhaustive. He tracked the deaths of first-born boys in your family through several centuries. What he found was hard to refute – always the same pattern, always the death on the eighteenth birthday. Every single time. Beyond coincidence. And not a fantasy.'

He paused. 'There's just one thing,' Deide said. 'Based on everything we've been able to find, it appears Sacha is the thirteenth Winters boy this has happened to. If the information we have on the curse is accurate ... the thirteenth is the last.' He held Sacha's gaze. 'The curse ends with you.'

Sacha felt like he'd been punched.

I'm the last?

Just one more dead kid hundreds of years ago and none of this would be happening to him now?

Fate was a bastard.

'But what does that mean, exactly?' Taylor was asking.

'It's the wording of the curse that's the problem.' Deide avoided Sacha's gaze. 'Nobody has studied this Dark practice in many years, so we don't fully understand it. The mechanism of it has been lost with time. But the books seem to indicate that, if we can't prevent Sacha's death, it will trigger something. Something awful. Something devastating.' His low voice echoed in the quiet. 'The curse wasn't designed just to punish one family. It was intended to punish the world.'

Sacha swallowed hard.

'What, exactly, will happen?' Taylor asked.

'We think it will unlease a demonic presence so powerful the world could be utterly changed by it.'

They stared at him.

'What ... An *actual* demon?' Sacha blinked. 'Like on television? They exist?'

'Not like on television.' The teacher's expression was dark. 'Much, much worse, if the old books are to be believed. More like a nuclear war than anything else we can conceive of.

We're not talking about a lizard with horns here, Sacha. This is pure destructive power.'

Sacha scanned his face for any sign that this was some kind of joke, but there was no humour there. Deide looked deadly serious.

How could this be real? What he was describing was madness.

'I still don't understand. What does Taylor have to do with any of this?' Sacha said. 'Why did you involve her?'

Deide looked back and forth between them, a hint of regret in his eyes.

'Sacha,' he said, 'you are the thirteenth first-born son of a man who was cursed by a Dark practitioner in the seventeenth century.' He turned to Taylor. 'You, Miss Montclair, are the thirteenth first-born daughter of the woman who cursed that man hundreds of years ago, as he killed her.'

Taylor made a small sound. All the colour drained from her face.

'If we are right about this, and for all our sakes I hope we are,' Deide continued, 'Taylor is the only person on the planet who can save your life.'

Twenty-four

The train from Paris to London took just over two hours. Throughout every minute of the journey, Taylor couldn't get Sacha's face out of her mind. She kept seeing his expression when Deide told them who they really were. Who she really was.

He'd looked horrified.

As the flat French countryside disappeared, replaced a short while later by rolling English hills, she tried to understand all she'd learned.

After dropping the bombshell, Deide had explained why they had to meet.

'Dark practice is a blood art. If we're to stop this curse from killing Sacha, Taylor, you have to do it.'

'What do I need to do?' she'd asked, conscious of Sacha's silence. 'I'll do anything.'

Deide's reply had been disappointing.

'That's the problem,' he said. 'We don't know yet. This is ancient power. Ancient practice. No one alive now has ever dealt with it.' Seeing Taylor's expression he added, 'We're not giving up. We're going to solve this. With your help.'

After leaving Deide's classroom, she and Sacha had walked in near silence to a Metro station. On the subway they left space between them, careful not to catch each other's gaze.

At the Gare du Nord station, the boarding area for trains to London was above the main concourse. They'd stood on the balcony, looking down at the crowds below, hurrying for trains, or greeting each other with hugs and kisses.

Their lives are so normal, Taylor had thought dully. *They have no idea.*

It had been the longest twenty-four hours of her life. It was impossible to believe that this time yesterday she'd been walking down the street in Woodbury, excited about going to Paris. Utterly unaware of what lay ahead.

'I'm sorry,' she said, finally breaking the long silence between them.

Sacha glanced over. His black sunglasses reflected her face back at her. 'For what?'

'For who I am,' she said, her voice quivering. 'Because, if what he said is true, and it's my family's fault this is happening to you ...'

He didn't let her finish. Removing his sunglasses, he reached for her hands, pulling her towards him until she was standing so close she could feel the warmth of his skin, and see the flecks of gold in his sea-blue eyes.

'You are not the person who did this to me, Taylor Montclair.' His voice was quiet but passionate. 'You're the person who will save me. Remember that.' He lifted her hand and brushed his lips lightly against the back of it. 'You have nothing to apologise for.'

A delicate pattern of goosebumps rose on the back of Taylor's neck. Not for the first time in the last twenty-four hours, she'd wished he'd kiss her. But he didn't.

'I want to believe that,' she'd said. 'I'm just ... scared. And confused.'

'Me too,' he'd replied. 'We'll figure it out. I know we will.'

At that moment, it had been easy to believe him. He spoke with such confidence.

Now, though, it was harder. How could she save him?

She'd seen impossible things in the last few days. She'd watched a boy die and come back to life. She'd seen her grandfather move energy at his will. She, herself, had nearly killed two grown men without so much as touching them.

The world she knew had lost its axis. Everything was spinning out of control.

But one thing was certain: She had to save Sacha. Somehow. She had to figure this out and keep him alive.

♊

'How was studying?' Taylor's mother glanced up from her paperwork.

She was working at the kitchen table ('A big project ...' she'd explained apologetically), which was covered in documents and hideous-looking spreadsheets.

She'd accepted Taylor's cover story without question, although she'd arched an eyebrow at the new outfit Sacha had purchased for her in Paris.

'Georgie keeps dressing me,' Taylor had explained. 'She thinks I choose boring clothes.'

In truth, she loved how she looked in these clothes. She never wore snug-fitting tops, she'd always worried that, with her curves, they wouldn't look right. So she'd worn loose tops. But now she realised wearing clothes that actually fit her, made her look ... good. She'd stood in that Paris dressing room staring into the mirror if she'd never seen herself before. The fitted black top and flared short skirt changed the way she looked completely. The skirt ended halfway down her thighs, making her legs look actually long.

The girl in the mirror looked strong. Confident.

Taylor didn't recognise that person.

But she liked her.

'It was good.' She shrugged. 'The usual.'

'Does Georgie have a hope of passing her exams?'

'She does.' Taylor affected a blithe tone. 'As long as I take them for her.'

It was beginning to disturb her how easy it was to lie.

Her mother chuckled and pulled a page from beneath the stack of papers in front of her. Her reading glasses had slid to the end of her nose and she peered at Taylor over the tops.

'Let me guess. Georgie did her nails while you did her homework?'

'How do you know these things?' Taylor filled her voice with mock surprise.

She grabbed a chocolate biscuit from the pack on the counter and ate half of it in one bite.

'I'm your mother. I know everything.' Her mother's smile was smug. 'Don't eat too many of those things. Dinner's in an hour.'

Taylor suspected this was optimistic, there was no sign that cooking had begun, but she didn't argue.

One thing about lying to your mother, it makes you want to be really nice to her the rest of the time.

Her phone chimed to let her know she had a message, and she pulled it from her pocket as she hurried from the kitchen.

When she saw Sacha's name on the screen, butterflies swirled in her stomach.

She'd only been home a few hours but she already missed him. It was all she could do not to text him constantly.

How do you spend one day with someone and decide they belong in your life? She couldn't explain it, but it had happened.

They'd been through so much together in those few hours in Paris. Now it felt weird being alone again. Like she'd left part of herself behind.

'Checking in,' his message said. 'Still alive. No bad guys. You?'

Before she left Paris, they'd exchanged addresses, phone numbers, all the information they'd need to find each other if anything awful happened. They'd also agreed to keep in constant contact from now on.

That was Taylor's favourite part.

'All good,' she typed in reply. 'Oxford tomorrow as planned.'

His response was instant. 'Be careful.'

But Taylor wasn't worried about safety right now. Because tomorrow she'd find out more about who she really was.

And she'd begin figuring out how to save Sacha.

♊

'*Maman?*' Sacha called as he walked down the corridor to the living room. 'Are you here?'

'In the kitchen,' she called. 'I'll be there in a second.'

It was her day off from work, and she'd been out running errands most of the afternoon. If she'd noticed his absence the night before, she hadn't mentioned it.

Maybe she was just used to it.

In the sun-filled living-room, he slumped onto the sofa, legs sprawled in front of him. He was exhausted.

He'd slept for five hours after Taylor left for England that morning. Now he felt like he could sleep five more.

Dying wore him out.

Maybe it wasn't just dying that had left him feeling strangely off-kilter – a little lost. He missed Taylor much more than he'd expected to.

They'd swung into an easy partnership when she was here. Having someone who knew the truth – who knew everything – had been such a relief. She'd lifted the weight of isolation from his shoulders.

As soon as she'd gone he'd felt lonely again. The journey back home from the Gare du Nord had seemed empty and grey. Without her in it, Paris seemed a little less beautiful.

It had taken everything in him not to kiss her at the station.

He just didn't know if she wanted that. She'd been so lost and confused – what if she didn't feel the same way?

It would ruin everything.

So he'd held back. But now he couldn't stop thinking about her.

His mother appeared in the doorway to the living room, clutching a coffee cup. Her short, brown hair was neatly styled, and she wore jeans and a loose, printed top. She was shorter than him now. Looking down at her made him feel strangely parental towards her.

He wished he was going to live long enough to get used to this – the way their relationship was changing.

Dropping into the chair next to the sofa, she began straightening the magazines on the coffee table into neat piles.

'How was school?'

'Interesting,' Sacha said, thinking of Deide. 'Actually, that's what I need to talk about.'

'Are you in trouble again, Sacha?' Her eyes narrowed. 'We talked about this.'

He bit back a sharp reply.

'Everything is fine at school,' he said evenly. 'I just need some information. From you.'

Taking a sip of coffee she leaned back in her chair and waited for him to explain, but her eyes remained guarded.

'You know I mentioned my English tutor to you before? Taylor Montclair?'

His mother froze.

'I think that name means something to you,' Sacha continued. 'And I want to know why. What do you know about her?

Her grandfather is Aldrich Montclair. He says he knew my father . . . ' His mother jumped, spilling her coffee.

Hurriedly, she turned to set the cup down on the low table, and fussed with a tissue mopping up the mess, avoiding his gaze.

Sacha's heart began to race.

'You know him, don't you? You know that name.' He leaned towards her, unable to disguise his eagerness. 'You have to tell me what you know, Who is he to our family? How do you know him?'

His mother's lips were tight. 'I don't want to talk about Aldrich Montclair.' She spat out the name. 'I don't want you anywhere near him. He's dangerous.'

Sacha's mouth went dry. 'I don't understand. How is he dangerous? What did he do?'

She crumpled the tissue in her fist.

'Your father trusted him. Aldrich kept telling him there was a cure, a solution for you. And that he could find it.' Her expression showed what she thought of that. 'Your father believed him. No matter what I said, he wouldn't listen. Believing Aldrich Montclair killed your father, Sacha. It was Aldrich he was visiting when he died. Aldrich who sent him on the road that day.' She pointed a finger at his face. 'Stay away from that man, Sacha. He'll ruin your life, like he ruined ours.'

Sacha's head dropped into his hands. He'd let himself believe in the idea of Aldrich Montclair. Believe in Taylor. And his mother was yanking that tiny lifeline away.

Leaving him with nothing.

He couldn't let her do that. Maybe she could accept his fate but he couldn't. And for once, he was going to call her on it.

'He'll ruin my life? What life?' His voice rose. 'Do you mean the next seven weeks? Because that's all the life I get.'

Her cheeks reddened as if he'd slapped her.

'Don't talk like that,' she said. 'You know I'm doing all I can. I've tried so hard to give you a normal life. To make sure that the years you have are ...' She stopped, blinking back tears. 'It's hard for us, Sacha. Your sister and me. Knowing we're going to lose you.'

He stared at her, disbelief slowly transmuting into rage.

'Hard for *you*? Are you serious?'

Leaping to his feet he faced her stiffly, arms crossed.

'Tell me how hard my death is for *you*. Tell me how hard you've fought to keep me alive. I want to hear all the things you've done to save me.'

She flinched, one hand shooting up, as if to physically block his words.

Guilt uncurled in his heart. He made himself ignore it.

For the last two years they'd both avoided the truth. Now there was no time left for lies.

'Please, *Maman*,' he said, softening his tone. 'I need you to stop accepting my death, and start *fighting it*. That's all I'm asking. You can begin by telling me everything you know about Aldrich Montclair.'

'You want to know about Aldrich Montclair? Fine. I'll tell you everything I know.' She rose to her feet. 'I know he's a monster and a fantasist. I know his crazy ideas killed your father. I know his family had something to do with all of this.'

She swung her arm at him. 'And I know if you get tangled up in his lies it will kill you, just like it killed your father.'

'I've got news, Maman,' he said coldly. 'I'm going to die anyway. And Aldrich Montclair has nothing to do with that.' He took a step towards her. 'Maybe there's no point in what I'm doing. Maybe I'll try everything and then I'll still die. But I'll tell you one thing – I intend to go down fighting.'

Pivoting on his heel he headed for his room, firing his parting shot over his shoulder.

'You should try it sometime.'

TWENTY-FIVE

The train shuddered into the station with a screech of metal against metal. They were ten minutes late.

Taylor stood at the door, fingers tapping impatiently against the 'Open' button. As the train jolted to a halt she stumbled, bumping hard into the grey-haired man next to her.

Springing back, she looked up at him apologetically. 'Sorry.'

He straightened his tweed jacket with deliberate movements that made his disapproval clear. His neat moustache and unlined face looked strangely familiar, although she couldn't place him.

Then the doors opened and she forgot all about him, leaping from the carriage to the platform.

She wound her way through the crowded station, avoiding elbows and suitcases, toddlers dangling perilously from their parents' fingertips and teenagers too lost in the music blaring from their headphones to notice the world around them.

On the street outside the crowds broke up, everyone going in their own direction. Moving with purpose, Taylor headed off towards the town centre.

It was a warm grey morning. The clouds overhead were heavy with the promise of rain. But even on a murky day, when the skies were scarcely distinguishable from the grey stone buildings below, and the streets were busy with traffic and tourists, Oxford took her breath away. Its soaring spires and crenulated rooftops stacked and stretched up all around her as if reaching out to touch the clouds.

She'd never been here on her own before – she'd always travelled with her mother. Still, the route was familiar enough. She turned this way and that down busy streets until she reached an intersection dominated by an ornate carved stone cross. From there she turned down a narrow, medieval lane.

On either side the street was enclosed by high stone walls, leaving the road perpetually in shadow. The walls had the effect of shutting out the sounds of the city completely; all Taylor could hear now were her own footsteps, steady as a heartbeat.

After a few minutes, the wall on her right grew gradually taller, until she reached a structure made of blood-red brick, topped with jaunty octagonal turrets three stories high, each with a colourful flag waving above it. This was the gatehouse to the College of St Wilfred.

Huge double oak doors, black with age, were secured with gigantic iron locks and hinges. Just next to them, a normal-sized entrance – by comparison it looked like a hobbit door – was propped open.

Taylor darted through, stepping high over the old doorstep, then stopped in front of a small, windowed office. Inside, a man in a black bowler hat sat writing something in very tiny handwriting in a ledger so wide it took up most of his desk. He spoke without looking up.

'One moment, please.'

Her toe tapping nervously, Taylor tried to hide her impatience as she waited for much longer than one moment.

'Now,' the man said after a significant amount of time had passed. 'How can I help you?'

Beneath the hat, he was bald. Taylor noticed his legs didn't quite fit under the antique desk.

'I've come to see Professor Montclair,' she said. 'I'm his granddaughter.'

'I see.' The man flipped the page of his ledger and looked through it as if seeking some hidden and important information. 'And your name is . . . ?'

'Montclair,' she said. 'Taylor Montclair.'

'Oh dear.' The man closed the book with a thud. 'I'm afraid Professor Montclair didn't notify us. Are you quite sure he's expecting you?'

Taylor's heart sank. Her grandfather *always* forgot to tell the gate. It drove her mother crazy.

'Could you phone his rooms please?' She made it sound more like a command than a question – a technique she'd seen her mother use to good effect on many occasions. 'He is expecting me.'

Two boys in torn jeans and T-shirts sloped by, passing through the door with a casual wave. Obviously recognising them, the doorman nodded in reply before turning in his chair to where an old-fashioned, heavy black phone sat on an adjacent table. After flipping through another book filled with tiny writing, he located a number and began to dial.

He held the receiver to his ear for a long time without speaking. Taylor had begun to fear her grandfather wasn't home, when the doorman straightened as if someone of authority had walked in.

'Professor Montclair? There's a girl at the gate claiming to be your granddaughter. She says her name is . . . ' He looked down to where he'd written a note. 'Taylor.' He nodded as if listening to a reply. 'As you wish, sir.'

The phone gave a slight musical protest when he set the receiver down. He looked up at Taylor. 'He says for you to go straight up. Do you know where his rooms are?'

She didn't bother to hide her triumph. 'Of course I do.'

Turning on her heel she walked through the dark stone archway into a quadrangle. Velvety green grass was bounded on all sides by tall buildings of carved stone that swirled up into jagged spires.

Taylor loved this place. The walkway around the edges of the square was partially enclosed in carved stone arches. When she was younger, she would play hide and seek here with Emily – the endless nooks and crannies made ideal hiding places.

She turned into a low doorway. Inside, an old, stone staircase led up into shadows. The steps were uneven and the lights weren't on, but she knew the way and her steps were sure.

When she reached the top floor, the staircase ended abruptly in front of an ancient, dark oak door. It bore no number or nameplate. Just a small, black metal knocker shaped like a fist. She thumped it smartly.

The door opened with surprising immediacy, as if her grandfather had been standing on the other side of it.

He smiled at her warmly.

'Taylor, how lovely to see you again.' He shuffled back a few steps making way for her in the narrow entrance hall. 'Do come in.'

He had the rich voice of someone who had spent his life speaking in crowded lecture halls.

She squeezed past him and he closed the solid door behind her. The flat was warm but not stuffy. It smelled just the way she remembered – of wood smoke and floor polish and Earl Grey tea. It was a subtle, pleasant scent, not unlike incense after it's had time to fade.

Gesturing for her to follow, her grandfather walked down the hallway. He was sprightly despite his age.

'Come in, come in,' he said. 'Let's have a cup of tea. I trust your journey was smooth?'

'Fine, thank you,' she replied politely.

As she followed, Taylor's eyes searched the flat, seeking out a small painting here, a tiny sculpture there. Everything was where it should be. The old wood floors were covered in faded

Persian rugs that softened their footsteps and gave the space a warm, russet glow.

Even though it was late morning, lamps had been switched on to light the darker corners. The windows were tiny, and only small light came through them.

In the crowded living room, the walls were lined from floor to ceiling with bookcases, each filled with heavy books of all shapes and sizes. The desk in the corner groaned under the weight of the stacks atop it. Even the battered, brass candlestick he used as a paperweight when marking essays stood atop a pile of books.

Her grandfather pointed to a chair near the fireplace. 'Have a seat. I'll get us some tea.'

'Is there any coffee?'

He gave her a disapproving look and shuffled into the kitchen, muttering to himself. Taylor thought she heard him say something about 'American drinks'.

The red floral fabric was fading, and the chair seat sagged in the middle but it had always been Taylor's favourite chair and she suppressed a happy sigh as she dropped into it. It was the kind of chair that seemed to fit anyone who sat on it – adjusting for their weight and then wrapping them in a warm, upholstered hug.

As she waited, she picked up a nearby book. Its soft leather cover bore no writing. Inside the text was entirely strange symbols. It appeared to be an ancient language.

'It's all Greek to me,' she muttered.

Her grandfather bustled back in a few minutes later, a tarnished tray crowded with a silver teapot, a tiny coffee pot, as well as mismatched china cups and a plate of biscuits. He stood helplessly, looking for a clear place to set it in the cluttered room.

Leaping up, Taylor cleared a mahogany side table of a stack of books and academic magazines, setting them all on the floor nearby. There was no dust beneath them and it occurred to her that this was unusual. It didn't look as if the place had been cleaned in years.

He sat down in the old chair next to hers, and poured dark liquid into a mug.

'Your coffee.' His tone said just what he thought of that.

'Thank you,' she said primly.

He handed her the plate of biscuits and she took one, finishing it in two bites.

His eyebrows winging up, he handed her the plate again.

'Perhaps you'd better keep this,' he said dryly.

'Thanks,' Taylor replied, through a mouthful of crumbs. 'Forgot breakfast.'

He poured himself a cup of tea, adding milk from a little silver jug with an ornate handle. With the ease of practice he used delicate silver tongs to extract sugar cubes from a silver jar and dropped one neatly into his cup, stirring it with a jingle of the spoon. Then, resting the cup and saucer on the arm of his chair, he turned to her.

'Now. I imagine you have a lot of questions.'

Taylor nodded, gulping down a scalding mouthful of coffee to clear her throat.

'Millions.'

'Fire away,' he said.

'Tell me about Adam Winters.'

He froze, his teacup halfway to his mouth.

'Goodness,' he said setting the cup back down. 'I wasn't expecting that.'

'It was you who made me meet Sacha, wasn't it?' Her tone was accusing. 'You set the whole thing up. Why did you do that? Why didn't you just tell me?'

The questions she'd spent the last two days thinking up tumbled out in a rush.

Her grandfather held up his hands until she fell silent.

'It's a long story,' he said after a moment. 'And a sad one. But, yes, I confess I did want the two of you to meet, and I didn't want it to be through a direct introduction from me. That would have been ... difficult to explain to Sacha's mother.'

Taylor still didn't understand. 'Why was it so important that we should meet?'

He met her gaze with steady eyes.

'You are starting in the middle of the story. I promise you we will come to that point, but it would be easier for both of us if you started at the beginning. Ask me the obvious first question. And we will build from there.'

Taylor hesitated. 'I guess ... I still don't understand who I am,' she said after a second. '*What* I am.'

'An excellent question.' Aldrich beamed. 'You are part of a select, very small group of people with unusual ... abilities.' He paused. 'We call ourselves alchemists.'

'*Alchemists?*' Taylor sputtered. 'Like, those old men in books who thought they could turn rocks into gold?'

Her grandfather tutted. 'My goodness, no, no, no ...' He

adopted a professorial expression. 'Alchemy was the precursor to modern chemistry. It is a science. The science of transmutation. Taking one substance and manipulating it into another. It dates back to Christ and even before. Unlike modern science, it was a mixture of the physical and the spiritual . . . ' Pausing, he peered at her. 'Surely you know *some* of this?'

She shook her head.

He gave a small dramatic sigh.

'Isaac Newton was a student of alchemy – many of his greatest discoveries came out of his efforts to prove the various theories.' He waved a hand, cutting off his own lecture. 'But that's not what you need to know. There are books full of this. Suffice it to say, alchemy became too popular. The science was *diluted* by charlatans and wishful thinkers lured to it by the thought of gold. They believed they could become unimaginably wealthy. Every lord in the land had so-called scientists working for him, trying to become the first to make it work. Because of their actions, their misinformation and lies, it was discredited. That is the alchemy most people know about – nothing but the science of chicanery.'

He leaned towards her. 'But here's the interesting part. *They weren't wrong*. Molecules can be manipulated. Energy can be altered. If you have the ability.' He leaned towards her. 'You see, there was one stage – one step – in the alchemical process where all of them failed. Even the great Isaac Newton.' His green eyes glittered. 'They called it "the secret fire." It was the great unknown. A fire that didn't burn but *transformed*. With it, the process would work. Without it . . . '

He held up his empty palm. 'It was all just so much smoke.'

Taylor had forgotten the coffee in her hand. 'What was it?' she asked. 'This fire?'

Her grandfather pointed at her.

'You. And me.'

She shook her head. 'I don't understand.'

'You see, it turns out the secret fire was not a *thing* you could find or buy. It wasn't mercury or some other chemical compound. It was an innate ability. This was the spiritual side of alchemy – they just didn't know it yet. No matter how much wealth and power a duke or an earl possessed, he couldn't purchase it. No matter how hard Newton searched he couldn't find it. You either have it . . . '

He held up his hand and the candle on the table by the window leaped into glowing life.

'Or you don't.'

Twenty-six

Taylor's gaze moved from the candle's steady flame back to him.

'Wait ... I still don't understand what it is, exactly?' she asked. 'The secret fire, I mean.'

He took a sip of tea. 'This is what we discussed in Woodbury. It's nothing more than an inherited genetic mutation. Something that allows you to do what the philosophers only dreamed of – take energy from one object and convert it into another form of energy. Or move energy from here to there. Do you remember the light bulb?'

She nodded.

'For that, I drew energy from the water – moving water contains huge power – and converted a small amount of it into electricity to power a light bulb. It's a very basic process. Edison accomplished it with wires and generators. For us it is somewhat ... easier.'

'And the candle?' she said. 'Just now?'

'For that I drew energy from the air around us, the electricity in the walls.'

He waved a hand and the candle went out.

Taylor set her coffee down on the little table.

It made sense. After what Sacha had told her, this sounded marginally less bizarre. A genetic ability? She could live with that. But it still didn't explain everything.

'And I can do this?' She pointed at the candle.

Her grandfather must have heard the doubt in her voice. Because his face grew more serious. 'Oh yes,' he assured her. 'You have the potential to be extraordinary.'

'If it's in your DNA, and it's in mine,' Taylor said, thinking aloud, 'then it must be in Dad's, too. Can he do what you do?'

Her grandfather's expression grew sombre.

'Your father, I'm afraid, is an exception.' He knitted his hands in his lap. 'Occasionally the power skips a generation. It's rare but it occurs; the gene becomes recessive. As it did in his case.'

'Oh.' Taylor tried to imagine how she'd feel if everyone else in her family had an ability and she didn't. But her accountant father had always been so practical and unemotional, it was hard to imagine him being able to explode lights with anger.

He'd never said a word to her about his family having special abilities of any kind, scientific, spiritual or otherwise. He'd kept it a shameful secret.

And then he'd abandoned them.

245

'He claims to be glad he's not part of it,' her grandfather continued ... 'Your father says he finds the whole situation ridiculous and dangerous. He has never shown any interest in being part of this world.'

Taylor leaned back in her chair. 'That sounds like Dad.'

'Your father missed more than this gene.' Aldrich's tone was thoughtful. 'I've never said anything before but I believe the way he treated you girls and your mother was abominable. I've barely spoken to him since.'

Exhaling audibly, he straightened his shoulders. 'But that is neither here nor there. What matters is you. And what is happening now.' He leaned towards her. 'You have great power inside you, Taylor. With great power comes great danger. You understand that now, though, don't you?' He gave her a significant look. 'After your trip to Paris?'

Taylor blanched. 'How do you ... ?'

'I told you we'd be watching you,' he reminded her. 'Trying to keep you safe. Correct me if I'm wrong, but I do not believe a secret trip to Paris was part of the plan we discussed.'

She sank deeper in her chair.

'The person watching the house saw you leave for school. It wasn't until Finlay noticed you weren't in class that we realised you'd run away. Monsieur Deide informed me of your unexpected visit.' Over the tops of his glasses he shot her a reproving look. 'He was afraid for you, and rightly so.'

Taylor straightened. 'I'm sorry I upset people. But I'm not sorry I went. I had to understand what was happening. And to meet Sacha.'

Aldrich sighed. 'Taylor, my dear, I want to help you. But if you run off without telling me, and to *other countries* for that matter, I will find it difficult to protect you.'

She couldn't argue with that.

'So it's all true?' she said, changing the subject. 'What Mr Deide told us?'

'I'm afraid so. The situation is desperate.' He cleared his throat. 'Sacha's father was a good friend of mine. A wonderful man. A great historian and a loving father. I promised him I would help his son and I do not intend to let him down.'

He paused, his expression thoughtful. 'There's something you need to see.'

He walked across the room to an antique, fold-down desk. Opening it, he began fumbling through the papers stuffed into the compartments inside. 'Ah. Here we are.' He moved to one of the windows and held a paper in the light to see it better. 'Most of the records of the prophecy that afflicts the Winters family have been lost to time. This is the only piece of real evidence we have.'

Taylor walked over to join him. The paper he held was a photocopy of a page from a book. The words were in Latin. 'What is it?'

'It's a page from a seventeenth century book on Dark practice. One of the only remaining historical texts. It says, "The curse of the thirteenth can be broken only by the thirteenth."'

Taylor frowned. Outside, someone shouted something she couldn't quite make out. 'That's it?'

He returned the paper to its cubbyhole in his chaotic desk. 'That's everything.'

'What does it even mean?'

'It means the thirteenth first-born daughter of the woman who issued the curse can undo it. That is why we wanted you to meet. Your powers hadn't yet manifested but time was running out. We thought finding each other might speed the process. And it did.' He watched her closely. 'You, my dear, are the key. And your next question will be "How?" And I will tell you that we are . . . working on it.'

'Working on it.' She repeated the words, despair threatening to consume her again. This couldn't be all they had. There had to be more.

'Grandfather, he only has a few weeks left.'

'I am very aware of that,' Aldrich said evenly. 'It is not easy to untangle a 300-year-old curse. But we will find a way.'

'This is why someone wants to hurt me? Just because I might somehow stop this thing?' Taylor held up her hands helplessly.

'If you prevent Sacha's death, you stop the fulfilment of the curse,' Aldrich said. 'Whatever his death was intended to trigger never happens. Somebody out there wants to stop you. They want the curse fulfilled.'

'But why? Why would anyone want to destroy everything?'

'For the same reason people do so many awful things,' her grandfather said. 'Power. And we must stop them. The first step is for you to learn how to fight.'

'Fight?' She stared. 'I can't *fight*. I can't do anything, really. I can't even play the piano. All I'm good at it is . . . is studying.'

Picking up the tray, he carried it to the kitchen; his voice floated back to her through the open door.

'Finlay told me there was an incident at school the other day. He said you picked a boy up off the ground and were in the process of slamming him into a wall when he walked in.'

Taylor sank back down into her chair, suddenly grateful he didn't know about the two men in Paris, too.

'It was an accident.'

Her grandfather gave her a stern look. 'It was an indication of how strong you are. And how critical it is that you learn to control your power. Which is why ...'

At that moment someone knocked at the door.

'Oh good,' he said. 'She's here.'

He hurried down the narrow corridor. Taylor heard the door open.

'Sorry I'm late.' It was a female voice. Young. Slight Liverpool accent.

'It's fine,' her grandfather said. 'I was just telling her about you.'

Taylor looked up with a polite smile that faded slowly when her grandfather appeared alongside the blue-haired girl she'd seen on the street the other day in Woodbury.

She wasn't much older than Taylor, but a little taller. Her hair was a vivid, turquoise blue. Her arms were covered in tattoos that snaked around her biceps and up her neck. A silver ring glittered in her nose, and she must have had five tiny earrings in each ear. She wore black biker boots with thick soles, and a short black skirt. Her bare legs were pale and muscular.

'Louisa, please meet my granddaughter, Taylor,' her grandfather said. Then he turned to Taylor. 'Taylor, this is Louisa. Your trainer.'

TWENTY-SEVEN

Taylor couldn't stop staring. This girl looked weird. Possibly dangerous.

Catching her eye, Louisa raised a sardonic hand, before turned her back on her and talking to Aldrich as if she wasn't there.

'How much does she know?'

Heat rose to Taylor's cheeks.

'As much as I've told you.' Her grandfather's voice held a hint of impatience. 'But she is very strong.'

'So everyone keeps saying.' Louisa sounded unconvinced.

'You will see for yourself.' Aldrich turned to include Taylor in the conversation. 'You'll train for an hour or two, then come back to see me.'

Still in her chair, Taylor looked back and forth between her grandfather and Louisa doubtfully.

'OK.'

Louisa rolled her eyes and headed for the door, but Aldrich stopped her.

'Remember what we discussed,' he said very quietly.

The girl shrugged with barely hidden irritation. 'Don't worry, Aldrich. I'll treat her like cut glass.'

But the way she said it made Taylor wonder exactly what she did with cut glass.

When she walked away, Aldrich cast a reassuring look at Taylor. 'Please pay very close attention. Louisa is extremely talented. A genius really, behind that absurd hair.'

'I'm sure it will be great,' Taylor said, doubtfully.

'Let's get going.' Down the hall, Louisa opened the door with a crash and stormed out.

Even from the hallway, Taylor could hear her heavy boots thumping on the stone steps. She dreaded the thought of spending hours alone with her.

Seeing the trepidation on her face, her grandfather steered her to the door. 'She's very good,' he said. 'Although her bedside manner needs refining. Now you'd better hurry. She won't wait.'

♊

Taylor caught up with Louisa in the quad. The girl moved like a tank, head down, ramming through crowds of students.

Nobody seemed to mind.

One boy leaped out of her way easily, grinning as she passed. 'Hi Louisa. In a hurry again?'

Louisa grunted a graceless reply.

Feeling an overwhelming need to apologise on Louisa's behalf, Taylor made a rueful gesture at him as she passed.

'Sorry!'

Louisa spun around. 'Don't do that.'

'OK,' Taylor said nervously. 'I mean, sorry.'

Louisa looked disgusted. 'Would you *stop* apologising? You're so . . . ' she made a vague gesture taking in Taylor's whole body, clad today in jeans and a striped top ' . . . white sliced bread.'

'Excuse me? I am not,' Taylor spluttered.

But Louisa was already heading through a stone archway and out into the wide green meadow that sprawled out behind the college. With no other choice, Taylor scrambled after her.

At this time of year the meadow was thick with flowers, and wild grasses grew nearly as high as Taylor's waist. She could see nothing but green, white and pink.

After they'd walked for ten minutes in stony silence, Taylor finally gave in.

'Where are we going?' she shouted, breathlessly. Louisa was well ahead, her blue hair a shimmering azure beacon.

'You'll know it when you see it,' she replied without turning back.

A few minutes later, they rounded a slope and Taylor saw the cold blue water of the river. Ancient steps led down to a long stone building on the sandy bank.

It looked like a boat house. Rowing is a popular sport in Oxford, but most boat houses were built closer to the colleges. And most weren't this old.

'Where are we?' Taylor said, catching up at last.

Louisa pulled a key ring from her pocket with a jangle. She pushed an iron key into the lock and turned it.

'We're here,' she said.

Then she walked inside.

With a resigned sigh, Taylor squared her shoulders and followed her.

The room was shadowy and cool. The small windows that lined one wall were so dirty almost no light filtered through. The room smelled faintly of fish and that soft, green smell all waterside buildings develop over time.

Louisa flipped a yellowed light switch, and a bare bulb flickered on overhead, illuminating a room empty save for a few boat cushions, scattered here and there on the damp, stone floor.

Candles stuck into bottles cluttered the window sills.

'Move.' Louisa stood in front of her, shoulders braced aggressively. Taylor scrambled to one side so the older girl could get to the door, which she closed and locked.

Taylor swallowed hard.

She wished she'd never come. Accidentally electrocuting Tom or Georgie would be much better than this.

Louisa walked up to her. Taylor looked at her warily. 'So . . . how do we start?'

'We start like this,' Louisa said, and then she kicked Taylor hard in the leg.

'Ow!' Clutching her shin, Taylor glared at her. 'That really hurt.'

Louisa looked exasperated. 'That was the whole point, idiot. It's supposed to hurt. Now I'm going to do this.'

Grabbing a handful of Taylor's curly blond hair, she wrapped it around her fist and yanked Taylor off her feet.

Stunned, Taylor reached up to try and free herself, but Louisa pulled her into a neck lock, one arm tight across her throat.

The pain sent tears to Taylor's eyes. She was frightened and angry and her hands began to tingle dangerously. She could feel her emotions going off-kilter, the way they had before she'd hurt the men in the park.

'Stop,' she gasped, her voice raspy from the pressure Louisa was putting on her throat. 'You have to stop.'

But Louisa pulled her tighter. 'Are your hands getting that delicious little tingle?' she asked sarcastically. 'Why don't you use it? Fight me.'

'I don't . . .' Taylor gasped, '. . . know how . . .'

'Yes, you do.' Louisa gave her hair another yank, and Taylor gasped, clawing desperately at her hands. 'I hear you gave your boyfriend the big heave-ho the other day. Literally.'

'He was,' Taylor whispered, 'a dick.'

Louisa chuckled. 'Well I'm a bitch, so . . . fight back, Blondie. Or suffocate. Because I am not your *Grampa*. And I don't give two shits about your super, amazing power.'

Taylor couldn't breathe. Black spots appeared at the edge of her vision. It struck her that Louisa was serious.

That same cold distance she'd felt with Tom and in the park in Paris settled on her and, with no other choice, she gave into it until it filled her heart. Her head. Her body. So quickly. Like a glass into which a cold, lethal liquid had been poured.

Louisa was nobody. She was nothing. She'd be sorry.

'*Stop*.' The word erupted straight from the source of her power.

Louisa's hands loosened, just for a second, but it was enough for Taylor to get a breath.

'Good.' Despite herself, her trainer sounded impressed. 'Do it again.'

Suddenly Taylor could feel something like a wave of heat emanating from Louisa's body.

Is that her power?

She took a deep breath and focused.

GET AWAY.

She didn't say it aloud this time. She thought it, but not in the usual, casual way. She thought it and felt it and meant it with her whole body, with every fibre of her being. She visualised Louisa flying through the air like Tom. Smashing into the wall.

But all that happened was Louisa let go and threw up her hands as if blocking a blow.

Taylor felt a heatwave of her power as it hit her again.

Dropping her hands, Louisa stepped back and grinned.

'Bloody hell,' she said. 'That was pretty good for white bread. If I was someone else you'd have thrown me in the river.'

Finally free, Taylor ran to the far end of the boathouse.

Crouching by the door, her back pressed to the wall, she took deep, rasping breaths. Her lungs burned from lack of oxygen. Her head pounded like something was hammering on the inside of her skull.

'Don't you ... *ever* ... do that ... again,' she said, panting.

Louisa studied her purple nails. 'OK, sure. I admit my methods are unorthodox ... '

'*Unorthodox?*' Taylor's voice rose sharply. 'They're criminal. You should be in prison.'

'Been there,' Louisa said coolly. 'Escaped that. Look, do you want to learn? Or do you want to complain? Because as first lessons go, if I do say so myself, that was a good one.'

'Good?' Taylor couldn't believe what she was hearing. 'If you're going to beat me up every time you want to teach me something, one of us is going to die. And it's not going to be me.'

Louisa barked a laugh. It was the first time Taylor had seen her do anything but snarl. It changed everything. When she smiled, she looked almost ... nice.

'Well, you're not as weak as you look. I'll give you that.'

'Wish I could say the same,' Taylor muttered.

Louisa ignored that. 'But you messed up. What you just did was to take your anger and your fear and use them to focus your own energy on attacking me.' She studied her with open curiosity. 'That was very good for a first-timer. Record-breakingly good, although I hate to admit it. Aldrich will be thrilled. But there are other things you should have done. Things that will make you stronger. Things that won't give you vicious headaches. That's what we're here to work on.'

Taylor watched her warily. 'OK ... '

'We need to work on where and how you source your energy,' Louisa said. 'At the moment you can only do it during moments of high emotion. You're drawing on your own energy, which is why you get the headaches. You need to learn how to summon power at any time from the energy all around you. Like I'm doing now.'

She waved her hand at the candles on the window sill.

Instantly, all of them came alight, glowing against the dirty glass. She waved again and they all went out.

Faint curls of smoke lingered in the air above them like question marks.

'What I just did,' she explained, 'was pull power at will from the environment around me and use it as I wished. It did not physically tax me. It didn't hurt me. It didn't cause any damage to anyone or anything. This is what you need to learn. Because, right now? If you tried to light those candles? I think you'd blow this building off the face of the earth and give yourself a brain haemorrhage.'

'Oh.' Taylor lowered herself to the floor. 'That would be bad.'

'Well, maybe no one would miss it but me,' Louisa said. 'But I like this place. And I want it to survive.' She patted the stone wall behind her. Then she turned back to Taylor. 'Now, let's get started.'

♊

They practiced for over an hour. First Louisa would explain the basic theory of a particular action, and Taylor would try to do what she asked for.

They tried lifting cushions, lighting candles, throwing candles, even breaking windows.

But the same problem arose again and again – unless she was frightened or angry, Taylor couldn't summon power from anywhere.

After trying and failing to make a candle shift an inch on a windowsill, she dropped down on a cushion, her face red and perspiring, her head pounding.

She lowered her head into her hands.

'This is pointless,' she said miserably. 'You're all wrong about me. I'm sorry I wasted your time.'

Louisa sat down near her, pushing vivid strands of hair out of her eyes.

'Look,' she said, 'if it's any comfort, I remember this stage of training well. It's a nightmare. Of course, I was twelve at the time. And also, don't be such a bloody baby.'

Taylor wanted to get angry but she was too tired. She leaned back against the wall and laughed wearily.

'Fine, whatever.'

'Think of it this way,' the other girl said. 'This ability is in your genes but you've never used it before. You can't expect it all to just work because, suddenly, you're aware it's there. You have to take it slow. You have to respect the process. And you have to want to be better.' She ticked the three things off with her fingers. 'If you do those things, you will be fine at this. Better than fine, actually. You'll be scary good. Otherwise, you'll end up in jail. Like I did.'

Taylor studied her curiously. She wasn't surprised to know Louisa came from a tough background – it was written all over her– but suddenly she really wanted to know more about her.

Plus, anything was better than trying to light candles that refused to cooperate.

'What did you go to jail for?'

Louisa stretched out her muscular legs. In the faint light filtering through the dust on the windows, the tattoos that climbed her calves looked like ancient symbols. A snake twined around one ankle, devouring its own tail.

'I was fifteen,' she said. 'I'd had a few lessons when I was younger, then my trainer buggered off. Along with my parents. I was living in a squat in Liverpool with some mates. Not like us. Just normal. One night they had a party. This bloke tried to cop off with me.' She stared across the boathouse, her expression blank. 'Over my objections. I didn't know him. He was older – twenty or something. I tried to make him stop but he was pissed. He wouldn't listen. I was so freaking scared. He was much bigger than me. He pushed me down ... And then the power just flashed from everywhere; I had no idea, how to control it.' Her molten gaze turned to Taylor. 'I threw him out the window.'

'God,' Taylor whispered. 'What happened to him?'

Louisa turned away again. 'You don't survive a fall from a fifth floor window.'

'He *died*?' Taylor was horrified.

Louisa nodded. 'And the squatters all grassed on me, so I went to prison.'

'For *murder*?'

'You do the crime, you do the time.' Louisa's tone was flat.

'But you're ... here.' Taylor gestured at the boathouse.

The other girl climbed to her feet in one athletic move, and held out a hand to her. After a brief hesitation, Taylor took it. Louisa pulled her up as if she weighed nothing and headed towards a door.

'That's the thing about us, Blondie.' She flicked her fingers at the door and the lock released with a rusty squawk. The door swung open.

'We don't stay anywhere we don't want to.'

TWENTY-EIGHT

'Give me the remote,' Sacha demanded, holding out his hand.

On the television screen a slim girl wearing a huge amount of makeup lip-synched to a popular pop song.

Her eyes glued to the screen, Laura shook her head. 'No way.'

Sacha grimaced. Laura had the *worst* taste in music.

As the bubblegum pop assaulted his eardrums, he checked his phone – nothing from Taylor. She must still be at school – it was an hour earlier in England.

He'd fully recovered from the stabbing in the park. For days, he'd followed the news avidly for reports of the unsolved deaths of two men, but found nothing.

The two thugs must have survived Taylor's vengeance.

She'd told him about the conversation with her grandfather.

That her powers were linked with alchemy. In French it was *alchimie*. He kept trying to replace his idea of an alchemist – a grey-bearded old man – with an image of her, so full of energy and youth, so sensible and sensitive. He kept failing.

'*I'm just gonna shake, shake, shake . . .* ' sang the dancing blonde American girl, as Laura watched, mesmerised.

Sacha let out a breath.

It was so hard to get his brain around what was happening. Taylor was spending all her spare time trying to light candles without matches. He was afraid to leave Laura alone in his own flat in case someone came to the door; either those *things* that had warned him to stay away from Taylor, or the men who'd stabbed him in the park.

It had been a week since Taylor's visit. A week of being trapped at home every night.

His phone vibrated in his pocket, and he pulled it out, expecting to see Taylor's name in on the screen. What he saw instead made him sit up so suddenly, Laura actually glanced up from the television to see if something was wrong.

Antoine.

Clutching the phone, he hurried out of the room. 'What's up?'

'Sacha!' Antoine sounded furious. 'What the hell did you do?'

'What are you talking about?' Sacha's stomach lurched.

'Those two guys – you know the ones – they were roughed up last week. Bad. Word on the street is, they say it was you.'

Sacha closed his eyes and sagged back against the kitchen counter. His bones felt like butter.

Merde, Merde, Merde . . .

'Sacha?' Antoine's angry nasal voice jarred him. 'Did you hear what I said?'

'I heard you.'

Antoine breathed heavily into the phone.

'Did you do it?' he asked after a second. 'Did you beat them up?'

'Does it matter?'

'I guess not,' Antoine conceded.

Rubbing his hand across his jaw, Sacha looked back down the hallway to where Laura still lay on the sofa watching the pretty girl dance. Was she safe? Could he protect her from all of this?

'Look,' Antoine said with obvious reluctance, 'I don't want to talk about this on the phone. Meet me at the usual place and I'll tell you what I know. They're going to come to me, Sacha. They know I know you. They're going to ask me where you live. I don't want to tell them. But . . . You know what they are. What they'll do to me if – when – I don't.' Sacha heard a loud crashing noise at the end of the line. It sounded like Antoine was punching something. When he spoke again, his voice was breathless, pained. 'We're screwed, you know that, Sacha? Really screwed.'

♊

Sacha stuffed his phone back into his pocket and, grabbing his hoody, returned to the living room, pulling it over his head as he walked.

'I promised *Maman* I'd go to the supermarket,' he lied casually. 'Will you be OK on your own for a few minutes?'

He hated to leave Laura alone, but things had been fine here for days. And he had to take care of this.

His sister rolled her eyes. 'I'm not a baby you know.'

Shoving his keys in his pocket he headed to the door.

'Lock the door behind me,' he instructed, 'and don't open it to anyone under any circumstances, OK?'

He emphasised the last words with a stern look.

She shrugged. 'Whatever.'

'I mean it, Laura,' he said firmly.

Outside, the sun shone, and the deep blue sky stretched out over Paris like a soft blanket. The street teemed with people going about their daily lives. They knew nothing of what really went on in this city.

If he told any of them the truth about his life, they'd think he was mad.

How could such different worlds exist side by side without noticing each other?

Pulling his phone from his pocket, he scrolled through his contacts until he reached Annie's name. They'd talked every day since that first call. Right now, he felt like she was the only person who really understood what was happening.

She'd been looking through his father's books – searching for answers.

'*Bonjour* Annie. It's me,' he said when she answered. 'Any luck?'

'Oh Sacha, I'm afraid not,' she said.

'There are so many of your father's books here,' she continued. 'It's just too much. I could use your help, to be honest.'

Sacha felt torn. If he went to help Annie, he'd be leaving his mother and Laura unprotected. He couldn't see a way to save himself and protect everyone else at the same time.

They talked for a few minutes more, and then Sacha ended the call, promising to think about it.

He was jogging towards the Metro station when his phone rang again. Assuming it was Annie ringing back, he answered it without looking.

'What did you forget to tell me?' He'd stopped outside a shop with a display of oranges so brightly coloured it hurt his eyes to look at them.

At first he heard nothing. He put his hand over his other ear to block out the noise of the street. 'Hello? Annie?'

Nobody replied. Then from the phone came a piercing scream.

Sacha's blood turned to ice. That wasn't Annie's voice.

Yanking the phone from his ear he stared at the name on the screen.

Laura.

He couldn't seem to breathe.

Whirling he began running. Back towards the flat. Back to his sister who was all alone.

'Laura, talk to me.' He tried to sound calm but his voice emerged thin and breathless. 'I need to know what's happening.'

He could hear the faint sound of sobbing, the rustle of the

phone against fabric. It sounded like she was holding the phone away from her head, perhaps cradling it against her chest.

The pavement was crowded and he shoved people out of the way, dashing around small children and vaulting over a tiny dog.

Frustrated, he leaped into the busy road and began running through the traffic.

An instant chorus of honking horns rose around him. Drivers gesticulated and shouted obscenities as they passed. Sacha ignored them.

He shouted into the phone. 'Come on, Laura. *Talk to me.*'

'Sacha.' Her voice was a terrified whisper.

Relief flooded through his veins like alcohol, leaving him dizzy. But he didn't slow his pace.

'What's happening, honey?'

'Men are at the door,' she whispered, so quietly he strained to make out the words. 'Scary men in black coats. There's something wrong with them. They don't look normal. They're trying to break in.'

At that moment, somewhere in the background began a steady, almost rhythmic pounding.

Laura whimpered and stifled a sob. 'Sacha who are they? What do they want?'

Stay away from the girl.

Sacha's gut tightened. He was still so far away – Paris had never seemed so big to him before.

'Is that them? Hitting the door?'

'Yes,' she whispered. 'It's locked but they're shaking it. I think they're getting in. I'm scared, Sacha.'

He could hear the panic in her voice and it broke his heart. He knew what it was like to feel trapped by things you don't understand.

'I'm on my way back right now. I'm coming as fast as I can. Hide somewhere and don't make a sound, no matter what.'

A splintering sound cut the air. Laura gasped. 'Oh God. I think they're in. Sacha, please hurry.'

The phone went dead.

Swearing out loud, he lowered his head and ran faster, until the city blurred around him.

The hot air was heavy with the smell of exhaust. A red light ahead warned of danger. The crossroad was a busy one, with cars and buses in all lanes. But there was no way he was going to wait.

After all, what was the worst that could happen? It wasn't like he could die.

Speeding past the queue of cars waiting at the light, he hurled himself into the stream of moving traffic.

A discordant squeal of screeching brakes rose around him. Someone screamed. The air filled with the acrid scent of melted rubber.

Gritting his teeth, he kept running.

When he reached the far side of the crowded road, a man stepped off the curve and jumped in front of him, arms outspread, as if to try and stop Sacha for his own good.

Shoving the man's hands away, Sacha shot by him without slowing his pace.

In his head he kept hearing Laura's frightened voice. *'Please hurry.'*

By the time he arrived at his apartment building, sweat poured down his face and his T-shirt clung to his torso. His throat felt raw as he skidded on the tiled floor in the quiet lobby.

He headed for the stairs but slowed when he passed the lift. It stood empty and wide open.

Like it was waiting for him.

It was ominous and unnerving.

Sacha wasn't about to get into it.

Shoving his way through the door leading into the stairwell, he vaulted up, taking the stairs three at a time. The building was quiet – he passed no one. He could hear only his heart thudding in his ears, and the harsh rasp of his laboured breathing.

When he reached the third floor, he crashed through the door into the corridor. What he saw froze him in his tracks.

His own front door hung off its hinges, three figures, white faced and clad in black, crowded around it. Each held out one arm, with their palms facing into the apartment building.

Goosebumps rose on Sacha's neck. But he showed none of his fear on his face.

'You again?' he called out to them. 'Are you *stalking* me?'

The three turned as one.

Just looking at them made his stomach twist – their appearance was inhuman. Their skin was unnaturally white, their sunken eyes far too black. Their faces like skulls.

They smiled.

Sacha's throat went dry. Still, he studied them with affected insouciance.

'I'm starting to think you're obsessed with me.'

With chilling silence, the three shapes slid towards him. He scrambled back – a little at first, then further and further. Soon, there was nowhere to go. The doors to the lift pressed against his back.

'Back off.' He tried to snap the words coldly but his voice came out shaky.

Without warning, he doors slid open behind him and he fell backwards. For one horrible moment he thought he'd tumble down the elevator shaft and he scrabbled for something to hold onto. Then he realised that, while he'd been facing off those things, the lift car had arrived. Unsummoned.

He stumbled into it, his eyes on the creatures in the corridor.

The pale men slid after him, their sliding steps eerily soundlessly across the floor.

Before Sacha fully understood what was happening he was trapped inside the lift with his back to the wall and the three figures clustered around him.

They were so close he could have touched them without stretching out his arm. The thought was somehow repugnant and he put his hands behind his back.

They exuded cold. There was a strange smell of earth about them – like damp soil.

Sacha tried to appear fearless, as if he was leaning against the back wall rather than pressing against it desperately.

'Well,' he said, 'isn't this cosy.'

The door slid shut behind them.

There was no way out.

The realisation hit him with icy finality. He took an unsteady breath.

He didn't know why the men terrified him so much. He wasn't afraid to die but he was afraid of being hurt, of being tortured for days without being able to escape into death. And he had the feeling they were capable of that.

'If you hurt my sister,' he made himself say. 'I will kill you.'

'You are the thirteenth son.' They spoke together.

Their voices were deep – unnatural. It made Sacha's skin crawl. And their words were disturbingly familiar.

Although their horrible grins hadn't changed, Sacha got the sense they were waiting for him to reply.

'So I'm told,' he said.

'You are the thirteenth son.' They repeated the words again, in unison.

'Yeah, I got the message.' Sacha leaned towards them, fists clenched. 'Now leave me alone. Leave my family alone.'

It didn't have the impact he'd hoped for. The tall one, at the back, watched him, a look of awful pleasure in his coal black eyes.

'You,' Sacha said, pointing at him. 'Talk. Tell me what's going on.'

To his surprise, the man spoke. His voice was flat, un-inflected. And deep as a grave.

'Sacha L'hiver. We are here to bring you home. It is the prophecy.'

Sacha didn't like the sound of any of this. He didn't like the word 'prophecy'. He didn't like that they knew his name. He didn't like the way they *smelled*.

He was starting to feel suffocated. The air had grown thin. As if somehow they *stole* the oxygen.

'I don't know what you want.' Too scared now, to feign sarcasm, he couldn't keep a pleading note out of his voice. 'And my last name is Winters. Maybe you've made a mistake. It could ... happen to anyone.'

Without warning, the lift jolted and started to descend. The whirr of the mechanism sounded unnaturally loud in the silent car.

Sacha's heart fluttered wildly in his chest. He thought of Laura, alone and terrified. He hoped there'd only been three of them to start with, and that he hadn't just left her alone with one of these *things*.

'Look, I don't want to go home with you,' he said, increasingly panicked. 'I live here so I *am* home. Technically. Now.'

'It is your destiny,' the tall one spoke again in his sepulchral voice, his eyes locked on Sacha's. 'It was decided long ago. We warned you to stay away from the girl. Now you must come.'

The floors passed one after another, glowing numbers on the screen by the door: ground floor, first underground, second underground ...

Sacha felt hypnotised by the man's black eyes. They seemed endless.

'Are you the ones who are going to kill me?' He hated the fear he heard in his voice.

The lift thudded to a stop in the basement car park.

The doors slid open to reveal a bored looking man in khaki shorts and a white, short-sleeved shirt. He was tanned, his hair perfectly blow-dried.

He took one step towards the lift.

With silent precision, the three swivelled to face him.

The man jumped back.

'I'll ...uh ... take the stairs ... '

He turned and ran.

'No!' Sacha cried out. 'Help me!'

But the man didn't stop. The tallest of the things flung out a hand. Somewhere in the distance Sacha heard something fall heavily with a sickening thud.

He took a step forward, but the doors slid shut again.

The lift shook and began to rise. The three pivoted back towards him, faces impassive and cold.

'The time has come,' the tall one said. 'The girl cannot help you.'

Sacha's throat tightened.

His mind whirled through a grim list of possibilities. If they could come here, these things, whatever they were, they could get to England. Taylor didn't know any of this was happening. He had to get away. Had to warn her.

'Leave her out of this,' he snarled. He lunged towards them, hands curled into fists.

As one, they each held out their arms, palms turned to face him.

Instantly, the lift filled with an overwhelming metallic stench of blood. Blood ran from the ceilings down the wall, puddling in viscous pools at Sacha's feet. He could feel it warm and sticky on his hands and shoulders, pouring over his face and hair. Hear it trickling like thick water.

He doubled over, retching, eyes squeezed shut, hands pressed to his ears, trying to block everything out.

The elevator stopped again, this time on the ground floor.

With a cheerful *ding*, the doors slid open.

Still bent over facing the floor, Sacha opened his eyes. The blood was gone.

The three creatures watched him with empty eyes. Behind them, a skinny little boy stood in the open doorway, staring at the three with his mouth open, an ice cream cone in one hand, dripping in the heat.

Sacha recognised him. He lived on the fourth floor. He was nice. A good kid. He was eight years old.

As one, the three swivelled moved towards him, and stretched out their arms.

'*No!*' With a strangled cry Sacha hurled himself at the Dark Men.

He expected them to be powerful, resistant. But their bodies seemed oddly insubstantial. It was like running through a field of tall, dry grass.

He passed right through them.

Grabbing the kid by the arm, he dragged him across the lobby and out into the street. The ice cream fell from the boy's hand, splattering onto the hot concrete.

At first, he was too surprised to fight. But when they reached the pavement he began to struggle in Sacha's grip, his face red with anger and fear.

'Hey, what's wrong with you? *Merde.* Let me *go.*'

Without loosening his grip, Sacha turned back to look into the lobby behind them. The lift stood open and empty.

Sacha gaped at the space where the creatures had been – it was as if they'd disappeared. Or never been there in the first place.

Shaking himself free of Sacha's hold, the boy shot off, running down the road as fast as he could go.

'You're welcome,' Sacha muttered as he watched his retreating back grow smaller in the distance.

He stood in the middle of the street staring up at his flat, his whole body shaking.

Laura.

Twenty-nine

He made his way back into the lobby, conscious all the time that the creatures could reappear. But the building was quiet.

The lift still stood open on the ground floor, gleaming like a cavernous mouth. Sacha wasn't getting back into that thing. He took the stairs running at a speed boosted by adrenaline.

On the third floor, he shoved past the shattered remnants of his front door. It sagged against the wall with a splintering sound.

The flat was cool and silent.

'Laura!' He ran down the corridor, his voice echoing in the stillness. 'Laura! It's me.'

His heart beating a violent rhythm, he checked behind every door. His room was empty. Her room was empty. The kitchen was empty.

What had they done to her? Had they taken her? Thrown her from a window?

Pressing his fingers hard against his mouth, he stifled a panicked sob. That was when he heard a faint rustling sound from his mother's room.

He ran back. The door was open. Light flooded through the tall windows. His mother's bed was neatly made; the room still smelled faintly of her perfume.

'Laura? Are you in here? It's safe.'

At least I hope it is.

The closet door swung open. She peered out warily from her hiding place, crouched among her mother's shoes and bags, her face streaked with tears.

With a gasp of relief, he pulled her into his arms.

'Thank God,' he said, holding her slim body close. 'Thank God.'

'Oh Sacha, I was so scared.' Her words poured out in a torrent. 'They kept pounding and pounding on the door. And then it was like everything exploded. I could hear them talking. They were looking for you. What do they want? Who are they? What did you do? Do you owe them money?'

Still holding her tight, Sacha shook his head. 'I really don't know who they are.'

He felt her shudder.

'They didn't look normal. They looked like monsters.'

Sacha thought of the blood-soaked vision they'd given him.

'They *are* monsters.'

'Will they come back?' Laura's voice was muffled against his chest.

'I hope not.' But his voice lacked confidence.

This was everything he'd feared. His messed up life was now threatening his family.

He'd wanted to stay here to protect them. But in reality, as long as he lived in this flat, they were in danger.

He'd had years to get used to the idea of dying but now that the time was closing in – now that he'd seen the things that would do it – he wanted nothing more in the world than to stay alive. To be a normal guy, with a normal life. To watch Laura grow up. To take care of his mother.

But he would never do any of that. He was sure of it now. He couldn't fight those things. He didn't know how.

Right then, holding his frightened sister in his arms, he made up his mind. He would go to Annie's first and look at his father's books. See if he could learn more. Then he'd hit the road. Get away from everyone he loved.

He'd lure those *things* away. If he wasn't here, they wouldn't be here. And Laura and his mother would be safe.

'I have to leave.' He hadn't meant to say it aloud – the words just came out.

Wrenching herself away, Laura stared at him. 'Leave? What do you mean?'

Her hand shook when she pushed her hair out of her face to see him better.

'Look, Laura, it's me they're after, not you. If I leave, they'll follow. You'll be safe.' He spoke with slow earnestness – he needed her to understand. If she was on his side she could smooth things out with their mother, make it all easier.

'No, Sacha. Where would you go? What if they get you?'

She reached for his hand, her blue eyes pleading with him. 'Sacha, please don't leave us. *Maman* needs you. And I need you, too.'

'I know,' he said gently, 'but I have no choice. This is the only way. If something happened to you two because of me, I'd go crazy.'

Laura squeezed his hand tightly.

A tear trickled down her cheek and she wiped it away. When she spoke, her voice was small. 'Where will you go?'

Sacha hesitated. The last thing he needed was for her or his mother to follow him to Annie's.

'I have an idea,' he said vaguely. 'A safe place outside the city.'

He tightened his grip on Laura's hand. It felt so fragile – such tiny bones. Thin skin. He had always protected her. And he needed to protect her again now.

Thirty

Taylor sat on the white and grey patterned rug on the floor of her bedroom, an unlit candle in front of her.

'Light.' She waved her hand at it.

Nothing happened.

'*Light*,' she said again, frustrated. 'You stupid bloody wax ... *stick*.'

The candle stayed stubbornly dark.

The first faint warnings of a headache pinged, and she brushed her hand against her forehead.

Muttering to herself ('Defective piece of ... '), she reached for a slim, antique leather-bound book. As soon as she touched it, her hands began to tingle.

The volume had no title on the cover. Instead, strange geometric symbols were embossed in the worn leather in faded gold indentations.

Her grandfather had pressed the book into her hands when she'd returned to his flat after her training session with Louisa.

Just holding it had given her the strangest feeling.

It seemed to vibrate with energy. 'This is a very old book of alchemical exercises,' he'd explained. 'My sisters and I used it to learn. My father used it before me. You must complete every lesson, starting at the front and working your way to the back.' He held up a cautioning hand. 'Never move on to the next lesson until you've conquered the one before. It is a process of ascension. Jumping ahead could be ... painful.'

'Pain,' she'd said, rubbing her bruised arms ruefully. 'Gotcha.'

His green eyes held a knowing glint.

'Louisa is tough, I know,' he said. 'But she is the best of all of us here. A natural, like you. And she was extremely impressed by you today.'

Colour crept into Taylor's cheeks. It surprised her how much the other girl's opinion of her meant.

Something he'd said struck her. 'You say she's the best of all of you. How many of you ... I mean, *us*, are there? Here?'

He turned back to his bookshelves and began searching, his hands running lightly across the old spines. 'Many.'

'Many?' She cocked her head. 'Like a dozen many? Or a thousand many?'

'St Wilfred's has been home to our kind since the thirteenth century.' As he spoke Aldrich pulled other books off the shelf and placed them inside a leather satchel. 'Its charter describes it as a place for the study of alchemy and the alchemical sciences.' He turned back around and held out the satchel. 'And that is precisely what it is, to this day.'

Taylor accepted the bag automatically. The worn leather felt buttery beneath her fingers.

'So everyone here . . . ?'

'Is an alchemist, yes.' He finished the sentence for her.

The idea that St Wilfred's was filled with people like her – that the students she and Louisa had passed as they'd barrelled across the quad were all alchemists – filled her with excitement and hope. What if they looked out for each other? What if they could all do the kind of things she could do?

On the train home later, she'd felt alight with energy and excitement. If she could just learn to do the things Louisa did, maybe she really could save Sacha. Somehow.

Now that she'd been trying to practice on her own, though, she was struggling.

The horrible truth was, she simply could not do what the book told was the first step. She had failed so far to complete a single lesson. And she'd practiced each day until her head pounded.

She'd already read and reread the section on drawing power from the natural environment around her but she couldn't seem to do it. The guidelines in the book made perfect sense in theory but when she tried . . . it simply didn't work.

She didn't care about the stupid candle and as long as she didn't hate the candle and wasn't afraid of the candle she couldn't light the candle.

'Oh my God, I'm such a crap alchemist,' she moaned, flopping onto her back. She let the book fall to the floor. There was no point in reading it again. She'd memorised the lesson days ago anyway.

She'd also done precisely what her grandfather told her not to, and skipped ahead to read the next exercise. It called for her to pick an object up without touching it with her hands. It suggested lifting something small to start, like a snuff box.

She'd had to Google 'snuff box'.

That book was *old*.

Her phone buzzed on the floor beside her. Without moving the rest of her body, she rolled her head to one side to see the screen.

Georgie.

Taylor hesitated. The phone vibrated again, insistently.

She'd avoided her friend ever since the fight with Tom. Georgie had sent dozens of texts and left at least as many voicemail messages, each increasingly hysterical.

It was starting to make Taylor feel annoyingly guilty. Worse than that, though – she really missed her. It was awful not having a best friend right now.

Slowly, she picked up the phone. Her finger hovered over the red button.

Then, with a sigh, she pushed the green button.

'Hi Georgie,' she said, her tone casual.

'Oh my *actual* God,' Georgie said dramatically. 'I was about to call the prisons and the morgue. Are you in *hospital*? I was freaking out!'

Taylor rolled her eyes. 'I was at school today, Georgie. I saw you in the corridor.'

(She didn't mention that she'd seen her from a distance, and she'd legged it.)

'Well.' Georgie's voice grew cautious. She'd clearly heard the cool asperity in Taylor's tone. 'I'm glad you're OK.'

'I'm good.' Taylor looked at her nails. 'Anything else?'

Georgie struck a bright tone. 'I have a question for you,' she said. 'And that is, how much do you want to help me with my maths homework tomorrow night? Is it a huge amount or just loads?'

Taylor bristled. How could Georgie ask her this after telling Tom about Sacha? How could she think everything was fine between them?

'Can't,' she said coolly. 'I'm busy.'

'Right,' Georgie said. 'What's up, Tay? I can tell something's wrong, I just don't know what it is. Spill, so I can fix.'

Taylor took a deep breath. *I must not get angry. I must not get angry . . .*

'I guess you haven't heard that Tom broke up with me.'

'But that's why I've been trying to reach you,' Georgie said. 'I couldn't believe it was true, or that you wouldn't call me to tell me yourself. I was really hurt, to be honest.'

Taylor gritted her teeth.

'Oh, really? Well, he accused me of cheating on him with Sacha, the French boy I'm tutoring.' Her voice was low and dangerous. 'The thing is, I never told him about Sacha. In fact, the only person I ever told about Sacha ... was you.'

Georgie went utterly silent.

'Georgie,' Taylor said. 'Did you tell Tom about Sacha?'

'No!' Georgie managed to sound both defensive and aggressive at the same time. 'I didn't say a word to Tom.'

'I see.' Fighting her temper, Taylor forced herself to be conscious of the solid floor beneath her back. She stared hard at the white ceiling of her room, making herself think about what shade of white it was, and whether it should be painted again – anything to stop the tingling in her hands. 'So how do you imagine he might have found out?'

Another long silence fell.

Georgie cleared her throat. 'I guess ... I mean, it's *possible* ... I might have told Paul.' She immediately launched into a defence. 'He swore he wouldn't tell Tom. Swore.'

Taylor couldn't think of anything at all to say. So she said nothing.

'How did Tom take it?' Georgie asked hesitantly.

Taylor thought of Tom, shoving her against the wall. Of the fear that had squeezed her heart like vise.

'Badly. Very, very badly.'

'Oh no,' Georgie whispered. 'Oh Tay, I'm so sorry. My big mouth. I shouldn't have trusted Paul. I shouldn't have told.'

'No,' Taylor agreed. 'You really shouldn't have. Because I asked you not to tell him and you *promised* you wouldn't. And then you just told him anyway. And now I don't think I can ever trust you again.'

The tingling was getting worse. The phone felt abnormally hot in her hand.

'Come on, Tay,' Georgie sounded scared. 'Don't say that. I made a mistake. I did something stupid. You know I do that sometimes. I talk too much. You have to forgive me. I couldn't bear it if you didn't.'

The lights in Taylor's room flickered ominously.

'You're just going to have to live with it,' she said. 'You always said "friends before boys", remember? But you chose Paul over me. And that's unforgiveable.'

She hung up without saying goodbye, dropping the phone onto the floor at her side. It might have been her imagination, but it seemed to smoke a little when she let go.

⚭

Taylor lay on the floor for a while after that. She couldn't seem to summon the energy to get up and try to light that candle again.

She told herself to get over it. Many worse things had happened lately. This wasn't as bad as watching Sacha die. Or nearly killing Tom.

But losing Georgie hurt like a kick in the stomach. She wanted her back. She wanted them to be friends the way they were before. She wanted everything that had happened between them to be undone.

Why can't I learn to do that instead of lighting a sodding candle?

Her thoughts were in such a tangle, she didn't know how much time had passed before her phone rang again. This time the screen read only: 'Unknown caller.'

She rolled over to pick it up. 'Hello?'

'You practicing?'

The voice was female, tough, with a Liverpool accent.

Louisa.

'Yes,' Taylor said without sitting up. 'But I'm a rubbish alchemist and my head hurts.'

'Quit drawing on your own power.' Louisa's disapproving sigh was so loud, Taylor held the phone away from her ear. 'How many times do I have to say it?'

'I don't know *how*.' Her voice rang with frustration. 'I've got Grandfather's stupid book and I'm trying and I'm still just sucking power from my own stupid head. I hate power. I don't want power. I just want to be a normal person.'

As she spoke, she stared at the light fixture above her head. It was vaguely unseemly. Like looking up electricity's skirt.

Louisa's response to her rant was a short command. 'Go outside.'

Taylor's eyes narrowed. 'Why? And by the way, how did you get this number?'

'How do you think?' Louisa said, and Taylor could almost see her bored expression. 'Go outside because I said so. Take your candle with you.'

Taylor reached for the candle automatically but midway there her hand froze.

'Hang on. How did you know I was practicing with a candle?'

'One of these days,' Louisa said, 'I will tell you about my powers. In the meantime let's focus on yours.'

285

But Taylor wasn't about to let this go. 'Can you see into my *house*?'

'Not exactly,' Louisa said. 'But sort of. Anyway, I'm standing on your front steps and it's boring, and your neighbours are really conformist and lookist and they're all staring. Now will you come outside?'

THIRTY-ONE

Grabbing the candle, Taylor shoved it into the pocket of her shorts and thumped down the stairs to the front door.

Louisa stood on the walk in front of her house, examining her short, purple nails with a bored expression.

'What are you doing here?'

Louisa shot her a disbelieving look. 'Do you always ask stupid questions? Or do I just bring that part of you out with my sparkling personality?'

She looked around, lips pursed. Two yummy mummies in exercise gear pushing expensive prams took in her blue hair and swirling tattoos with open suspicion. Louisa stared back at them with such intensity they both looked away, flustered.

The air buzzed with the angry sound of lawnmowers and leaf blowers. It was a warm day and everyone seemed to be outside, cutting things down.

'Where can we practice? Your street's a bit Nappy Valley, if you know what I mean. Two nubile young alchemists summoning nature's power might not go unnoticed.'

For a second, Taylor wasn't sure how to respond to this. Then she pulled herself together.

'The water meadow,' she said after a few seconds' thought. 'I sometimes go there to read. They don't cut the grass so nobody's ever there but me. People seem to like short grass for some reason.'

With a look that said she didn't really care about the details, Louisa gestured impatiently. 'Lead the way to the long grass.'

For a while, they walked in silence. Taylor found herself suddenly afraid to say anything. Every word that came out of her mouth seemed loaded with a double-thick coating of idiocy.

Louisa didn't seem to mind the lack of conversation. Her brow furrowed as they turned onto the main street heading into the town centre.

To her surprise, Taylor found that she liked the looks people gave them when they passed. Ever since she'd been to Paris, she'd been trying out a different style. Darker. More daring. Today she wore black shorts and a fitted long grey vest with the boots Sacha had bought her in France.

It occurred to her that her outfit was not unlike Louisa's – as usual she wore combat boots and a short black skirt that showed off her muscular legs.

'My grandfather sent you, I guess?' she said after the silence grew too long.

'Mm-hmm,' Louisa said. 'He's worried about you being in the boondocks without knowing how to use your energy.' She shot her a sideways glance. 'You're a combination time bomb and victim-in-waiting until you get the hang of this stuff.'

'I nearly blew up my phone a few minutes ago,' Taylor said.

'Really?' Louisa studied her with new interest. 'Maybe you were drawing from it without realising. That's a good sign.'

Taylor hoped that was true. She was sick of failing. She'd never failed at anything in her life.

The town centre was crowded with families out doing whatever families do on sunny Saturdays. Louisa ploughed through them without apology, sending small children scattering.

'Now see here . . .' an older man remonstrated as she barrelled past. But she never looked back.

For a change, Taylor didn't apologise either.

It felt good not being sorry.

'Here,' she said, pointing at the turning into the park.

It was cooler in the grass, and the route beside the stream was quieter, although the grass was covered in sunbathing teenagers.

After about five minutes, the path entered the high grass of the water meadow and the crowds thinned, eventually disappearing completely.

Taylor led the way off the main path onto a rougher track. The grass brushed against her bare legs as she walked. Gold and orange flowers peeped out at her through the myriad shades of green.

It was much quieter here. The sounds of the street disappeared, replaced by the gentle hum of wind through the grass. The sun beat down on her skin and, for a second, she turned her face up to soak it in.

Eventually, the footpath led down to the edge of the stream. An old wooden bench sat under a nearby tree, looking out over the slow-moving water.

Louisa stood on her toes to see if anyone was around, but soon satisfied herself that they were alone.

'Perfect,' she said, dusting her hands. 'Good spot.'

She took off her shoes and socks and set them under the bench. Then, barefoot, she walked into the water until it covered her feet.

'Blimey, it's cold,' she announced. The light caught her hair and made the blue sparkle.

Glancing back at Taylor she gestured for her to follow.

'Come on,' she said. 'In the water. Feet first.'

Taylor, who'd expected more candle lighting, hid her puzzlement.

She fumbled with her boots, then followed her into the stream.

The water chilled her feet, sending involuntary shivers up her spine. The mud squelched pleasantly between her toes as she stepped carefully towards the other girl.

When she reached her side, Louisa held her gaze. Her toffee-coloured eyes were lined with thick, black lashes that curled naturally at the ends.

She's really pretty, Taylor thought, wondering why she'd never noticed that before.

'Now, we're going to try something. I want you to take my

hands. I am going to try to push energy against you, and I want you to push back.'

Hesitantly, Taylor took her proffered hands. Louisa's fingers were strong, her fingertips rough.

The other girl looked up to the sun and closed her eyes. After a second, Taylor did the same.

The water tugged at her ankles as it moseyed past. Water weeds tickled her feet. The only sounds she could hear were birds calling to one another, and honeybees buzzing in the meadow flowers.

'Can you feel it?' Louisa asked after a moment.

Taylor, who could feel nothing in particular, frowned with effort.

Then, suddenly, she felt a wave of heat, pushing at her. The force was so tangible she imagined she could see it if she opened her eyes. But then she did open her eyes and all she saw was sunlight.

'Yes,' she whispered, awed. 'I can feel it.'

'Good,' Louisa said. 'Now, imagine the river and the sun feeding you energy. If it helps, think of it as something you can touch, something physical.'

Remembering Finlay's suggestion, Taylor imagined the power as a strand of shimmering golden thread she pulled towards her.

The thread unravelled easily.

Taylor's pulse began to race. 'It's working,' she breathed. 'I think I'm doing it.'

'Good,' Louisa said. 'Now push the power at me. Like I just did to you.'

Taylor imagined the thread flowing towards Louisa in a steady, shining stream, weaving it around her in a glowing circle. It was so easy. It danced and moved wherever she wanted it to go . . .

'Woah.' Louisa jerked her hands free and took a splashing step away. She stared at Taylor wide-eyed.

Taylor blinked. 'What happened? Didn't it work?'

A grin spread across Louisa's face. 'Oh, it worked alright.' She pointed down. 'Look.'

Puzzled, Taylor looked where she indicated.

The water that had trickled over their ankles was now up to their knees. She hadn't even noticed it happening.

'What . . . ?' she heard herself whisper.

The river had stopped flowing and pooled around the two girls, as if drawn to them.

Ahead, the stream bed lay empty and exposed. Green-black water weeds sagged flat to the muddy ground.

Around them, the water was rising.

Bewildered, Taylor turned to Louisa. 'I don't understand.'

'Aldrich isn't joking about your strength.' Louisa shook her head. 'You're *nuclear*.'

'Wait,' Taylor reached down to touch the cold water that now swirled around her knees. 'You're saying *I* did this?'

'Yes I am.' Turning, Louisa splashed towards the shore. 'Come on,' she said without looking back. 'Let's get out before you cause a tidal wave that drowns Woodbury.'

Taylor scrambled after her, slipping and sliding in the mud.

This was all bewildering. She couldn't light a candle but she could stop a river from moving?

I didn't do that, she assured herself. *It's impossible.*

But in her heart, she knew she had. She'd felt the exhilaration of the energy around her. It had poured into her veins like a drug.

When she reached the shore, she looked back.

For a moment, the water continued to rise, blocked from heading downstream as if by an invisible dam.

Then, with a sound like a sigh, it began to flow again, down the stream bed. Soon the sigh turned into a rush, and the water poured away, pushing pebbles and weeds ahead of it, tiny waves tumbling until the stream was almost back to normal.

Taylor exhaled audibly.

Louisa was sitting cross-legged on one end of the old wooden bench. She motioned for Taylor to follow suit.

The sun-baked bench was warm beneath her legs.

'How's your head?' the other girl asked.

Taylor paused. 'Fine,' she said, surprised. 'It doesn't hurt at all.'

Louisa gave a satisfied nod. 'Not using your own energy makes all the difference.' She held out a hand. 'Got that candle?'

Taylor pulled the stubby, white candle from her pocket and handed it over. Louisa shoved it into a crack in the wood of the bench between the two of them.

She held out her hands, palms up. 'Let's try this.'

Taylor's heart sank.

'I can't,' she said, shrinking back. 'I've been trying all morning and I just ... can't.'

The look Louisa gave her was incredulous.

'Taylor, what you just did?' She tilted her head at the river.

'That was much harder than lighting a candle. It was a hundred times more complex. To be honest, I know you can light this thing. I'm just curious to see if you shoot it into the sun like a rocket.' She grinned and her nose ring sparkled. 'It's an experiment.'

Taylor doubted all of this. But moving the water had been surprisingly easy. Having Louisa with her made her feel more confident. Maybe she could light the stupid candle.

Settling down on the bench, she took Louisa's hands.

'Find that same energy,' Louisa told her. 'Visualise it the same way you did a few minutes ago. Make sure it's coming from the river and the air around you. Know the source. You should be able to sense it.'

Taylor closed her eyes.

It was easier this time. As if doing it once had opened a door inside her, revealing things that had been always present, but hidden until now.

She saw shimmering golden strands of energy everywhere. It came from the fields, from the grass, from the air, from the water . . . she was surrounded by it.

She didn't even know where to begin.

Carefully, she chose one strand and directed it towards the candle.

Light, she thought.

It flowed around the candle like honey.

She opened her eyes.

The candle glowed.

Pulling her hands free of Louisa's grip, she clapped delightedly. 'I did it!'

Louisa looked up with a smile that soon faded as she looked around them.

'Uh, Taylor . . .'

When she followed her gaze, Taylor drew in her breath sharply.

Hundreds of tiny lights floated in the air around them, surrounding them in concentric circles of gold. Each was like a tiny candle flame glowing and flickering, but there were no wicks or candles.

Taylor could have cried.

'No, no, no,' she said, frustrated. 'I just wanted *one* candle. Just one.'

An odd sound from the end of the bench made her look up. Louisa was shaking with laughter.

Taylor's cheeks reddened. 'It's not funny.'

'I don't even,' Louisa gasped, hands clutching her sides, 'have any idea how you did that. You set the *air* on fire.'

'It was an accident,' Taylor said, but she found herself giggling, too. 'Just a tiny accident.'

Louisa wiped her eyes. 'Well, you'll have to make them go out now before the whole field goes up in flames.'

Taylor looked around in alarm. She'd never considered the flames might be real fire.

'How do I do that?' she asked, panicked.

'Do the same thing again.' Louisa's voice was calm. 'Only now you must imagine the power receding.'

Taking a deep breath, Taylor stared at the flames.

Out.

Nothing happened.

She frowned and tried again. This time she pulled the power in first and then pushed it out with all the force she could muster.

Go out!

The lights blinked out instantly.

She turned to Louisa with a look of triumph, but before she could say anything an electricity pole on the far side of the meadow exploded with a retort so loud it momentarily silenced the birds.

They both stared as sparks tumbled down in a hissing arc.

In the distance Taylor heard people exclaiming, and, seconds later, the far-away whine of a fire engine siren.

'Huh,' Louisa said, reaching for her shoes. 'Maybe give it less juice next time.' Then she stood up and stretched. 'Is there any place around here to get coffee?'

♊

The sun was still high when the blue-haired girl walked into the train station to check departure times. The next train to Oxford was in ten minutes.

Good, she thought.

She glanced around, pretending not to notice the narrow glances and disapproving looks at her tattoos, her nose ring, her boots, as if she posed a personal threat to the community's affluence and general sense of contentment.

I need to get the hell out of here.

The guard checked her ticket with a thoroughness that seemed entirely unnecessary before letting her through the barricade.

Louisa resisted the urge to use her energy to give him a sudden outbreak of adult-onset acne.

She was too mature for such petty things, as Aldrich was forever telling her. She was twenty now, and needed to put her childhood rebelliousness behind her.

Easy for him to say. He'd never slept in a hostel bunk bed on a frozen night when the sound of cars outside was so loud you couldn't hear yourself breathe.

Wait until I tell Aldrich what Taylor did today, she thought, as she climbed the pedestrian bridge to platform three.

Excitement sang in her veins. The day had been exceptional. Taylor was unbelievably powerful and her strength seemed to double each time she saw her. She was the only one with more power than Louisa herself possessed. There was no doubt about her untapped potential. She'd never used her power and today she'd moved the *stream*.

She was going to be the most powerful alchemist of her generation. If she kept working with Louisa and Aldrich, they could be unstoppable . . .

A startling sensation, like pinpricks against her back, interrupted her thoughts in mid-flow. Louisa's heart stuttered.

Through sheer will, she kept the shock from her face, and her stride remained steady as she crossed the footbridge. But as she made her way down the stairs her eyes swept the sparse crowd searching for the source.

She found him standing on the opposite platform – a grey-haired man in a tweed suit. With his thin moustache and flat cap, he looked like someone's natty granddad.

But Louisa could sense his strength like a wave of ice, and she fought the urge to shiver.

A Dark practitioner? she thought uneasily. *Here?*

It couldn't be a coincidence. He had to be here because of Taylor.

Turning, she headed down the platform at a slow pace, glancing casually at posters and time tables as if they were hugely interesting.

Finally, she found a spot in the shadows behind a cluster of chattering teenagers. She leaned back against a pole and allowed her gaze to drift back towards him.

Her breath caught.

He was looking right at her. And his look told her he knew exactly who she was. And that she was afraid.

This time she couldn't seem to tear her gaze away. His eyes were depthless pools of hate and darkness and she was sinking in them. Her heart thumped so hard it hurt, and she could hear her own blood slowing in her veins.

The thing about her tattoos that she'd never mentioned to Taylor was that the symbols were all carefully designed. She'd worked with a very skilled alchemist to fashion them – each had powerful protective properties. Combined they acted as a shield – or ward – against Dark power.

Protect, she thought, pulling energy from the thick electric cables that ran through the tracks.

It was as if an invisible wall was raised between them. The cold sensation ceased. The sun's warmth enveloped her again.

Louisa's heart began to beat normally again.

She drew a shaky breath.

A train rumbled into the station. On the opposite platform, the man smiled at her, very faintly. With two fingers he tilted his cap in acknowledgement.

Then the train growled in between them, hiding him from view.

Louisa sagged back against the pillar, her hands squeezed into fists. She needed to talk to Aldrich. Right now.

Thirty-two

Sacha pushed open the new front door; it swung with
smooth silence.

The flat was hushed; empty.

He locked the door behind him.

Things had been quiet since the day the *creatures*, as he'd
come to call them, attacked Laura. They hadn't returned.

His mother believed there'd been a burglary attempt.

Sacha had convinced Laura that lying to her was the only
option. 'She'd never believe you if you told her the truth.'

Insurance had paid for the new door. It was better, they all
agreed, than the old one. It also had twice as many locks. It
felt more solid.

His steps echoed hollowly as he walked down the short
hallway to his room. His mother was still on day shifts and
Laura was at school. So there was no one to say goodbye to.

That was the way he wanted it.

He'd waited several days – time for the new door to be installed and tested. Time to meet with Antoine and give him enough cash to convince him to get out of town too, until things cooled off.

Now, with everything finished, it was time to go.

Annie was expecting him, and the longer he stayed here, the more likely it was those things would come back.

He hadn't been back to his aunt's house since his father died. The thought of going there now was bittersweet. He'd always loved her place. But it was intrinsically associated in his mind with his father. Everything would be different without him there. Besides, he was no longer a child. He wouldn't be climbing the trees in her orchard, or splashing in the lake.

He'd be trying to save his own life.

Moving with mechanical efficiency, he filled a small bag with clothes, throwing in his father's notebook and a map he'd printed of the route. He tucked a thick stack of cash into a zipped inner pocket.

There was only one thing left to do before he could leave. And it was the hardest.

Carefully, he chose a clean sheet of paper from the drawer of his desk. For a long moment he held a pen poised above the blank, white expanse. Then with slow, deliberation, he began to write.

Dear Maman and Laura

By the time you read this, I'll be gone. Don't try to find me, because I'm going away for your own protection. As

*long as I'm here, you're both in danger. If anything
happened to you because of me, I couldn't live with
myself.*

*I'll be in touch as often as I can. Please don't worry
about me.*

I love you.

Sacha

Blinking hard, he folded the letter and slipped it into a large
envelope. He stuffed all the remaining cash in with it, then
took the bulging package into the living room and left it on the
coffee table where his mother would be certain to find it.

He tried to convince himself the money would make everything better. But he knew it wasn't true.

When your family consists of just three people, the loss of
one is excruciating.

Nothing would make this better.

He could hear the rumble of traffic outside, the sound of a
dog barking nearby – the familiar sounds of a Paris morning.
But already he'd begun to feel distanced from this place.

As if he didn't live here anymore.

His jaw set, he grabbed the bag and his helmet.

In the doorway, he paused for one last look. He wanted to
remember everything just as it was, with summer sunshine
pouring through the windows. The living room was tidy again
now that his mother was back on days. The soft brown sofa
sagged in the middle as it always had. The sturdy kitchen
table where they'd argued and laughed together over so many
meals was empty now, and waiting for the next conversation.

He took a shaky breath.

What if I never see it again?

He couldn't bear that thought. He had to come back here. He had to live.

He swiped the back of his hand across his eyes. Then he closed the door.

♊

Getting out of Paris was the hardest part. The traffic was heavy, and the streets, once Sacha had left his own neighbourhood, were confusing. He took several wrong turns, and was forced to backtrack.

He kept his eyes on the motorcycle's side-mirrors, constantly checking that he wasn't being followed. But he never saw the same car twice.

Once he'd left the urban tangle behind him, the roads opened up and he began to feel safer.

The familiar, almost animal roar of the bike's engine comforted him. He opened the throttle and bent low over the handlebars. The machine was powerful beneath him. The wind blew past him with huge force, making his jacket snap and crackle. The city suburbs became a haze.

Once he hit the motorways, the route was straightforward. In two hours he found himself on the outskirts of the pretty town of Troyes.

For Sacha, who could remember exploring the town with his family as a child, seeing the tilted half-timbered buildings of the town's old centre was like stepping back in time.

Except it all looked so much smaller now.

He stopped for fuel at a petrol station on the outskirts of town.

At this time of year, the countryside was crowded with families escaping the cities. There were people all around him, kids running barefoot across the tarmac, parents shouting for them to *Arrête! (Stop!)* No one paid any attention to a teenage boy on a motorcycle.

It was a hot day and he was sweating beneath his helmet; he pushed damp strands of hair out of his eyes as he frowned at his map. The route grew more complicated from here.

He kept an eye on the roadway, but he saw nothing to indicate he'd been followed. He seemed to have made a clean getaway.

A few miles from the petrol station, he turned off the main road onto a narrow country lane, lined on both sides by thick forests. The road twisted and turned and the scenery gradually began to look more familiar.

Soon, purpling grapevines appeared, covering the rolling hills, dotted here and there with church towers, sharply pointed, like witch's hats.

He recognised the crossroads where he turned to reach Annie's house, but the road was rougher than he recalled, and he was forced to slow the bike to a crawl, navigating carefully to avoid treacherous potholes.

The narrow dirt lane, which ran between two sprawling vineyards, ended at a cluster of four stone houses.

Annie's was the furthest of the four, built so close to the vineyard it was almost part of it. Fat green grapes grew along the old stone wall and tumbled into her garden in heavy clusters.

Sacha pulled up in front of the house and switched off his engine.

The sudden silence was deafening. It took his ears a moment to adjust, but then he began to hear the breeze rustling through the vines, the jangle of a wind chime hung near the door, the complaints of crows.

He was just pulling off his helmet when the door swung open with a thud. A tall, thin woman stood on the porch, a tea towel forgotten in one hand. Her raven black hair was cropped short, and her eyes were a vivid blue.

At the sight of her much-loved face, Sacha felt instantly better.

'Hi, Aunt Annie.' He grinned at her. 'Mind if I drop in?'

'Sacha! You made it.' She rushed out to hug him. 'I can't believe you're really here. It's been too long.'

She spoke French with a faint English accent – like his father, she'd moved to France from the UK two decades earlier. Sacha found himself clinging to her slim shoulders. She smelled of lavender soap and fresh air, just as he remembered.

She leaned back to look at him again, smile lines crinkling around her eyes. The sun glinted off a few silver strands among the jet black of her hair. Those hadn't been there the last time he'd seen her.

'Look at you! You're all grown up. You look just like . . .' Her voice trailed off and she smiled again, but this time he saw a hint of sadness in her expression. 'Well, you must come in and tell me everything.'

Sacha's own smile dimmed. 'It's a long story.'

She patted his shoulder. 'I've got nothing but time.'

Inside, the old farmhouse was just as he remembered it – the large, sunny living room had the same worn leather chairs, over-filled bookcases, bouquets of herbs and dried flowers.

A black cat, curled up on the sofa, opened one golden eye to gaze at him.

'Nothing's changed,' Sacha said, pleased.

'Why should it change?' Annie pointed to the chair. 'You have a seat. I'll make some coffee. Then we can talk.'

When she opened the kitchen door, a little brown dog of no discernible breed dashed in and hurled itself against Sacha delightedly, its tongue lolling from its mouth.

'Pikachu!' he exclaimed, staring at the dog in disbelief. 'He's still alive?'

'He's not as fast as he used to be, but he's still here.' Annie stood in the kitchen doorway, watching the two of them affectionately.

Sacha knelt and hugged the dog close, burying his nose in the short, smooth hair behind its ears. 'Pika. I can't believe you're still here.'

The dog, which had found its way to Annie's door more than a decade before, had been his constant companion on his visits as a child.

Pikachu licked his face gently.

Minutes later, Anne bustled back in with a tray of coffee and fruit. Clearing his throat, Sacha let go of the dog and followed her to the sofa.

Evicting the cat from its spot, she settled down and handed Sacha a steaming mug, sliding a plate of sugary cookies and sliced peaches in his direction.

'Now,' she said. 'Tell me everything. But first, does your mother know you're here? I need to know what to tell her in case she phones.'

He shook his head, and wrapped his hands tightly around the warm mug.

'She can't know. If she knows I'm here she might come after me. I can't risk that. I want her and Laura to be safe.' He added, with a hint of bitterness: 'The safest place is as far away from me as possible.'

'I wish I could tell you that wasn't true.' The shallow lines on Annie's face deepened with worry. 'Have there been any more visits from those men?'

Sacha shook his head. 'Not since they knocked the door down. But I have a feeling they'll find me.' Setting the cup down on the coffee table, he rubbed the palms of his hands on his jean legs. Just talking about this made his hands sweat. 'I don't want to put you in danger, either, so I can't stay here long. We'll probably be safe for a few days but no more.'

'Don't you worry about that.' Annie's lips were set in a tight line. 'Stay as long as you need to. I'm tougher than I look.' Sacha opened his mouth to argue but she held up her hand. 'Just tell me more about them so I know what I'm up against.'

He told her what they looked like – the strange wide grins, the dark hair and cavernous eyes and the way they smelled of death.

'They can make you see things,' he said. 'Horrible things. And they make you give up. Somehow they make you quit fighting.'

307

'Your father thought something like this might happen around the time of your eighteenth birthday. Last night, I found some notes he made. He was afraid they'd send someone to find you, to assess you. He found records of that happening to previous boys.' She looked down at her cup. 'He'd always planned to run when that time came – with you. To get you as far away from them as he could.'

'Those . . . things,' Sacha said hesitantly. 'Are they the ones who killed him?'

A long moment passed before Annie replied.

'I don't know,' she said finally. 'But your father's death was no accident, I'm sure of that. He knew someone was after him. He was worried about it. That's why he sent all his papers home before that last trip. He wanted to be certain his work wasn't lost. He wrote me a note that came with the box. It said, if anything happened to him, I should save all his work. For you.'

Sacha's emotions swirled between pain and white hot rage. If those *things* killed his father, he would destroy them. He would find a way – even if it cost him his life, he'd do it.

But he had to be practical. They were strong. He needed to know more – about them, and about what his father knew.

'I've got a lot of work to do, then,' he said.

Setting down her coffee, Annie stood and motioned for him to follow. 'Come with me.'

Sacha followed her from the living room to the creaky wooden staircase. In the wide, shadowed hallway on the first floor, she opened a door.

She pulled a cord and a dim light switched on. Ahead, steep wooden steps led to the attic.

Under the high, tilted roof, a round window let in a circle of light, illuminating a large open space with a rough wooden floor. In the middle a polished mahogany desk stood in incongruous magnificence, surrounded by two matching bookcases, each stacked with books.

Sacha's feet felt rooted to the old oak floor beneath his feet.

It was his father's desk. His bookcases. His entire office.

Everything was arranged exactly the way it had been in their house in the countryside years ago.

'You saved it.' He breathed the words.

Annie stood by the desk, watching his reaction.

'I saved everything,' she said.

THIRTY-THREE

'**D**escribe them to me again.' Louisa set her coffee cup down with a thud. The liquid inside sloshed dangerously. 'The things that attacked Sacha – what did he say they looked like?'

They'd just finished another training session down by the stream during which Taylor had not destroyed any municipal utilities, and they were celebrating with cake and coffee at Caffeine Daze.

This was becoming routine for them. Louisa had been in Woodbury every day since that first visit. She told Taylor it was because she needed more training. Which was true, in part.

She was also there because of the Dark practitioner at the train station.

When Louisa had told Aldrich what happened, he'd sent her straight back along with a few others from St Wilfred's.

They were working in shifts now, watching Taylor's house day and night. Waiting.

She hadn't explained all of this to Taylor, though. Aldrich wanted to have that conversation himself.

'You can be a bit ... undiplomatic,' he'd said, diplomatically. 'This needs to be handled with great care. We need her to be aware. Not terrified.'

'Fine,' she'd replied. 'But she needs to know. This guy, whoever he is, he's pure power. And I'd lay money he's behind everything that's happening right now.' Remembering how helpless the man had made her feel – how afraid she'd been – she tightened her hands into fists at her sides. 'We've got to find him, Aldrich. Fast.'

'Leave that to me,' he'd said. 'You focus on keeping Taylor safe.'

And so she was here, day after day, watching the girl wrestle with her new abilities. One thing was clear – Taylor was pure power, too. The feats she performed effortlessly, Louisa would have worked for hours to learn when she was her age.

I mean, blowing the electricity transformer?

Louisa wasn't convinced she could do that now, even if she wanted to.

Taylor had done it by accident. Like knocking over a glass.

Yet she still had no control over her ability. It took her time to find the energy around her, to draw on it. She drew on her own energy instinctively.

This was normal – practice was everything. But she needed to learn faster.

Time was one luxury they did not have.

That said, nothing had happened – there'd been no further sign of the Dark practitioner since that day at the station. No indication of any threat at all.

The mood had been light until Taylor told her what she'd learned from Sacha when they'd chatted online the night before.

'He's left Paris,' she'd explained again. 'He's hiding in the countryside somewhere, with an aunt. He said these things came to his house and attacked his family. They have pale faces, like skulls. They move oddly. They made him see things – awful things . . . '

'What kind of awful things?'

'I don't know . . . Like, visions, hallucinations. He said . . . ' Taylor paused. 'He said they make you feel like you're going to die.'

Louisa's stomach curdled.

'And they said "Stay away from the girl"?'

Taylor nodded. 'They said other things, too. That they'd come to bring him somewhere. That it was a prophecy.'

Louisa slid down in her chair until her muscular legs jutted out into the aisle. She stared at the ceiling as if she'd find answers there.

She knew Aldrich didn't want her to scare Taylor but . . . Bloody hell. This was bad.

I'm going to need more coffee.

Taylor was watching her closely. 'You know what they are.' she guessed. 'You know what all of this means.'

Louisa sat up straight again. 'Bringers.'

'Bringers?' Taylor blinked. 'I don't . . . What are they?'

312

Monsters. Sickening monsters from our nightmares brought to life to destroy us.

But she didn't say that.

'Harbingers.'

'Harbingers of ... what, exactly?' Taylor watched her closely.

Oh you know. The usual: doom.

'It's hard to explain.' *Without scaring you to death.* 'They're not human. They're not even *real*, precisely. They're more like ... minions. Servants. Dark practitioners use them to get whatever they need. *Whoever* they need. They don't take no for an answer, these things. I've never seen one myself but they are legendary.' She let out a long breath. 'They're bad news, Blondie. Seriously bad news. Whoever this Dark practitioner is, he's working some major mojo if he's got Bringers.' She pushed a strand of vivid blue hair out of her eyes. 'But I guess we knew that already.'

'Do we have any idea who they're minioning for?' Taylor asked. 'What does he want?'

She wasn't stupid, this girl. Her clear, green eyes watched Louisa's every move with wary concern, reading her expression.

Aldrich might not want her to do this, but things had just become too dangerous. It was time to tell the truth.

'We think he wants Sacha,' Louisa said. 'We think he's the one who wants the curse to be fulfilled and the world to basically end. We think he believes, as we do, that somehow you can stop that from happening, and because of that ... '

'He wants to stop me.' Taylor finished the sentence for her.

'By any means necessary.'

'You mean he'd kill me.'

Louisa nodded. 'And I think he'd enjoy it.'

Actually, Aldrich really was right about her and diplomacy.

They stared at each other across the table in the sunny cafe. The faint jazz of a bossa nova song floated from the speakers above their heads.

'That about sums it up.' Louisa picked up her coffee. 'Tune in at ten for the latest headlines.'

Taylor's expression darkened. 'I don't know how you can be so . . . *whatever* about it. You'll die too, you know.'

'I'm not whatever,' Louisa snapped. 'I'm trying to look calm so you don't freak out. *Jesus.*' She glared. 'It is impossible to comfort you.'

'You're the worst comforter I think I've ever met.' Taylor picked up her cold hot chocolate and looked away.

'Thank you.' Grabbing her phone, Louisa typed a quick message to Alastair in the lab at St Wilfred's. When she'd finished, she tossed the phone back down on the table.

'What was that?' Taylor pointed at the phone.

'Just letting the guys at St Wilfred's know the Bringers are coming.' Imagining how Alastair would react when he saw her text, she added, 'They'll want to roll out a welcome mat.'

'But they aren't *here*, here.' Taylor tapped her finger on the table. 'They're in France. With Sacha.'

'For now.' Louisa shot her a look. '"Stay away from the girl," right?'

Taylor nodded.

'They're hunters, Taylor,' Louisa explained. 'It's what they do. They can find anyone. They'll find Sacha eventually, wherever he's hiding. And then they will find you.' Her phone buzzed and she picked it up, glancing at a message from Alastair:

```
BRINGERS?? HOLY SHIT YOU HAVE GOT TO BE
JOKING!!
```

She typed a quick response and set the phone down.

'So Alastair knows now,' she said pleasantly. 'He's not worried. But we're going to need reinforcements.'

'What kind of reinforcements?'

Louisa's smile had a dangerous glint. 'The St Wilfred's kind.'

'But what about Sacha?' Taylor leaned towards her. 'He's all alone out there.'

'Everything he's doing is right,' Louisa said. 'He needs to stay on the move, stay out of sight. Sounds like that's what he's doing.'

'Can't we do anything, though? To protect him?'

Taylor's tone was pleading, and she had a point. If the Bringers were after Sacha now, they could easily lose him. Then Taylor would never have a chance to save him.

Aldrich was going to need to come up with a plan, and fast.

'We'll figure something out,' she promised. 'It's just a bit . . . tricky. A lot of this stuff we didn't even think was real until recently. We've got five guys in the Bodleian Library right now, digging for whatever they can find. More are working on our own books.' She took a breath. 'We'll get there.'

It was nearly closing time, and the coffee shop was mostly empty. The staff had begun cleaning up behind the counter, putting things away for the day.

No one paid any attention to the two girls, who sat in a corner by the windows, talking quietly about demons.

'Grandfather seems so sure we can handle this,' Taylor said. 'That we'll save Sacha. I just ... wish I was that certain.'

Louisa frowned. 'Aldrich is the best in the world. If anybody can win this, he can. But I'm not going to lie to you; it's going to be dangerous. Really, really dangerous.'

Taylor swallowed hard. Could things get more dangerous than they were? More dangerous than Paris?

Louisa thought for a moment, absently tapping the side of her cup with the rough edge of a short fingernail. 'I'd like to move you out of Woodbury now and get you to St Wilfred's. But we need to keep you here as long as we can. As soon as we move you, whoever's behind all this will realise we're on to him. Then things could get messy.'

'Why would I be safe at St Wilfred's?' Taylor asked.

'Think about what we do,' Louisa said. 'We manipulate molecular energy, right?'

Taylor nodded.

'A bunch of us working together can create a smokescreen, of sorts. It would, effectively, make you invisible to an outsider.'

Taylor blinked.

Seeing her expression, Louisa shrugged. 'It's not that hard to do actually. I'll teach you.'

Her phone buzzed again. She picked it up and pushed a button. An image flashed into view. Grimacing, she glanced up at Taylor.

'I asked the guys to send me a picture of a Bringer,' she said. 'I want you to see what we're dealing with.'

She turned the phone around.

On the screen was a black and white illustration from a very old book. Taylor could see the yellowed paper and the way the ink had blurred with time, but the image was clear. It had a skeletal head, with empty black eyes. Its smile was horrible. Like a grinning skull.

The colour drained from her face.

'*That's* a Bringer?'

Louisa nodded. 'Ugly bastards, aren't they?'

Taylor leaned back in her seat. 'Bloody hell.'

Louisa beamed. 'Why Taylor Montclair, Miss Goody Two Shoes. Did you just actually swear out loud? In *public*?'

'Shut up, Louisa.'

Louisa laughed. 'I'll make a delinquent out of you yet.'

♊

After she left the coffee shop, Taylor ran all the way home.

Louisa had been as reassuring as she could be, promising her St Wilfred's would be watching her house, looking out for her.

But their conversation had left her unnerved. She kept seeing that drawing of a Bringer – its eyes as vacant as skull.

By the time she reached her own neighbourhood, it was almost seven o'clock. The streets were quiet. Everything seemed perfectly ordinary.

When she turned off the busy main street onto her road, though, she felt an odd sensation, like cold pinpricks down her back.

She'd felt it before, once, on this same street a few weeks ago.

It made the fine hairs on the back of her neck rise.

She was being watched, she was sure of it. She didn't know how she knew, but she knew.

She tried to convince herself it was all in her mind. The last time she'd had this feeling, nothing had happened. There'd just been Georgie, checking on her. But the feeling was so clear. So disturbing.

She tried to keep her steps steady, her back straight, her eyes ahead, but her skin began to crawl. She could *feel* the person watching her. And something worse. She could feel their loathing. A hatred so fierce it turned her stomach.

Finally she couldn't take it any longer.

She spun around, fists raised.

The long street stretched behind her, completely empty. A car rolled slowly by, the family inside didn't seem to notice her.

I'm getting paranoid, she told herself.

Still, she was so relieved when she reached her own house and locked the door behind her that she leaned her back against it, while she caught her breath.

Fizz appeared, winding around her ankles and uttering occasional hoarse yaps of happiness. Taylor scooped her up and held her close. She could feel the dog's small heart beating beneath her fingertips, a rapid flutter of joy.

Her own heart began to steady.

'Is anyone home, Fizz?' she asked.

The dog licked her nose in reply.

'Mum?' She called up the stairs. 'Emily?'

But her voice echoed back in the hollow hush.

'Where'd they go, Fizz?' she asked, dropping her bag.

Fizz skittered around as she walked into the empty living room, each question making her happier. Taylor sat on the chair by the front window, and moved the curtain so she could see the street. There was no one there except a dapper, grey-haired man in a flat cap.

She was still watching the man when the sudden violent buzz of her phone made her jump.

Dropping the curtain, she glanced at the screen. 'Hi Grand-father.'

'Hello, my dear,' Aldrich said. 'I've just had Louisa on the blower. I understand Sacha had a run-in with Bringers. Hideous creatures.'

Taylor didn't argue with that.

'Listen, Taylor,' he continued, 'the presence of Bringers changes things somewhat. I don't know what Louisa told you but no one alive has ever fought these creatures before – it's been a hundred years since anyone's seen one.' He cleared his throat. 'But if the books are right, they are unpleasant creatures.'

'Well,' Taylor said, 'they sure don't look very nice.'

'Their looks are the least of it,' Aldrich replied. 'They are toxic to our kind. Their very presence is poisonous. And there is no known way to kill them.'

'Oh.'

The news kept getting worse. Sacha was being pursued by monsters they couldn't even fight? How would she save him? How would anyone?

'Your house is being watched but I'd like you to come up to Oxford again on Saturday,' her grandfather continued. 'We can brief you on what we know. You can train with Louisa. You'll be safe here and we can decide what to do next. We may need to change our tactics.

'Things are much more dangerous for us all now.'

THIRTY-FOUR

That evening, at the desk in the attic, Sacha was deep into the complex task of scouring his father's papers for clues.

As with anything involving Adam Winters, it was not easy.

Looking through his files was like walking into the middle of a confusing film. There was one simply labelled 'Known Eighteenth Century Deaths'. Another called 'Acts of The Brotherhood'.

The contents of the files didn't bring much clarity, either. His notes tended to be cryptic.

'Remember page 930,' read one.

'Possibility of blood war???' read another.

After a while, Sacha gave up on the files and decided to look through the books instead.

Large mahogany bookcases were arrayed on either side of

the desk. He stood in front of one, running his fingers down the spines, looking for something that could help ground him in his father's research. Most of the books were very old. Some had leather bindings while others were bound between hard sheets of what might have been wood.

He pulled a book off the shelf at random. It appeared to be about eighteenth-century farming practices in France. The print was tiny; the lines very close together. It was six hundred pages long.

He put the book back on the shelf.

For hours, he pulled books off shelves, looking for notes, signs, *something* that stood out.

The books mostly focussed on the late 1600s but beyond that the information they contained seemed random. One book was filled with yellowing maps of southern France. Another held only transcriptions of court cases in the French city of Carcassonne. Many were academic books about witch trials. One appeared to be a very old travel book, with hand-drawn sketches of the French countryside.

There were almost no obvious elements connecting the books, and after three hours, Sacha had made only one note: 'Carcassonne'.

As the light outside faded and the round attic window changed its view from blue sky to stars, he fought the urge to panic. He had so little time left. Even if he avoided the creatures and spent all his time here, he couldn't read all these books before his eighteenth birthday. There were hundreds of them.

And yet, giving up was not an option. He had to keep looking. The answers were here.

Somewhere.

He pulled another book from the shelves. And started again.

♊

He must have fallen asleep while reading. When he woke, his cheek pressed hard into the wood of the desk, his neck stiff and aching, bright daylight streamed through the round window.

He sat up slowly, rubbing his neck. Downstairs, he could hear his aunt in the kitchen, and smell the sweet scent of baking bread.

He lumbered stiffly down to the bathroom where he made himself presentable before going to meet Annie in the kitchen.

Taking one look at his face, she shoved a cup of strong, sweet coffee in his hands before slicing him a thick piece of brioche, soft and warm from the oven.

She let him finish chewing, the bread melting in his mouth, before she asked the obvious question.

'Any luck?'

He shook his head glumly. 'There's so much to go through.'

She didn't seem surprised. 'I had the same problem. Your father never kept anything he didn't think was useful. Unfortunately, he didn't indicate why he thought things were worth keeping.'

She busied herself wiping down the already clean counter with a tea cloth. Sunlight poured through the wide kitchen windows, highlighting the sharp planes of her cheekbones and turning her eyes the colour of sapphires.

'I know you can do it,' she said, with quiet conviction. 'Just take your time.'

'The problem is there's no one place where he put everything together.' Sacha didn't try to disguise his frustration. 'It's all scattered – a few notes here, a few there – and it's so hard to understand.'

Taking the cup from his hand, Annie refilled it for him, half thick black coffee and half scalding hot milk.

'I loved my brother,' she said. 'But he was never organised.' She leaned back against the counter, eyes thoughtful. 'He had a huge brain. And he kept everything in there. That's the problem you're having now.' Folding the tea towel into a neat rectangle, she set it down next to the sink. 'Try to think like him. He would never go for the biggest book or the most obvious solution. Look for something small that seems unimportant. Start there, and see what you find.'

'I'll try,' Sacha promised.

But in his heart he wasn't sure there was enough of Adam Winters in him to do what he had to do.

♊

After breakfast, Annie headed out to work with her foreman in the vineyard. She took Pikachu with her, leaving Sacha alone with his father's books.

But when he sat down at the desk in the attic, he didn't start reading right away. Instead, he turned on his phone.

He was keeping it off most of the time – it could be traced. But once or twice a day he'd turn it on for a few minutes, just in case someone from home had been in touch.

Home ... it had only been a couple of days since he left, but it already felt like an eternity.

His phone buzzed like a living thing, then beeped loudly as if for emphasis. The shrill modern sound seemed out of place in the old farm house.

His mother and Laura had each left several text messages. He winced as he scrolled through them – he could sense the pain in their words. And their fear for him.

His signal was very weak at Annie's house, but he managed to text them both back.

'I'm fine and safe,' he wrote. 'Promise to be in touch again soon. *Bisous*. S.'

Taylor had sent one text. He read it last.

'The pale men that came to your house are called "Bringers". They are v. dangerous. They're hunters. They will find you. Let me know you're OK. Txx'

They will find you.

He flipped the phone over in his hand as anxiety churned in the pit of his stomach. If Taylor was right, he had even less time than he'd thought. He had to figure out what his father knew. Today.

His jaw set, he turned back to the shelves, and pulled off a book.

♊

He worked steadily as the hours ticked by, leaving the attic only for water or to grab a piece of Annie's bread and a hunk of cheese and bring it upstairs with him. Late in the afternoon, when she returned from the fields, she brought up a bowl of fresh, sweet strawberries, which he devoured as he worked.

'You're the talk of the town. My nephew back to visit after so long.' She patted him on the shoulder. 'Jean Claude next door has fallen in love with your bike.' She paused in the attic doorway. 'He says they're very expensive. How could your mother afford something like that on her salary?'

'Oh, I'm the one who bought it.' Sacha kept his voice casual. 'I had a job. And I got a really good deal on it, anyway.'

'Hmm.' A doubtful line appeared between Annie's eyes. But she let it go.

The food renewed his strength and his optimism but the books were in no hurry to reveal their secrets. By the time the sun began to sink in the sky, his father's desk was covered in stacks of papers, and his head had begun to pound. His neck still ached from sleeping at the desk the night before and he could feel his chances slipping away.

It was all beginning to seem hopeless. How could he figure out in a few hours what his father had spent years learning? Still, he kept going.

It was late that evening, when, having looked through dozens of thick, dusty books, he came across a slim volume. It was so small, so ordinary looking, he almost bypassed it. But something made him stop and pull it out.

The title engraved on the battered leather cover was hard to read and he peered at it for some time before figuring out what it said.

'*La Famille de L'hiver*'.

His heart skipped a beat.

L'hiver was his family's original French name. In English, it meant 'Winter'. They'd changed to the English name generations back after emigrating to England.

'Guess they got tired of everyone pronouncing it "Liver",' his father used to joke.

He carried the book over to the desk, shoving other books out of the way to make space for it.

Before he lifted the cover he closed his eyes for just a moment.

Please be something I can use, he prayed.

The book was fragile from age, and he opened it carefully.

The first pages appeared blank at first. It was only when he went to turn them that he realised they were folded inward, hiding their contents.

Carefully, he unfolded the brittle, yellowed paper, revealing a long and extensive hand-drawn family tree.

It went back centuries but appeared to be nothing more than an ordinary record of the family. Marriages, children and deaths were all duly noted and connected by straight lines drawn long ago and faded with time.

The book started in 1643. The spidery handwriting was hard to read in the earliest part of the chart, the ink faded. But the box at the top held one name: 'Matthieu L'hiver'.

In the early nineteenth the handwriting changed, becoming clearer, easier to read. The name also changed, as he'd expected. 'L'hiver' became 'Winters'.

At the base of the tree, in his father's familiar left-slanted handwriting he found the name 'Adam L. Winters'. Beneath that, neat lines led to his name and to Laura's.

As he studied it, he noticed odd marks in the margins by certain names. Leaning closer, he saw that the marks were really numbers. A 'one' very high up beside the name of Matthieu L'hiver's grandson, Jean-Pierre. Then a 'two' a row down next to another name. Then after a few rows, a 'three'. And so on. Each number was written next to the name of a first-born son in the direct line of Matthieu L'hiver. The last was at the bottom, next to Sacha's own name.

The number stared up at him. Unlucky as hell. *Thirteen.*

He looked at the list again, reading the names. Tracing them with his fingertips. Twelve dead boys. And soon he'd be one of them.

Unless he could figure out how to stop this.

He folded the family tree away and turned the page. It quickly became apparent the book was a written family history. The first few pages were mundane details of the L'hiver family in the late 1600s. Their prominent position in the community. The location of the family estate. Numbers of livestock. Numbers of servants.

Then, five pages in, something happened.

A paragraph signalled the change:

The Brotherhood was convened in the year of our Lord fourteen hundred and twenty-seven to protect France from the darkest evil. For two hundred and twenty-five years it worked tirelessly to keep the people safe. But in the year sixteen hundred and fifty-two, at the request of the Grand

Inquisitor and representatives of King Louis XIV, the Brotherhood was dissolved. They declared that evil had been vanquished. That the fires had burned too long. We know now the fires should never have stopped.

The elaborate handwriting and confusing language conspired to make it very difficult to understand, and at first Sacha thought he must be wrong. But as he went on, it became clear he wasn't.

The book told the tale of a family of vigilantes. His family. Each page told of new exploits. New occasions when they'd sought out alchemists (also described as 'wyches') and killed them.

They were systematic. Ruthless.

They called themselves 'The Brotherhood'.

It was clear they thought they were doing the right thing. They passionately believed the world was threatened, that these alchemists and healers were communing with demons. The church was on their side – a local priest blessed their murderous rampages.

But there was nothing holy about their work. They had killed many, many people. Page after page of them.

The hour grew late and Sacha read on, numb. Seeing his own family's name associated with page after page of unimaginable violence.

Murder after murder was detailed in sickening detail. Men, women, even children, tied to stakes and burned. Their ashes left to scatter in the wind. Even the person recording their exploits seemed to grow weary of it.

Our task is unending. Satan's armies refuse to yield. Our victories are hard won, yet still his legions rise. Each night we ride, to seek them out and engage in battle. It is decided that we shall leave Toulouse and ride to Carcassonne. The holy Fathers say that is where the devil makes his home, and with him converge unnatural Alchemistes and wyches, there to commit their foul deeds. We must strike the belly of the beast. We depart on the morrow.

The tales of destruction and death was hard to take after a while, but Sacha couldn't stop reading. He turned the pages faster, skimming the details. Hoping the litany of death would end. Because of that he almost missed it.

In the end it was the name that stopped him from turning the page – leaping out at him.

Montclair.

His heart racing, he backtracked, finding the beginning of the section and reading it more slowly. It was another burning. Another woman described as an 'alchemiste wyche'.

But this one was described in incredible detail, as if the person writing the book had not been told of what transpired, but had been present – had seen the woman die. Had perhaps even killed her.

Sacha read the pages twice through to make sure he wasn't missing anything. Finally, he stared up into the shadows. His chest felt hollow.

At last he understood how the curse came to pass. And why.

It was so fantastic, he wouldn't believe it if he hadn't experienced everything he'd been through. If he'd never seen the Bringers.

But he had seen them.

He knew what evil looked like.

Outside the round window the light began to fade. Night was coming.

Carcassonne 1693

'Isabelle Montclair. You have been convicted of witchcraft. The sentence is death by the flame.'

The man in the mask sat atop a pale horse, his dark coat snug against his shoulders. The feather on his hat shivered in the cool evening breeze. His accent was refined. His voice clear and triumphant. He'd hidden his face but the condemned woman recognised him none the less.

'Matthieu L'hiver.' Isabelle's voice was low. She'd been beaten, and her dark eyes peered out through bruised and swollen flesh. Contempt dripped from her words. 'At last you get your wish.'

She yanked at the ropes that bound her like a barnyard animal prepared for slaughter, but the restraints were well tied. She could not move. Power crackled within her but she was too weak to focus it on her enemies. She was defeated.

The full moon illuminated the scene with ghastly clarity. The tall stack of wood. The masked men arrayed around it, each holding a burning torch. The crowd of townspeople who watched with the quiet fascination of long experience.

There had been many burnings in Carcassonne.

From her position atop the pyre of stacked wood and brush,

the woman was higher than L'hiver on his horse, and she looked down on him, her lip curled in disgust.

L'hiver smiled. 'Before you die, do you wish to make your confession?'

'I have nothing to confess to a coward,' she hissed. 'We were tried in no court. You are not the law. The law forbids burnings. And still you send your filthy brethren to attack us in our homes. To kill our families. To enslave us.' She struggled futilely against the ropes, her face taut with rage. 'All because you are afraid of what you do not understand. You think you have won. But you are a fool, L'hiver. For you have won only grief. And despair.'

L'hiver's horse stamped nervously; he steadied it with one gloved hand against its neck, his eyes were fixed on Isabelle.

'So you do not deny your guilt. You are a student of the dark arts. The devil granted you unholy power. In return, you would raise a demon and give it dominion over God's land.' Through holes cut in the dark mask, he held the woman's eyes with a steely gaze. 'I will not allow that to happen. This ends tonight.'

Without waiting for her reply, L'hiver held up his hand. The torch-bearers stepped forward. Each wore a fabric mask exactly like his, disguising their features. With a sharp movement, he dropped his hand to his side.

The torches arced through the night, golden rainbows of death shooting down into the dry tinder beneath the woman's feet.

The flames caught instantly. The crowd murmured as the fire began to climb.

But she did not shift or stir, even as the flames began to bite at the hem of her torn skirt. As the smoke rose around her head, she did not cough or struggle.

Her stillness was disturbing, and the townspeople clustered together, whispering anxiously.

The burning agitated the horses who jerked at their bridles, eyes rolling. Somewhere overhead a bird, awakened by the violent night, cried out, though none could see it in the dark sky.

Then Isabelle's voice rose above all other sound, ringing out with the clarity of a church bell.

'Matthieu L'hiver: I curse you. I curse your family. I call upon Azazel and Lucifer, I call on Moloch and Beelzebub, I call upon all the demons in hell to hear my plea. Your sons, and the sons of your sons I curse. Thirteen times may your first-born sons be taken from you before they are men. Thirteen times, may their blood feed the demons and bring about all you have tried to destroy.'

The flames had begun to lap around her skirt and the choking wood smoke mingled horribly with the acrid stench of burning skin. And still Isabelle's voice was strong.

'In this way you shall fulfil the prophecy. You will finish my work through the sacrifice of your own blood.'

In the shadows, the townspeople crossed themselves and murmured hushed prayers. For, though they believed God to be more powerful than the Devil, they none the less feared this woman's words.

L'hiver didn't flinch. His head high, he held the woman's gaze for as long as they could see each other through the fire. Then the flames climbed above her head, hiding her from sight. And yet still she did not scream.

She burned in unnatural silence.

God protect us.

Thirty-five

It was late. The air in the attic seemed stale, suffocating; dead. The walls were too close. Sacha needed to get out. Stuffing the book into the pocket of his jacket, he crept down the wooden steps.

The living room was dark and silent. He fumbled across it, hands stretched out in front of him, feeling for obstructions. Somewhere along the way he barked his ankle on a low table and swore quietly. That woke Pikachu, who'd been curled up on the chair. His claws clattered on the wood floor as he hopped down and trotted over to see what was happening.

'Pardon, Pika,' Sacha whispered. 'I didn't mean to wake you.' He ran his hand across the dog's soft, warm head, scratching his ears.

He slipped out the back door onto the small terrace. The moon was full and high; its soft light illuminated the rippling vines, turning them into dark waves, rolling over the hillside.

Pikachu followed, his stumpy tail wagging, pleased with this unexpected nocturnal outing.

The cool night air smelled of rich soil and fragrant flowers as Sacha made his way down the stone steps to the garden and across the grass into the vines, his feet sinking in the soft earth. The moon cast everything in unearthly shades of blue.

The dog darted ahead, chasing moon shadows between the vines.

'This is good, isn't it, Pika?' Sacha's voice sounded too loud in the quiet night. He lowered it to a whisper. 'Like old times.'

They both knew he was lying. In the old times they were happy. And Sacha knew nothing of death.

Pulling his phone out of his pocket, he turned it on, waiting impatiently for it to find a signal.

He glanced at the clock. It was two in the morning in England. But he needed to talk to Taylor. She was the only one who would understand.

One ring.

Two rings.

Three.

He was losing hope when she answered. 'Sacha?'

Her soft, British voice was hoarse with sleep and worry. But she sounded so close – so alive – that for a moment Sacha didn't trust himself to speak.

'Where are you?' she asked. 'Are you OK? Did they find you?'

'Everything's fine,' he assured her. 'I just needed to make sure you were safe.'

He heard her sit up in bed. He could imagine her tousled curls, her cheeks flushed with sleep.

'I'm fine,' she said. 'What's happening there? Did you find something?'

He dug his heel into the dirt, unsure of where to start.

'I found a book about the history of my family. About the curse.' He hesitated, before telling her the rest. 'Deide was right. My family was cursed by a woman named Isabelle Montclair. My family murdered her. I found a passage in the book about it all. Taylor, it was so real. So detailed.' He exhaled audibly. 'It's like I was there. Watching her burn. Listening to her curse me. It was . . . intense.'

'I'm so sorry.' Taylor sounded miserable. 'It's so horrible. I wish it wasn't true. I hate that my family did this to yours. To you.'

'It's not your fault,' he reminded her. 'Besides, my family killed her. They brought this on themselves.'

'But you've suffered because of it all your life. I swear to God, Sacha.' Her voice was fierce. 'We will figure this out. We'll undo it. Lots of good people are working on this. I'm going to Oxford tomorrow to talk with them about things we can do to fix this. Please believe me: you're not alone. *We* are not alone.'

Sacha's heart twisted.

He wanted to believe it was possible. That he could live.

But he knew enough now to think it was unlikely, if not downright impossible, that they had enough time to find the solution his family had sought for centuries.

Time was slipping by so fast. The new day would start in a few hours, then it would be gone. Then the next. And soon there would be no time left at all. And his life would be over.

He longed to tell her every thought in his head. How scared he was. How tired he was of feeling death just at the end of his fingertips, waiting for its moment. How much he longed to be a living, breathing *boy*. Instead of a victim.

But he couldn't bring himself to say it.

Besides, she so wanted to believe her grandfather would save him. He didn't want to shatter that dream.

Still, there were some truths he could share with her.

He lowered himself into the dirt until he was sitting on soft soil, vines stretching above his head like dark curtains. Through the leaves he could see the sky. It held more stars than he'd thought possible.

Pika sat next to him, pressing his little body against Sacha's side, warm as a blanket.

'I'm so glad you're here,' Sacha said.

'Me too,' Taylor whispered.

'Could you just . . . I don't know. Talk to me for a while?' he said. 'I don't want to be alone.'

Her reply was instant and warm – like a hand reaching out to hold his.

'I'm not going anywhere.'

♊

Sacha woke with a start and looked around in confusion. He was sure he'd heard something – a shout. A crash. But now all was quiet.

He was surrounded by leaves and fat bunches of pale green grapes.

He sat up, blinking.

What the hell am I doing in the vineyard?

In a rush it came back to him.

He'd been talking to Taylor. He must have fallen asleep. Looking down, he saw his phone was still on the dirt beside him. Pika must have left at some point. He was alone.

He stood up slowly, muscles groaning from a night spent on damp soil.

A glance at his watch told him it was early – just before six. Outside, birds chattered and trilled a cacophonous chorus. Everything seemed normal.

He'd just decided it was a bad dream, when from the house Pika began to bark viciously, snarling and growling with fear or rage.

In all his life he'd never heard the dog make those sounds.

Sacha was already running when something shattered. A piercing scream split the air.

His heart hammering in his chest, he upped his speed, hurtling through the gate and up the steps to the terrace. He crashed through the front door into the living room.

'Annie?'

No one replied. The dog's frantic barking was coming from the kitchen.

He ran across the room, skidding to a stop just inside the kitchen door.

'Annie . . . ?' he began. Then his voice trailed off.

His aunt was cornered, her back pressed hard against the kitchen cabinet. In one hand, she clutched a butcher knife.

'Get *back*,' she shouted.

Broken glass covered the stone floor at her feet, sparkling with dangerous beauty in the sunlight.

Pikachu crouched among the shards, snarling and snapping, his lips curled up to reveal small, pointed teeth.

The back door hung loose on its hinges. Three Dark shapes stood inside it, their bodies shrouded in black.

A strange cold calm descended over Sacha. He'd been afraid of these things from the moment he first encountered them. But he was sick of them now.

Besides, nobody could kill him.

'Get away from her,' he ordered, his voice low and threatening. 'Now.'

The three turned toward him in a perfect coordinated movement.

'You cannot escape us,' the tall one said.

Ignoring that, Sacha turned to his aunt. 'Are you OK?'

She nodded, her face contorted with fear. 'Run, Sacha. Don't worry about me.'

But he had no intention of leaving her alone with those *things*.

Hands curled into fists at his sides, he turned back to the three.

'You have no right to be here. Get out of this house.'

Cocking his head to one side, in a curiously human movement, the tall one studied him. His dispassionate assessing gaze made Sacha's blood chill. He was the scariest one. Something about him conveyed authority.

'Enough. The time has come.' The thing's deep voice was

powerful – it seemed to exist inside Sacha's head, as if he spoke to him alone. The sound of it left him dazed; he felt dizzy, drugged.

His aunt gasped, and he looked up sharply. The three had advanced – now they surrounded him. Leaving her free. But she didn't run.

He wanted to tell her to run but he couldn't seem to form the words.

The musty scent of damp earth overwhelmed him, making him gag. He stumbled back too slowly.

Pika's barking grew hysterical.

'Leave us alone,' he said thickly.

But they had no intention of doing that.

The tall man moved with such impossible speed he seemed to blur. Before Sacha could react, his long fingers had grabbed his wrist, holding it in an iron grip.

'You must come with us.' The voice was sepulchral. 'It is time.'

The hand on his wrist was cold as death. The awful chill of it crept into his veins and climbed his arm, numbing him. Weakening him.

He looked at the hand in disbelief. He wanted to fight but couldn't seem to move.

Darkness crept into his vision. He felt himself beginning to crumple.

A scream jerked him back into the room. Annie threw herself at the shorter of the dark men, plunging her knife into his back.

The creature didn't even blink. Slowly his head swivelled

341

towards Annie, turning much further than should have been possible.

Annie's body began to convulse. She shook violently. Her throat made a gurgling sound. She clawed at her neck desperately, her face gradually turning red, then purple.

Sacha tried to call out to her, but the words wouldn't come. He couldn't move.

As he watched in horror, her body flew across the floor and slammed into the wall with an awful snapping sound.

Pika began to howl.

The thing turned towards him and lifted his hand.

'*Stop.*'

Sacha's voice was raw with pain and he shivered violently from whatever the Bringer had done to him. 'Leave them alone. I'll go with you. OK? Do you understand?'

The creatures pivoted to look at him, their black eyes blank and soulless.

'I'll go with you,' he said again, his teeth chattering. 'Voluntarily.'

Instantly, the sickening coldness seemed to relent.

'We go now.' The man holding his wrist turned towards the door.

But Sacha hung back. He was catching his breath. His brain had begun to work again.

'I need to take my bag with me.'

The thing stared at him, eyes as empty as a freshly dug grave.

'We go now,' he repeated.

'I will not go.' Sacha spoke through gritted teeth. 'Without my bag. I will not cooperate with your summoning. I will not be your *thirteenth*. Without. My. Bag. Do you understand?'

He wanted to punch them. To kick them and stab them. But he'd seen how they reacted to the sharpest knife in this kitchen. Across the room, Annie still hadn't moved. Fury and fear for her steadied him. Helped him focus.

For a long moment, the three studied him with identical expressions of incomprehension on their bony faces.

Then Pikachu shot across the room and sank his teeth into the tall one's ankle. All three pivoted to look at the dog.

Seizing the moment, Sacha wrenched his arm free and ran.

He hurtled across the living room, leaping over the coffee table, crashing through the front door. As he ran, he pulled the small, silver key from his pocket where it had been since he arrived.

He didn't dare look back.

His bag was on the motorcycle where he'd kept it since he arrived. His helmet dangled from the handlebar by the strap.

He'd always suspected he'd need to leave in a hurry.

He inserted the key. The bike roared into life.

Sacha gunned it.

The bike shuddered and wobbled violently on the rugged lane but he didn't slow down.

His heart ached for Annie and Pika. But he had to go. Otherwise everything would be lost. He had to get away from those things if he was ever going to figure out who they were. And how to destroy them.

Besides, the only thing he knew for certain was, if he ran,

they would follow him. And then Annie and Pika had a chance.

Still his hands gripped the handles so tightly his knuckles turned white, and it took everything in him not to turn back.

He was nearly to the end of the lane when an almighty *bang* exploded behind him.

In the side mirror, he saw the front door of Annie's house fly off its hinges and crash into the vineyard.

The three creatures glided out of the house and into the front yard. He saw them raise their hands toward him, heard a strange, dangerous humming sound in his head.

But then he turned the corner and accelerated. The bike responded like a living creature.

In seconds he'd left them far behind.

♊

Sacha drove without stopping until he reached a sizeable village. It was a picturesque place at the edge of a slow-moving river. Flowers spilled out of window boxes and flowed over fences. The houses were all made from a pale limestone that glowed in the early morning sunshine.

He barely noticed any of it.

Tears blurred his vision as he slowed and turned off the road into a car park overlooking the water. Wiping his eyes with the back of his hand, he pulled his phone from his pocket and called the police.

When an official voice answered, he gave Annie's address.

'Someone's broken in. Beaten her. I don't actually know what happened. She's lying on the floor in the kitchen. Unconscious. I saw three men in black coats. Please, hurry.

Bring an ambulance.' His voice broke and he struggled to keep it together. 'I don't know if she's alive.'

When they asked for his name, Sacha ended the call.

Swiping the back of his hand across his eyes, he switched his phone off.

He'd done all he could for now. Every part of him wanted to go back to his aunt but he knew he couldn't. The three would never let him help her. If he fled now, the things would pursue him. And then Annie might live.

He hated himself for putting her in danger in the first place. For foolishly believing he could escape those things, whatever they were.

Taking a shaky breath, he pressed his fists against his eyes so hard he saw bright flashes of light.

Annie, please, be OK.

Then he turned the bike back onto the road, and roared away.

Thirty-six

When the train pulled into the grey walls of Oxford station, Taylor was standing impatiently at the doors. She hopped off the second they opened, and dashed through the station.

There was so much to do. She was desperate to get started.

Everything seemed even more urgent after Sacha's phone call last night. She could sense how scared he was, though he never said it. Time was running out. She had to convince everybody to hurry. Whatever they were doing at St Wilfred's they needed to do it *faster*.

This journey was very different from her last trip to Oxford. This time she wended her way with practiced ease down the busy main streets, in such a hurry she barely glanced at the students rushing by on their way to exams, black robes fluttering around them like dark wings.

She half-ran down the narrow medieval lane leading to St

Wilfred's, and by the time she reached the red brick gate, which fairly glowed in the summer sun, she was breathing heavily.

The porter at the gate was different this time, short and fat, rather than angry and angular.

She didn't want to wait and she was sure her grandfather would have forgotten to put her name down again.

Making her face look as bored as possible, she hustled by him, raising her hand in a nonchalant wave as she'd seen the real students do when they walked through.

As she'd hoped, he raised his hand in automatic reply, and she bounded into the quadrangle, which looked straight out of a fairytale this morning, the sun capturing the copper and gold gild on the tops of the carved pikes and making them gleam.

But she'd only gone a few steps when a voice called after her. 'Hey! You there. Come back here.'

Turning, she found the porter running after her, his face red from exertion. He was waving a notebook.

Taylor's stomach tightened.

'Yes?' she asked, as haughtily as she could.

'I'm sorry miss,' he panted, 'but I don't recognise you. Have you made an appointment?'

'Yes,' she said. 'With Professor Montclair.'

'I am sorry, miss,' he said. 'I don't usually work here. I'm filling in, you see. The regular man didn't show up this morning.' Leaning forward he confided, 'It's all a bit chaotic, under the circumstances. Nobody seems to know what's going on.'

Taylor did not have time for this. But she hid her impatience.

'It's OK,' she said, forcing a smile. 'I'm happy to help.'

'I need to put your name in my book if you're an associate of the professor's,' he said, pulling a notebook out of his pocket. His movements were deliberate, unhurried.

Come on, come on! Taylor thought, drumming her fingers against her leg.

He flipped to the last page, and placed the stub of a pencil between his fingers, poised to write. Then he looked up at her.

She didn't wait for him to ask.

'I'm Taylor Montclair. The professor's granddaughter.'

His eyes widened. 'Of course you are. Of course.' He scrawled a few words in the notepad. 'Well, I'm sure he's expecting you, Miss Montclair. I'll take care of everything down here – you run right up. Would you like me to ring him to let him know you're on your way?'

Relieved, Taylor shook her head. 'No need. He knows I'm coming.'

Turning she began to hurry away.

The guard called after her. 'Now you be careful in this heat. They say it's going to be over 30 today.'

Taylor waved a hand to show she'd heard, but she didn't slow down, speeding around the cloistered walkway that edged the courtyard.

Students walked by her in pairs and groups, talking and laughing – none paid her any attention as she raced to the little door leading into the stairwell.

Inside, the temperature dropped instantly. The old walls were so thick even the hottest sunny day couldn't penetrate them.

She hurried up, her shoes tapping briskly on each stone step. At the landing, golden light poured through a narrow window in the wall, throwing blade-shaped shards of light.

When she reached the top, she knocked lightly on the door, then waited impatiently.

But seconds ticked by and no one came to the door. She heard nothing at all inside the flat.

Puzzled, she knocked again.

Again, there was no reply.

Her heart sank.

Where was he? She pulled her phone out and checked it – Louisa hadn't texted again. Maybe she was meant to meet them at the boathouse? But no one had said.

She leaned back against the door, preparing to write her a quick text.

The door swung open under her weight, nearly sending her toppling.

Startled, she grabbed the door frame to catch her balance.

She stared at the open door. It wasn't like her grandfather to leave the door open unlocked. He hated for anyone to visit him unannounced. He was obsessed with privacy.

Cold fingers of apprehension crept up her spine.

'Grandfather?'

There was no reply.

Tentatively, she pushed the door so it swung open further.

'Grandfather?' she called again, louder this time.

Her voice sank into the shadows. The flat was heavily silent. Not as if it were simply empty. But as if something had been removed from it.

The entrance hallway looked perfectly normal. A stack of books teetered perilously by the door. An umbrella stand was stocked with sturdy, black umbrellas with the St Wilfred crest in silver.

'Grandfather?' she said again. 'Are you here?'

Her voice echoed back at her mockingly.

With cautious steps she made her way down the narrow hallway.

The second she walked into the living room, she saw him. His body lay crumpled on the floor, face-down. As if it had been dropped from a great height. The little table, where she'd eaten cookies and rested her books, was crushed to kindling underneath him.

'Grandfather?' The word came out as a whisper.

Taylor tried to run to him but her feet seemed to be operated by someone else. Then somehow she was kneeling beside him. Reaching for his shoulders; rolling him over.

But there was nothing she could do. No one could help him now.

Her own scream seemed to come from far away.

THIRTY-SEVEN

'Drink this, miss.' Someone pressed a cardboard cup into Taylor's hands. She accepted it numbly.

The cup scalded her fingers. Steam curled up from the brown liquid.

All around her was frantic activity. The police had taped off the quadrangle as soon as they arrived. An ambulance rushed up only to leave a short time later, replaced by a police van with the word 'Forensics' painted on the side.

She was being kept in an administrative office, reached through one of the many doors on the quadrangle. The little room was nondescript – bare, scuffed walls, stacks of paper everywhere, a modern metal desk and plastic chairs.

People kept asking her if she was OK. She just shook her head. It all felt like it was happening to someone else.

She'd spoken briefly to the police when they arrived. After

that they'd taken her phone away and left her here, ordering her not to move. She'd been here ever since.

She didn't know how long. Hours.

Teams of investigators just kept arriving – she could see them through the open door.

Periodically she closed her eyes tightly, willing this to all be a dream. Then she opened them again and it wasn't.

The moments after she found the body were a blur. She'd run from the flat and pounded on every door at every landing. A man opened the third door, and stood there in a tweed jacket, staring at her in surprise as she sobbed, 'Help me, please. My grand ... Professor Montclair is hurt.'

While he ran upstairs with surprising nimbleness, she'd remained slumped outside his door, weeping.

When the man reappeared, his face was pale and set.

'Come with me,' he'd said, grimly.

Gripping her by the elbow, he'd marched her back down the stairs to his flat where he'd called the police.

From there a constant stream of people had spoken to her, but their words came from too far away to make sense.

'I think she's in shock,' she heard someone say.

'Oh, bloody hell,' the chubby porter murmured unhappily at one point. 'This would have to happen on the day I fill in.'

She heard herself ask for Louisa. Someone murmured that she was on her way.

But once the police arrived, no one else had been allowed to speak to her.

In her mind, she kept seeing her grandfather's face, bloodied and smashed. The awful image would not go away.

With a sob, she bent forward, resting her face on her knees. Her stomach churned a warning and she wondered if she would vomit again. She couldn't believe there was anything left to throw up.

A shadow fell over her, and she straightened slowly. A man stood in the doorway. The sun was so bright behind him that, at first Taylor couldn't make out his features. He was just a dark figure surrounded by a halo of blinding light.

'Miss Montclair?'

She nodded, wiping away the tears from her cheeks. 'Yes.'

'I'm DI Rogerson. I need to ask you a few questions.'

'OK.' Her voice was barely above a whisper.

He stepped inside. A woman in a police uniform walked in behind him and closed the door. As her eyes adjusted, Taylor was able to see them properly. DI Rogerson was about her father's age, with dark hair. He wore a navy suit that must have been hot in this weather but he wasn't sweating.

'This is PC Jones,' he said, gesturing at the female officer. 'She'll observe our interview.'

Taylor's gaze swung to the new figure. PC Jones had blonde hair, bound tightly and tucked under her police hat. Unlike the detective, she was perspiring.

The office was small and, with the three of them, it was at full occupancy.

PC Jones remained standing by the door while the detective navigated around an ill-placed column and a bin before lowering himself into the chair across from Taylor.

Biting her lip nervously, she watched as he pulled a device

out of his pocket and switched it on, holding it close to his mouth.

'DI Rogerson with PC Jones and ...' With his free hand, he pulled a notebook from his pocket and referred to it. '... Taylor Montclair, the witness. It is ...' He glanced at his watch, '... 13.33.'

He set the recorder on the desk next to them and raised his head, studying her with astute, distant eyes.

'Why don't you tell us in your own words what happened?'

Clutching the cardboard cup, Taylor told him all she knew. The stairs. The door. The body.

As she spoke, the detective watched her closely, scrawling occasional notes in the notepad resting on his knee.

'And why were you here today?' he asked. 'The porter says your name isn't on the list of expected guests.'

Taylor gave him the story she'd had plenty of time to prepare. It was as close to the truth as she dared to go.

'I visited my grandfather a week ago,' she said. 'He was working with me on a history project, and I'm planning to go to university here so he was helping me with that, too.'

A tear escaped from her eye, and she struck it away with the back of her hand, ignoring the tissue she clutched.

'He always forgot to put my name on the list. He ...' She faltered. '... forgot things.'

His pen scratched across the paper.

'Did you and your grandfather have some sort of an argument? The neighbours reported hearing loud voices.'

Taylor shook her head so hard her pony tail hit her cheek. 'I didn't get to ... to speak to him.' Her voice thickened and she paused to gather herself. 'He was ... like that when I found him.'

The scratching of the pen seemed loud in the hush of the office.

'Did you see anyone come out of the flat? Or pass anyone on the stairs?'

She shook her head. 'No one.'

He glanced up. His eyes were piercing. 'You're certain?'

'Yes.'

He made more notes, talking as he wrote. 'Did your grandfather have any enemies? Anyone who would want to hurt him?'

Taylor froze. She thought of the Bringers. She thought of the Dark practitioner. The sickening sensation of being watched.

So many enemies. So much danger.

Then she remembered Aldrich asking her if she'd called the police. *'Nothing about this in their books ... '*

He was right. He had no enemies of the kind she could mention to an Oxford homicide detective.

She shook her head. 'He was just a professor. A nice old man who loved teaching. Everyone loved him. I don't know who ... '

Her voice broke and she looked away.

The detective and the female police officer exchanged a glance. Heaving a sigh, Rogerson stood.

'I think that's all we need for now,' he said. 'PC Jones will take you to the station. I assume we have your contact details ... '

Taylor stood shakily and followed the two towards the door. Rogerson got her phone back from one of the officers outside and handed it to her. She slipped it into her bag without looking at it.

They walked her to the front gate at a brisk pace. PC Jones' utility belt jangled heavily with every step. Rogerson's hands were shoved deep into his pockets.

The quadrangle was littered with police equipment. As the porter had predicted what seemed like a thousand years ago, it was brutally hot.

When they reached the elaborate Tudor gate, the flags atop the towers hung limp in the heat. Striped yellow and black crime tape had been strung across the main entrance. Outside, dozens of police cars were parked in an unruly cluster. A crowd of curious onlookers gathered nearby, speculating in hushed voices.

DI Rogerson held up the tape for Taylor and the female officer to pass. He stayed on inside.

Numb, Taylor began to follow PC Jones to her car, but she'd only gone a few steps when Rogerson called her name. He motioned for her to return.

When she'd made her way back to the crime tape, he reached across to hand her a card.

'This has my number on it – call if you think of anything that could help us find whoever did this.'

As she tucked the card into her pocket, he she was conscious of his piercing gaze, searching for any indication that she might be capable of murder. But when he spoke, his voice betrayed only the professional compassion of an experienced police officer.

'I'm sorry for your loss.'

♊

PC Jones spoke very little on the short ride to the station. It was early afternoon and traffic was heavy, but she manoeuvred her way through the city with ease.

Outside the grey station, she pulled the police car to the curb.

'This is your stop,' she said briskly.

Taylor felt dazed. Was she really just going to go home now? What was she going to tell her mother?

And where the hell is Louisa?

When she didn't move, the officer misunderstood her hesitation. Her stern expression softened.

'Look,' she said, 'what you saw today can be very hard to deal with. Can I offer you some advice?'

Taylor nodded, wiping away a tear.

'Join a victims' support group. Talking to other people who've gone through something like this can help. Your local police can find one near you.'

Like they could help, Taylor thought bitterly.

'And call us if you think of anything at all,' the woman continued. 'We want to find the people who did this to your grandfather just as much as you do.'

Suddenly Taylor didn't want to be here anymore. She believed the police officers wanted to help but she didn't for a moment think there was anything they could do to keep her, or any member of her family, safe. And now that she thought of it, if someone had killed her grandfather, why not her mother next? Or Emily?

Fear sent a shard of ice into her chest.

She had to get home.

Scrabbling for the seatbelt, she pulled it open with almost painful force.

She climbed out of the car so quickly she only vaguely heard PC Jones tell her she was sorry for her loss before the door slammed shut and she was running into the station, tears streaming down her cheeks.

Sorry for your loss.

What did that even mean? It wasn't like she'd *misplaced* her grandfather. Someone had smashed his face to bits until all that was left was blood and fragments of bone.

Nothing had been lost. Something had been stolen.

Something precious.

Taylor saw the train timetables through a watercolour blur of tears.

Pushing her ticket through the machine, she passed through the barricade onto the platform and ran down to the end, far away from other people.

Then she pulled her phone out of her pocket and pushed a button.

Somewhere far away, a phone rang and rang. Finally Sacha's recorded voice gave a terse message in French. A beep jarred her.

Taylor wanted to stay calm and tell him what had happened rationally and intelligently. She didn't want to frighten him. But the sound of his voice seemed to trigger all the emotions she'd kept bottled up since she'd first stepped into that cool, shady flat this morning.

She began to weep in great heaving sobs.

'He's dead, Sacha,' she heard herself say. 'My grandfather's

dead. Something killed him. Something awful. And he was ...
And I ... I have to go home but I think it can find me there,
whatever it ... it is. I don't know what to do. What if it comes
for me? What if it comes for my *mum*? I can't ... I have to ...
to leave. But, where am I going to go?'

Despair overwhelmed her and she sagged forward, resting
her forehead against a dusty support column. The iron was
cold against her skin. Her lungs hurt from sobbing but she
couldn't seem to stop.

'Oh God, Sacha,' she whispered, 'I'm so scared.'

♊

After his brief stop to phone the police, Sacha didn't stop
again for hours. He drove at full speed down narrow country
roads shaded by tall trees, through peaceful villages where the
beauty was lost on him. When he reached the motorway, he
turned south. He had no destination, no goal except to get as
far away as he could from everyone he loved. And to bring
those creatures with him.

In the end, the only thing that could stop him was the
simple reality that his motorcycle's fuel gauge was pointing
firmly at empty.

Even so, when he rolled into the petrol station, he made a
careful perusal of the grounds before stopping – as if the
Bringers might leap out from behind the tired-looking hedge,
or step out of the nearby convenience store.

He had little idea where he was. He'd quit looking at
the signs long ago.

When he climbed off the bike after all that time staring

at the gray ribbon of the road, his legs trembled. He held onto the handlebars until he felt steadier.

He didn't know if Annie was alive or dead. He didn't dare call anyone to find out. He just had to hope. To pray.

The guilt was overwhelming.

Everything he touched was destroyed.

He knew he had to make decisions about where to go, and what to do, but he couldn't do that right now. He kept seeing the moment Annie's body flew. Hearing Pikachu howl.

The tears he'd fought to hold back stung his eyes. He dashed them away. He didn't have time to grieve.

With mechanical movements, he filled the engine, checked the oil and water.

Inside the station, he said the right things to the person on the till, paid for the fuel and bought a bottle of water, cold from the refrigerator. It had been a long time since he'd last eaten but the very thought of food turned his stomach.

He wheeled the bike into the shade of a tree nearby. He knew he needed a break to think this through. He had to stay sharp.

Taking his phone from his pocket he stared at it for a long moment before switching it on. It dinged four times, letting him know he had voicemail messages. He sat on a nearby bench and, with his eyes closed, listened to all of them.

The first few messages were from his mother, begging him to return home, or at least to call.

The fifth message was odd. At first there he could hear only uneven breathing. In the background a mechanical English voice made announcements he couldn't quite understand.

Then he heard a sob.

It was Taylor.

He was on his feet as she began to speak. By the time she finished he was on his bike.

His lips set in a tight line, he shoved the phone back into his pocket. He pulled on his helmet and started the engine.

Then he turned the bike around.

Now, at last, he knew where he had to go. What he had to do.

THIRTY-EIGHT

The journey home from Oxford seemed endless. As the train rolled across the countryside, Taylor called her mother's mobile and the house phone over and over, getting voicemail each time.

By the time she finally arrived at the station, she felt sick with anxiety.

Leaping out of the train before the doors were fully open, she sped down the platform, ignoring the irritated looks from the other passengers she shoved past.

She had to get home and make sure her family was safe.

It was Saturday and the streets were packed with shoppers. She ran through the crowds, barely even noticing them, until someone grabbed her arm, pulling her back.

She looked around wildly.

'Taylor?' Georgie's dark brown eyes were filled with concern. 'What's going on?'

Seeing her face, Taylor felt her soul break just a little more.

Why aren't we still friends?

She longed to tell her everything, but she couldn't.

'I can't talk right now.' Taylor tried to pull her arm free. But Georgie's grip was determined.

'Tell me,' Georgie insisted. 'Something wrong, I can see it.'

'I ...' Taylor's voice trailed off because, what could she say?

'Monsters killed my grandfather and I'm afraid they might get my mum.'

She couldn't tell anyone what was going on.

Georgie wouldn't let go. 'Taylor, come on. You're scaring me.'

Suddenly tears were streaming down Taylor's face.

'Oh George,' she whispered. 'It's awful.'

The worried look on Georgie's face deepened. She pulled Taylor into her arms, and quickly walked her away from the busy high street.

When they'd turned off onto a quiet lane she stopped and turned Taylor to face her. She smoothed her hair out of her face so she could see her eyes.

'Now. What happened?'

'My ... my g-grandfather died today.' Taylor decided she could share that much. But saying the words made her feel worse. Like making a still-fresh wound bleed again. 'I was the one who ... found him.'

'Oh no,' Georgie whispered. 'I'm so sorry, Tay. That's horrible. No wonder you're upset.'

One arm around her shoulders, Georgie guided her down the pavement. 'Come on. Let's get you home.'

Taylor knew she shouldn't let Georgie go all the way to the house with her. It wasn't safe. But she let her anyway.

For a while they walked in silence. Then, Georgie shot her a contrite sideways glance.

'Look, I know it's not the right time. But I just want to tell you I'm sorry again about saying those things to Paul. I was stupid. And you were right to be angry. I was just excited about being with him and it made me act like an idiot. You're more important to me than any boy. And you always will be.'

Taylor's arm tightened around her friend's waist. She'd been longing to forgive her. There were more important things in the world than Tom and Paul. More dangerous things.

'It's OK,' she said. 'I think I'm over it.'

She could see the relief on Georgie's face.

'You know what's weird?' Georgie said, glancing at her. 'Tom has been so strange since you broke up. Like, he won't talk about you at all. I tried to find out what happened that day, and he says he doesn't remember anything about it. Like he sort of . . . I don't know. Forgot it. I don't believe him, of course. But isn't that crazy?'

Taylor thought of Mr Finlay's soft, whispered words as he guided Tom out of the gym and repressed a shudder.

'I'm just glad he's not in my life anymore.'

'Are you still talking to that French guy . . . What was his name?' Georgie wrinkled her nose as she thought. 'Sacha?'

This time Taylor did meet her gaze. 'Yes I am,' she said firmly. 'We're friends.'

As they neared her own house, her eyes swept the brick building, looking for any signs of danger. But nothing seemed amiss. The glossy blue door closed tight. All the windows glittering in the afternoon sun.

Still, when she pulled her keys from her shoulder bag her fingers shook, making the keys clatter as she fumbled with the lock.

Georgie was right beside her when she walked in. She knew she should tell her to go home. That she'd be fine now.

But she didn't want her to go. She didn't want to be alone.

Inside, the house was cool and quiet.

'Mum?' she called. 'Are you here?'

The heavy silence was an eerie twin of her grandfather's flat that morning. Her heart rose to her throat.

'Emily?' Her voice sounded weaker this time.

There was no reply.

'Doesn't Emily have dance class on Saturdays?' Georgie leaned against the doorframe. 'Like, always?'

'I'm just going to check,' she said, glancing up at Georgie. 'Stay here.'

She rushed back down the hallway, checking every room before hurtling up the stairs. Her mother's bedroom was empty, the bed neatly made, and Emily's door stood open, so she could see the lemony walls and rumpled bed.

The house was empty. Fizz was gone, too, so her mother must have taken him with her. That wasn't unusual.

So why was she still so anxious?

An awful sense of impending doom seemed to settle on her like a blanket. Something was horribly wrong.

'I'm making tea.' Georgie's voice came from the kitchen. Taylor heard the burble of water pouring into the kettle. 'I don't think I've ever seen anyone who needed tea more than us, right now. And I don't even *like* tea.'

Georgie chattered away but Taylor wasn't listening. Because suddenly she felt like she was going to be sick. Her heart pounded in her ears. It was too loud.

She clutched the banister and wondered if she was having a heart attack.

The last thing she heard Georgie say was, 'Where does your mum hide the good biscuits . . . ?'

Then the door blew off its hinges.

Thirty-nine

The three men standing in the doorway all wore long black coats. Their skin was pale as ice. They had eyes the colour of death.

They were smiling.

Taylor stood frozen on the stairs, pinioned in their collective gaze.

'What the hell was that?' Georgie appeared in the hallway from the kitchen.

The Bringers all cocked their heads at once. The smooth inhuman coordination of their actions made Taylor's blood run cold.

Georgie's voice spurred her to action. She leaped down the last remaining steps to place herself between the Bringers and her friend.

Keeping her eyes on the smiling men she called over her

shoulder. 'Georgie, go to the kitchen and close the door.'

'What? Why?' Georgie was still coming, she was within view. 'What was that noise?'

Why would she never *listen*?

Turning towards her, Taylor drew power from wherever she could.

'Go to the kitchen.' This time her voice didn't sound like her own. It was a command.

Meekly, Georgie did as she was told.

Taylor's head began to pound. She'd drawn on her own power.

Stupid, she thought.

She turned back to find the Bringers standing right in front of her.

How had they moved without her hearing them?

Stifling a scream, she scrambled back, but they followed, with disturbing smoothness – their steps almost like floating.

They looked human in every way, but they were painfully thin. And there was a smell to them – a stench of wet earth and decay so overpowering she couldn't breathe.

She thought of what her grandfather had told her. *They are toxic to our kind.*

Taylor could feel herself beginning to panic, her breath came in short gasps.

'What do you want?' She tried to sound powerful, but her voice was thin and reedy.

The tall one held up a hand. His fingers were unnaturally long, the sight of them made Taylor's skin crawl. She began to hear a strange, low humming sound, like a million insects swarming.

The pounding in her head grew louder. It was hard to think. To focus.

'Get out of my house.' But it was only a whisper. No one would be afraid of that.

Then she heard the voice. 'Thirteenth daughter.'

The tall one at the back held her gaze. His eyes were black holes of hate.

'You would interfere with the summoning. This is forbidden.'

The humming noise grew more intense. She thought she could make out words in the sound now, words in a language she'd never heard. Awful, horrible words.

Suddenly her left arm swung outward, as if someone else had lifted it. Taylor tried to lower it but it wouldn't respond. As she watched in horror, a slash appeared on her forearm, dripping blood on the floor.

It's not real, she told herself. *It's an illusion.*

But the pain was real – her arm burned like fire.

Panic had its claws in her in earnest now. Her heart fluttered in her chest.

Then her right arm flung out, and another burning slash appeared.

Blood poured from the cuts, pooling at her feet.

She could feel the blood, warm and wet. Hear it dripping to the floor.

This was no illusion.

Taylor tried to scream.

The three dark men stood directly in front of her now, each

holding up one hand so the palm faced her. She stared at them in confused pain, seeing them only as dark shadows looming over her.

The hallway around her started to sway; she was losing consciousness.

She wasn't going to make it through this. Everyone had been wrong about her.

I'm sorry Sacha.

'All right, gentlemen. That's quite enough fun for one day.'

The voice sounded familiar. Fearless. And very pissed off.

The three men turned in unison.

Louisa stood in the doorway behind them, blue hair shining like an azure halo. Her face was puffy, as if she'd been crying. But she didn't look sad now. Right now she looked furious.

Relief flooded into Taylor's veins like a drug, followed instantly by fear for her. These things were too strong.

They'd kill her.

'Louisa, *don't*,' she heard herself whisper

But the other girl didn't even look at her. Her eyes steady on the Bringers, she made a come hither gesture with her fingertips.

'Come on, kittens. Right this way.'

Taylor wanted to help her, but she was dying. Wasn't she? She could still feel the blood trickling down her hands.

Gathering her strength, she forced her gaze down to her bloodied wrists.

Only now there were no slashes. No blood pooled at her feet.

Wonderingly, she turned her arms over, back and forth – they were smooth. Perfect.

Taylor became aware that the chanting had changed, taking on a querulous note. Looking up, she saw the Bringers closing in on Louisa.

If killing Taylor had been their job, it was clear that killing Louisa was going to be a pleasure.

Still the other girl's face showed no fear.

'That's right boys.' Her voice was low and ominous. 'It's me. Let's see how you like it when they fight back.' Louisa held up one hand. A strange, geometric symbol had been tattooed on her palm. It looked like a triangle with an eye inside it. It was so new it was still red and angry around the edges.

Taylor felt the concussive heatwave of Louisa's power as she flung it at the Bringers.

They recoiled as one, voices rising in protest. Then the tall one straightened and made a sharp movement. A jagged piece of wood flew at Louisa's head like an arrow.

Taylor gasped, but Louisa swatted it away with a bored flick of her fingers.

'Is that all you've got?' The ridicule in her voice was cutting. 'That's pathetic, gentlemen. I expected more. You've got a reputation, you know.'

But she was gritting her teeth, and Taylor could tell she was using all of her strength to hold them back.

As if she'd heard her thoughts, Louisa's eyes darted towards her. 'A little help here?'

Her words were like a splash of cold water.

What am I doing? Taylor thought, horrified. She was leaving Louisa to fight alone.

She moved towards the fight. Her head and hands felt heavy, as if someone had drugged her, but the more she moved the stronger she felt.

The Bringers stood between her and the other girl. She'd have to shove past them but some instinct told her not to touch them.

She shot Louisa a desperate look. The other girl shifted her eyes, very briefly, to the wall behind the Bringers. Perspiration gleamed on her forehead now, and her face was red from exertion. She was fading.

At first Taylor wasn't sure what she meant, but then she got it.

Two silent steps to the wall. She braced herself against it. Then, closing her eyes, she sought the power around her.

It was everywhere. Golden strands of energy. The presence of it was dizzying. She felt as if it wanted her to use it. It all leaned towards her enticingly.

Among the gold, though, she saw three scars of oozing black.

The Bringers.

Their Dark energy was like toxic waste among the silken, shimmering gold.

There was no time to waste. Grabbing the first strands of energy she could find, Taylor flung up her arm and focused everything she had on the Bringers.

Out.

Instantly, the three pivoted towards her.

Startled, Taylor pressed her back harder against the wall and grabbed for more energy.

'Ouch,' Louisa commented tartly. 'I'll bet that stung.'

Two swung back towards her, while the tallest kept his focus on Taylor.

They were dividing them. Weakening them.

Taylor pulled energy from anywhere she could grab it, heedless of its source. Her hair flew around her face in a cloud. She could feel the power crackling around her. It was so tangible she could smell its scorched scent; like the aftermath of a fireworks show. Or an electrical storm.

She could sense the creatures' confusion. The chanting was rougher now. Uneven. They hadn't counted on this interference. Louisa noticed it, too. She took a step towards them.

'We will put you,' she said coldly, 'into the ground. Why don't you sod off and save us the trouble?'

Unfortunately, this seemed to infuriate them. For a moment, the noise intensified. Then one of the men raised his hand so the palm faced up.

Louisa followed the gesture with her eyes. 'Oh bollocks.'

Two things happened at once. Taylor heard a deafening *crack*, and Louisa threw herself at her so hard they both tumbled into the living room, landing in a heap on the floor as something crashed to the ground where they'd stood seconds before.

The force of the fall knocked Taylor's breath from her lungs. Wheezing, she struggled to sit up and see what had happened. The air was white with dust. The hallway floor was buried in rubble.

Half the ceiling lay where they'd just been standing.

She craned her neck to try to see the Bringers.

'Don't bother.' Louisa had landed by the sofa, where she was calmly brushing dust from her tattoos. 'They're gone.' She wrinkled her nose. 'God, they *stink*.'

Taylor scrambled onto her knees to look, but Louisa was right. The doorway was empty. Outside there was only blue sky and a quiet suburban street.

Slowly her heartbeat began to return to normal. She turned back to Louisa. 'Are you OK?'

Louisa met her gaze; her eyes were filled with pain.

'No.' Her voice was choked. 'I'll never be OK again.'

She wasn't talking about the Bringers any more.

Taylor took a step towards her. 'I asked them to call you.'

Louisa shook her head. 'As soon as I heard I wanted to be there but . . . the police were there.' Taylor had never seen her look so helpless. 'I couldn't have them check my background. I'm sorry you were left alone with that. I didn't have any choice. It was just so . . . messed up. So messed up.'

She pressed the back of her hand against her eyes.

Taylor swallowed hard. The horror of that morning would be fixed in her memory forever. A place she could go to when she needed to remember what grief and fear felt like.

'Taylor?' The tiny voice came from the kitchen.

Instantly alert, Louisa stared down the hall. 'Who the hell is that?'

'Oh balls. I forgot about Georgie.'

Picking her way through the rubble in the corridor, Taylor ran to the kitchen and threw open the door. Georgie stood inside, her brown eyes huge.

'I can't seem to get out of this room for some reason,' she said, her voice timid and apologetic. 'It's so odd.'

'What did you do to her?' Louisa had followed Taylor and now stood in the hallway behind her, peering over her shoulder at Georgie as if she was a lab rat.

'I don't know,' Taylor confessed. 'I just needed to keep her away from those *things*. How do I undo it?'

They were both talking about Georgie as if she wasn't right there. Her eyes darted back and forth between them anxiously.

'Tell her it's OK,' Louisa said. 'At this point she's mostly scared.'

'Georgie,' Taylor used her most soothing voice, 'you really can come out now.'

Slowly, Georgie stepped out into the destruction in the hallway. 'Oh my God. What happened?'

'Gas explosion,' Louisa didn't hesitate. 'Luckily it was a minor one. Otherwise, someone could have been hurt. You should probably go now.'

Georgie blinked. 'Who are you?'

'I'm from the gas company,' Louisa said unbelievably. Placing a hand on Georgie's shoulder, she spoke to her quietly. 'You need to go home. Taylor is fine. It was a minor accident. Nothing much really happened anyway.'

Georgie turned to Taylor. 'I have to go. I'm glad it wasn't serious.'

Taylor's shoulders slumped. She knew it was necessary but she hated to have anyone mess with Georgie's mind.

'Yeah,' she said, unable to keep a melancholy note from her voice. 'Me, too.'

Georgie's expressive brown eyes were hazed with sympathy.

'I'm so sorry about your grandfather. Are you sure you're really fine?'

'I'm really fine,' Taylor lied.

Georgie picked her way through the rubble. When she made it to the other side, she looked back at her through the dust.

'Your mum is going to freak.'

Taylor's lips curved into a bittersweet smile. 'Tell me about it.'

FORTY

'Practical things first.' Louisa started talking as soon as Georgie was gone. 'You need to call your mother and tell her there was an accident. Say you came home from Oxford and found it like this.'

Standing ankle-deep in plaster, Taylor shook her head emphatically. 'No, Louisa. She can't come back here. It isn't safe. She and Emily have to go somewhere else. Oh my God.' She pressed her fingertips against her forehead. 'How am I going to tell her about Grandfather? What am I even going to *say*?'

Too much had happened. Too much horror. She felt dizzy with it all. Sickened by it.

I'm not ready for this. I'm just seventeen.

'Good point.' Louisa stopped to think.

They stood staring at each other, surrounded by the ruins

of Taylor's front hallway. In the sudden quiet, a final piece of plaster fell to the floor with a soft thud.

Beyond despair, Taylor looked at the wreckage around her. Plaster dust covered everything. Bits of the ceiling had fallen into the living room and onto the stairs. The front door was gone.

Hi Mum. Grandpa's murdered and monsters just trashed the house. What's for dinner?

Luckily Louisa was keeping it together. 'Ok,' she said after a second. 'Here's what you do. You have to tell her the truth about Aldrich. The police will tell her anyway. But lie about this.' She pointed at the rubble.

Taylor shook her head, 'What about those *things*, though? The Bringers. What if they come back when Mum and Emily are here? How will I even . . . '

'They won't come back tonight.' Louisa sounded confident. 'I'll stay nearby and they won't want to take the two of us on again. But I think we have to get you out of here. Soon.' She pulled out her phone. 'Let me work on that. You call your mother.'

Taylor climbed through the wreckage, stepping carefully over the light fixture that had hung from the ceiling for as long as she could remember. Her bag was still where she'd dropped it by the front door.

Shaking the plaster dust off the leather, she pulled out her phone and scrolled to her mother's number. Her hands were unsteady.

'Remember,' Louisa called after her. 'You came home and found it like this.'

Voicemail. Her mother's familiar voice.

A hot rush of tears filled Taylor's eyes.

Beep.

'Mum, something's happened. Something ... bad.' Her voice broke.

She just wanted her mother here. Now. But she couldn't seem to find the words.

'It's Grandfather. And I think someone tried to break in here. The house is ... Everything is ... You just ... You just have to come home. Please. I don't know what to do.'

When she hung up, she stood still, taking in the ruins of her home. After a second, though, she straightened and dried her eyes. There was no time for tears.

Louisa's voice floated down the corridor from the kitchen. She was talking to someone on her phone.

'We'll need three or four of them,' she was saying. 'Right away, Finlay. This situation is not under control.'

The shattered plaster crunched under Taylor's feet as she walked, sending up tiny clouds of pale dust. She found Louisa sitting at the table with a cup in front of her. She put down her phone when Taylor walked in.

'Your friend made tea,' she said, sliding a cup in her direction. 'Which was helpful of her.' For a moment, Taylor stood in the doorway. Every muscle in her body ached. It was like everything that had happened today had weight, and it was crushing her. Clocking the look on her face, Louisa shoved a chair back for her.

'Sit.'

She did as she was told.

Louisa pushed the tea cup closer to her. 'Drink.'

That was when Taylor lost it.

'How the hell did it happen, Louisa? I thought St Wilfred's was *safe*.' Her voice rose on the last word. 'Something smashed his face in. Something picked him up and threw him. Who killed my grandfather? Who did this?'

Louisa exhaled, a long, slow breath. 'St Wilfred's is safe. Or it was. And it will be again. The thing is . . . ' She bit her lip, as if she almost couldn't bring herself to say what she said next. 'This Dark practitioner – the one controlling the Bringers. We think he's one of us.'

Taylor was stunned. Through the broken door, she could hear a car rumbling by. Kids were playing in a nearby garden. Such normal sounds seemed incongruous as a backdrop to the conversation they were having.

'What do you mean? An *alchemist* did this? Someone like me? I don't understand. I thought we were the good guys, Louisa.'

The look Louisa gave her then was tormented.

'We were betrayed. There's no question this was an inside job. We think this guy came up through St Wilfred's, that's how he knew how to bypass the protections we put in place.' Louisa's voice was tight. 'Believe me, that school is Fort Knox for our kind. It's the safest place on the planet. To get in, you have to be one of us. Those things?' She gestured to the damage the Bringers had done. 'They'd never get in. A Dark practitioner would never get in.' She paused. 'Unless he was one of us to start with.'

Taylor shuddered. This made things so much worse.

'Do you know who it was?'

Louisa shook her head. 'Not yet. There are a few possibilities. Everyone's working on this now, trying to work it out.' She leaned forward, holding Taylor's gaze. 'We will figure it out, Taylor. We will get this guy.'

But Taylor didn't want reassurances. 'Tell me how it happened.'

Louisa took a slug of tea, like it was whiskey. 'Our usual guard didn't show up that morning. Didn't call in. It wasn't like him, but we assumed he was ill. This afternoon, we found his body in his house.'

Taylor remembered the grumpy, thin guard who'd given her a hard time and felt a rush of guilt for having disliked him so much.

'The replacement wasn't one of us,' Louisa continued, her voice steady but weary. 'It was a mistake. It should never have been allowed. But nobody thought . . . ' She cut herself off. 'The replacement was easily manipulated. Whoever this guy is, he just walked right in.' She shook her head, obviously bewildered by the day's events. 'It's never happened before. In all of St Wilfred's history, we've never been infiltrated. It's unheard of. Now everyone's panicking. We're working as fast as we can to change the protections. To enhance security. It will take time, but we'll make the college safe again.'

'Did he hurt anyone else?' Taylor asked. 'Aside from the guard and Grandfather?'

Louisa shook her head. 'Everyone is accounted for. He just took out the most important alchemist in the world –

the first person who ever cared about me. And walked away.'

Her voice shook and she brushed the tears from her cheeks with impatient fingers.

There's something devastating about seeing a tough person get their heart broken. They seem so surprised. Like they didn't realise their heart was there at all. Until it shattered.

Without even knowing she was doing it, Taylor found herself reaching across the table to her. Louisa's nails were blunt and chipped around the edges. Her hand was cold when she gripped it.

'I'm so sorry.'.

Louisa gave a tearful laugh. 'I can't believe you're saying that to *me*. You lost your grandfather. I wasn't even family.'

'But you *were*.' Taylor insisted. 'You were his family. Anyone could see that. He loved you.'

Louisa let go of her hand and covered her face. She took a deep, shaky breath.

'The thing is, I think I saw the guy who did this. Once, when I was here.'

Taylor stared at her.

'What?' she said. '*Here*? In Woodbury?'

Louisa nodded. 'At the station. The man I saw ... ' She shook her head. 'He reeked of Dark power. He knew I recognised it. The thing is ... I can take your average Dark scumbag without even trying. But this guy ... He wasn't afraid of me. He was laughing at me. Toying with me. Aldrich was looking into it. I don't know. Maybe he should have been more cautious ... But then we found the book and everyone got distracted.' She blew out her breath. 'I think that's how he got in.'

Her words came out in a tangle and it was hard for Taylor to know which part to grasp. She chose the one that puzzled her the most.

'What book?'

Louisa blinked. 'Oh, bollocks. You don't know about that. I forgot. We were going to tell you today.' She cleared her throat. 'One of our researchers found it in the Bodleian. You know, the library?'

Taylor nodded. She knew all about the famous library with its massive collection of historic books. She'd dreamed of studying there since she was 6 years old.

'Aldrich thought he'd seen every book published on the subject in the time period but he'd never seen this one before. We only found it because this researcher had a brainwave and asked the librarian for books in any language.'

Taylor's brow creased. 'What language is it?'

'That's the thing. It's entirely written in ancient alchemical symbols. To any ordinary person it would look like gibberish. It was filed under "No known language".'

Taylor was still perplexed. 'If he can't read it, why did Aldrich think it was important?'

'If it's the right book, and he thought it was, this book is referenced several times in other writing, and it's unbelievably valuable.' Louisa sounded almost reverential. 'It's meant to be a kind of a blueprint, I guess. An instruction book, for dealing with Dark practitioners. How to fight them. How to repair what they destroy. It's the missing link. The only problem is . . . ' Her lips curved into an ironic smile, 'we can't read the bloody thing.'

How to repair what they destroy.

Hope leaped in Taylor's heart.

'Grandfather thought the solution was hidden in there?' she asked eagerly. 'A way to break Sacha's curse?'

'He thought it could be.' Louisa's tone held a hint of caution. 'The book is from the right time. Its content has been carefully – even forensically – hidden. Everything in it is written in code. Even Aldrich couldn't read it. Whatever it is, though, it's important. It might be why this is happening. Maybe he knew Aldrich had it.'

Taylor stared. 'He didn't get the book, did he?'

'No. The book is safe. Aldrich isn't.'

The phone rang, making them both jump. Taylor grabbed it off the counter.

Her mother's panicked voice erupted from the receiver. 'Taylor, are you OK? You scared me to death. What happened to your grandfather? And the house?'

Hearing her mother upset somehow calmed Taylor down a little, and she found herself being the steady one.

'I think you should just come home,' she said. 'I don't want to talk about it on the phone.'

'I'm on my way now,' her mother said, her voice echoing as it always did when she used the speaker phone. She could hear the sound of the car engine in the background. 'I'll be there in about ten minutes. I've got Emily with me.'

Taylor didn't know how she was going to tell her about her grandfather. Where would she find the words? She'd never felt more grown up. And never longed so much to be a child again.

As soon as she finished the call, Louisa stood.

'Look, I better go. If your mum sees someone who looks like me standing in the middle of her ruined house things might get messy ...' she eyes flickered towards the rubble in the corridor '... er.'

Taylor didn't want her to go. But she was already headed down the corridor, her heavy-soled biker boots crunching on the remnants of the ceiling.

'Wait!' She rushed after her trying not to look as afraid as she felt. 'You could stay, if you want. My mum won't care.'

From the doorway, Louisa shot her a disbelieving look.

'... much,' Taylor added weakly.

'Don't worry Blondie. I'm not going far. I'll stay nearby and keep an eye on you. Finlay's heading over, too. Some of the guys are on the way from Oxford to help.'

Taylor didn't want anyone else. She wanted Louisa. But she couldn't say that without sounding childish.

'Oh sure,' she said. 'We'll be fine.'

Louisa's expression softened.

'You *will* be fine.'

The unexpected gentleness in her voice made Taylor want to cry again.

Louisa lingered in the shattered doorway, the sunlight making her blue hair gleam. 'We fought those things pretty well together, Blondie. And I want you to know I'm honoured to have Aldrich Montclair's granddaughter on my side. He'd be proud of you.'

Then she turned on her thick, black rubber heel. And strode away.

FORTY-ONE

I t was after midnight by the time Sacha pulled in to the
port city of Calais.

The town was quiet at this hour, but the streets were
confusing in the dark. At one point, thoroughly lost, he
stopped to ask for directions from a jovial looking group of
drunk men stumbling home in a cluster.

'You go left at the end of the street,' one said helpfully.
'Then right. Then I think ... left. No! Wait. Right.'

'Idiot.' His friend shoved him so hard he nearly fell over, then
peered at Sacha blearily. 'You go right at the end of the street.'

He stood back, satisfied, as if this explained everything.

The third shook his head in intoxicated disgust. 'Don't
listen to them. They're drunk.'

But he offered no alternative directions.

'Uh ... thanks.' Sacha began pushing the heavy motorcycle
slowly down the street away from them.

'Wait!' The first one had recovered and was stumbling after him, filled with the desire to help. 'Just remember, left then left. Then, I think . . . Right. Or left.'

The last thing Sacha heard before the roar of his engine drowned them out was the second man complaining, 'You're so stupid.'

In the end, though, he found what he was looking for. There were signs.

He parked in front of the ferry port's ticket office and lifted his helmet. The ocean breeze felt cool against his sweaty skin.

A profusion of street lights emitted a sulphurous glow against the velvet black of the night. He couldn't see the sea, but he could hear the waves somewhere nearby. Smell the salt tang in the air.

He'd stopped only for petrol on his journey. He needed rest. Food. But that had to wait.

When he walked up to the ticket office, though, a sign in the window read 'Fermé'. Behind it, a cashier was counting the register.

'We're closed,' he said brusquely when Sacha waved for his attention.

Sacha's heart sank. 'But I need to buy a ticket.'

The man gestured impatiently. 'Last ferry's gone. There's not another one until morning.'

Sacha followed the line of his hand. The faint glimmering lights he could see in the distance were not another town as he'd thought, but the ferry, sailing away.

His shoulders sagged. Had he travelled so far, worked so hard, for nothing?

He checked the list of departure times posted on the window. The cashier was right – he'd missed the last ferry by less than five minutes. Could *nothing* go his way?

He pounded his fist on the aluminium counter so hard it shook. '*Merde!*'

'Hey!' the man snapped, jumping from his chair. 'There's no need for that. Get lost, kid, or I'll call the cops. Come back in the morning like everyone else.'

In his hand he clutched a forgotten 20-euro note, which he waved at Sacha like a weapon. It would have been funny under different circumstances. Right now, though, Sacha could have punched him.

But he was rational enough to know getting arrested right now would ruin everything. And it wasn't the cashier's fault he was too late.

He held up his hands.

'*Désolé,*' he said, stepping back from the counter. 'Please excuse me. I'll go.'

'You'd better,' the man muttered.

As he walked away, Sacha watched the man from the corner of his eye to see if he picked up the phone. But he'd returned to counting money, grumbling to himself about the state of French youth.

For a while after that, Sacha walked the streets near the port.

He weaved a little as he walked – he knew he needed to eat something. Drink something. But everything was closed.

Even though it was a warm night, he couldn't stop shivering. In a park near the waterfront his energy ran out. He sat on a bench and buried his head in his hands.

He thought of Annie and Pika, his mother and Laura, and Taylor's broken sobs.

He couldn't ever remember feeling lonelier in his life.

He'd failed everyone.

'I'm sorry,' he whispered. 'I'm sorry.'

After a while, with the sound of the sea in the distance, he curled up on the hard bench, his head pillowed on his bag, and fell asleep.

♊

The shrill sound of cars honking pulled Sacha from an uneasy dream.

His eyes blinked open. The sky was a hazy grey-white. Seabirds wheeled against the pale backdrop, their mournful cries piercing through the sound of the waves and the rumble of lorry engines.

The memory of where he was flooded back, and he sat up with a start, wiping sleep from his eyes before checking his watch.

It was just after five. The ferry would be leaving in a few minutes.

Swearing under his breath, he threw his bag over one shoulder and ran towards the ticket office.

The queue at the window was short, and Sacha skidded into the last place in line, breathless.

Thank God, he thought. *I'm not too late.*

But the line moved slowly, and by the time it was his turn, the ferry's engines were rumbling.

He was relieved to see the cashier was not the man he'd yelled at last night. This one was younger and female. She glanced up from the register as he stepped to the window, pulling cash from his pocket.

'One please,' he said. 'For me and my motorcycle.'

'One ticket for a boy and his bike,' the cashier said cheerfully, typing something into the computer. 'One way or return?'

Sacha hesitated. He didn't know the answer to that question. He didn't know if he'd ever come back. He had less than five weeks left to live. He could end up going somewhere else entirely. Maybe he and Taylor would flee to America. Hit the road. Drive to California. Always staying ahead of those things.

But he knew in his heart that wasn't going to happen.

He would get to Taylor and make sure she was safe. They would decide what to do next. And then he would come back here and fight for his life.

There had to be a way out of this. He'd barely even begun to live. It couldn't be over already.

Seventeen years is not a lifetime. Seventeen years is a *start*.

He looked back up at the ticket seller.

'Return.'

FORTY-TWO

'How did your mum take the Bringer damage?'
Louisa stirred her coffee with a slow jangle of her spoon.

'She freaked out.' Taylor winced. 'Called the police. Called the gas company. Shouted at the insurance man. Shouted at everyone.'

Caffeine Daze was quiet, only a handful of customers had left their homes on a Sunday morning. The smell of coffee filled the air like caffeinated incense.

Louisa arched one eyebrow. 'And what did *they* say?'

'Police said it wasn't a crime. Gas company said it wasn't gas. Insurance company said they'd send someone today to have a look.' Taylor recited the facts off at a rapid clip. 'They said maybe it was damp.'

'Damp.' Louisa snorted. She paused for a beat. 'What about Aldrich? You told her?'

'She was really upset,' Taylor said quietly.

She kept her face neutral but, in reality, it had been awful. Her mother sobbing. Emily inconsolable. And the whole scene had played out while the repair guy put the door back up and pretended not to notice.

'Must have been grim,' Louisa said.

Taylor's reply was barely audible. 'The worst.'

Louisa let the moment pass, quietly sipping her coffee until Taylor felt ready to continue.

'No strange visitors of any sort, though?'

'Nothing like that,' Taylor affirmed. 'Peace and quiet.'

What she didn't tell her was that she hadn't been able to sleep. And that at three in the morning she'd looked out her bedroom window and seen Louisa standing under a street light like a blue-haired guardian, keeping watch. And after that she'd dozed for a couple of hours.

'What about you?' she said. 'Did you sleep?'

Louisa stretched languidly. As usual, she looked absurdly cool. Today she wore two vests layered – one grey and one army green. Her tattoos were ink-black against her pale skin.

'I never sleep, don't you know that by now?' Louisa demurred. 'I'm like a bat.'

'Bats sleep during the day.'

'Then I'm not like a bat,' Louisa said. 'There must be something that doesn't sleep. A wombat, maybe.'

'OK, you're a wombat.' Taylor had to smile but she quickly grew serious again. 'Look, I just wanted to say ... That thing yesterday. I don't think I ever thanked you. So ... thanks for looking out for me.'

Louisa considered her for a moment without replying. Then she reached into her bag and pulled out an envelope. Setting it on the table, she slid it across to Taylor.

'I'd like to keep looking out for you,' she said. 'And I think we both know you need to get yourself somewhere safer so . . . here's your golden ticket, Blondie. Welcome to the chocolate factory.'

Taylor studied the envelope suspiciously. It had her name and address on it, and a large, official looking stamp.

When she didn't pick it up, Louisa made an impatient gesture. 'Open it.'

Carefully, Taylor lifted the flap and pulled out a sheet of heavy paper. The first words were so stunning she squeezed her eyes tight and opened them again to make sure she wasn't dreaming.

*I am pleased to inform you that **Taylor Elizabeth Montclair** has been accepted for early admittance into the Advanced Summer Programme (ASP) at **St Wilfred's College** at the University of Oxford for studies in Medieval History. The programme commences the fourth week of June and continues until the second week of August. All arrangements will be handled by Dean Jonathan Wentworth-Jones and his staff. This programme is open to only a few excellent students every year. Successful completion of the programme counts strongly towards full admission to St Wilfred's. Congratulations on being one of the nation's truly outstanding young scholars!*

Taylor felt like someone had just punched her in the stomach.

There'd been a time – only weeks ago – when a letter like this was all she wanted. Her whole life would have been made.

But everything was different now. She didn't know how to feel. What to think.

She held up the letter. 'Is this real? Or is it all fake?'

Louisa pursed her lips. 'What's your definition of "real"?'

When Taylor didn't smile, she looked a bit exasperated.

'It's *real*. The dean insisted your grades meet the requirements before agreeing to admit you. I mean, God's sake, Taylor. You could get in anywhere with those scores. When he saw your records he practically tripped over himself to write this letter.'

Taylor folded the paper carefully and slid it back into its envelope. So it was really happening.

She was going to Oxford.

All her old dreams were coming true. Only now her grandfather wouldn't be there to welcome her. And Sacha might not be alive. Maybe Oxford wouldn't even exist by the time she got there.

On the other hand, she'd be at the heart of the action. Able to help fight back against everything that was happening. She'd learn more about what and who she was.

Louisa was waiting for her to say something.

'Thank you.' Taylor's voice was genuine. 'I'm so happy that I'll work with you more. And be part of this. I just wish ... '

Her voice grew uneven and trailed off.

'I wish Aldrich was here to see this.' Louisa finished the

sentence for her. 'And I'm sorry he's not. But this is what he wanted. You at St Wilfred's. Training with people he believed in.'

Taylor knew she was right. She owed it to her grandfather to make this work. To do as much as she could to complete his work. To save Sacha.

She sat up straighter in her chair. When she spoke again her voice was steady. Determined.

'When do we start?'

Louisa shot her an approving look. 'As soon as possible. The dean will call your mother to give her the news. We want to get you out of here today. He'll explain that you should come in sooner, and she should come too, to help deal with your grandfather's effects. Maybe bring your little sister.'

Taylor didn't admit how much better this made her feel. It would be so nice if she could keep her mum and her sister with her for a little while longer.

Louisa arched one sardonic eyebrow. 'Now that you're one of us I guess I'll have to teach you the secret handshake and everything.'

'Maybe give me one of those tattoos,' Taylor gestured at her arms.

'That can be arranged.' Glancing at her watch, the other girl stood abruptly and grabbed her bag from the floor. 'But first, you need to get home and pack. The van's coming in an hour. There's no time to waste.' She headed for the door. 'It's time to start your new life fighting evil and saving the world. Don't forget to pack your toothbrush.'

♊

Louisa and Taylor parted on the corner in front of the coffee shop.

'I've got to run to meet Finlay at the school,' Louisa explained, holding out a fist for Taylor to bump awkwardly with her own. 'But I won't be long. I'll be at yours before the van gets there. Anyway,' she added, 'this will give you a chance to talk with your mum and your sister without me getting in the way.'

It struck Taylor that Louisa was always finding excuses not to meet her family. She wondered why. But now wasn't the time to ask.

She hurried home, her thoughts in a whirl. There was so much to do. She had to pack her things. She had to deal with her mother's inevitable questions.

For example, how did she get early admission without ever technically applying?

Good question.

She also really needed to talk to Sacha. He'd never replied to her voicemail message about her grandfather. His silence was starting to worry her.

She hoped he was safe at his aunt's house and just busy. But it wasn't like him to disappear.

Just as she neared the intersection with the road leading to her house, the sun disappeared behind a cloud, sending shadows shooting across the town. The winds began to rise.

A storm was coming.

She quickened her pace. The boots Sacha bought her in Paris made a rhythmic thumping sound against the pavement as she turned down the tree-lined street. There were only a few other people on the street, and they were all rushing to get out of the wind.

Above her head, branches swayed, shoved around by the strengthening breeze. The wind picked up grit from the road, hurtling it at Taylor's skin, like tiny needles.

She was nearly home when she heard it. A low, ominous humming.

Her blood turned to ice water.

She whirled.

The three men in dark coats turned the corner as one, and glided down the street towards her. They were smiling.

They can't be here, she told herself, too stunned to think straight. *There are people everywhere . . .*

But Bringers didn't seem to care whether people saw them. They didn't seem capable of caring about anything.

And they were heading straight for her.

'Oh God,' Taylor whispered, stumbling backwards. She'd fought them yesterday and survived, but only barely. And not on her own.

She spun away from them and started to run.

Someone would be at her house. Someone from St Wilfred's. They could protect her.

But her feet wouldn't seem to work properly. The strange chanting sound rose with each step she took. Her legs felt heavy – as if they were weighed down with bricks. It took all her strength to move.

After a few steps, her feet stopped moving altogether.

Panic rising inside her, she struggled wildly. But she was trapped.

The Bringers encircled her, their frozen grins hideous and unchanging; their eyes soulless.

In unison they lifted their hands, palms facing her, and began to chant.

It was as if all of them were crushing her at once. All of them strangling her. It was hard to breathe. Impossible to think. She felt herself being pushed down, buried beneath them. Her breath gurgled in her throat as she struggled to breathe.

It was different this time. This time she could understand them. Not the words they were saying but the thoughts behind those words.

'We will tear you apart.'

'We will taste your flesh.'

'We will destroy you.'

Across the street a middle-aged man strolled at a leisurely pace. He was one of her neighbours. He often waved when she was on her way to school.

'Help!' she heard herself scream. 'Mr Elstead. Help me.'

He didn't seem to see her.

'Please,' Taylor sobbed. 'Someone help me.'

The Bringers moved closer, their hideous faces looming over her. Taylor closed her eyes. As soon as she did, the world sprang into extraordinary life.

She could see power all around her. It wasn't just gold this time. It was green and blue and red. The vivid colours streamed around her.

And she could see *them*. The three Bringers. Dark shadows like black holes in the world, sucking the colourful power into themselves, absorbing it.

Come to me, instead. She didn't know where the thought came from. Just suddenly it was there. She held out one hand, palm up and open.

Come to me.

The strands of power flowed towards her like colourful water. Filling her. Flooding her spirit with unbelievable strength.

She straightened slowly.

Her resilience seemed to surprise the Bringers. Their chanting intensified – she sensed them throwing energy at her – she could see it shooting towards her like arrows.

She raised her hand, palm facing them.

Stop.

The nearest man recoiled, as if she'd struck him. The chanting weakened – just for a second, but it happened.

Taylor's breath caught.

I can hurt them.

The realisation was emboldening. But the things had already resumed their efforts. The chanting grew louder, more determined. More vicious.

She could feel their power like hands on her neck, throttling her. It was hard to breathe, and she heard herself gasp for air. Her heart hammered against her ribs in protest. But she let them touch her. Let herself be afraid.

The power within her rose instantly, with a kind of uncontrollable rage.

'STOP!'

The word seemed to roar out of her in a voice that didn't sound like her own, and the men leaned back, as if she'd struck them.

The chanting stopped, leaving a deafening silence.

Taylor took a step back. And another. Before she could run, though, they began to recover. They raised their hands again. This time, though, the chanting was different. It was louder – a constant, deafening, shriek. It burned her like fire; tore at her skin like knives.

She screamed.

A steady mechanical whine cut through the fog of sound and pain they'd created. It grew louder and louder, closer and closer.

Whatever it was, it seemed to distract the Bringers. Their chanting slowed, only for a second, but that was enough to give Taylor the chance to turn.

It was a motorcycle. Roaring towards them. The engine screaming.

The rider was bent low over the handlebars. His features were hidden behind a silver helmet, but it seemed to Taylor that he was intentionally aiming right for them.

The Bringers kept their focus on Taylor. They were still chanting when the motorcycle crashed into them, sending them flying.

The chanting stopped.

The rider yanked off his helmet, revealing sandy brown hair and sea-blue eyes.

She stared. 'Sacha?'

'Taylor! Are you OK?' He leaped from the motorcycle and ran to her.

'What are you doing here?' she asked, wonderingly.

'I got your message . . .' was all he had time to say.

Then the Bringers were up again and heading towards them. Sacha froze, she could see fear in his eyes.

'Hurry,' he said urgently, his French accent thickening in panic. 'We have to go. I can't fight them.'

He grabbed her hand.

Taylor gasped.

Suddenly the power inside her was a torrent. A raging river.

She was sick with power. Overwhelmed by it. There was too much. She couldn't control it. It wasn't around her anymore. It was in her. She *was* power.

She couldn't explain it. But something about Sacha made her stronger. Her hair flew around her face in a golden cloud. And she knew what she had to do.

'We can fight them together,' she heard herself say.

Sacha was looking at her strangely, as if he could see the difference in her. But there was doubt in his eyes.

'Taylor, they're too strong.'

She held his gaze. 'Do you trust me?'

His response came without hesitation. 'Yes.'

'Then don't let go.'

The Bringers turned towards them but now their chanting seemed to come from far away.

Taylor hated them. With every fibre of her body she wanted them to die. The hatred consumed her.

They had to be destroyed. And now, she could do that.

Turning towards the closest she held up her free hand, palm facing him.

Die.

He exploded.

A concussion of energy sent hard fragments of what looked like bone flying through the air.

Swearing, Sacha spun Taylor around, putting his body between her and the shrapnel.

'What the hell ... ?' she heard him say.

Flushed with power, she looked up at him. 'We did that.'

He stared at her. 'How ... ?'

'I don't know,' she said. 'Just ... don't let go.'

He squeezed her hand so hard it ached.

'Don't worry.'

The remaining two Bringers turned to each other. Then without warning, they pivoted in unnatural unison and glided towards Taylor and Sacha. The tall one was in front. His black eyes burned with rage. His hatred washed over her like a sheet of fire. It burned.

He turned towards Sacha and raised his hand.

Taylor felt Sacha's body tense, anticipating a blow. But he didn't let go.

'*NO!*'

She barely recognised her own voice. It seemed to come from everywhere. From the sky. From the trees.

For a split second her gaze met that of the tallest Bringer. She saw his black eyes widen as she pulled power to her with all the strength she could summon. Then she flung out her left arm and opened her hand.

The two Bringers burst into flames.

She and Sacha watched in horror as the Bringers spun around the street like burning dervishes.

Their chanting turned to screaming and then to an awful keening sound.

And, finally, silence.

The grey ash that blew on the breeze smelled of damp earth and rot.

We did it.

Taylor felt sick. She was definitely going to puke. She let go of Sacha's hand.

Her legs gave way.

Sacha caught her as she fell. He looked as dazed as she felt. 'What just happened?'

She took a shaky breath trying to steady her pounding heart.

'I think we just found out why they didn't want us to meet.'

FORTY-THREE

'Where are they? We have to leave *now*.' The man's nasal voice was sharp. He looked worried.

'No one's saying we don't, Finlay,' the blue-haired girl said patiently. 'The guys are on their way. The dean is talking to Taylor's mother right now, making sure everything is arranged.' She held up her hands in a calming gesture. 'Five minutes. Just ... stay calm.'

She looked so intense, with her sparkly blue hair, biker boots and tattoos. Sacha liked her instantly.

They were all in Taylor's living room. Sacha sat on the sofa next to Taylor watching the other two squabble.

The man she called Finlay paced the living room. First to the windows, then back to the sofa, then to the windows again.

It was making Sacha dizzy.

'There's no time. We simply must move quickly,' he

reiterated. 'Killing Bringers is unprecedented. This will bring trouble. And fast.'

'Killing Bringers ...' Louisa sounded awed. 'Can you believe it?'

The thin man stopped pacing. For the first time, he smiled. 'It's incredible.'

They'd arrived just as the fires burned out. The blue-haired girl, Louisa, appeared first, red-faced and panting, as the last of the Bringer ash blew away. The thin man, the one called Finlay, arrived came a few minutes later, white as a sheet.

Taylor had called them, her fingers shaking as she dialled.

'They're like me,' she'd explained.

Sacha could tell Finlay and Louisa both found their story hard to believe. Until they saw the evidence.

'You can pick up pieces of them on the pavement,' Louisa told someone on the phone, astonishment in her voice. 'Bringers don't get deader than this.'

Sacha was still trying to process all that had happened. The second he'd touched Taylor's hand he'd felt something not unlike an electrical shock. But it had affected her much more. He'd seen the change in her. Her spine arced back. Her hair rose around her face, her clothes had fluttered, blown by a wind he couldn't feel.

He could sense the power pouring through her. It radiated from her skin.

They'd talked about it briefly with the others.

'It's like Sacha's an amplifier,' Taylor explained. 'He made me much stronger.'

Now the blue haired girl and the thin man, Finlay, kept

talking about some book, and how they had to get to it as soon as possible.

They also said the Bringers worked for someone. And that person was the really dangerous one. And he might be coming here now, looking for vengeance.

He cast a sideways glance at Taylor, who sat next to him. She was watching the other two, a worried crease between her eyes.

'Are you OK?' he whispered.

She nodded, lips curving up.

Her hair was in tangles, and she wore no makeup at all.

He wasn't sure he'd ever seen anything so beautiful.

Those green eyes . . .

'I'm alive,' she said. 'Which is kind of surprising under the circumstances.' Her gaze swept his face. 'What about you? Are we freaking you out?'

'Nothing freaks me out anymore,' he said.

Her smile widened.

'Have you got in touch with your mum?' she asked. 'Is your aunt OK?'

He'd told her what had happened in France, and how he'd ended up here. Taylor had ordered him to phone them, there and then.

He nodded, relief coursing again through his veins. 'She's in hospital, but they think she's going to live. Thank God.'

She squeezed his hand, which somehow had ended up in hers again. 'Thank you so much. You risked your life for me.'

'I can't die, remember?' he reminded her. 'Besides, where else would I be?'

'I hear the Bahamas are nice.' Her tone was dry.

His lips twitched. 'No Bringers?'

'White sand beaches,' she said. '100 per cent Bringer-free.'

'Damn,' he snapped his fingers. 'I should have gone there instead.'

Taylor grew serious again.

'I know Louisa wants you to stay in Oxford.' Her voice was hesitant. 'They think we'll both be safer there. And ... maybe we can figure this out. You know ... together.' Her eyes searched his. 'But you don't have to. Maybe you want to go home now. Back to your family. That would be fine. I just ... want you to know that.'

I want to be wherever you are.

He wasn't entirely certain where that thought came from. But he knew as well as he knew his own name that he wouldn't leave her. The only way they could win this thing was if they fought together. He'd seen it today.

Besides, his father had loved Oxford. He'd talked about it so much when he was a boy. He could walk in his footsteps.

He'd feel closer to him there.

'Oxford sounds cool,' he said. 'Let's go there.'

Taylor beamed at him.

'This is it.' Louisa ran from the front window, where she'd been keeping lookout, to the door. 'The van's here. Grab your things, everyone.

'We're going home.'

♊

The unmarked white van idled on the street in front of Taylor's house.

As they walked towards it, the doors opened; three young men about Louisa's age leaped out and arrayed themselves beside the van.

In their T-shirts and jeans – and one in surfer shorts and sandals – they didn't look like anything special. But Taylor knew they'd be natural alchemists, just like her.

Well, maybe not *just* like her.

'Right,' Louisa said. 'Taylor, Sacha, meet Shahid, Sam and Alastair.'

The three studied them with avid interest.

'They really did it?' the one she'd identified as Shahid said to Louisa. 'Seriously?'

Dropping the bag she carried, Louisa reached into her pocket and pulled out a piece of something stone-like, the colour of ivory. It gleamed in the light.

'This was the biggest piece of Bringer I could find.'

The guys took it and passed it around. One of them gave a low whistle.

'Unbelievable,' the blonde one whispered as he held it in his hand.

They all turned to stare at Sacha and Taylor again.

Taylor squirmed a bit in the light of their attention, but Sacha showed no emotion at all. He just stared back at them with cool, blue eyes. As if daring them to say anything he didn't want to hear.

Finlay broke the tension.

'No dilly-dallying,' he announced, clapping his hands. 'Let's get moving.'

The surfer-shorts guy grabbed Taylor's bag and threw it in

the back, climbing in after it. Louisa and Finlay were talking with the blonde one, who held the keys.

Sacha's bike was still where he'd left it when he arrived. Looking at it, Taylor suddenly realised they wouldn't be travelling together.

Sacha seemed to have the same realisation.

For a second they stood uncertainly at the kerb.

Everything was happening too fast. She was going away without saying goodbye to her mother. After everything that had happened. She just wanted to hug her. To make sure she was fine.

And she didn't want to leave Sacha. Even for the few hours of the journey. Whatever had happened with the Bringers – whatever had passed between them in those moments – she felt connected to him now. The need to stay with him was as overwhelming as fear.

Sacha seemed to sense that something was wrong. He shot her a questioning look.

Louisa tilted her head at the van.

'Climb in, kiddo,' she said. 'Sacha's going to follow us.' She glanced at him. 'You've got the directions, right?'

But Sacha's gaze was still on Taylor.

'I've got an extra helmet,' he said. 'If you want to ride with me.'

Her heart leaped. 'Really? You wouldn't mind?'

Sacha turned to Louisa. 'Taylor's going to ride with me.'

'What? On *that*?' Louisa pointed at his bike accusingly. 'I don't think so . . . '

Sacha ignored her tone.

'It's what she wants. Right?' He glanced at Taylor.

She nodded enthusiastically. 'Yes. Definitely. Yes.'

'Taylor . . . ' Louisa warned.

'I'll be fine,' Taylor promised.

Sacha handed Taylor a helmet.

Still grumbling, Louisa climbed into the van and shut the door.

Sacha got on the bike first and showed Taylor where to put her feet. She climbed on after him.

It felt weird. Strangely bouncy. Incredibly dangerous.

She liked it. Hesitantly, she placed her hands on Sacha's waist. She didn't quite know where to hold him.

He turned the key and the motor revved. The bike seemed to come alive.

Sacha glanced back at her. His visor was up, and his sea-blue eyes were the only part of his face she could see.

'You're going to have to hold on tighter than that.'

She tightened her grip. She could feel the bones of his ribcage; the taut muscles below.

He gunned the engine.

The bike shot down the street.

Soon Woodbury was behind them like a memory.

And Oxford lay ahead.

Epilogue

T he white van rolled through the tall medieval gates and headed slowly down the narrow drive towards an imposing, gothic building. Behind it, a gleaming black motorcycle carrying two riders followed with an ominous growl.

Overhead, the banner of St Wilfred's College crackled and waved in the steady breeze.

Dean Jonathan Wentworth-Jones stood on the front steps of the administration building with his assistant dean and head of research, Alec Milford, watching the two vehicles approaching. To a casual passerby the dean's expression would be hard to read. But anyone who knew him well would have seen the tension in the lines of his patrician face. The way his hands flexed and released at his sides.

Behind them, the building's 400-year-old limestone walls stretched up, culminating in jagged spires. From the eaves, four storeys above their heads, stone gargoyles, mouths wide open, leered down at them.

Mysterious geometric symbols surrounded the arched doorway in which they stood, concentric circles, six-pointed stars, curved lines and triangles within triangles. Each carving was a symbol of alchemical power. All had been carefully arranged many centuries ago to protect St Wilfred's and its inhabitants.

Each had failed them the morning Aldrich Montclair was killed.

'Do you think it's true?' Milford glanced up at his superior. 'Do you think it's possible she killed Bringers?'

The dean's eyes stayed on the motorcycle. The two riders wore matching silver helmets that hid their features, but he knew it was them. The slim boy at the front, in jeans and black T-shirt, was Sacha. The pale girl in the black short skirt was Taylor Montclair.

He knew why Milford was asking. Every book they had – every bit of their history – told them Bringers could not be killed. They could be chased away. They could be repelled. But no one had ever succeeded in killing one.

The idea that it might have actually happened sent his pulse racing. It was so hard to believe.

'Finlay and Louisa are quite convinced.' His lips barely moved when he spoke but he knew Milford could hear him perfectly. 'They've gathered the remnants for us to examine in the lab.' He glanced at his assistant. 'I think it's unlikely they're mistaken.'

He and Milford had been having a conversation very much like this one ever since Finlay phoned them a few hours earlier.

They'd told very few people the details he'd relayed. Waiting, instead, to see the evidence. To be absolutely certain there was no mistake.

'Do you think this means ... ?' Milford couldn't seem to bring himself to complete the thought.

Fixing him with a steely look, the dean finished the thought for him. 'That they can do this? That those two *children* can take on the greatest Dark practitioner our kind has encountered in centuries? That they can save us all?'

The van had reached the end of the lane. The engine cut off.

The motorcycle stopped at the foot of the stairs. Its powerful engine fell silent.

The boy took off his helmet first, revealing a shock of fine brown hair. The girl lifted hers, sending blonde curls tumbling over her shoulders.

They climbed off the bike and stood side by side looking up to where the two deans stood at the top of the steps.

An ordinary person would have noticed nothing unusual about them but, even from that distance, the dean could sense their extraordinary energy. The girl, in particular. Her power was like nothing he'd ever encountered.

It didn't stream as energy normally did it. It projected outward, like a pulsar.

Looking at it directly was like staring into the sun.

The dean never answered his assistant's question. Instead, he held out his hands.

'Welcome,' he said, 'to St Wilfred's.'

CJ's Acknowledgements

This book started in the way all wonderful things begin, with a conversation in Paris over coffee. Carina and I had both just signed books for three hours straight at a book fair, and then sneaked away to recover and ice our fingers. We talked vaguely about writing a book together – something thrilling and romantic. Then I went back to England to work on the Night School series. Months passed. Then one rainy Saturday I got an email from her that said, 'I've had some ideas about our book.'

So, my first thanks are to Carina, for being brave enough to write in English, and game enough to try co-writing with me. It's been a fascinating journey, and I've loved every step.

Huge thanks are due to Karen Ball and Sarah Castleton at Atom Books, who both instantly *got* Sacha and Taylor's story, and helped nurture this book into being. They saw the potential, loved the characters as much as we did, and helped bring the best of the story into the light. I'm so grateful for your patience and your skill.

Thanks also to our wonderful agent Madeleine Milburn, who got an email from me saying 'I want to co-write a book with a French writer I just met . . .' and didn't run away as fast as she could, but instead said, 'Tell me about the story.' And then when I told her about the story said, 'Come back when you have three chapters.' And when I came to her with six chapters instead, said, 'Go write this book.' Thank you so much for your faith, Maddy.

Thanks are very much due to Glenn Tavennec, our editor at Robert Laffont in France, who introduced me to Carina at the Salon du Livre book fair with the fateful words, 'I think you will like each other.' Less than a year later we were writing a book together. *Merci beaucoup*, Glenn!

Huge thanks to Doris, Maia and Christina at Oetinger in Germany, to Monika at Otwarte in Poland, to Oliver and everyone at Bookouture, and to all of *The Secret Fire*'s international publishers. We are so grateful for your energy and your belief in this new series.

Thanks also to Holly Bourne and Alexia Casale for being there and being awesome. What would I do without you?

To the writers in YAT, thank you for putting up with me. Yours is the first group I've voluntarily joined since 1991. You almost make me less of an introvert. *Almost.*

And finally, as always, to Jack. Who never doubted we'd pull it off. You believe so much more in me than I believe in myself. Thank you for making everything amazing.

Carina's
Acknowledgements

All of this amazing adventure would never have happened without the wonderful C. J. Daugherty. The idea of writing a book together was born during a book fair in Paris, and, at first, it seemed like something really, really crazy. But to achieve amazing things you have to be a little crazy. So, we did it. We combined our different styles to create something strong and wonderful. This book is not only a journey for Taylor and Sacha, but it is also one for us, and I want to thank CJ for being an amazing writer and friend. And for being as crazy as I am. Thank you for those extraordinary months of writing. It was fun and fascinating, and I'm happy we still have another book to write together.

I also want to thank my new publishers in England: Atom Books. Especially Karen Ball and Sarah Castleton, for trusting me – trusting us – and this story. Their terrific work helped make it the best it could be.

I want to thank my agent, Madeleine Milburn, who instantly saw the potential of *The Secret Fire* and believed in us and in this very unusual collaboration. These are my first steps writing in English, and being published in the UK. I hope she knows how many Christmases she offered me.

A huge thank to Glenn Tavennec at Robert Laffont in France. I met CJ because he had the brilliant idea to sit us next to each other at a book fair. He was sure we would get along and he was so right! He is the godfather of this book.

Thanks to all the publishers all over the world who already believe in *The Secret Fire*. I can't wait to meet you all and work with you.

And finally, I send all my love to Leo, my son, and to my parents, who are always there to support me, to believe in me, whatever the challenge. Without them I wouldn't be where I am today.

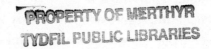